IRONHEAD

or, Once a Young Lady

IRON

HEAD

or, Once a Young Lady

by JEAN-CLAUDE VAN RIJCKEGHEM

Translated by KRISTEN GEHRMAN

LQ

LEVINE QUERIDO

Montclair | Amsterdam | Hoboken

This is an Em Querido book
Published by Levine Querido

LQ
LEVINE QUERIDO

www.levinequerido.com • info@levinequerido.com

Levine Querido is distributed by Chronicle Books, LLC

Originally published as *IJzerkop* by Querido

Library of Congress Cataloging-in-Publication data is available

ISBN: 978-1-64614-048-0

Printed and bound in China

Published February 2022
First Printing

J'aime l'oignon frit à l'huile, j'aime l'oignon quand il est bon.

Au pas camarades, au pas camarades, au pas, au pas, au pas
Un seul oignon frit à l'huile nous change en lions.

I love an onion fried in oil, I love an onion when it's good.
In step comrades, in step comrades, in step, in step, in step
Just one onion fried in oil turns us into lions.

(*Chanson de l'Oignon*, marching song of Napoléon's army)

For Lowie, Marieke, and Irene
For Virginie
For Dries
And always for Bernadette

I

STANCE

Ever since my brother started at the Latin school, with all those sons of French officers and Flemish factory owners, he really thinks he's somebody. Whenever he's home on holiday, he parades around Ghent in his school uniform, as proud as Charles V's cat. Of course, he thinks he's way too important to help me with the laundry. This morning he made sure to attend the second Mass—that wafer-swallowing dolt—just to get out of helping me with the wash! By the time he gets home from church, it's already ten o'clock. He shows up with a prayer book under his arm and a look of devotion on his face that reminds me of a simpleton or an old nun. It took him half a year to find his way home from the cathedral. But I waited for him. I wasn't about to lug all that laundry down to the river by myself.

"Was there a long line for confession or something?" I ask.

He gazes at me as if there's a halo over his head.

"I have nothing to confess," he says. "Laundry is your job. Not mine."

"No way, church mouse," I say. "When you're home from your stupid school, you help me with the laundry."

I've already lifted one end of the basket. Pier takes his time neatly arranging all his church paraphernalia on the proper sideboard shelf in the dining room. When he finally returns to the basket, the reluctance is practically dripping off his shoulders. Together we lift the heavy basket off the table.

"You're not going out like that," a voice behind me says.

Mother stomps into the room in her wooden clogs. I try to look as innocent as possible. What's wrong? My skirts are down to my ankles, my white blouse is buttoned up to my neck, and my hair is neatly braided.

"Where's your bonnet?" She plucks that awful hat with the round brim from the hook under the shelf, pushes it down onto my head, and stuffs my braid up into it. I can no longer look from side to side, but at least my blessed face is now completely concealed from the prying eyes of young men. Mother ties the wide ribbons under my chin so tightly you'd think it were some kind of war helmet to protect my virginity.

"Ow, not so tight," I say.

"Don't whine, Constance," she says. "These bonnets are all the rage in Paris."

"Yeah," I reply. "Back when Grandma still had her baby teeth."

Mother ignores the comment and turns to my brother. "Pieter, keep an eye on your sister."

"You can count on me," says Pope Pieter the Pious.

Pier and I lug the basket down the street with the tall pile of laundry bouncing back and forth between us. We're careful not to walk too fast so as not to drop any shirts or socks along the way. It's cold. There's smoke rising from the chimneys, and the streets are all but deserted. A couple of boys covered in soot are hauling bags of coal from door to door. Down on the quays of the Lieve Canal are two floating platforms where women and housemaids scrub the laundry with lumps of hard white soap. In the mornings, you can smell the fresh scent from miles away and the dark water is covered in a blanket of white foam. The Lieve must have the cleanest fish in all of Ghent. Pier and I walk across the first raft to the second, where there is still plenty of room. We set down the basket. Most of the women here are maids for wealthy families, but my mother doesn't need a maid—she has me.

The women on the raft roll up their sleeves and, with bare arms, they soap, scrub, and rinse each item of clothing at a frantic pace. I take my time while my lazy brother lounges on the raft in his expensive school uniform. He's going to get those fancy white knee socks dirty, just wait. He doesn't dare to take off his boat-shaped hat. He's afraid I'll throw the thing into the water just to see if it floats.

I chat with Mie De Peeze—now there's a gossip. She's this chatterbox who never got married and likes to rattle on about her employer, the brewer Hans De Grote, and his wife, who can't stay away from the beer, and how their children are always swinging from the rafters like wild monkeys. At least, that's her version of the story.

"And guess what?" she says, finally getting to the point. "The brewer delivered a ton of beer to the widow Coppieters in his donkey cart. But he didn't drop it off at her pub; he took it up to the Franciscan monastery. There's going to be a boxing match there today."

"On your feet," I say, passing Pier a corner of the sheet I've been washing. He stands up. We twist it in opposite directions, making water droplets rain down on the raft.

"And not just any boxing match," Mie whispers in a conspiratorial tone, as if she's about to say something God shouldn't hear. "It's a match between two women."

Pier drops his end of the clean sheet and makes the sign of the cross.

"May God have mercy on their souls," Mie De Peeze says. She crosses her heart three times and asks herself what our country is coming to now that the monks have been expelled from their monasteries, our Flemish boys are marching in the French army, and marriage—that sacred, eternal, unbreakable union—can simply be annulled down at the Ghent Town Hall with the stroke of a clerk's pen.

"We're living in Godless times," Mie De Peeze laments as she scrubs the brewer's sweaty nightshirts. "It all started with that French mob murdering their king. And poor Marie Antoinette too."

Mie De Peeze shakes her head as if she's still grieving for

that spoiled shrew. Pier looks so grim you'd think Marie Antoinette was his first cousin. But I couldn't care less about that spoiled sovereign. I'm a child of the Revolution. I whistle "La Marseillaise," the former national anthem of France, as I fold the sheet—just to get on their nerves. They don't even notice. Mie's already chatting away with somebody else.

Fifteen minutes later I wring out the last shirt and toss it to Pier. My hands are white from the icy water.

"We're going to watch that boxing match," I say.

Pier looks at me as if he's just had his ears twisted by the hand of God. Then he folds Father's shirt without looking me in the eye—he never looks me in the eye when I have a fantastic plan he doesn't like. What a milksop. He tosses Father's shirt onto the pile and picks up the basket by one of the handles.

"Come on, lift," he commands.

I take the other handle, and we lift the basket together; it's even heavier now that the laundry is wet. We take a big step off the raft and climb the twelve stone steps up to the quay without a word. The basket leaves a trail of drops behind us. We set it down on the quay. I roll down my sleeves. The color is returning to my tingling fingers.

"Did you hear what I said, Spiering?" I ask. "We're going to a boxing match." A spiering is an ugly little fish—that's what I call my brother when he gets on my nerves.

"We're going home," he says. "You still have to hang this laundry on the line. Come on, lift."

We carry the basket a bit farther, but when we reach the

bridge overlooking the castle ruins, I stop. I lower my side of the basket to the ground and drop the handle. The laundry almost topples out. Pier drops his side of the basket too.

"You can't carry that basket home alone," I say. "We went out together, we go to the boxing match together, and then we go home together."

Pier straightens up, trying to make himself taller than he is.

"We're not going! If Mother finds out, you'll get such a beating that people will read about it in the *Gazette.*"

"Good, then I'll finally make the *Gazette,*" I say.

"Stop it, Stance," Pieter roars. He's actually imagining tomorrow's paper: *On Sunday, the sixth of March, in the year eighteen hundred and eight, Constance Hoste, the eighteen-year-old daughter of the famous Ghent mechanical engineer and inventor Leopold Hoste received such a beating from her father that the young lady is henceforth of limited capacity.*

"You know what your problem is, Spiering? You don't have any guts. You're as boring as they come," I say.

"A boxing match? Between two women? It's immoral! And on a Sunday, no less, on the Feast of Saint Colette," he says. "It's a sin. We'll have to confess."

"You can confess for both of us," I say, "and we'll split the Our Fathers as penance. Come on, we're going."

"No, we have to be home in time for lunch."

"We'll just tell them the washing took longer than usual," I say, "that all the maids in Ghent were out on the rafts and we had to wait our turn."

"No."

"Five minutes, Spiering, that's all. I just want to see it. We'll take a quick peek and leave. In and out. I promise I'll never call you Spiering again. I'll be nice to you."

"The day you're nice to me is the day Easter and Pentecost fall on the same Sunday."

"Damn it, Spiering, aren't you just a little curious? Boxing women. You can brag about it next week at your Latin school in front of all your aristocratic friends."

Pier sighs as loudly as possible. He knows I'm more stubborn than the two donkeys on Noah's Ark.

The city bells are ringing eleven o'clock as Spiering and I push open the wooden door of the monastery. We worked up quite a sweat carrying that bloody basket. The Franciscans used to count their prayer beads and recite Psalms in this church. But apparently God's not home today. The Lord's temple is full of hundreds of men drinking and shouting as if they were in a tavern. They're all gathered around a roped-off ring in the center of the chapel. I stand on the tips of my clogs, but I still can't see what's going on. There are too many men in front of me. But judging by their excited cries, the match is in full swing. Pier kicks at some rat droppings in the sand and accidentally trips over his own clogs. He falls onto his knees, and I just barely manage to keep the basket upright. My brother doesn't always have control of his limbs. At home, he runs into everything, trips over every step, and is constantly dropping things. He's already broken a dozen porcelain teacups. Mother often wonders how she ever got such an uncoordinated son.

◎ ◎ ◎

Pier points to an empty corner by the baptismal font. We walk over and set the basket down. The girls from the Black Magpie, the local brewery, are tapping beer from a barrel into people's mugs. Their mother, the widow Coppieters, is smoking a pipe. The old biddy is wearing a thick woolen coat that's been out of fashion for a hundred years. She counts the money people give her and stashes it in a cigar box. There are a couple of daring women in the crowd. Most have loose hair and plunging necklines, as if their breasts need room to breathe. They're probably from one of those houses of ill repute, where men go to buy love and Bibles are used as fire starters. They hang on the arms of men in expensive boots, riding coats, and white collars.

We've barely set down the basket when all the men start roaring at once—a deep ferocious cry, as if from one throat. Pier nearly wets his pants.

"We have to go back," he says with his hat in his hands.

"We just got here, altar boy. Go pray if you feel scared."

I step forward, closer to the spectacle.

"Stance, stay here," says Pier, but I'm already weaving my way through the crowd. From all the shouting, it sounds like the fight is almost over. I push my way into the crowd. I didn't carry that damned basket all the way up to here to miss the entire show. There, in the middle of the chapel, is the battlefield, a rectangle marked off by wooden stakes.

"Shouldn't you be at home making lace?" says a man to my left. I can barely see him around the brim of my bonnet.

He reeks of beer, sweat, and onions. He pulls his cap off his head, slaps it against his knee, and puts it back on again. Years of sun and knee-slapping have stripped the cap of all its color.

"I've already finished my lacework for the day," I say without turning my head. "It's not over yet, is it?"

"No, the third round's about to start," the man says. "Say, are you one of the girls from the Black Magpie? I love your beer. Can you get me another one? For free? I'll give you a kiss for it."

He hands me his earthenware cup.

"Get it yourself," I say, turning to look at him. He looks about as rough as his old hat. "And as for that kiss, my brother's an officer in the gendarmerie. The last guy who asked me for a kiss sure was sorry."

The idea that Pieter the Pious would last a single day as an officer of the law is laughable, but this sorry drunk doesn't know that.

"Oh," the man says.

"But he's recovering," I say. "The doctors think he'll be able to chew again in a month."

For a moment, the man looks perplexed, but then he smiles.

"A gendarme," he says. "Now isn't that something."

"Just tell me who's winning," I ask.

"Mad Nel, of course. That's who I've got my money on."

"And who's the other one?"

"Get me a beer and I'll tell you."

"Leave her alone," shouts a familiar voice behind me. Well, what do you know? It's the Holy Spiering with his guppy lips and fish brain. All he's missing is a halo. The man looks surprised.

"I'm her brother," Pier says, trying to sound as tough as possible.

"The gendarme?" the man asks with a thundering laugh. He gives Pier a friendly slap on the shoulder as if he were an old drinking mate. Pier nearly collapses. Then he wipes the dirty man's beer spittle off his face.

"You wouldn't know by the looks of him," I say, "but my brother can bend an iron rod with his teeth."

The man with the ugly cap can't stop laughing.

"That little lady of yours is a real pistol," he says.

Pier braces himself for another slap on the shoulder, but it doesn't come.

"I think this man is drunk," Pier says.

I roll my eyes.

"Me, drunk?" says the man, feigning surprise. "Never on a Sunday!"

"Let's go, Stance," Spiering squeaks.

"Just a little longer."

I look at the two women sitting in opposite corners of the ring. One has short blond hair and is wearing a silk blouse, a dirty purple skirt, and leather gloves. She's clearly a woman of means. And of stature: She has broad shoulders and long arms, but other than that there's not much meat on her bones. Her skin is soft and pale.

"She goes by Courage," says the man. "That's it. No one knows who she is or where she's from."

Judging by the bruises on her face, her heavy breathing and bloody lip, I suspect that Courage is not winning.

"I'll knock your jaw crooked for the rest of your life, you bourgeois pig," her opponent shouts from the other corner.

The other one I recognize. It's Cornelia, the coal trader's eldest daughter. She's a fortress of a woman, a matron with thick skin and fists like coal shovels. Whoever came up with her nickname, Mad Nel, probably ended up cut into quarters with a blunt pair of nail scissors. But she's suffered her share of damage too. Her right eye is swollen and bleeding. I wonder if she can still see out of it.

"No man'll want you after I'm finished," Nel shouts at her opponent. She takes a swig of beer and wipes the foam and blood from her lips.

"Mad Nel's a feisty one," says the man with the faded cap.

Suddenly, a gentleman wearing a brand-new riding coat that's much too large for him and a hat with a giant plume in it takes Courage's bruised hand and tries to convince her to leave the ring and come with him. But Courage jerks back her hand and starts yelling. She's angry. I can see it in her eyes. I can't make out what she's saying over all the noise, but there's one word I can read on her lips: "Never!" She points at a jug of gin on the floor.

The gentleman grabs the jug, takes a swig, puffs up his cheeks, and sprays it into Courage's bruised face. She recoils from the sudden, stinging pain and perks up. Her eyes are wide and alert.

A man in a French sergeant's uniform steps into the ring and shouts, "Gentlemen, messieurs, your attention please, votre attention s'il vous plaît." I hear a Ghent accent in his French *R*s. His uniform is missing a few buttons and is full of holes. He has a pistol in his hand. The cheering crowd goes silent.

"Round three," he shouts. "Le troisième tour."

He points his pistol at the ceiling and fires gunpowder at a mural of Saint Francis sharing the Gospel with the birds and wolves. The smell of rotten eggs permeates the room.

Nel gulps down her beer, licks the foam from her upper lip, and throws the cup into the crowd. People cheer.

"Go get her, Nellie!" shouts the drunken oaf beside us.

Courage and Mad Nel step forward, circling each other, barefoot. Arms bent. Fists wrapped in gloves. Eyes locked on each other. Nel loses patience. She swings, trying to hit her opponent square in the face. Courage rears her head, and Nel misses her three times in a row. Courage moves left, then right, but Nellie blocks her every time. When Courage hits the wooden wall, Nel seizes her chance. She pummels Courage in the arms and shoulders over and over again. She throws a blow to the head, and the audience screams.

"Finish her!" shouts the man in the dirty cap. Courage hurls herself with all her might into Mad Nel, hooking her skinny arms around Nel's giant body. Nel tries to pry herself loose. She stomps on Courage's feet and kicks against her shins, but Courage clings to her like a leech.

In the middle of the battlefield, Courage finally lets go of her opponent and pushes her away. Nel launches another attack, vicious, like a tortured animal. Courage ducks and dodges. What she lacks in brute force, she makes up for in limberness and skill. The spectators are screaming their throats raw. They're calling for blood. For a winner. I untie the ribbon under my chin and rip the stupid bonnet off my head. My braid tumbles down my back, and before I know it, I'm screaming too—there, in the middle of that wild, sweaty crowd of peasants.

"Don't take that, Courage!" I yell. "Knock her lights out, God damn it!"

"Behave yourself, Stance," Pier shouts in dismay. I've just cursed in public. But I can't take my eyes off those two ferocious women swinging their fists at each other.

Pier has had enough. He tries to escape but gets pushed off balance and smacks into a wooden barrier. His hat falls off. Somebody steps on it.

"I can't take you anywhere," I laugh.

He clambers to his feet and shouts that we have to go home at once. That Mother said I have to listen to him, even though he's four years younger than me. He begs. Tears of powerlessness well up in his eyes. But I just keep right on shouting—"Come on, Courage, don't give up!"—as if I go to boxing matches every Sunday. Nel stays on the attack, but Courage covers her head with her arms. She's not going to let herself be cornered again.

"Punch her teeth out!" the dirty cap shouts at Nel. "No mercy. Make that blue blood eat dirt!"

Puffing and sweating, Nel punches Courage hard in the gut. I gasp for air as if someone's just hit me in the gut too.

Courage falls onto her right knee. Nel cocks back her arm to deliver the final blow. Here comes the sledgehammer. But Nel's not quick enough. Courage ducks out of the way and springs to her feet. Reeling from the missed punch, Nel loses her balance, and Courage finally seizes her chance. Before Nel can brace herself for another hit, Courage slams her in the face with her fist. Mad Nel's nose breaks, spewing blood out into the crowd.

A few splatters land on Pier's shirt, and he screams.

The pain must be searing through Nel's head. She stumbles backward. Before she can regain her balance, before she can find her footing in the sand, Courage deals her three more punches straight to the temple. Mad Nel collapses. She hits the ground like a sack of coal, facedown in the sand and rat droppings. The ringmaster is stunned. He can't believe the match is over. Then, he raises Courage's arm in the air.

"Winner. Le vainqueur!" he shouts. "Mademoiselle Courage wins the pot of forty-three francs."

But Courage is exhausted. She's on the verge of collapse. Out in the crowd, coins are changing hands. The men who bet on Courage collect their winnings from the ones who were too stupid not to. My drunk companion with the empty cup rips off his dirty cap, beats it three times against his knee, and curses the crucifix. The young man in the oversized riding coat helps Courage to her feet. He puts her arm over his shoulder, hoists her up, and leads her out of the church. I push my way through the crowd.

Out in the courtyard, I see Courage's companion helping her into a red berline, a small, closed carriage with room to seat four. Then, the gentleman hurries back inside. I walk toward the carriage, jump up on the step, and peek in the window.

Courage is holding a wet cloth against her face. Then she sees me. She looks me straight in the eye and grins. Her teeth are red with blood. Her face is scratched and bruised but beaming with pride. The man with the plumed hat runs back out and climbs into the coach from the other side. In his haste, he bangs his head on the roof and loses his hat. He puts it back on—it's much too large for him, just like the riding coat. Is his tailor nearsighted, or are those his big brother's clothes? He sits down across from the battered woman.

"I got the money, chérie," he says to Courage and kisses her on the mouth, the cheeky buck. Then he sees my dumbstruck face peering into the coach. He smiles—a beautiful, warm, and mischievous smile. There are earring holes in his earlobes. Then he taps the roof of the carriage with his cane. The coachman clicks his tongue, and the horse pulls the coach forward. I jump down from the step.

Pier jerks my arm and says we have to go.

"That man with the plume," I say. "Did you see him?"

"What about him?" he asks.

"It was a woman," I say.

Pier looks at me, confused.

"What are you saying?"

I shake my head. Never mind.

"We're going home."

Pier heads back into the monastery church. Who were those women? Does one of them have a husband off traveling somewhere? Or are they both unmarried? Or do they, God forbid, live together like a married couple? Why on earth would Courage want to be beaten to a pulp between four wooden stakes in front of a crowd of half-drunken men and a couple of women, all screaming their heads off? And that grin! It was the kind of grin that laughs at life and turns the order of things upside down.

I walk back into the chapel and find Pier standing by the baptismal font. He looks at me, ready to burst into tears. He points down at a dark wet spot in the sand where we left the laundry. It's gone.

2

PIER

That afternoon, Stance tells her story at the table. She explains how that morning, while we were bringing home the laundry basket, she was suddenly so overwhelmed by the dreadful state of the world and the sadness of human existence that she asked me to take her to the cathedral, where, in a cloud of incense, she might find stillness and inner peace in God.

"We left the heavy basket at the entrance to the church," Stance says. "After all, it wouldn't be right to enter the house of God with a dripping basket full of wrinkled sheets, shirts, and undergarments. We were only in the cathedral for a few minutes, just long enough to say ten Hail Marys, but when we went back outside, the basket was gone."

Stance looks at me.

"Gone," I confirm. I don't dare to look my parents in the

eye. I still haven't recovered from all the emotions of this morning: the noise of the men, the smell of spilled beer, the two women beating each other to a pulp, and all that in the house of the Lord. And then there was that idiot who smashed my hat.

"Who would steal a basket of laundry on the Feast of Saint Colette?" Stance wonders indignantly.

Little Eddy, who's barely five, grabs hold of Stance's hand and rests his head against her shoulder to comfort her. Eddy is the runt of the family. Mother pampers and coddles him in every way. He never gets a spanking, and every little thing he learns—from walking to sitting on the pot to his first words—is nothing short of a miracle.

"Shall we eat?" Father asks. He's heard enough about the mystery of the missing laundry.

"Why are your clothes so dirty?" Mother wants to know. She points to all the dust and stains on my school uniform. I feel my face turn red.

"Pier was so upset by the theft that he lost control," Stance replies. "One moment he was on his feet and the next he was sprawled out on the ground in rat poop. He was absolutely beside himself. Imagine, our laundry basket stolen at the door of the cathedral! I had to call out his name three times before he finally calmed down. He's such a sensitive boy."

My younger sister, Rozeken, who has been standing quietly in the corner for the duration of this scandalous exchange, shoots me a worried look with those dark eyes of hers. I melt with shame. Stance is making everything worse. Father puts his hand on my shoulder. I jerk back my head, expecting a slap. But his face is friendly.

"It's all right, son," Father says. "There's nothing you could've done. Isn't that right, Clara?"

"No, there was nothing Pier could have done," Mother says.

Her voice is about as warm as an icicle. Nothing gets past her. She shoots Stance a foul look.

"You wouldn't be caught dead in a church," Mother says.

Stance looks shocked, as if she is on a Christian-name basis with all the angels in heaven.

"That basket was stolen by one of those Austrian soldiers," murmurs Grandma Blommaert, my mother's mother. She only has four teeth left and has to repeat the statement three times before we understand what she's saying.

"The Austrians have been gone for almost twenty years. Emperor Joseph is dead," Mother says loudly. Grandma Blom nods as if she's satisfied to hear that Mother agrees with her. Grandma is as deaf as a post and has a crack in her brain that makes her think we're still living in the wig era.

"Surely you mean a French soldier took it, Grandma," Stance hollers, "and you're right. Those frog eaters ran off with five shirts, eight sheets, twelve undershirts, and twenty pairs of socks. Father should write a letter to Emperor Napoléon himself and ask him to compensate us for the stolen laundry. Let him foot the bill."

That Stance is a nasty piece of work. She doesn't know when to stop. Sometimes it almost seems as if she wants to be punished. I feel my head burning.

"Those Austrian bastards," mumbles Grandma Blom. Then she draws a cross on Stance's forehead to protect her from further calamity and gives her a kiss. Since she doesn't have any teeth, it's more of a splotch of wet saliva. But Stance doesn't mind. She doesn't even wipe it off her forehead.

"Thank you, Grandma," she says.

Everyone falls quiet. There's snorting and pounding in the stable behind our house.

"Achilles is hungry," Stance says.

Father bought Achilles when he was still working as a mechanic and traveling to weaving mills around Ghent. Now he has his own factory and doesn't need the old horse anymore. These days, Achilles is nothing but a bag of bones in a saggy fur coat, but Father doesn't have the heart to sell him to a glue maker or a skeleton scraper. Stance is attached to the animal and takes him for a walk through the city every few days.

"I'm coming, my Greek hero," Stance hollers.

The horse eats everything Stance feeds him. Hay, old vegetables, rotten fruit, and even pieces of newspaper—only the good news though, Stance says.

"The poor animal will have to wait," Mother snarls. "We're not done here."

"Calm down, cookie," Father says. "We should be happy that nothing happened to Constance and Pieter."

"Praise the Lord," Grandma Blom mumbles.

"Exactly," Father says and makes the sign of the cross with his left hand. He's not nearly as religious as my mother and grandmother are. It's one of his few flaws.

"Admit it," Mother says to Stance. "You went to the fair at Saint Michael's. You left the basket so you could watch the musicians and impress the boys. And when you and Pier went back for it, it was gone."

"But Mother," Stance says indignantly, "I would *never* do such a thing."

Mother looks at me. I shake my head. No, we didn't go to the fair, and she certainly didn't impress any boys. How could she? She's scrawny, with long gangly arms and a chin like a shoe last. She couldn't be attractive if she tried. And that cackling laugh of hers is enough to drive you crazy. Grandma Blom might be convinced that Our Lord hasn't forgotten Stance, but I'm pretty sure He has.

"Let's just eat," Father says to Mother.

Mother folds her hands in prayer. I follow her example, glad to see the crisis averted. The others fold their hands as well. Mother asks the good Lord to protect her family and her laundry from any further disasters and to forgive her husband for not going to church. One day he, too, will see the light. I peek at Stance through half-closed eyes. She is pretending to be fully absorbed in prayer. Her story has taken on the form of the Gospel. Mother asks God to show Stance the path of virtue and obedience. She prays for my two sisters in heaven and for the sawing machine in Father's factory, which hasn't been working very well. Finally, she asks for God's blessing over the bread and cheese on the table.

"Amen," we say and eat lunch. Mother has already chewed Grandma Blom's food for her. She hands her the bowl of mush. Eddy scarfs down everything on his plate. My good father eats slowly, his thoughts elsewhere. The candle on the table is planted in a shoe last with a hole drilled in the middle.

My father's father was a cobbler and tanner. Grandfather Hoste cleaned pigskins to be made into shoes and clogs. He soaked the skins in a deep pit, which he insisted his children pee into every day. The more piss in the pit, the more acidic the water became and the faster the pigskin would come clean. After letting it soak for a few days, my father and his brothers would pull the skin out of the pit, roll it up, and rinse it in the river. After that, they'd sit on the quay for hours pulling out hairs until the hide was completely clean. The Carmelite monks taught my father and his brothers to read and count, but they weren't allowed to sit with the other children because they smelled like piss and dead animals. But Father doesn't stink anymore. Nowadays, he dabs himself with eau de Cologne before heading out the door. As a child, I liked to press my nose into his neck and breathe in the sweet smell of oranges and grapefruits. "Little Devil," he'd say.

Grandfather Hoste stopped tanning leather the autumn he lost his two eldest sons and his wife to typhus. According to the doctor, the disease had something to do with the fumes from the piss or with the dirty water itself, but he didn't understand the details of it either. The Lord giveth and the Lord taketh away. Grandfather Hoste nailed a lid on the pit and placed a giant pot with a honeysuckle bush on top of it. It hasn't been opened since. Today, the honeysuckle grows all the way up to the first floor and smells sweet in the summer.

Stance has always been afraid of that pit. She always walks as far around it as she can and sometimes even makes the sign of the cross, which is something she almost never does. It's as if she believes the ghosts of the dead children are still under that lid and the pit leads straight down to the underworld.

Grandfather Hoste wasn't the same after his wife and children died. All the money he'd earned making shoes and clogs was used to pay for the studies of his only surviving son, my good father, Leopold. That's how my father was able to attend the Latin school from the age of twelve to eighteen. After school, he helped his father in the shop. Every evening, after he had hung the shoe lasts on their hooks and washed the dark polish off his fingers, he'd leaf through books on mechanical engineering and read from the great French encyclopedia, parts of which he still knows by heart. At night, he'd use a pencil, compass, pen, and triangle to create sketches of strange contraptions and carry out complicated mathematical calculations. And when he ran out of paper, he would continue his calculations on the wallpaper of his study. My father went on to become an inventor. An engineer. A businessman with his own factory.

"Your father is a genius," Grandma Blom murmurs, and she's right about that—even with the crack in her brain.

The day before I'm supposed to return to the Latin school, Father storms into the house and slams the door. He calls Stance and me into the kitchen. We sit down on two stools at the table. Rozeken and Eddy are out brushing the horse in the courtyard, and Grandma is sleeping in the chair by the fireplace. Father asks us—hardly able to suppress the rage in his voice—if we went to the Franciscan monastery last Sunday. My stomach lurches with fear. But Stance doesn't flinch. She asks him why on earth we'd ever want to go to that Godforsaken pile of rubble.

"I hear it's infested with rats," she says.

Father repeats the question. For a moment, all goes quiet. Then Stance swears on Saint Peter that she has never set foot in that monastery. Father turns to me. Can I also swear on a holy apostle that my sister and I were not in the monastery where men were drinking and a boxing match was going on?

"Where *heathens* were drinking and a *wicked* boxing match was going on," Mother specifies.

"I swear on an apostle," I repeat in a trembling voice.

And just as I—the coward, the church mouse, the little brother with the poor sinner's face—am gripped with panic, ready to fall to my knees and confess everything, Stance says as innocently as Mary in Bethlehem, "Did you hear that, Pier? Heathens drinking at a wicked boxing match. I'll say, we really missed something on Sunday."

Mother slams her fist on the table. She's heard enough. She wants to know how it's possible that her eldest daughter can sit here and lie through her teeth. Didn't she raise her to be a God-fearing child? Mother cries. Over the last few years, she's had to watch her daughter's mind be polluted with sin. Now she tells lies left and right. Doesn't she understand that her father is an entrepreneur, that he doesn't have time for this kind of nonsense? Doesn't she understand that his factory, which is facing so many difficulties right now, depends on loans from a French bank and that an employee of that very bank saw her take off her bonnet and shout at a *woman* boxer? That she was seen with her head uncovered, chatting with some drunken idiot? Doesn't she realize what will happen if the bank decides to stop extending her father's line of credit? He won't be able to repay his debts, and then what? Stance tries to interrupt Mother's tirade, but Mother's voice just gets louder and shriller.

Mother always has the last word at home—and the second-to-last word too. She keeps track of the money and makes all the household decisions. That way Father doesn't have to worry about such things, and she can spare her husband—her thinker, her engineer, her great inventor—whose thoughts are consumed with flywheels, pressure systems, revolutions, and all those forces that fly around their center points.

"I'll ask you one more time," Mother concludes. "Were you at that monastery?"

She glares at Stance with fury in her eyes. But Stance is as stubborn as a mule. Her next words are slow and deliberate.

"We did not set foot in that monastery, Mother. Right, Pier?"

She looks at me with those haughty eyes of hers. My sister has brought this family nothing but misery. Mother waits for me to respond. Her eyes burn through my skin. My lip is trembling; my face is as red as a tomato. I say nothing, but my silence says it all.

"God damn it, Pier, you're such a killjoy," Stance finally says.

"Oh, she curses now too. Leopold, do something."

Without a word, Father grabs Stance by the hair and jerks her off the stool.

Stance screams like the Devil in a barrel of holy water. Father shouts that the Good Lord and the Holy Spirit must have been playing cards when they bestowed Stance with ears, legs, and mind in the warm womb of our innocent mother.

"Children are like waffles," he says. "No matter how well you butter the iron, the first one always fails." And of Father's children, Stance was the test waffle, the one that fell apart as soon as it was pulled off the iron.

It's not the shouting and screaming that frighten me; it's the ripped-out hair. Father has grabbed Stance by the hair many times before, and every time thick clumps are left behind on the tiles. Enough hair to fill a whole pillow.

Having heard the screams, Rozeken and Eddy come running into the room.

"Don't, Father," Rozeken begs.

"Don't hurt Stance," cries Eddy.

"You're my daughter," Father roars. "Behave yourself!"

Mother doesn't say a word. Her crooked teeth are chattering with rage. She looks as if there's a lump of burning coal in her throat. All the commotion wakes up Grandma Blom in her easy chair. She's sitting with her back to us.

"Is it the Austrians?" she cries out in alarm.

"No, Mother, it's nothing," our mother says.

"Father is trying to kill me," Stance screams.

Suddenly, our neighbor Gilbert De Paepe appears in the

front room and asks what's going on. There's a hammer and a pair of pliers sticking out of the pocket of his leather apron.

"Save me, please!" Stance screams. She's lying on the floor in a pile of her own hair.

Gilbert tells my father to calm down before something unfortunate happens. Wouldn't it be better to just shove a bit of tobacco up his nostrils, snort, and sneeze? It really helps a person relax.

Father throws my sister into the attic room and bolts the door shut. I can hear them shouting—my good father versus my destructive sister.

"You forget that you're the daughter of an engineer and an industrialist," Father yells.

"Oh really? I forget which university you attended," is Stance's muffled reply. "Where's your diploma?"

"Enough."

"Why doesn't your invention work?"

"Silence!"

"Why is your factory so quiet?"

"I said silence, God damn it!"

"You're nothing but an old clog maker," Stance screams, and then she sings the rhyme the neighborhood children used to taunt him with when they walked by and saw him working with his father: "Shoemaker, shoemaker, dirty little lice raker."

Poor father. How did such a brilliant man end up with a such a witch for a daughter?

3

STANCE

What in God's name possessed my mother to marry a cobbler who thinks he's too good to shit in his own ditch? A clog maker who dared to tell the bankers and the members of the Ghent elite that he was a mechanic and an inventor? A man who won't step out the door without dousing himself in enough eau de Cologne to make the flies fall from the sky? Mother should have known better. The gossip Mie De Peeze once told me how beautiful Mother used to be, back when she was still in the spring of life.

"She had a voice like the angels in heaven," Mie said. "At the cathedral, all the faithful—whether they were rich or poor, kneeling on the hard church floor or praying on an embroidered cushion in their own private chair—would look up in anticipation when Clara Blommaert would go stand next to her father the sexton at the organ and sing 'Ave Maria.' It was as if the back door to heaven had been opened."

My parents' marriage was the work of Grandfather Hoste, who contracted a lung infection on a cold autumn day and had to stay in bed. The doctor said he'd recover with a bit of bed rest and warm milk, but the old cobbler already knew the Lord was preparing his place in heaven. And he didn't want his pipe to go out without seeing his only surviving son married. Young Leopold was twenty-four at the time and spent his days carving clogs and hammering soles. In the evening, he wore his eyes out reading books. He had no interest in going to the fair, looking at the girls, or any kind of fun. Grandfather Hoste must've been desperate. How could a girl with an ounce of brains want a dry herring like Leopold? So, it was up to him—the old, dying tanner—to find a suitable match for his son.

On his sickbed, my grandfather told Sexton Blommaert how his son was no ordinary shoemaker: He knew Latin and was educated in the sciences. He would be a good match for Clara, who Grandfather knew could write in French and had a voice that made the angels envious. The sexton wouldn't have to worry about a dowry. Leopold would inherit sheets, silverware, crockery, and a beautiful house from him in the near future. And the sexton, that pathetic pea counter, couldn't have been more delighted. This was a chance to marry off his daughter to a cobbler in good standing without having to loosen his own purse strings. Less than half an hour later, the sexton and the old cobbler had reached a marriage agreement. Now their children just needed to meet. The sexton proposed the following: His daughter had a pair of old bottines that were in bad shape, and he would have her take them to the young Leopold for repair.

It was a trap, and my mother, the billy goat, walked right into it.

"I'm not going to be a cobbler forever," was one of the first things my father said to my mother. "I've read the great French encyclopedia from A to G. I know all the definitions by heart. I've also read the Latin books on machines and mechanical engineering that they use at the university in Paris."

"What kind of machines?" she asked.

"Miss Blommaert," he said, "the era of draft animals, muscle power, and windmills is behind us. The future is steam. Steam is energy. Steam is power. Steam is life."

Mother should have grabbed her old bottines and run. She should have gotten as far away from that pathetic dreamer and his shoe shop as possible. But Clara did her best to smile politely, which only heightened my father's enthusiasm.

"The steam engine is going to change everything, Miss Blommaert," he said. "It's already being used in Rotterdam to drain ponds. But I intend to make a steam-powered sawing machine."

Clara Blommaert knew where Rotterdam was—somewhere north of Antwerp and south of the North Pole. A machine for emptying ponds didn't seem very practical to her. After all, where would a woman do her laundry after all the ponds had been emptied? Leopold rattled on about cylinders, pistons, expansion energy, and flywheels. Clara didn't follow. In her eighteen years, she had never met such a strange fellow or heard such difficult words. But the man had a sparkle in his eyes and contagious energy. As he went on and on about centrifugal forces and revolutions, she couldn't help but notice that he still had most of his teeth and that he was actually pretty adorable.

"At the center of it all is Watt's centrifugal governor," Leopold said.

He paused dramatically so Clara could feel the significance of his words. She had no idea what he was talking about.

"Watt's what?" she asked.

"Watt's centrifugal governor," Leopold said. "Invented by James Watt, the British mechanical engineer."

"Of course, James Watt, who else?" Mother said, blushing.

Leopold nodded.

"A colleague of yours, I presume," she said earnestly.

At those words, Leopold swelled with pride. He took her old bottines and told her they'd be ready by the end of the afternoon. Mother flashed him her most beautiful smile. One month later, they were married.

"That first year everything was fine," Grandma Blom told me once, before she got that crack in her brain. She scooped me into her lap and searched my head for lice. Her breath warmed my ears as she told me the story. "When my daughter had you, she was prettier than ever." But then her second and third children died within two weeks of being born. Mother thought it was her fault. That God wouldn't let her keep those children because she sang fairground songs on Sundays, daydreamed in Mass, and chewed on the wafers. When she got pregnant for the fourth time, she didn't make any more mistakes. She murmured all the prayers at Mass, let all the wafers melt in her mouth, and never sang fairground songs on Sundays again. She made the sign of the cross before every statue of Mary she passed and became as pious as the nuns themselves. She was rewarded: Pier and Rozeken survived. Mother couldn't thank heaven enough. She wouldn't make any more mistakes.

I still remember very clearly when the two men from the British Isles came to stay with us. They had come to assemble the steam engine for Father's sawmill. Every evening, Mother cooked a small feast for the guests. One of them was a skinny Englishman named Michael. He drank a glass of port every night after dinner. His Irish assistant, Connor, was a colossal redhead with a thundering laugh that rattled the porcelain in Mother's sideboard. Connor loved thick, creamy soup, and Mother's soup became thicker by the day. And every night, they would sing. She'd sing her old Flemish fairground songs with their dirty lyrics, and he'd sing Irish ballads full of longing for his homeland. Those islanders smoked their pipes constantly, and Mother smoked right along with them. She didn't say a word when Connor stretched out his legs and rested his feet on the corner of the table. Father wouldn't dare to do such a thing!

The men stayed with us for six weeks. The day they finally fired up the steam-powered machine for the first test, there were rumors flying around that the Emperor was going to close the sea borders with England and cut off all trade with the British Isles. A few days later, it was there in black and white in the newspaper. A coach was coming that very evening to take Michael and Connor to Ostend, where they, along with hundreds of their compatriots, would pay a skipper a small fortune to sail them across to Dover.

At the Korenmarkt, a large stagecoach was waiting. The clunky cupboard on wheels would take Michael and Connor via the old Roman road to the coast. The wind was howling and it was pouring rain. Mother begged them to stay another night. She had bought a sheep's leg and marinated it in mustard, garlic, and fresh thyme all day and was planning to roast it for dinner. She'd also made a lentil soup so thick a mouse couldn't drown in it. They could all sit around the stove. What difference would one night make? They could leave first thing the next day. One more night with us, she begged. Connor hesitated, but Michael was unyielding: they couldn't take any risks. The sooner they got to Ostend, the better chance they had of finding a skipper. Tears were streaming down Mother's face. I had never seen her cry before.

"Crossing the Channel in October!" she cried. "You could die! A person should burn candles and pray rosaries in the church for at least seven days before attempting a trip like that."

Father didn't understand. He laid his hand on Mother's shoulder. "Calm down, Clara," he said. "We will pray for them."

She pushed him away.

There was no more room inside the carriage. Michael took a seat next to the coachman, and Connor found a spot amongst the luggage on the roof. Our two guests would arrive in Ostend completely soaked. I saw Mother take three steps toward the stagecoach. It was almost as if she were ready to climb up on the roof and sit down amongst the luggage with a blanket on her lap and go to England with them. Then she turned away from the carriage, clenched her fists, and threw her arms up in the air. She ran home, as if she'd suddenly remembered the thick lentil soup on the stove.

In the early summer of the following year, Mother gave birth to a sixth child. The midwife severed the umbilical cord with her teeth. The infant was strong and heavy.

"This little boy weighs as much as a small turkey," the midwife exclaimed. "Nothing like that chicken-boned brother of his."

After the midwife had skillfully shaped the baby's skull, I was allowed to wash him in a bucket of warm water and wrap him in red cloth. I shouted to Pier to go fetch Father. To tell him he had a son. A second son. His name was Edmond.

◎ ◎ ◎

It wasn't until hours later, when the sheets were hanging out on the clothesline and night had fallen and the baby was suckling Mother's breast for the first time, that we heard Father come home. Pier had delivered the happy news that afternoon, and Father went straight to the Black Magpie and bought a round of beers for every tanner, manure shoveler, fishmonger, and drunk in the pub. Six children, and finally another son. When he finally walked into Mother's room that night, he had to lean against the doorframe to keep himself from falling over. I was sitting on a stool next to the hatbox. Father was carrying a candlestick with a flickering candle in it. He gawked at the child, who had fallen asleep at Mother's breast. Then he conjured up a bouquet of roses from behind his back; two of them had already lost their heads. I took the flowers and put them in a water jug. Then Father came closer and kissed Mother on the forehead, smothering her with the smell of tobacco and rotten beer. Mother told him her duty was done. She had brought six children into the world.

"Cheers to that," cried Father, for a moment forgetting that he was no longer in the pub.

"Six is enough," Mother said dryly.

Father looked speechlessly at his wife and then chuckled. Whenever his thoughts collided, be it from doubt or drink, and he no longer knew what to say before God, he'd just laugh. Mother didn't look the least bit amused. She was clearly exhausted, he said, his tongue limp from alcohol, but he knew that she'd be back to her old self in a few weeks.

"Of course," Father nodded. In his drunken state, Father

didn't see the corners of her mouth trembling or hear the certainty in her voice. He staggered out of the room.

Mother passed the baby to me. I wiped the drops of milk from his mouth and laid him against my shoulder. He let out his first burp. I wrapped him in red cloth and laid him in the cradle. When I turned around, Mother's face was wet with tears.

"What is it, Mama?"

She didn't answer. Her fingers were shaking, and I could tell she was struggling to swallow, as if there was a lump in her throat.

"Mama?"

She shook her head. "Nothing, it's nothing." Her lips formed the words, but no sound came out.

"Just say it."

She buried her head in the pillow and screamed. It was a raw scream, full of madness. A cry that wouldn't stop. I didn't know what to do. Should I wake up my father, who was too drunk to recite the alphabet? Or call our neighbor Gilbert De Paepe, who was surely sleeping between his stoves? Or a doctor? Everyone was asleep. It was late in the night. We were all alone in the world.

"Mama," I said. "Stop it, Mama!"

She just kept screaming into that pillow. Her whole body was shaking. I stood there, clutching the oil lamp as if the flame were our only hope of salvation. Finally, I set down the lamp and pulled Mother out of the pillow by her shoulders. Her head was red and hot. Her cheeks were a web of thin purple lines—the veins that had burst during childbirth.

"What am I doing here?" Mother wailed. "I have to get out of here. I don't want to be here. I have to get out of here, Stance. I need to leave."

I didn't understand what she was saying.

"Father will be sober again tomorrow," I said. "He's proud of his son."

"His son," Mother mumbled. "His son."

Then she started giggling like a lunatic.

I could feel the hairs on the back of my neck stand up as I suddenly remembered how Grandma Blom had told me how small and scrawny we all were when we were born. This little one weighed at least eleven pounds and had fox-red hair. I looked at my mother in astonishment, and she knew I'd guessed her secret. She gripped my hand as if I were her trusted confidante. As if I were suddenly an adult. I was only fourteen at the time. She squeezed my hand to mush.

The weeks after the birth, Mother prayed one rosary after another. In front of the crucifix in the drawing room, she recited Our Fathers and Hail Marys by the dozen and with such devotion that all the bells in heaven must have been ringing. Edmond lived, and Mother calmed down. Heaven had forgiven her mistake. But she hated me. She'd shown me the bottom of her soul, and now she regretted it. I asked her if she still wanted to leave. She told me to keep my mouth shut. That I had misunderstood. That I had too much imagination. She sent me out to fetch water from the pump. To buy bread. To wash sheets. And above all, to stay away from her. Mother wouldn't let me look into her soul again. She didn't squeeze my hand anymore.

A few weeks later, at the fair, I kissed a boy for the first time. He was a few years older than me and tried to strike up a conversation. I pushed him against a hedge, pressed my body against his, and kissed him. And I made sure Mother could see me. Our lips were locked for nearly half a minute when she showed up beside us.

"Constance, shame on you!" she shouted.

The guy nearly wet himself. I cackled with laughter, and Mother slapped me in the face. But I just kept laughing. Father showed up, grabbed me by the hair, and dragged me home. Since then, it's become a kind of family tradition, dragging me around by the hair.

My punishment for going to the boxing match lasts one day and one night. On the morning of the second day, Mother opens the door to the attic room and says that Spiering has left for the Latin school and will not be home until Easter.

"Good riddance," I say.

I follow Mother downstairs with my full chamber pot between my hands and dump it out in the street. Then I head into the dining room in search of a piece of bread. I'm chattering away when I notice that something has changed. Our beautiful Empire-style salon chair is gone. "When you sit in it, you immediately feel like you're in Paris," Father used to say, and then he'd let us take turns sitting in the expensive chair with the laurel wreath carved into the backrest. We felt rich in that chair.

"Sold it to the stove maker," Mother said.

"Why?"

"We're going to have to live more simply," Mother says.

"Do we have money problems?"

"No," she says.

"Is Father's sawing machine still broken?"

Mother doesn't respond.

"How is that possible?" I ask disparagingly. "He's got that centrifugal governor, doesn't he?"

"Stop talking about things you don't understand," Mother snarls. "Your father will get his machine working. And he's going to the bank to take out an extra loan. Everything is going to be fine. God will take care of us."

I hear the baker tooting his horn outside. He's come with fresh bread.

Mother hands me the crocheted wallet with the Emperor's face on it.

"Go get some bread," she says.

The wallet feels awfully light.

God will take care of us. Tell that to the mice, Mother.

4

PIER

According to my good father, there is no better place to learn French, mathematics, and Latin than at the boarding school in Pecq, near Menen. This is the school where my father used to teach and where he cultivated his taste for science. The Jesuit fathers from my father's time have since been replaced by noncommissioned officers of the French army. I travel to school by trekschuit, a boat pulled down the canal by a team of horses. At my side is Albert "Bertie" Lallemand. His father owns a company that makes uniforms for the French army and is one of the richest people in Ghent. Bertie is my only friend at school, and he makes me laugh. He's a master at imitating sounds. In the cabin on the boat, he squeaks like a mouse—it sounds so convincing that the skipper's wife jumps in fright. Then he buzzes like a horsefly tapping against the windows. It's enough to drive the woman crazy.

At the end of our journey, Bertie tells me that my father came to his house.

"Why?" I ask.

"I'm not sure," Bertie says, "but I think he asked my father to lend him some money. He said he had a sturdy daughter who might be a good match for my older brother."

"What?" I exclaim. "Your brother and Constance? She's as ugly as the night."

"My brother thinks she's charming," Bertie replies.

I shake my head. Charming! He has no idea.

"Why do you hate her so much?" Bertie asks. "Didn't she save your life once?"

It's true; she did. I was about ten years old when I fell in the Lieve. The water was ice cold; it seeped into my woolen clothes and pulled me down. Stance jumped in after me, grabbed me by the collar, and pulled me to the ladder on the quay. People came running up to help and wrapped us in blankets. Yes, she saved me. But what else was she supposed to do?

"Well, your father left empty handed," he says.

"My father will get the money from the bank," I say. "And as for your brother—he should consider himself lucky."

Bertie and I share a room with Toine, the son of a major. He's French, but he doesn't mind sharing a room with two Flemish boys. There are three beds to a room, each with a narrow wardrobe and bedside table. At dinner, there's a lot of talk about the Emperor and the war. Most of the boys want to join the army later. They can't wait to become officers in the cavalry and charge at France's enemies. "Long live the Emperor!" they shout, and me and Bertie join in. We don't want to stand out in a school full of boys from rich French families. Every morning we wake up to the sound of a drumroll from the courtyard, and within ten minutes, we have to present ourselves fully dressed in our school uniforms. We are divided into companies of twenty-five. Artillery Sergeant Leroy teaches us mathematics and geometry in full military dress, including his black, two-pointed hat. He shouts his lessons because he can't hear very well anymore. And he has very little patience. When he interrogates me about acute angles and it takes me too long to answer, his face turns red.

"When we pointed our guns at the Russians, we did not hesitate, Hoste," he rants. "At Austerlitz, there was not a doubt in my mind that if I wanted to blow the Russians to smithereens, my cannon had to be positioned at a forty-two-degree angle." The way he talks, you'd think the Emperor owes France's victories to him personally.

Subjects like French, history, and science are taught by corporals. One of them makes us stand at attention for fifteen minutes every day. We're not allowed to move a muscle—not even if a wasp lands on our nose. He promises that he'll make men out of us and teaches us to march in step, one behind the other, in perfect rows, so that we can go straight into the army after we finish school. Corporal Wasp runs with us through the woods, and when we collapse after a couple of miles, he shakes his head with pity. No, we're not men yet.

There's one teacher who is different from the rest: Father Charles. Under the Emperor, members of the clergy are no longer allowed to teach, but Father Charles has been around for so long he's practically part of the building. He's as old and knotty as the furniture. Sergeant Leroy couldn't find any officers who could teach Latin, so he quietly let Father Charles stay on.

A few days after we arrive at school, we're ambushed in the orchard by a company of older boys. They hurl rocks at us and then charge at us screaming and brandishing sticks with their compass needles attached to the end. Bertie and I make a run for it, but they still get us. They scrape us with the compasses and tear the sleeve off my jacket and the buttons off of Bertie's shirt. Our white knee socks get covered in mud. "The Emperor hates cowards," one shouts. We don't say anything back.

That night, Marie-Ange, the kitchen maid, assesses the damage. All the maids and servants at the school speak Flemish. Sometimes they slip us an extra stick of licorice or a sugar cookie and help us when we need it. While Marie-Ange is sewing my sleeve back on, Bertie and I hear a cat screech. Marie-Ange immediately makes the sign of the cross. The screeching, she tells us, comes from the Devil, a black cat that lurks around the school and rarely shows its face. Every night, it sneaks its way into the cellar to steal some sausage or a dead pigeon. After it's had its fill, it sprays the contents of its accursed bladder against the cellar door.

"There's not a soap in the world that could get that stink out," Marie-Ange complains, and she kisses the picture of Our Lady hanging on a chain around her neck.

"It's as if the Devil is mocking us," says Beatrice, another kitchen maid, who's ironing shirts. Every day after the evening prayer, the maids bolt the cellar door shut, but that cat still gets inside.

"We even followed Father Charles's advice and sprinkled the door with holy water," Marie-Ange says. "But it didn't help."

"What a bunch of superstitious sheep," Bertie whispers as we walk back to our room.

Late that night, after the last candle has been extinguished, Bertie sneaks out of bed, pushes open the window to the courtyard, and imitates the long, piercing cry of a cat in heat. It sounds so mournful that you'd think he hasn't seen a female in years. Suddenly a light flickers downstairs. Toine and I peer through the window. We see none other than Father Charles—barefoot and wearing nothing but his nightshirt—step out into the courtyard with a giant knife in his right hand and a candle in the left. His eyes are wild, full of vengeance, ready to ram the blade into the Devil's ribs himself. Bertie and Toine bite their pillows to keep from laughing.

The next day, Father Charles De Bruyne—or the Porpoise, as we like to call him behind his back—recounts the story of Caesar and Scipio as if he were right there with them when they marched into battle and stood face-to-face with an army of screaming barbarians spitting on their shields.

I hang on to his every word. I hammer the Latin vocabulary into my head, recite the declensions as if they were verses, and during the lessons, I'm completely focused. I'm one of the best in the class, and I hope that one day Father Charles will pat me on the shoulder and call me amicus, a friend.

In the third week of March, Sergeant Leroy informs me that my school fees have not been paid. Father has asked them to postpone the deadline for his payment. The sergeant has given him one week. I'm so embarrassed.

"Master Hoste, does your father think that his son can attend this school free of charge?" Father Charles rants later that day. "Imagine, free tuition! What would become of the world, Hoste? The fathers of all your classmates pay very promptly for the fresh sheets, the meals, and yes, even the lessons we provide at this school. Those men understand that we teachers, the ones who fill your heads with knowledge every day, do not work for free. Everyone pays on time—everyone except your father, Pieter Hoste."

The boys in the classroom chuckle. My eyes are glued to my wooden bench, which is full of scratches and scribbles from earlier generations of pupils.

"I had your father in my class, you know," Father Charles continues. "He learned about as much Latin in this classroom as a calf in High Mass. If it weren't for his aptitude for mathematics and the kindness of my colleagues he would have never finished school. Your father should've stuck to his clogs and shoe polish after he graduated. But no, Mr. Hoste had to put feathers on his hat and curl his ponytail. He had to be a gentleman. Play the businessman. The inventor. And now he's asking us to give him an extension on his payment."

I feel the steam rising in my head.

"Your father is a shoemaker," Father Charles concludes. "Once a dirty cloghead, always a dirty cloghead."

The following evenings, I get my revenge when Bertie stands at the window and moans like a cat for minutes on end. I imagine the woeful cries cutting through Father Charles's sleep like a guillotine through a human neck. Night after night, we behead his sleep. And the next day the old Jesuit shows up for class with dark circles under his eyes, looking like the walking dead. Just to annoy him, Bertie makes sure to ask if he slept well. Apparently, the sergeant and the corporals are able to sleep right through it. But the maids look worried. "It's the Devil," we hear the kitchen maid Beatrice mumble. "The Devil."

But then one day, we hear Father Charles De Bruyne whistling through the corridors to the tune of "Alas, and Did My Savior Bleed," and it seems that nothing can steal his joy. That afternoon, Marie-Ange tells us that Father Charles murdered the Devil. Caesar and Scipio's brother-in-arms had set out a saucer of mutton drenched in blood that he'd laced with a thimble of arsenic bought from a painter in Tournai.

"The Devil lapped it right up," Marie-Ange whispers. "Every last drop of the poisoned blood. But we still haven't found his body."

"I'm sure he's dead," Beatrice says, but she makes the sign of the cross to be extra sure.

"Amen," Bertie says and gives me a wink. "Come on, let's go find the Devil."

We search the coal cellar and check behind the woodpile; we search the old stables and the fields. Finally, up along the road, we see it: the Devil's curly tail sticking out from under a rhododendron bush. We crouch down and push away the low-hanging branches. The Devil is one of the biggest cats I've ever seen. His fur is blacker than coal and ink combined. His tongue is hanging out of his mouth. The arsenic dried him out. He dragged himself here from the cellar to die.

"Let's take him and put him in the Porpoise's room," Bertie says.

"You're crazy," I say.

"No wait, I have a better idea," says Bertie. "Take off your jacket."

"Why?" I ask.

"Just do it. The Porpoise called your father a calf, didn't he?" Bertie says. "You! You speak Latin better than the Pope, God damn it!"

"That animal stinks."

"Your coat!"

I give in.

Bertie wraps my blue coat around the filthy animal and hands the bundle to me.

"Why do I have to carry it?"

"I'll go make sure the coast is clear," Bertie says. We walk across the stone-walled courtyard. I'm afraid someone will see the tail dangling out of my jacket. We head up to the dormitories.

When Toine sees the giant, dead cat lying on my bed, he's stunned.

"Mon Dieu, Bert! Is that the Devil?" he asks anxiously. "Are you sure he's dead?"

"As dead as Caesar and Scipio," Bertie reassures him.

Then Bertie walks us through his plan. Toine thinks it's brilliant. I think it's terrible. I want no part of it whatsoever.

"What are you going to do, then?" Bertie asks. "Sleep with the Devil on your bed?"

I don't answer. He's got me in a tight spot, all right.

"Nobody's ever dared to attack my father like that," Toine jokes. He doesn't speak much Flemish yet, so he probably only understood half the insult.

"When we pointed our guns at the Russians, we didn't hesitate, Hoste," Bertie roars, imitating the sergeant. My roommates laugh, and I can't help but chuckle along with them. Then we take an oath of eternal secrecy.

After the clock strikes midnight, me, Bertie, and Toine sneak out of our room carrying the Devil between us and walk through the corridor to the stairwell. We scamper down the stairs, cross the courtyard, and slip into the school. We tiptoe past the classrooms and up the stairs to the attic. The door is locked. But Bertie has already planned for this. He pushes his compass needle into the keyhole and wiggles it around.

"This lock is nothing," he says. Toine and I are on high alert. We're afraid of even the slightest sound. The creaking of a staircase. The squeaking of a door. A voice. I mumble a Hail Mary, and all of a sudden the lock clicks open.

"Shhh," Bertie warns. He pushes the door open. We step into the attic. Broken chairs and benches are stacked in a corner. Piles of notebooks bundled together with string are stacked in an open cupboard. Maybe my father's notebooks are around here somewhere. Our bare feet leave prints in the dust. Bertie points to the ceiling. There's a small window in the roof. He climbs up on a crossbeam and crawls over to the window. Then he stands on his tiptoes and pushes it open. He motions for us to come. Toine hands me the Devil. I accidentally drop him and just barely manage to catch him by the tail.

"You've got two left hands all right," Bertie says.

"Hoste, if you'd been born in Sparta, they would've thrown you into the ravine," Toine jokes.

But I'm the one holding the giant cat under my arm. I inch across the crossbeam toward Bertie. He takes the Devil and hurls him out the window with a swoop of the arm. The cat hits the slate roof, slides down, then falls over the edge and lands in the gutter with a quiet thud.

"It worked," Bertie whispers.

A few minutes later, we're creeping down the stairs on our tiptoes. When we get back to our beds, we can't stop laughing.

The next day, the weather is mild. When we enter Father Charles's classroom, he asks us to open the windows so the classroom can air out a bit. Before we know it, a rotten stench has permeated the room. It's so bad that we can hardly concentrate on the grammatical cases of ancient Rome. The Porpoise wants to know where the foul smell is coming from. Nobody says a word, so he starts sniffing around. We open our bags and desks, and eventually the old Jesuit concludes that it must be coming from outside. He sticks his head out the window, looks down, sideways, and finally up. He jumps when he spots the Devil's stiff tail hanging from the gutter. A pigeon is pecking at the rotting carcass. He slams the window shut, his face white as a sheet. He looks as if he's wondering whether the Devil actually does live in black cats, as the kitchen maids claim. How else could a dying cat, after ingesting a dose of arsenic large enough to take down a grown man, drag itself in all its pain and agony all the way up to the roof of the school to die in the gutter right above his killer's classroom? Father Charles makes the sign of the cross at least three times and touches the rosary on his chest. He closes the window, but the smell remains.

During the break, the old Porpoise, in his long black robes and three-pointed hat, marches out to the sergeant and corporals, who are smoking their pipes in the schoolyard. He asks them to go up to the roof and fetch the black cat from the gutter, but they all refuse. It's not that they're superstitious; they're just not interested in climbing up on the roof for a stupid cat.

By the afternoon, Father Charles can't take it anymore. He grabs a broom, stomps through the classroom, kisses the cross around his neck, rolls up his sleeves and trousers, and throws open the window. Without a word of explanation to his students, he steps out onto the ledge. He grips the window frame with one hand, and with the other he wields the broom like a Trojan War hero ready to attack the Greeks with his javelin.

"Go get him, sir!" Bertie shouts with a sly look on his face, and Father Charles orders him to go stand in the corner and recite the conjugation of *essere*. Bertie does as he's told, but his eyes are locked on the window so as not to miss the life-threatening act of heroism that his Latin teacher is about to perform. My stomach twinges with fear. If Father Charles falls and breaks his neck, it'll be all my fault. I will go to hell. I look at the statue of Christ on the cross and murmur a string of Our Fathers at top speed.

The Porpoise looks down at the twelve meters below. Then he curls his lips as if he has nothing but contempt for the terrifying height. He stands on the tips of his lacquered shoes and taps the gutter a few times with the end of the broom. The gutter dates back to Burgundian times. "Indestructible," the sergeant once called it. After a lot of frantic jabbing, the Porpoise manages to nudge the Devil's carcass. The cat's butt appears over the edge of the gutter. Father Charles gives the indestructible gutter one final poke, and it promptly crumbles into pieces.

Rocks and dust come crashing down on the Porpoise's head, filling the collar of his teaching robes, followed by the Devil, whose body has been ripped to shreds and eaten away by maggots. The fact that the Porpoise, in his billowing teacher's robes, didn't fall off the ledge is nothing short of a miracle. He charges back into the classroom with a beastly roar, knocks over two benches and rams his elbow into the face of Toine, who was standing far too close to the window. Toine collapses like a rag doll. The Porpoise brushes the rubble off his neck like a lunatic. He curses like a sailor, rips off his robes and then his shirt. He rubs the Devil's remains off his clothes and shakes the wriggling maggots out of his hair. Everyone stares at the Devil's body on the floor of the classroom. I make the sign of the cross, and everyone else does the same. Everyone except Bertie, that is, who's still facing the wall and practically wetting his pants with glee.

At dinner, Toine—with a goose-egg-sized bump above his eye—keeps asking the others what he missed while he was unconscious. The only topic of conversation at every table is Father Charles's spectacle, and the whole dining room is roaring with laughter. Every once in a while, Corporal Wasp stands up and shouts for silence at the dinner table. But even the petty officers can't get enough of the story. We can hear them snickering. It's Saturday, and we each get half a waffle with a dash of butter on it. I'm just about to bite into mine when Marie-Ange, the kitchen maid, comes to tell me that the sergeant has asked to see me.

I knock on the door of Sergeant Leroy's office and greet him politely. Outside the evening sky is streaked with red. My legs are as heavy as lead. Did somebody snitch? Was I seen crossing the courtyard yesterday with the Devil in my arms?

"Pieter Hoste from Ghent," he says, without looking up from his writing. There's a medal hanging on his uniform next to the shiny buttons. The two flickering candles on his desk are the only light in the room.

"Yes, Sergeant," I reply.

I hear his quill scratching on the paper. He sets it back in the inkwell and blows the paper dry.

"You're going home tomorrow," he says without looking up.

"Tomorrow," I say. "But it's not Easter yet."

"Your father has just informed me that he cannot pay your tuition," Sergeant Leroy says. "I'm sorry."

Only then does he look up at me. His eyes are soft. He's not the worst.

"But I want to stay in school."

"Rules are rules, Hoste. A school is not a charity. You understand that, don't you?"

I nod. He hands me a coin, a silver napoléon.

"That's for the boat. I've reserved a place for you. You leave at seven. Marie-Ange will pack you some bread and cheese for the trip. You'll be home the day after tomorrow."

I close the door and walk through the corridor back to the dining room. The Porpoise comes down the stairs. He's wearing clean clothes and smells like eau de Cologne and dead cat. I lower my eyes.

"What are you doing here, Hoste?"

"I've just come from the sergeant, Father Charles."

"Do you have to leave?"

I nod. He looks at the floor and growls.

"I take it things are not going so well for your father?"

He says it in a flat tone, without mockery or malice.

I shrug.

"That fool," he says.

I don't know what to say to that.

"Don't give up, Hoste," he says. "Keep your chin up."

I nod.

"And above all," he says, "don't forget your Latin."

I shake my head.

Then he turns and walks to the dining room, his long robes flapping down the corridor.

That evening I gather my things and say goodbye to Toine and Bertie. They saved my waffle for me. I eat it cold. I tell them I'll be back soon. My father will find a solution. He's an inventor, after all.

5

STANCE

It is the first Sunday in April in the year one thousand eight hundred and eight. Pier is home from school and sulks around the house. Sometimes I hear him whispering Latin inflections. He is afraid he'll forget everything.

"Pieter, you go with your sister," Mother shouts just as I'm about to leave for the Ghent Town Hall, where they're drawing conscrits for the Emperor's army. Whenever a man gets too close and tries to strike up a conversation with me, Spiering is supposed to puff up his chest and tell the dumb clod that I'm a young lady of stature and that he better get lost. Rozeken asks if she can come too, but I tell her the soldiers' lottery is not a spectacle for snot-nosed kids and that she should stay home and play with her dolls.

We walk through the city as if there's nothing going on. I'm wearing my finest dress, a red-and-white bonnet with flowers and ribbons, and even leather boots. But Pier and I both know that Dad has given up his sawing machine. The oaks, elms, and lime trees are piling up in his factory. His workers have to cut the trees by hand. He says he doesn't even want to look at trees anymore. Even the scraggly apple tree in our courtyard makes him feel depressed. Father sold his expensive steam engine for half of what he paid for it to an entrepreneur in Rotterdam who plans to use it to pump the water out of the marshes and transform them into farmable land. But Father is still in debt. The men from the bank come by every week. He tells them that he's working on a new machine. His sketchbooks are filled with formulas, and when he runs out of room, he writes on the wallpaper. But the bankers are getting impatient. They want money.

Despite the spring chill in the air, the Botermarkt is especially busy that morning. The stone counts and countesses of old Flanders look down from their niches in the Ghent Town Hall at the boys who will soon be sent off to war. There are also mothers, sisters, and curious onlookers with parasols. A few of the young men are dressed in their Easter best, wearing expensive coats, knickers, polished boots, and plumed hats. They're the sons of counts, marquesses, and factory owners. Their names could be drawn too, of course, but they don't seem very worried. They look around arrogantly as if the very cobblestones in the square belong to them.

"It looks like most of them have dug deep in their clothes trunks," I say.

"It's not every day that you meet the mayor and the prefect," says my brother, the killjoy.

The rest of the young people in the square aren't exactly dressed for church. Some are walking around in gray rags with straw in their clogs. They're farmers' sons from the villages around Ghent. A peddler in a top hat walks through the crowd calling himself "Gaspar the Egyptian" and telling people that he's selling "infallible talismans" that he brought back from the pyramids of Egypt himself. His talismans bring good luck, he says, and a guarantee that the owner will draw the right number. A number that will exempt him from military service. And in the unlikely event that he draws the wrong number and has to join the Emperor's army, the talisman will protect him from bayonets, swords, bullets, and cannonballs. A nervous young man with a puffy collar buys a talisman in the shape of a sphinx for ten francs. Then Gaspar the Egyptian walks deeper into the crowd until he comes to a group gathered around Fons De Keghel, the son of the grocer from Sint-Jacobs. Fons loves his beer and doesn't shy away from a fight. All the girls in the neighborhood call him "Mr. Adonis." When I was fourteen, he dared me to throw burning pieces of cork through the Coppenholle spinsters' open cellar window and shout "Fire in the hole!" He'd barely finished his sentence before I'd already thrown three blazing pieces of cork into the cellar. Pretty soon, the smoke was rising out of the window, and Fons started screaming "Fire! Fire!" like a madman. Less than a minute later, the women came rushing out of the house hysterically, wearing nothing but their nightdresses and caps. The two old figs fainted in the street. By then, Fons the scoundrel was already long gone. The neighbors came with buckets of water, and I was blamed for everything.

"Why don't you think before you do something stupid?" Father shouted before twisting my ears and pulling me up to the attic by my hair.

As the peddler is making his sales pitch, Fons takes off his wooden shoe and claims that it came from Egypt too.

"Won it from a mummy in a card game. The poor guy had to go out in his socks," he says and motions as if he's about to sell the peddler a slap with his wooden shoe. Gaspar the Egyptian ducks out of the way. I burst into laughter. Fons sees me.

"Well if it isn't Stancie from the Kraanlei quay," he says.

"If it isn't Fonsie from Sint-Jacobs," I reply without lowering my eyes. Pier gives me a shove. A come-on-keep-walking shove. But I shove him back. Fons seems to find this funny too.

An elderly man in a tidy gendarme uniform walks up the steps to the Ghent Town Hall. The crowd falls silent. The man twiddles the ends of his long mustache—a badge of honor grown by men who have fought for the Emperor. This man served under the French flag. He's been through the fire, and now he's been made gendarme. He shouts that today is a great day, that seventy-one young men will have the honor of joining the Grande Armée of Emperor Napoléon the First. Each young man of twenty years of age present here today will walk into Town Hall and draw a piece of paper from Prefect Gijsens's hat. Then, they will present it to the two gendarmes who will read the number written on it aloud. If the number is higher than seventy-one, the young man can go home and continue his life as a citizen of the great French Empire. If he draws a number lower than seventy-one, he will immediately receive his medical examination in the Town Hall. If he's declared fit for duty, he will join the Emperor's army this summer or fall and might even have the chance to climb up in the ranks and achieve fame. The lottery is fair, the gendarme emphasizes, because in the eyes of the Emperor all men are equal. Each one will be judged on his courage and merits, not on his family tree or the color of his blood. Those days are over. At that, the gendarme proudly shows off the stripes he earned in the French army.

"My family tree is at home in the garden," Fons shouts. "I've been pissing on it my whole life."

Fons's friends burst into laughter. I laugh too. As loud as I can.

"Quiet," hisses Pier the Nag.

A couple of the young men who do have an impressive family tree and a fancy last name stare at the ground to avoid the others' mocking looks.

"Those rich people will get the last laugh anyway," Fons says. "If they draw a low number, they'll just find a replacement."

Fons spits on the ground in the direction of a young nobleman standing nearby. The young man looks up, clearly annoyed. It's Geoffroy de Soudan, the son of the marquess who lives on the fancy Veldstraat. They visited my father's factory a year ago for a demonstration of the steam-powered saw. My father even introduced me to Geoffroy, and I made small talk with him in my best French. His father, the marquess, stood there beside us with his nose in the wind as if I were some farm girl unworthy of his son's attention. Then the demonstration began. Father's saw split a giant oak tree in six minutes and thirty-two seconds. It was the highlight of his career. We had money back then. An Empire chair with a laurel wreath carved in it. Fish on Fridays and meat on Sundays. And a fresh newspaper to read every day.

The young nobleman doesn't flinch at Fons's spit. His eyes linger on my face. He recognizes me and nods. I nod back, and that makes Fons jealous.

The gendarme reads a letter from the Emperor aloud, praising the soldiers who followed him from victory to victory and helped him establish peace in Europe. His men are the defenders of the French Revolution: freedom, equality, or death. Our enemies, the Emperor tells us in his letter, find it easier to mock the eagle of France than to defeat him on the battlefield. When our great France is finally complete and the prosperity of all is within reach, the soldiers will return home. All they will have to do is say that they fought for the Emperor, and every man will want to shake their hand and thank them for their courage.

The gendarme ends his speech with "Long live the Emperor! Vive l'Empereur!" Everyone at the Botermarkt repeats the cry in unison—all the anxious young men, the girls with their parasols. It makes me tear up. Freedom, equality, or death. It sounds so good.

"Poor boys," says someone behind me. "They know when their military service starts, but no one can say when it will end."

Fons says he doesn't want to join the army. How will his parents manage the store without him? He's hoping he'll draw a number higher than seventy-one.

"But surely you don't believe in an Egyptian talisman," I say.

"No," Fons replies, "but I do believe in a lock of hair."

"A lock of hair?" I repeat in surprise.

"Yes, a lock of your hair," he says. What a charmer.

"Might I kindly request that you go find someone else to give you a lock of hair?" Pier demands, sounding like a chick who thinks he's a rooster.

"Please," Fons begs, suddenly a little less tough. "A lock of your hair will bring me good luck."

"Stance, it's time to go," says my brother.

"Fine, you rascal. You got a pair of scissors?" I ask Fons.

Pier looks angry, and Fons looks relieved. He marches right over to a knife sharpener's stand and grabs a pair of scissors. The man looks at him in shock. I take off my bonnet, and my brown braid falls down on my shoulder. I loosen my hair. It's a lovely feeling. Fons stares at me. All that loose, full hair has quite an effect on him. I take the scissors out of his hand and snip off a large lock of hair. I pull a ribbon out of my bonnet and tie it around the lock.

"Hey snotnose, why don't you go take these scissors back," Fons says to Pier, whose face is purple with rage.

I carefully tuck my hair back into my hat, a little more slowly than necessary. Fons slips the lock into his breast pocket. He's glowing. It's true, he is pretty handsome.

"I think you'll need more luck than that," I say.

Then I stand on the tips of my boots and kiss Fons on the mouth. He doesn't even look surprised—as if that happens to him all the time.

Pier yanks me by the arm.

"Are you out of your mind? Everyone can see you," Spiering moans and jerks me away, away from Mr. De Keghel. From the grin on Fons's face, you'd think he was the richest man at the Botermarkt.

Pier is as nervous as a mouse in a cat basket. His eyes dart back and forth like a madman's. He's really going to get it when Mother hears that I kissed a boy on the mouth with him standing right there next to me.

"Why do you always do this to me?" he shouts.

"He tasted like summer apples," I tease. "Sour but juicy." I can feel my cheeks glowing with excitement.

Pier keeps walking with his arm through mine.

"Where do you get these ideas?" he groans.

Finally, he stops at the edge of the Botermarkt in front of a couple of souvenir sellers with their wares laid out on the ground.

"Are you done?" I ask.

He doesn't answer. He pretends to be interested in the souvenirs—French flags, eagle pins, tricolored ribbons, and little busts of the Emperor with a two-pointed hat on his head. The vendors sit by their trinkets waiting for the young people to pour out of the Ghent Town Hall and buy them. The ones who are off to war will have just received their stipend and have some money to spend. Those who managed to escape might buy something out of sheer joy.

"Come on, Spiering, stop sulking," I say.

"People are watching you," he says. "The wild inventor's daughter who goes around kissing boys in public!"

Then, to my horror, Binus Serlippens, the son of the baker on Lammerstraat, is standing in front of us. His face is covered in pimples. Something about him gives me the creeps. He asks for a lock of my hair too.

"Soon all of Ghent will be asking for one," moans Pier.

"Ask your mother, Binus," I say. "Leave me alone."

"Please, Stance," Binus asks. "I don't want to be sent to the army."

"What are you whining about, Binus?" I ask. "With all those pustules on your face, you'll probably be refused anyway. They'll never let you join the army."

Binus looks disappointed. Sorry, but my hair isn't for everyone.

"Don't be sad, Binus," Pier says sympathetically. "There's a man selling Egyptian talismans."

Despite my lock of hair, Fons still draws the number eight from the hat and has no choice but to become a soldier of the Emperor. Fons spends all the draft money he got from Prefect Gijsens at the Black Magpie. The whole afternoon, people in the pub shout, "Vive les conscrits!" and "Long live our soldiers!" By nightfall, Fons is completely drunk. He stands up on a stool and shouts, "Where is Stancie from the Kraanlei quay?" The question is shouted over and over again by his drinking buddies. Then he falls off the stool, hits the floor, and breaks two teeth. He doesn't even feel the pain.

Of course, Mother hears the story of the public kiss and takes me to the Chapel of Saint Rita, the patron saint of the hopeless. She dips her fingers into the shell of holy water and makes three signs of the cross, flinging drops wildly as she does. Then she pushes me to my knees in front of the statue of Saint Rita, the one the French found too ugly to steal. There's a bloody gash on Rita's forehead, and against her chest she holds Christ's crown of thorns. In front of the statue, Mother lights an animal-fat candle that smells like something dead. She bought a rose at the market to put in the stone vase in front of the statue. While I am kneeling there, Mother prays to Saint Rita.

"Our Constance needs wisdom, Saint Rita." Her words rustle through the chapel. "And an ounce won't be enough. Give my daughter a whole pound of wisdom so that she can preserve her decency, use her working hands, keep her big mouth shut, and, above all, understand that obeying her parents is the way to happiness. Amen."

The candles around Saint Rita flicker for a moment. Mother looks down at me and says, "One hundred Hail Marys." I nod and try to look as pious as possible. She gives me a slap on the side of the head. "Wipe that smile off your face!"

When we walk out of the cathedral, Mother gives some money to the beggars, most of whom are victims of the plague or missing a limb. Apparently, a little charity gives your prayers more weight in heaven. In the square, Mother buys an amulet of Saint Rita and tells me that from then on I will wear her ugly face around my neck.

A week later, Fons shows up at our house and stands at our kitchen window. He's combed his hair and smells faintly of tobacco and Cologne.

"Mrs. Hoste," Fons says to Mother. He takes off his hat and bows deeply. "How are you this evening, madam?"

"I'm still standing," Mother replies as I step outside to greet him. "And mind your manners. I've got my eye on you, grocery boy."

She beckons to my watchful protector and pushes him out the door with us. Pier nods at Fons, and Fons nods back. The front door remains open. Mother sets the table loudly, so I don't forget she's there.

Fons tells me that the pimply Binus has to join the army, too, and that he'll never survive. He says that Binus is thinking of running away, but there are high fines for the parents of deserters.

"And the Emperor's gendarmes will always find you," Fons adds.

"I'm sorry my hair didn't help," I say. "You should've bought an Egyptian talisman instead."

"Yeah, well, I ran into Geoffroy de Soudan at the pub, you know, the marquess's son. He bought one of those talismans, the stupid bluestocking. And he still drew a low number. He tried to tell the mayor that he was physically unfit for the army. But the doctor listened to his heart, checked his tongue, and declared him fit for service. It took less than a minute. The Marquess de Soudan offered two thousand francs to anyone willing to take his son's place, but so far no one's volunteered."

"Two thousand francs," I whistle. "For that kind of money he's sure to find somebody. He still has a couple of weeks, right?"

"I don't give a damn about the marquess," Fons whispers. "All I care about is you."

"Excuse me, I'm still here," my shadow sputters.

"Then close your eyes, Spiering," I say and lean in for a second taste of that summer apple. Sour and juicy. I can't get enough of his lips.

"That's enough!" shouts Pope Pieter the Superfluous.

Five seconds later, Mother steps outside. She looks at me and then at Pier, then she says it's getting late. Very late. She makes no effort to suppress the disdain in her voice. Fons wishes Mother a restful evening and bows again. Mother looks at him as if he personally nailed Jesus to the cross. Fons gives us a short nod and walks off in the direction of Oudburg. You'd think he's got feathers under his shoes the way he floats off into the night.

"What a calf," says Pier.

I nod.

"You're driving that guy crazy."

"Crazy is right," I say.

My brother sighs.

"Maybe I'll follow him into the army this fall," I say. Pier looks at me, trying to judge whether or not I'm actually serious. I feel wild, almost intoxicated from the taste of summer apples.

"Father would never allow it," Pier says.

"I can cook for the army. I can do the laundry. That's what I do at home anyway."

"Then you'll have to marry Fons first."

"Or I could just go as his sweetheart. His girl."

"I thought you hated laundry and cooking?" He looks at me with that righteous Latin-school smile of his, the milk-sop. I feel like smacking that grin right off his face. But Pier is right. I'm not going to run away with Fons. I was bluffing. Am I supposed to follow in my mother's footsteps and just marry the first fool who comes along?

"Maybe I will do it," I say with just a little too much conviction in my voice.

"You go right ahead," Pier says. "I'm going to bed."

"You'll miss me when I'm gone," I say.

"Not for a second," he says.

6

PIER

On a day in early June in the year one thousand eight hundred and eight, Father announces that his friend Lieven Goeminne is coming to dinner. I've been out of school for two months already. He says we need to make sure it's a festive evening. Not only is Lieven considering taking over Father's debts, he is also thinking about financing one of his latest inventions. He's already paid him an advance. An advance! Lieven is our salvation.

Stance and Mother sweep, mop, and scrub all day long. They shine the doorknobs with copper polish, scour the floors with green soap, and rub the silverware with sour milk. I have to go shopping with Stance at the Botermarkt. The butcher's son, a hefty guy with a bullish neck, goes out of his way to help Stance. He shows her the best cow tongue and the meatiest rabbits. He blushes so red that it looks as if all the blood has drained from his tiny brain. Can't he see that Stance is too ugly to dance for the Devil? The butcher's son asks if we would like to buy the rabbits and beef on credit because for her that could certainly be arranged. What a dumb Joseph that guy is. I jingle the wallet and say we'll pay for it immediately—and for any outstanding charges as well.

"My dear brother," Stance says. "Why can't you just nod and smile for once?"

While paying, I accidentally drop a few centimes in the sheep's kidneys, and Stance tells the butcher's son that her little brother is so clumsy he wouldn't be able to pluck a chicken without dropping it. And boy, does that make the idiot laugh!

Mother is in the kitchen, cooking as if her life depends on it. Stance helps her with the cow's tongue broth and fills the fish rolls with pine seeds, grapes, and sweet herbs. My mouth is watering. The main course is a rabbit-plum stew, and for dessert they're making nun fritters, soft gingerbread balls kneaded with cloves and cinnamon. I steal one of the balls from the plate, and Stance whacks me with a wooden spoon.

"Get lost," she says. Mother doesn't even bother to correct her. Stance grins. What a shrew.

Mother goes next door to borrow a large, pumpkin-shaped porcelain bowl from the wife of the stove maker Gilbert De Paepe. The handle on the lid is shaped like the stem of a gourd.

Mother insists that Stance wear a blue frock with a white

bonnet. She wants her daughter to look like the statue of Mary in the church, the picture of innocence. Stance plucks spitefully at the dress.

"This damned thing itches," she says.

"Watch your mouth," Mother snaps.

Stance looks grumpier than the north wind. Pretty soon, she's going to bite back. She looks nothing like the Virgin Mary.

Around noon, Lieven Goeminne arrives. He parks his horse in front of our house. He's wearing a modest wig with a short ponytail, a white shirt with a collar up to his ears, a cloak, and wide beige trousers. He looks as if he just stepped out of a painting. Rozeken giggles that he looks silly with that old-fashioned wig on his head. I tell her that's how important people dress. The spurs on his boots tap against the floor. He's carrying a walking stick with a silver handle in the shape of an eagle spreading its wings. He hands it to Mother, and she walks around with it in her hand for a few minutes, unsure of what to do with it. Finally, she lays it on the sofa. After the greetings have been exchanged, we all sit down. The whole house smells of fish, rabbit, and nun fritters. Lieven has come with gifts. He hands Mother a linen pouch with beans in it. She holds it up to her nose and sniffs. Then she inhales deeply.

"Coffee?" she asks, as if she can't believe her nose. Lieven flashes her a wide smile.

"Say nothing more," he winks at Father. I have no idea how Father's friend managed to get his hands on coffee. The English are the only ones who can import coffee from

America, and no one on the European continent, from Ghent to Moscow, is allowed to trade with the English. They've even cut off all post to the British Isles.

"Stance and I love coffee," Mother says. "We've had enough of all that chicory, haven't we, Stance?" She holds the coffee up to Stance's nose so she can smell it. Lieven has more presents: an iron fountain pen and inkwell for me, a drawing of the Emperor and his beloved Joséphine for Rozeken, and a tin soldier for Eddy. We thank him with a nod.

Lieven nudges a little box with a ribbon around it toward my father. We all watch over his shoulder as he loosens the bow and pulls off the lid. Inside are at least fifty rolled papers with tobacco inside.

"Cigarettes," Lieven explains. "A new product from an American tobacco factory I have shares in."

Father immediately takes three of the cigarettes out of the box. He gives one to Lieven and one to me. Lieven lights them for us with a sulfur match. My father and Lieven inhale the smoke. Father examines the tobacco with appreciation. I inhale the smoke too.

"Delicious," I say as I feel the smoke seeping out from every hole in my head. My stomach churns.

"So I hear you're studying at our dear old Latin school?" Lieven asks. "Is that old Porpoise still there?"

I nod, but suddenly, I don't feel so well. Maybe the tobacco was rotten or something.

"Even my father had lessons from the Porpoise," says Lieven. "How old is the man anyway?"

"He's indestructible, practically a piece of furniture," I

reply, and I have the feeling that the whole dining room is a lot bigger than it was a second ago.

"Pieter is good in Latin," says Father, "but his marks in mathematics and science are disappointing."

"I do my best," I say. All of a sudden, I taste the leek soup I had for lunch in my mouth and, before I know it, it comes spewing out along with the other contents of my stomach.

Luckily, Father and Lieven step out of the way just in time.

"I do my best," I repeat before falling to the ground.

Mother swoops in with a wet towel. She wipes my mouth roughly and gives me a slap on the face, as if it's my fault I threw up. Father shakes his head, wondering how he ever ended up with such a blunderbuss of a son like me. Stance just stares. There's laughter in her eyes.

"Oh Pietie," she snarls. "Such a tender stomach."

She's relishing in my humiliation, that monster.

"I've got something for Constance too," Lieven says. My sister almost looks frightened for a moment. Our guest places a package on the table. There's something soft inside. Stance glances at Father and Mother, who look at her as if they already know exactly what it is. The smile disappears from Stance's face. She unties the string around the package and unfolds the paper. It's a silk scarf.

"Silk from the Himalayas," Lieven specifies. None of us knows where the Himalayas are. The only people I've ever seen wearing silk scarves are the rich young ladies on the Veldstraat. Just last year, Mother claimed that the delicate fabric is life-threatening—if a woman doesn't cover her neck and shoulders properly she could catch a deadly cold. But tonight she doesn't say that. Tonight she can't resist touching the silk in Stance's hands.

"I've never felt anything so soft," Mother says.

Apparently, Lieven's scarf isn't as life-threatening as the other silk scarves in this city.

Stance doesn't know what to do with the long piece of cloth. Rozeken grabs one end of it and starts walking. The fabric seems to stretch on forever. The scarf is almost as long as the room is wide.

"Put it on," Mother says. With Rozeken's help, Stance drapes the scarf around her neck and shoulders.

"It looks lovely on her," Lieven says, and Stance nods.

"You could be a bit more enthusiastic, young lady," Mother scolds.

"Thank you, Mr. Goeminne," says Stance.

"Please, call me Lieven," he replies.

We spend the entire afternoon eating—the broth, the fish rolls, and the rabbit stew. I slump in my chair, overwhelmed by all the food. My belly feels like it's about to burst.

"Why don't you sing for us?" Mother asks Stance.

She shoots my mother an irritated look.

"I taught Stance to sing," Mother says.

"You sing so much better than I do," Stance says. "Why don't you sing for us, Mother?"

"We'll sing together," Mother declares. "For our guest."

Lieven smiles, his eyes full of expectation.

Mother starts singing a French song about love, loyalty,

and happiness. Stance hesitates for a moment, but after a poke from Mother, she starts singing along. Mother transforms into another woman when she sings. Her voice of iron and stone turns into something fragile and delicate, like crystal. As Mother's voice climbs higher, Stance's remains low and deep, almost masculine. Their two tones dance together, teasing each other. They exchange smiles as they begin the final strophe. For a moment, a very brief moment, you'd almost think my mother and sister actually like each other.

When the song is over, Father and Lieven applaud exuberantly. Eddy runs over to Stance and jumps into her arms.

"My little Coppertop," Stance says.

"Stance sings to me every night when she tucks me in," he says.

We all smile. That little Eddy is too mischievous for words.

"Stance is very good with children," Mother says to Lieven.

Mother blows the dust off the coffee grinder, pours a handful of coffee beans into it, grips the thing between her knees, and grinds like crazy. The sound of the grinding beans reverberates through the house. Father and Lieven smoke a pipe while they wait for their coffee. A cloud of tobacco hangs above the dining table.

"I'm a businessman," says Lieven. "I bring my customers whatever it is they don't have. Coffee, for instance. Or cigarettes. But other things as well."

Lieven grins mysteriously to keep us in suspense.

"I import blue dye from South Carolina," he says with pride. "I sell it to the French army for their uniforms. The officers call me the Master of the Blue."

He chuckles.

"But where do you get all these things?" Stance asks.

"Now, Stance," Father reprimands her. "That's none of our business."

I want to say, "*Well said, Father.*" And if Stance hadn't given me a kick under the table, I would have said it too. But Lieven is still smiling. He's not the least bit annoyed with Stance's unruly tongue.

"Can you keep a secret?" he whispers.

"To the grave," Father grins.

"My business partner is a customs officer," Lieven says. "We trade with the English."

"But that's illegal," Stance retorts. "It's smuggling. You're betraying the Emperor."

"The Emperor needs my blue dye and my coffee for his army, dear child," Lieven replies. "A large portion of my wares is sent to Paris. The Emperor turns a blind eye. Let me assure you, the man does not drink chicory."

"Have you met the Emperor yourself?" asks Mother as she pours the ground coffee beans into a paper sack.

"A couple of times," Lieven replies, as if it were the most normal thing in the world.

"The Master of the Blue," Mother whispers in admiration. "You are an extraordinary man."

"And you are an extraordinary cook, Mrs. Hoste."

Mother gazes lovingly at father. She's delighted that he

has invited such a courteous man into their home. She takes the kettle off the stove and pours the hot water.

"Ah, the smell of real coffee," she exclaims.

"And the smell of smuggling," Stance murmurs, and my good father has to restrain himself from smacking her on the spot.

Only Lieven smiles.

"That daughter of yours wears her heart on her tongue. I find it absolutely refreshing. I love girls with fire in their bones," Lieven says.

Lieven doesn't know what he's saying. That'll only encourage the shrew.

"Well, she certainly is fiery," Father says with a clumsy chuckle.

Then, all of a sudden, the room goes quiet. Stance looks worried. She stands up and asks to be excused. It's getting late.

"Don't be so unpleasant, Stance," Mother says. "Just last week you said you'd trade your faith for a cup of coffee."

"I'm feeling a bit nauseated from all the food," Stance says. She reaches for Eddy's hand, but he's already running upstairs. He's had to sit still for too long. Stance makes a little curtsy. Lieven stands up, pushes back his chair, lays down his pipe, and takes Stance's right hand in his.

"Your hand is rough," he says softly.

"I do the housework around here," Stance replies.

"Yes, but not without grumbling about it," Mother snaps.

"Thank you for the scarf," she says.

Lieven lets go of her hand and smiles broadly. Then he gives my good father a slap on the shoulder.

"You didn't tell me she was funny," he says.

As we devour the nun fritters and coffee, my father talks about his plans. Where is most of the Emperor's money going? he asks. To the war, of course. Which is why Father intends to invent something that the Emperor can use in the war.

"The Emperor is undefeatable on land," Father explains, "but the English rule the seas. The Emperor needs new cannons for his ships."

"That's true," Lieven encourages.

"At sea, a cannon is fired horizontally through a wooden hatch," Father continues excitedly, "but those cannonballs are nothing more than lumps of lead that they send barreling into the sides of ships in the hope that the wooden planks will break. But suppose"—he pauses dramatically for a moment—"suppose you could create a time fuse that works at sea."

Father lets the idea sink in for a moment. Lieven grins, curious to hear where this is going. Rozeken doesn't understand. I explain to her that cannonballs with a time fuse are only used on land. A time fuse is a fuse inside a cannonball. The rest of the cannonball is filled with bullets or nails. It doesn't explode until it reaches the enemy, causing maximum casualties.

"Imagine, dear Lieven," my father continues, "that you fill a cannonball with gunpowder. You light the fuse and fire. The second the ball hits the enemy ship, it explodes. The ship's wooden sides would burst right open."

"It sounds like a dangerous weapon to me," says Lieven. "If the fuse burns too quickly and the gunpowder catches fire before the ball is shot, the whole cannon will fly into the air."

"The ball would have to be heavier." Father nods. "And maybe a different shape. The cannon would have to be different too—with thicker iron and a longer barrel. But it is possible."

"Perhaps it is," Lieven says.

"The army with the best artillery rules the world," Father concludes.

"Leopold was already making sketches of machines in Latin school," Lieven explains to the whole table. "A catapult that could shoot hot coals, a ladder you could unfold to the stars."

"The fantasies of a child," Father growls.

"The Latin school," Lieven muses. "Remember the battles we fought in the orchard?"

Father smiles.

"Remember how they used to call you 'Cloghead'?"

Father's smile fades, but Lieven doesn't seem to notice.

"But, tell me, your saw factory isn't doing so well these days, is it?" he asks.

"The steam engine works fine, but it's like a wild beast," Father sighs. "It's too powerful. The machine keeps destroying my saws."

"But a cannon doesn't need steam, Leopold," Lieven encourages him.

"True. Designing such a cannonball is pure mathematics," Father agrees.

"You're good at mathematics," says Lieven. "You always let me cheat."

"I could design such a cannonball and a cannon to go along with it," says Father, his voice swelling with confidence. "I can already see it. It will be the future."

It's getting late. I say goodnight to Lieven and light the last stump of a candle in a candlestick. I walk up the stairs to my room, where Eddy is already sleeping. In the glow of the candlelight, I see Stance standing at the top of the stairs. Her eyes are wide and fierce.

"What are you doing here?"

She looks at me for a moment and turns around.

"I was waiting for you to untie the knot behind my back," she says. "I can't breathe in this stupid dress."

"Couldn't Rozeken do it?"

"Untie me!" she snarls.

I set down the candlestick and loosen the knot. Then I loosen the cord behind her back. She peels the thing off her arms as if it were a disease. I catch a glimpse of her small breasts.

"What a man, that Lieven," I say, just to annoy her.

"Drop dead, Spiering," she says.

She keeps her dress pressed against her chest.

"Are you just going to stand there in the dark?"

"Shut up. Leave me alone."

We can hear Lieven and Father's muffled voices downstairs. Then Lieven declares, "We're going to be partners," and Father shouts, "The company of Hoste and Goeminne."

I go into my room and close the door. I lie down on the bed next to Eddy and blow out the candle. The room goes dark. The floor on the landing creaks. Stance is still out there eavesdropping.

7

STANCE

It's late when I hear Lieven leave. I listen to his horse's hooves slowly fade into the distance. Finally. I'm too annoyed to sleep. You might like me, Mr. Goeminne, I say out loud, but I don't like you one bit. My hands are much too rough for you. Stay away from me, Master of Blue, smuggler of coffee—I don't need you. We are doing just fine here without you.

I wake up to the sound of carts clattering on the street. I overslept. I get dressed, but my head is still heavy from all the wine yesterday. My whole body feels like lead. I walk down the stairs and trip over the last step. I crash into the doorframe. Mother doesn't even look up. She is setting the table and humming softly. She seems cheerful. On the stove is the neighbors' pumpkin-shaped porcelain bowl with the final leftovers of last night's stew simmering inside.

Father asks if he can speak to me. I follow him upstairs to the most beautiful room in the house. This is where my parents sleep. The shadow of the honeysuckle vines dances across the wood floor in the morning light. In the small bookcase are books on mechanics and the first seven volumes of the French encyclopedia, from A to G. Father ran out of money for the rest of the alphabet, and I always wondered if, back when he was working as a cobbler and spending all his free time studying, he wouldn't have been better off designing a machine that starts with one of the first seven letters of the alphabet, instead of the S of *saw machine.*

Father closes the door.

"Lieven and I talked for a long time," he says.

He pronounces the words as if they each weigh a pound. I stare out the window and watch the sloops carrying coal and barrels of beer being pushed along the water. The men on the boats aren't wearing jackets. It's going to be a warm day. But inside, here in this elegant room, there's a chill in the air.

"Lieven believes in my new invention. He even offered to take over my debts to the bank."

"So instead of owing the bank, you would owe Lieven?"

He nods.

"Hoste and Goeminne," I mumble.

"We'll start the company together and share the profits," Father explains. "And I'll use my share to pay him back my debt. And while I'm working on my new invention . . ."

"Your cannon," I add.

". . . I'll get a monthly salary. Lieven and I will work together, as business partners. You know, Stance, in life it's important to have someone who believes in you."

I want to tell him that we do believe in him. That goes without saying. He shouldn't be so dramatic. But I bite my tongue.

"Lieven is a cathedral of a man. He's well-traveled. He has seen the world. He has made his fortune."

Father falls quiet. I say nothing and cross my arms in front of my chest. It's freezing in here.

"Now Lieven has reached an age where he wants to start a family. His greatest wish is to have a son."

Father looks at me as if he'd like nothing more than for me to pull a baby boy out from under my skirts.

"He's a good match for you, Stance. He'll give you prestige. It will be an honor for you. For us too. He thinks you have a lovely figure. And you can read and write. You can teach his children to read and write as well."

I'm going to catch pneumonia in this room. And everyone knows what happens to people who get pneumonia: they end up between four planks with a cross between their fingers and a wafer on their lips.

"Come on, Stance, say something."

"Can we go to the dining room? With the others? It's freezing in here."

I get up to leave, but he grabs me by the wrist.

"Stance, do you hear what I'm saying? Lieven has asked for your hand in marriage. You're eighteen. You have a bright future ahead of you."

"Marry Lieven," I say, each word doing a cartwheel in my throat. "I'll marry Lieven when the apostles and devils dance the German waltz together," I retort.

Maybe I shouldn't have added that bit about the "German waltz." Everybody knows the waltz is a danger to one's health and morals. I jerk my wrist out of his grasp. And before he can grab me by the hair, I run out of the room and down the stairs to the dining room where the stove is. The rest of the family is sitting around the table. The room falls silent when I walk in. All you can hear is Grandma Blommaert grunting in her wicker chair and the simmering of the rabbit stew on the stove. Pier and Rozeken look at me. I can see in their eyes that they know exactly what Father just asked me. Mother told them. Father pushes me into the dining room.

"Act like an adult for once," he says.

"If I marry Lieven, I'll die giving birth," I shout and hear my own voice skip.

"Nonsense," Mother says. "You'll bear six children just like I did. You're a sturdy woman. You're strong."

"Be reasonable, Stance," Father says. "Without Lieven, I'll go bankrupt. Then what will we do? They'll send me to the Rasphuis!"

Mother makes the sign of the cross.

"What's a rat's house?" Eddy asks, worried.

Nobody answers him.

"Pier won't be able to finish school," Father continues. "How is your mother supposed to feed the children?"

Rozeken makes the sign of the cross too, then she whispers a Hail Mary.

"You're a cobbler, aren't you?" I ask.

Father falls silent for a moment. He looks at me and shakes his head.

"No, Stance," he says, as if he were some Godforsaken prophet. "I am an inventor."

"No, you're a clog maker," I shout, "and a clog maker should stick to his clogs."

"Come here," Mother shouts. I lift the bowl of stew off the stove.

"I'll drop it," I threaten. The porcelain pumpkin is burning hot. I can feel the handles searing into my skin.

"Calm down, Stance. Marriage isn't the end of the world," says Pier. "Lieven is a fine, cultivated man."

Of course, my brother, the Latin school know-it-all, just has to say something too. For a second, I feel the urge to dump the pot of plum-rabbit stew over his cultivated head.

"Why can't Stance marry who she wants?" Rozeken asks.

Mother whips around and slaps Rozeken on the side of the head.

The handles are too hot. I can't take it anymore. I drop the porcelain pot on the stone floor. Mother shrieks.

"The Austrians, the Austrians!" screams Grandma Blommaert, who hears the crash and thinks the invasion of Ghent has just begun. Eddy starts to cry. Rozeken takes his hand.

"Not the neighbors' porcelain!" Mother moans three times.

"Come here," Father growls, but I grab the long meat fork on the sink and brandish it in front of me.

"Try to pull my hair again, and I'll stab you," I shout.

"No, no, don't do it," Eddy screams. "He's our papa!"

"Stance, stop it," Pier yells. "You're out of your mind."

"Put down the fork," Father says.

"You sit down," I shout back.

My voice quivers in my throat.

The room falls silent again. All we can hear is Grandma Blommaert's unintelligible mumbling and the licking and smacking of the two cats who've scurried in from the courtyard to devour the remains of the stew. The two skinny, rotten felines are as happy as can be.

Father sits down. Mother does too. Pier pulls Rozeken and Eddy close. Everybody is looking at me with eyes as wide as saucers. I taste a salty tear in my mouth and feel angry at myself. I sit down and drop the meat fork on the white linen. I wipe away my tears. My hand is shaking. Everyone is holding their breath.

"What's a rat's house?" Eddy asks again.

"The Rasphuis," Rozeken corrects him. "It's the prison." She says it almost too softly to hear.

"At least think about it, dear," Mother says. "We're your parents. We have your best interests at heart. I know you're sweet on Fons De Keghel . . ."

"What? Fons De Keghel?" says Father. "The grocer's son? Why not with the son of a manure shoveler, then?"

"Stop it, Leo," says Mother.

Father shuts his mouth.

"We are convinced that Lieven will be a good husband for you," Mother continues quietly. "This is the chance of a lifetime."

"I'm not in love with Lieven," I say.

"All the better," Mother says. "I wasn't in love with your father either."

Father gapes at Mother in amazement. A silence drifts across the room. All we can hear is the licking and smacking of the cats.

I look at Mother. She was eighteen too once. I search for the young woman in her eyes. The woman who sang dirty Flemish songs to Connor, the great Irishman with his red hair, sweet voice, and booming laugh. Wasn't she wildly in love with him? Wasn't she ready to climb up on top of the stagecoach and ride away with him into the night? Mother knows that I know everything. I, who was her confidante when she screamed into that pillow after Eddy was born. I, the daughter who comforted her.

"I'm madly in love with Fons," I lie. "He wants to marry me."

"You might think that," Mother says softly. "But he's got other girls. That boy is a cock in a henhouse."

"He's a nobody," Father shouts. "And you know what? His parents are nobodies too."

"Cookie," Mother tries to interrupt him.

"Grocers with flour and cornmeal for brains. They couldn't tell a pearl from a pea!"

"Will you be quiet, for once!" Mother barks.

Father stops talking.

"What's a pearl?" Eddy asks.

But no one answers him.

I could run away, grab Fons by the scruff of his neck,

drag him to the altar, follow him into the army, bear his children between the battles, and hope that he survives the war and that—who knows—later on, if the war ever ends, that he'll earn money to . . . to . . . But, of course, it is true what they say: he'll never amount to anything. When Fons got his stipend of ten napoléons, he spent every last centime in the pub and gave none of it to his parents, who just barely scrape by. And I am well aware of the fact that I'm not Fons's only girl. He's also sweet on Lewieze La Belle, the daughter of the ironsmith on Onderstraat, and, according to Mie De Peeze, he sometimes stands at the window of Marie Scheldewaert, the daughter of the hatmaker from the Lange Munt.

I grab hold of Mother's hands. My burnt fingers wince from the pain. I look her in the eyes, and she knows what I am asking. *Mother, don't make me marry that old stick in the mud. Don't sell me off to some arrogant man who wants nothing more than a womb with a warm body around it.* I can tell Mother is conflicted. She grinds her crooked teeth. But then she looks at me sternly.

"Stance, you must obey," she says.

"No," I shout.

"He has a bathtub," says Father.

I look at Father. I have no idea what he's talking about.

"Lieven. He has a bathtub. At his house, you won't have to wash in a tub of cold water anymore," Father explains. "He has a real bathtub that you can sit in. A red copper one in the shape of a wooden shoe. He pays the water carrier to collect buckets of water from the village pump to fill it up. He can even heat that water. Imagine, Stance, a warm bath. Isn't that something?"

"What's so great about a warm bath?" I ask.

"Be reasonable," Mother says. "Lieven is a kind man. A handsome man. A thoughtful and intelligent man. You will learn to love him . . ."

Like I learned to love your father, she almost says but can't bring herself to do it. I think back on the boxing match. I think of Courage, who, as battered and bruised as she was, still got back up to fight Mad Nel. But I'm not as strong as Courage. My fingers ache.

"I burnt myself," I finally say.

Mother puts my hands in cold water and then rubs them with ointment. I breathe more calmly. Father sits down.

"Shall I let Lieven know that you'll accept his offer?" he asks.

I don't reply.

"Stance," Mother presses.

I look down at my poor fingers. They're covered in blisters. My hands will sting for days to come. The tears start rolling down my cheeks.

"Stance?" Mother repeats.

I shrug.

"Let Lieven know that Stance was deeply touched," Mother says for me.

A week later, Father and Lieven draw up two contracts. The first is a business contract with which I, as a woman, have no business. The second is my marriage contract. Father doesn't have to pay a dowry. Mother makes sure that the contract includes a clause stating that Lieven has to show me Paris and take me to the opera. And that he has to provide me with coffee every day. Lieven has no problem with any of this. He offers me a basket of clothes as well as earrings, cosmetics, and a few vials of Eau de Ninon, a perfume made from the extract of orange blossoms, which are known to calm a woman and make her glow. When I go down to the washing rafts with Rozeken for the last time, all the women congratulate me. They say that if there ever was a woman who fell into the butter churn, it's me. They wish me luck and many healthy children. On the way home, Rozeken and I carry the basket between us. She looks up at me and says she's sure I'll be happy.

The girl in the mirror is wearing a dark-blue wedding dress. Her teeth are bleached, her hair is pulled back with her mother's silver hair pin. She is wearing new shoes that her father made specially for her. Her mother keeps saying that this is the most beautiful day of her life. She sprinkles the girl with holy water for happiness and braids daisies through her hair to ward off evil. I stare at the girl in the mirror. There she is, Stance the Bride. We try to smile at each other, me and Stance the Bride.

In the cathedral, the priest asks if I promise to help and obey Lieven in all things, as long as we both shall live. I can feel my heart pounding all the way in my feet. When I say "I do" in that cold house of God, Mother bursts into tears and squeezes Father's hand to mush. And then the tears start streaming down his face too. Stupid cloghead.

Afterward, there's a party. There's singing. There's dancing. Drinking. Eating. Burping. Dirty jokes about the wedding night. My mother calls my father "Cookie" and kisses him. My father's friends congratulate me. Girls I grew up with from the neighborhood wish me luck.

After the sun goes down, my husband decides it's time to go. Our carriage is waiting. I say goodbye to Rozeken and Mother. Eddy has fallen asleep on the sofa. I give him an extra-long squeeze. He doesn't wake up. I cry; what a stupid goose I am. Outside by the carriage—a small English coach of Lieven's—my father and my husband are deep in conversation. Pier is standing there with them. Lieven passes them some snuff tobacco. Pier and Father shove the tobacco up their noses and snort. My brother must be feeling like quite the bigwig tonight.

"Good luck, sis," he says with a grin.

Just as I'm about to slap that smile off his face, he sneezes really hard. So hard that a string of snot shoots out of his nose. I can't even bring myself to laugh. All of a sudden, it occurs to me how pathetic he is, my clumsy little brother tripping over his own two feet.

"You're going to miss me," I say.

"Not for a second," he says between sneezes.

8

STANCE

Lieven Goeminne lives in Lovendegem, a half hour's trot from Ghent. They call it a country house, but it's really more of a small French-style castle in a park with hedged gardens and flower beds, enclosed by a wall. There is a small terrace at the entrance and a large veranda around back. Inside, an oak spiral staircase winds its way up to all the floors. The curtains on the windows are dark, heavy, and dusty. The walls are covered in wallpaper with a natural motif: horns of plenty overflowing with flowers, garlands, and fruits. There's a coachman who also serves as gardener and two maids, both daughters of a local farmer. One of the girls walks with a limp in her right leg. The coachman lives in the cellar, and the two maids go home in the evening. Lieven cheerfully gives me a tour of the house. He walks with a spring in his step and looks younger than when I first met him.

The drawing room overlooks the park. On the wall are gilded frames containing prints of the Emperor in Egypt. In one of them, he's speaking to his officers and pointing at a large pyramid as if he had just excavated it from the desert sand himself. In the corner is a dark-brown secretaire desk with drawers. It is locked. On the floor are thick carpets, and against the wall is a clock ticking away the time. On either side of the fireplace are red, upholstered chairs with curved legs and lion's heads carved into the armrests. These are armchairs for wealthy behinds. The room is heated by a fireplace and lit with the latest oil lamp, all the way from Paris. It's a mechanical contraption with a timer in it that feeds the rapeseed oil into the wick. It can stay lit for up to ten hours without interruption.

"Isn't it magnificent?" Lieven says, and I nod. What luxury! Maybe I really did fall into the butter churn.

For the first time in my life, I take a bath—in steaming hot water scented with cloves. I sink down into the tub and let the warm water embrace me. It's intoxicating. I close my eyes. Never have I felt so light. The maid with the limp pulls me up to a seated position, plucks the daisies out of my hair, and insists on washing me. She combs my hair, works it into a braid, brushes my teeth, scrapes my tongue, and perfumes my neck as if I were a lady. The girl tells me to take off the necklace with the amulet of Saint Rita, but I don't want to. Then she helps me into a nightdress and tells me to stay put. She hobbles around me for a minute, inspecting me from every angle. She adjusts a lock of hair, tugs the nightdress down a bit on my shoulders, until she's satisfied. Then she leads me into the bedroom. The room is cold and smells like camphor. The chill in my body returns. She sits me down on the giant bed, which is strewn with freshly picked wildflowers. It makes a creaking sound. The maid giggles and winks at me—what a silly goat. Finally, she leaves the room. There's a bust of the Emperor on the dresser; he looks down at me sternly. Beside the statue is a vase of silk flowers. My clothes are lying on a chair upholstered with yellow cotton. In a moment, I will share in every woman's fate. There are no exceptions. My parents want the best for me. I will learn, as Mother said, to love Lieven.

My new husband doesn't keep me waiting for long. He enters wearing a white nightshirt that reaches down to his calves and still has his knee socks on. He places a candlestick with a long candle in it on the nightstand and chuckles when he sees me sitting upright on the bed. He blows out the flame and sits down beside me. Then he pushes me down onto my back. I can smell the dank cellar air on his breath. I feel his hands pressing on my nightgown and then his knee pushing my legs apart. He licks my face. The bed starts creaking.

Lieven comes to my bed every night. On the third evening, I say it hurts and ask if he can wait until tomorrow, but he says the pain will pass. He's in a hurry, after all. The man needs a son. He is already forty-five. He promises that as soon as I get pregnant, he'll leave me alone. Then he pushes my legs apart with his knee and licks my face. The creaking begins.

Every night, while my husband is fast asleep, I lie awake in bed. Sometimes I get up and go sit in the chair with my clothes on it and think about nothing. Will my whole life be in this room? Is this the furniture that I'll spend my whole life wearing out—that bed, those chairs, that table, and that oval mirror that folds so elegantly into a wooden box? Will I have to listen to the clock ticking on the mantelpiece like a predator for the rest of my life? Will the bust of the Emperor always be there, staring me down? Will I always have to look at that horrible wallpaper? Seventy-eight horns of plenty. All with exactly the same stupid flowers, the same ribbons, and the same fruits tumbling out of them. After a week, I am ready to rip it off the wall. I want to smash the clock—the clock that's ticking away my youth. I want to howl. But finally, after the night has progressed so far that it no longer has a name, I lie back down beside my husband and fall asleep.

A few weeks after the wedding, I wake up to the sound of shouting. Lieven is not lying beside me. I get up and walk over to the window. The park around the house is lit with torches. Along the road and in front of the house are men in long coats. A covered cart pulls up to the house, and the men scramble to untie the canvas. Underneath are chests, which are quickly loaded off the cart. The men work swiftly. Two of them have guns in their hands. Their eyes are on the road. Lieven is out there talking to a giant man in a thick cloak. They walk into the house together.

I get dressed and go downstairs. Lieven and the man are standing there, drinking wine. Lieven catches my eye.

"My wife," he says.

"You sly old fox," the man says as he walks up to me. His muddy boots leave a dirty trail on the floor. I take a step back. The man stops in front of me and takes off his hat.

"Auguste Dupin, at your service," he says and kisses my hand. He has chestnut-brown hair, stubble on his face, and a scar above his mouth. There's a black mark on his right cheek, as if he were branded by the Devil himself. He speaks Flemish with a strange accent.

"Auguste is from Zeeland," my husband says. "We do business together."

Men in long coats burst in through the back door. They're carrying a heavy chest and already know the way down to the cellar. Nobody wipes their feet.

An hour later, the sun is barely up, and the men are already gone. They disappear with their big cart in the direction they came from. Most of the goods were taken down to our cellar, but some of them were loaded onto two other carts that left in the direction of Ghent. It's all contraband. My husband and Dupin have retreated into the drawing room and are not to be disturbed. The maid is limping around the kitchen making bacon and eggs for our visitor. At least five eggs go into his omelet. She pushes it all onto a plate and places a hunk of black bread beside it.

"That man eats like a wolf," the girl complains as she hobbles back and forth.

"I'll take it."

The maid looks at me as if I have insulted her, but she doesn't dare to object. I take the tray out of her hands. I want to know what my husband and his business partner are up to. I walk into the drawing room with the tray and find Dupin and my husband sitting on two chairs in front of the secretaire in the corner. The desk is folded open and covered with sheets of paper. There are stacks of money on the writing tray.

"Breakfast," I say and bring the tray closer. In the top drawer of the desk, I see a small pistol with a few cartridges lying beside it. Lieven carefully closes the drawer. He frowns at me, looking annoyed, but Dupin is delighted to see me. He grins with the few gold teeth he has left.

"I'll say, that girl takes good care of you," he says.

"I won't be but a minute. I don't want to disturb you," I say.

"You're not bothering me," says Dupin as he wolfs down the omelet.

"Oh, that's a relief," I say.

"We're just doing some bookkeeping," Lieven says nervously. "Just money and goods going in and out. Calculations. Logging numbers. Not for women."

"We have to keep a good record of everything for the tax

service." Dupin chuckles and tosses a few sheets into the fireplace. The flames swallow the paper without a sound.

"That all sounds very serious," I say, and I leave with a nod.

The paperwork lasts until mid-morning. Afterward, Lieven and Dupin get drunk. They empty two bottles of wine before lunch, then they drink more wine, followed by cognac. The two men laugh and smoke. I'm allowed to stay and play listening ear to all their adventure stories. Dupin served as a cannoneer in the Emperor's army for several years. He lost his front teeth in an explosion and was discharged from military service.

"Because you lost a few teeth?"

"You need them to tear open a cartridge before you load it into your rifle," he says. "You can't break it with false teeth. The paper is too stiff."

"So now you're a customs officer?" I ask.

"Yes, near Sluis," he says. "I'm responsible for a stretch of the sea border."

"And do you catch a lot of smugglers?" I ask.

My husband and Dupin burst into laughter.

"Auguste has the smugglers working for him," my drunk husband blurts out. "He's the master of Zeeland's smuggling network."

Dupin flashes his gold teeth.

"The whole village is working for us," my husband explains. "Sailboats from England bring over crates of contraband. We drag the boats onto the beach and load the crates onto a large cart."

"The cart that arrived this morning?" I ask.

The customs officer growls. He doesn't want to talk about it. But Lieven can't help but brag.

"Auguste and his men travel at night," Lieven says. "Much quieter."

"And everyone in your village in Zeeland participates?" I ask. "Nobody's reported it to the gendarmes?"

"Anyone who snitches to the police should make themselves right with God," my husband says with a chuckle. "Because sooner or later they'll end up with a rotten fish down their throat."

"You're full of horseshit," Dupin says, and he gives Lieven a shove, causing him to spill his wine. It leaves a deep, red stain on his shirt.

"Damn it, Auguste, this shirt is made of silk," he says. "Do you have any idea what that costs?"

"It'll cost you a lot more if you don't stop blabbing," Dupin says. "A man doesn't talk business with his wife. He talks about making children."

Lieven looks aggrieved. Then he smiles at me.

"My business partner is a little rough around the edges," he says.

"Tell me more about your courtship," says Dupin.

"Very short," I say flatly, "and very businesslike."

That makes Dupin laugh.

"A golden deal," says Lieven. "Her mother gave birth to four healthy children. My wife is as fertile as the spring."

"You sure about that?" Dupin teases his host.

Lieven looks at Dupin in surprise and then looks at me.

It's as if, all of a sudden, he's starting to wonder whether it was such a golden deal after all. If, perhaps, I am too good to be true.

"In Zeeland, they say you can smell if a woman is fertile," says Dupin.

"How?" my husband wants to know. His good humor is gone. He's lost his taste for the wine, and Dupin is starting to get on his nerves.

"Listen carefully," says Dupin with the seriousness of a professor of the female anatomy. "If a lady puts a few cloves of garlic in her sacred hole"—he lets out a cognac-induced hiccup—"and her breath smells of garlic the next morning, then there are no blockages in her system. All the body fluids are flowing, which means she's in perfect health and will be pregnant in no time."

"That sounds very logical," my husband replies, as if his guest is surgeon to the Emperor himself.

"And who told you all this, Mr. Dupin? A gnome from Zeeland?" I ask.

Lieven laughs.

"I told you she's a funny one. My Ghent flower," he says.

"But I don't think she's pregnant yet," Dupin replies.

He looks down at my breasts and licks his lower lip, as if he's looking forward to catching me alone sometime without my husband around.

As the sun starts to set, I bid the two gentlemen a good evening and head back up to the bedroom. I take a knife with me, just in case the anatomy professor decides to pay me a visit. But an hour later, it's Lieven who stumbles into the room, and he's too drunk to take off his pants. He lies down beside me and states the obvious: "Here I am."

He smells like a mix of stomach bile and musty cellar.

"You're my lovely little wife," he blows into my ear.

He tries to hoist himself on top of me, but his arm slips on the edge of the bed. He tumbles over the side and hits the floor with a smack. For a moment, I think he's broken his neck. But a few seconds later, I hear loud snores coming from the floor.

9

STANCE

Fifteen weeks into my marriage, I'm still menstruating. I welcome the blood on my petticoats. It's as if the blood is there to tell me that all is not lost. That I can still run away.

I smell autumn in the air. The scent of earth and wet leaves, the salty northern wind. The fall makes me happy.

"Husband, it's Friday. Market day in Ghent." Lieven looks up from his papers in surprise. The secretaire is open. On it are little towers of coins neatly stacked in a row. A cloud of tobacco smoke swirls around his head. He pushes some of the drawers shut, including the one with the pistol and ammunition.

"The coachman can take me, and the maid will help me carry things," I say.

Lieven sighs irritably, but in the end I get my way. My

maid helps me into a bluish-gray, Roman-style dress trimmed with lace. I wear my scarf from the Himalayas; a yellow-and-purple hat with a cloth rose sewn into it; and a pair of shiny, black leather bottines. When I ride into Ghent in the carriage, I look just like a lady from the Veldstraat.

The Friday market is as busy as ever. My maid, the little nag, doesn't leave my side for a moment as I push my way from stand to stand. The butcher's son doesn't even recognize me and addresses me as *madame,* as if I were suddenly ten years older. I tell him it's me, Stancie from the Kraanlei quay.

"You are Madame Goeminne," the kitchen maid corrects me.

I could have set that ninny's hair on fire. I smile at the butcher's son. He used to sell me everything on credit and always gave me a few ounces extra too. But now he hardly dares to look at me. He swats a few flies away from his meats and asks, "How may I help you, madame?" Going to the market isn't as much fun as it used to be. He wraps up a few slabs of meat in newspaper for me, and I take out my wallet to pay. Out of the corner of my eye, I spot a young man who looks vaguely familiar to me. I look again and notice that his riding jacket is much too big for him. He removes his hat for me, as he would for any lady. I greet him with a curt nod and notice the plume in his hat. That's when it hits me. It's Courage's companion. The woman in men's clothes. He's carrying books under his arm that he must have bought at the stand run by the little old monk. He greets a few gentlemen, who nod courteously and wish him a pleasant day. He whistles for the carriage and tips his hat for another lady, who responds with a short bow. Nobody knows that he's a she.

"Are you going to pay, madame?" the maid asks. I open the wallet; my fingers tremble as I take out the coins. One of them slips out of my hand. The maid bends down to pick it up. I tell her to excuse me for a moment and push my way through the crowd. A little ways ahead, I spot the red carriage with a coachman on top and see a plumed hat climbing in. I run after it.

"Wait!" I shout to the coachman and hop onto the side of the carriage. The coach tilts under my weight. Inside, the plumed hat is seated beside the girl I cheered for at the old monastery. Her short hair is tucked under a hat. The top buttons on her collar are open, revealing her neck. Her shoulders are narrower than I remember, her wrists finer.

"You're Courage," I blurt out. "I've seen you fight."

She beams with pride and straightens her shoulders.

"You jumped onto my coach that day too," she says.

She recognizes me. A wide grin stretches across my face.

"Are you here for another boxing match?" I ask.

"No," she says. "We're just passing through."

Her companion nods and holds up the books he bought from little old monk.

"My, you're so strong," I say.

It comes out sounding terribly silly, but Courage smiles.

"Not as strong as Mad Nel," she replies.

"But you still beat her," I say.

She nods. "At first, I thought there was no way I could

win. But Nel was slow," she says. "And I've got a hard head."

Then she grins. I know that grin. It's the grin that looks life straight in the eye and laughs, a grin that can turn the order of things upside down. There's nothing more for me to say.

"Good luck," she says.

I step off the coach.

The carriage jolts forward and rattles away down the street. It disappears in the direction of the Kortrijk Gate, out of the city. I stand there watching it go, until my nagging kitchen maid tugs at my sleeve.

"What on earth are you doing, madame?" she gasps. She's carrying the package of meat under her arm. The meat is so bloody that it's soaked through the paper and the flies are already going after it.

"Someone I used to know," I say.

I decide to pay my family a visit, but the only person home is my mother. She receives me in the front room as if I no longer belong there. She tells me that Rozeken and Eddy are out and Pier is helping my father write letters to his suppliers.

"Pier can write in perfect French," Mother says. "He's going to go far, that boy. On Monday, he's going back to the Latin school."

"So everything is back to normal," I say.

Mother asks me if I'm pregnant yet. I tell her I'm not.

"Make sure you give that man a son," she replies irritably. "Don't test his patience."

The maid asks when we're going back. I don't answer. I still want to wander through my old city, my Ghent. I tell her I still need to buy some bread from Binus on Lammerstraat. The girl groans and complains that we could have bought bread at the market. Lammerstraat is out of our way. But that prissy little peasant can bite me. I tell her to go wait in the carriage while I buy a loaf of bread.

I smile at the sight of Binus's pimply face. He too needs a moment to get used to my expensive dress with all the fancy lacework on it. He just keeps nodding his head and refuses to look me in the eye.

"Has Fons left for the army yet?" I ask.

Binus nods.

"His parents said that he's in the artillery," he says.

"What about you?"

"I'm off tomorrow morning," he says. "This is my last day at the bakery. I leave tomorrow at seven o'clock."

"And you," he says, nodding at my clothes. "You're a proper lady now, aren't you?"

"Yes, I married money," I answer. "My father arranged it."

"Are you happy?"

"Oh yes, very," I lie.

"When I see Fons, shall I tell him you said hello?" He asks.

"Yes, that would be nice."

"I'm sure he still has your lock of hair."

I smile. Sure, he's still got my lock of hair all right, along with locks from Lewieze La Belle from the Onderstraat, Marie Scheldewaert from the Lange Munt, and who knows who else? That Fons.

That night, after three minutes of puffing and creaking, for which I thank my dear husband, I lie in bed wide awake, thinking about Courage. She was so tough, so cunning, so quick. She made her opponent eat dust. I ball my fists and feel my heart racing in my chest. I slip out of bed and try to recall every step of that boxing match, from the first punch to the final blow. I remember exactly how Courage ducked down on one knee, dodging that major blow, and bolted upright to throw the final punch that broke Nel's nose and decided the match. And as I replay the match in my mind, I start moving my feet and jabbing my arms, as if I were the one in the ring breaking noses. All of a sudden, I feel my husband's seed dripping down my right thigh like drops of poison leaking out of my body. It's a miracle I'm not pregnant yet. And once I am with child, I will never leave this room again. I rub the portrait of Saint Rita around my neck.

I am a hopeless case. But I too have a hard head.

My husband's clothes are draped over the yellow chair. I pick up each item of clothing one by one. The blue knickers with gold piping down the sides and the silver buckle, the white shirt that smells like an armpit. I can just picture her: Courage's companion wearing that oversized riding jacket and hat. How she walked across the square as if she owned it. She greeted men and women alike, and each one greeted her back as if she were a young gentleman. She fooled them all. I pull on the knickers first. They're too big, but then I put on the shirt and tuck it into the pants. That's better already. Then I pull on his coat with its fancy buttons and ribbons.

"What are you doing?" Lieven mumbles.

I whip around, but the room is so dark that all I can see is his silhouette.

"Nothing," I say. "I couldn't sleep."

He grumbles something unintelligible.

"I'll be back to bed in a minute, dear," I say. "Go to sleep. Dream away, darling. Dream about me."

He doesn't respond. The black lump on the bed that must be his head doesn't move. I hold my breath. And then, after what seems like an eternity, I hear his rhythmic breathing and snoring again.

Moonlight floods into the room. I take Lieven's hat and place it on my head. I can't believe my eyes. There, looking back at me in the mirror, is a young man. He looks like someone I've known for years; I've just never gotten a good look at him. What magnificent eyes he has. Big, brown eyes. Fiery eyes. Mysterious eyes. He grins. I want to kiss the mirror. I want to pull the young man toward me, run my fingers through his hair, and blow into his ear. It's love at first sight. I can hardly look away, and when the clouds float back in front of the moon and the darkness returns, I feel different. I stare at the silhouette of my husband snoring in bed, and I can't imagine myself sharing a bed with him ever again. I see the long bluish-gray Roman dress with the lace collar hanging on the chair, and I can't imagine myself ever putting it on again. All I want to do is to gaze at that boy in the mirror.

The clock strikes two. My husband, the black lump on the bed, is still snoring. It's now or never. I pick up his boots, take his walking stick with the silver handle, and tiptoe down the stairs barefoot. On top of the closed secretaire is a wallet with some money in it—I take that too. I shove it down into my shirt, and for a second, my fingers get caught on the chain around my neck. It's as if Saint Rita is clutching my fingers, as if she doesn't want me to leave. I'm so nervous I accidentally break the chain. The little portrait of Saint Rita falls to the floor. I feel around for it in the dark, and when my fingers land on it, I feel relieved.

I unlock the back door and walk barefoot through the high grass in the park. The coachman's room is completely dark. Every night, he makes his rounds with a loaded gun, but he must be asleep by now. I walk up to the iron gate, which is locked with a chain. The top of the fence is lined with rusty spikes that could spear me like a hare on a spit. The chain rattles loudly as I climb up on the fence and wedge my body between two of the posts and drop down on the other side. But my husband's jacket gets caught. I rip it off and jump down. At first I manage to land on my two feet in the sand, but then I stumble backward and hit my stupid head against the fence. My fall makes an awful racket, as if the big iron fence is protesting my departure. I throw myself on the ground. The coachman must have heard me. He's lighting his lantern right now. He's going to shout, "Who's there?" and cock his rifle any second. If he sees a shadow moving in the dark, he'll shoot. But no lantern flickers on. All is dark in the coachman's room. I lie there in the sand for a few minutes. He didn't hear me. He didn't see me. He's probably in his bed snoring like an idiot, just like my husband.

I sit up in front of the fence and put on the boots. Then I pull myself up with the walking stick. That's when I notice that I tore a nail while climbing. My finger is bleeding. I wrap it with a dirty handkerchief that I find in my husband's pocket. Then I run off into the night. I follow the muddy road to Ghent. The spurs on Lieven's boots tap against my heels. I clutch the walking stick tightly in my fist. What if I run into vagrants? Or deserters? Or drunk farm boys?

"But wait," I whisper almost loud enough to hear. "I'm not a woman anymore! I'm the boy in the mirror with a walking stick in my hand and spurs on my boots."

I run as fast as I can, but it's a cloudy, starless night, and the half moon only peeks out its head every once in a while. When the road disappears into the trees, the darkness is so thick that I have to hold the stick out in front of me just to stay on the road and make sure I don't run into a tree. All of a sudden, I hear rustling behind me. I look over my shoulder. There's something moving, but I can't see what. It's an animal. Something panting. Something pattering. Surely not wolves? My heart is racing. No, please don't feed me to the wolves. I'll say my Hail Marys. Fifteen. No, fifteen hundred. Anything to keep the wolves from tearing me to shreds. I keep running through the blackness until I emerge in a row of trees and can finally see my surroundings again. The moon is back out. I look behind me. For a moment I think I imagined the panting and pattering feet. But then I see them. Wild dogs. They're moving toward me, skinny and dirty, their tails curled. They growl and gnash their teeth.

There's no way to tell if the beast snarling in front of you is rabid or not. And if a rabid dog bites you, well, you can bet the Devil you'll start foaming at the mouth too, and sooner or later the madness will eat you alive. Eventually, you'll be screaming like a witch at the stake until your voice finally cracks, and two days later you're six feet under. There's no herb that can save you from rabies.

"Don't run," I say out loud. "Whatever you do, don't run."

There are five of them. The largest one steps closer. The animal drops its head, moves a few steps to the right, then back to the left. He's looking for the best angle to launch his attack, while the other dogs—those impatient monsters—egg him on with their growling, barking, and drooling.

"Holy Rita," I beg, clutching the walking stick. I make myself as small as possible and wait, just like Courage did in the boxing match. I look the big, nasty beast straight in the eyes.

"You're going to attack me first, aren't you, bitch?" I shout. "Well, come on, then. Jump my throat. Attack. Bite me in the jugular. Do it."

The dog jumps, but he's not quick enough. I take a step back, just like I saw Courage do. The dog misses me. As he's bracing for a second attack, I seize my chance. My only chance.

I whack him as hard as I can with the silver handle of the stick. The silver eagle splits the dog's skull. Blood sprays in all directions. The beast convulses, and a few seconds later it's all over. The other four dogs are confused and stand there grunting stupidly at one another for a second. Then, I scream all the air out of my lungs, wave the stick, and kick with the spurs on my boots. The dogs run away. I throw my arm into the air. Le vainqueur! Victory. Constance Hoste wins the pot of forty-three francs. Except I'm no longer Constance Hoste, not anymore. I'm someone else.

Two hours later, I push open the back gate of the bakery on the Lammerstraat. My legs are shaking. My undershirt is drenched with sweat. I can see Binus and his father standing by the oven through the dampened window. Binus is wearing his travel clothes. I've never been so happy to see his pimply face. He pulls a loaf of bread from the oven. His father squeezes his shoulder. Father and son are baking bread together one last time before the son goes off to the army. It's almost touching. I tap on the window. Binus opens the back door and holds the oil lamp up to my face.

"Can I help you, sir?" he asks. I can't help but laugh. I take off the hat, and my braid falls down on my shoulders.

"It's me, Binus," I say.

Binus's jaw drops. I hear his father asking what's going on. Binus says it's nothing, that it's just a friend. He steps out of the house and into the courtyard to speak to me.

"I ran away."

"What? But why?"

All of a sudden, Binus steps back and points to the blood stains on my pants.

"Your husband, you didn't . . . ?"

I burst into laughter. I'm laughing so hard I almost fall to my knees. Binus looks at me with a mixture of confusion and horror.

"That's from a dog," I say.

Binus smiles.

"Let me take your place, Binus," I say.

"What?"

"Give me your draft orders and let me go into the army as Binus Serlippens."

His jaw drops again. It's like some kind of twitch.

Mr. Serlippens opens the door. He takes off his white baker's hat when he sees me. He has flour on his cheeks. He has no idea what's going on.

"But, Stance, you can't be serious?" Binus stutters.

"Think about it, Binus," I say. I do my best not to raise my voice, not to fly into some crazy rant like a maniacal housewife and get him all shaken up with a spitfire of words and arguments. "This is your chance. Your only chance. I've been thinking about it all the way here. I can go into the army in your place. And you can stay here, far away from the war. You can stay here and help your parents and not leave the house until the war's over. As long as no one sees you. Your parents can work out front in the shop, and you can stay back here with the oven. Nobody will come looking for you, nobody will miss you because officially you're in the army."

"You mean lock myself up? Hide from everyone?"

"I'll join the army under your name. I'll be Binus Serlippens."

"But what if . . . what if . . ." Binus stammers.

"What if they find out I'm a woman?"

"Exactly," Binus sputters.

"They won't," I assure him. "You've already stripped down for the doctor at the Ghent Town Hall. You've been approved. So I've been approved. Nobody needs to see me naked."

He stares at me in amazement.

"They measured your height and weight," I continue. "All right, so I'm a little taller than you, but no one's going to check."

"I don't know. I have to think about it . . . I . . ."

"Binus," I say. "Pretty soon the servants are going to wake up and the maids will discover that I've run off with my husband's clothes."

He hesitates.

His pimply face is stricken with doubt. My stomach is in knots. I can feel my insides churning. I am terrified that I'll have to go back to my husband after all. Binus is my only hope. He looks at his father, who is standing there with his baker's hat in his hands and flour on his cheeks. The old man has heard everything.

"I can't do it," Binus says.

"What can't you do?"

"What kind of man lets a woman take his place in the army? I'll live the rest of my life in shame."

"But there's nothing to be ashamed of."

"Of course there is. If something happens to you, I'll think back on this night for the rest of my life. That it was my fault."

"I want to go to the army," I shout. "Send me back to my husband, and I'll die. Maybe not right away, maybe not even in a few years, but sooner or later it will kill me."

Binus stares at me.

"Listen, Binus, I won't get shot," I say. "And if I get hit by a cannonball, there'll be so little left of me that they'll never know I was a woman."

His father turns his back toward us. He doesn't want any part in his son's decision. Perhaps he's silently praying. *Let the girl go, dear Lord, don't take my son.* Binus looks me straight in the eyes. Then he nods. He extends his hand to me as if I were a man, and I give it a good hard shake.

"Are you going to report to the gendarmes dressed like that?" he asks.

For a moment, I'm perplexed. I hadn't thought of that.

"A baker's son doesn't wear clothes like that," says Binus, and he pulls off his jacket and shirt. I take off my clothes too. Binus turns around.

Five minutes later, I toss Lieven's gold-piped knickers into the bread oven. Flames burst from the inside, releasing a foul odor. Binus shuts the oven door. I hand him the walking stick with the silver handle. He hands me the papers, a loaf of bread for the road, and a leather pouch.

"That's the money they gave me at the Town Hall. My military stipend."

"Give that money to my family," I say. "Make sure my mother doesn't know it came from you. If she finds out, she won't leave you alone. The woman is as sly as a fox. She'll lure you in with her chatter and then question you until you break. She won't let you go until you've confessed everything."

He nods. His father walks up to me and makes the sign of the cross on my forehead with his thumb. His eyes are filled with gratitude.

"One more thing," I ask and grab my long braid. "You got any scissors? I'll give you a lock of hair."

An hour later, I'm presenting my papers to two gendarmes at the Bruges Gate. One of them is Flemish; the other is French.

"Binus Serlippens?" the French gendarme asks, and I nod. I take off my cap, slap it against my thigh like men do, and rub my fingers through my hair. It's so wonderfully short; I can feel the wind running through it. The French gendarme hands me, Binus Serlippens, my papers and wishes me bonne chance. I thank him. The Flemish gendarme points to a wall covered with posters announcing the upcoming fair. A group of drafted soldiers is waiting in front of it. I walk up to them and hope that none of them knows Binus Serlippens. But then I remember that only women go to the bakery, and Binus rarely shows his face at the pub. I stand next to a bench where five guys are sitting. One of them is in tears. Another is staring at an amulet of Our Lady in the palm of his hand. I give them each a big, firm handshake and tell them my name is Binus. I can't get enough of my new name. I am Binus. My name is Binus. Just Binus. They look at me as if I'm out of my mind. As I'm shaking hands with the fifth guy, I realize it's Geoffroy de Soudan, the son of the rich marquess from the Veldstraat. He's headed off to war wearing a new pair of pants, his Sunday coat, and an expensive linen shoulder bag with a rose embroidered on it. His mother's bag, no less! He doesn't recognize me.

The two gendarmes sling their guns over their shoulders and collect their bags. They shout in French and Flemish that it's time to go. One of the gendarmes leads the way, and the rest follow. I can hardly conceal my excitement as I say to the second gendarme, "So, we're off to war."

His only reply is, "Keep up. We have to make it to Kortrijk by nightfall."

And so begins our march to Paris. I take one last look at the towers of Ghent. In the thick morning mist, they stand like three ghostly shadows.

10

PIER

On a windy September afternoon—the day before I'm supposed to leave for school—Lieven Goeminne storms in. His coat and pants are splashed with mud. His face is red with fury. A neighborhood boy is standing outside holding the reins of his horse. My brother-in-law is completely beside himself. He asks if Stance is here with us. Mother is too shocked to answer. He pushes past her and bursts into the living room, where Rozeken and I are setting the table. "Constance!" he shouts up the stairs. "Wife!" Father comes downstairs. He hasn't even buttoned his shirt yet, and his loose collar is flapping up and down.

"What ever is the matter, my dear Lieven?" says Father.

"What's the matter?" Lieven exclaims, as if the whole world—everyone except us—already knows of his misfortune.

Lieven looks back at Mother and then again at Father.

"That's some daughter you have," he shouts. "She's run away. Like a thief in the night."

I stare at Lieven. His face is warped with rage and heartache, the poor soul.

"Are you sure?" Father asks, as if his business partner is one to imagine things.

"Surely, you've taught her what her place is in this world," Lieven shouts. "She knows her duties, doesn't she? She knows we have a contract!"

Father nods. Rozeken's face is as white as chalk. Eddy has come downstairs. From the back room, we can hear Grandma Blom's soft voice asking what's going on.

"Where is Constance?" Lieven asks.

"She can't be very far," says Father. "Where could she have possibly gone?"

"That woman's not right in the head!" Lieven screams. His voice slides from his throat and comes out as a high-pitched squeal.

"That's not possible. My husband and I have slapped that head on straight," says Mother dryly.

"Stance got all the beatings she deserved," Father confirms in a calm tone. "And I admit that my eldest daughter is not the most docile woman in the Christian world . . ."

"You're certainly right about that," Lieven snarls.

"But if I were Saint Peter at the gates of heaven and had to take stock of all her graces and flaws, I would certainly . . ."

"Stance is not dead," Mother interjects. "What's all this nonsense about the gates of heaven?"

Rozeken makes the sign of the cross. She takes hold of Eddy's hand.

"Where do you think she might have gone then, Mrs. Hoste?" asks Lieven, a little calmer now.

"Stance has always been a brooder," says Mother. "Maybe she was overwhelmed by the first weeks of marriage. Maybe she was feeling desperate because she didn't get pregnant. Maybe she just needed to get out of the house. Catch her breath."

Father and Lieven stare at Mother as if they want more of an explanation.

"Stance wouldn't be the first woman who wanted to escape."

What a strange thing for Mother to say.

"But I'm sure it's just a whim," Mother continues, as if she's experienced it herself. "A moment of weakness. She's probably sleeping on a chair in a pub as we speak. She'll be back."

Stance sleeping on a chair in a pub. I make the sign of the cross. Rozeken and Eddy follow my example.

"Go find Stance," says Lieven.

"Find her?" Father asks. "But I've just started working on the drawings for a new design, and . . ."

"Go find her," Lieven shouts, "and bring her to me immediately. We have a contract, Hoste. A contract!"

Lieven turns and marches out of our house.

◎ ◎ ◎

Father visits every pub in town and asks if anyone has seen his daughter. "So, Mr. Saw Factory!" an old drunkard shouts. "Your daughter's snuck off, has she?"

A few hours later, Father returns home. He reeks of beer and tobacco. Nobody has seen Stance. Mother declares that she's probably back home in Lovendegem by now, sitting next to her husband by the stove.

"Yes, she must be," Mother repeats three times. "Stance is back home with her husband."

But there is no way Stance is sitting with Lieven by the stove.

My father won't let me return to school until Stance is back. My trunk was all packed. My uniform was ironed. It's enough to drive me mad. Once again, thwarted by Stance! Just when everything was all settled. Just when Father's been relieved of his debt and found someone who believes in his talents. Just when our father, the scientist, is about to make a name for himself as an inventor. Three days later, when there's still no sign of Stance, Mother lights a candle before bed and leaves it burning all night. As if Stance is lost in the underworld, in the shadows of Hades, and has to find her way home. But she never comes.

I write a letter to Bertie, asking him to keep notes for me, especially of Father Charles's lessons. I don't want to fall behind on my Latin vocabulary. Bertie writes me back and tells me that he and Toine have a new roommate, some guy from Paris who's as boring as a rock and does his homework every night. *Come back soon, Pier,* Bertie begs in his letter.

A week after Stance's disappearance, Lieven comes by to pick up me and my father. He wants us to go down to the Ghent Town Hall with him. We scramble to get our coats and follow Lieven through the streets of Ghent just as the first autumn rain starts to fall, washing the summer's dust off the streets.

Prefect Gijsens receives us in the Austrian Salon in the Town Hall. The dry parquet floor creaks under our feet. The portraits of the former Austrian Archduke and Archduchess on either side of the marble mantelpiece are covered with a sheet, as if they're not allowed to see or hear what is being discussed in their salon. The prefect is sitting by the stove and is so warm that he takes off his wig and arranges it backward on the Emperor's bust, so the ponytail hangs down over his plaster nose. His nails and fingers are covered with ink from drafting documents all day long. There are two dozen goose-feather quills sticking out of a copper vase with the Emperor's head etched into it. Most of them are bent, but a few of them are still standing upright, fresh and immaculate.

The midday bells haven't rung yet, but Prefect Gijsens is already enjoying his lunch: white wine with cheese, white bread, and a hard-boiled egg. He greets Father warmly, much to Lieven's annoyance. "How's business?"

"I can't complain," Father says with a smile.

"This man is an inventor," he says proudly to Lieven and

me, as if we don't already know that. "He's the Archimedes of Ghent."

Father blushes.

"And is this your son?" he asks. "Is he studying at the Latin school as well?"

"He helps me with my correspondence," Father replies.

"Here at Town Hall, there is always work for young men who can write well," the prefect says kindly. "What can I do for you, my dear engineer?"

Silence falls over the room.

There are no chairs in the prefect's office. Lieven seems irritated that he has to tell his story standing up, as if he were a farmer here to complain about a neighbor who stole his apples and pissed in his well.

"Go ahead, sir," says the prefect. He drums his fingers impatiently on the stained, green blotting paper on his desk.

Lieven tells him what happened. He explains how he first met Stance and how my father assured him that if there were ever a virtuous woman on Earth it was his daughter.

Prefect Gijsens shoots Father a sharp look, but Father's eyes are glued to the floor. Lieven goes on to say that Stance abandoned their marriage bed three and a half months after promising him eternal fidelity and left the house without a word. In the middle of the night. There was no warning, no reason, not even a letter.

"Ah yes, what a daughter you have, Leopold," says the prefect with a hint of admiration in his voice.

Father smiles.

"She's the Whore of Babylon!" shouts Lieven.

Father's smile disappears from his face. I'm not sure what Lieven means, but I have a feeling that Babylon wasn't known for its virtuous women.

"My patience has run out," Lieven declares. "I want my marriage to Constance Hoste dissolved. Now! Today. I was deceived. Trapped. I am the victim of a conspiracy." He points at Father. "This man lied to me about his daughter's character, piety, and fertility."

No one says a word. The only sound is the dull ticking of the clock. Then the prefect leans back in his chair and says in a calm, businesslike tone, "A marriage cannot be unilaterally dissolved. As absurd as it may sound, a divorce requires consent of the wife. As long as her signature is not on an official document"—he raises his hands as if he has just washed them of all responsibility—"the marriage cannot be dissolved."

Now Lieven is speechless too.

My father is still staring at the tips of his shoes.

"There are plenty of reasons to demand a divorce," Lieven concludes.

"Of course there are," says Prefect Gijsens as he cleans the last pieces of cheese from his plate and refills his wine glass.

"She was disobedient," says Lieven. "A wife owes her husband her full, unconditional obedience."

Prefect Gijsens chuckles; his round, rosy cheeks jiggle up and down on his face. "A donkey is supposed to obey his master," he says, "but when the master isn't looking, it'll kick over its trough."

"Constance is infertile," Lieven shouts. "I've tested her. With garlic."

We all look at Lieven in surprise.

"A garlic test?" Prefect Gijsens repeats as if he hasn't heard correctly.

Lieven nods and avoids the prefect's eyes, as if he doesn't need a lesson on the womb and its secrets.

"Infertility can only be invoked as a valid reason for divorce after three years of childless marriage," the prefect snarls. "That is what is written in the Emperor's new code of law. Three years. And it doesn't say anything about garlic."

"And if that snake never comes back?" Lieven asks, his voice trembling with rage. "How can I remain married to a woman who isn't here?"

"Was the woman somehow dissatisfied in the marriage?" the prefect asks.

"Dissatisfied?" Lieven retorts. "She had a warm bath and a silk scarf from the Himalayas, for God's sake! And fresh coffee every day! What else could a woman possibly want?"

Lieven looks at us. Father doesn't reply.

"Nothing," I say. "She fell into the butter churn."

The three men look at me, and Lieven nods gratefully. I feel sorry for the man. If I had married my sister, I would have kicked her out of the house after one day. But Lieven lasted fifteen weeks with Constance the Contrarian.

"You could file a lawsuit," the prefect suggests. "But any judge will tell you that a marriage can only be dissolved after the wife has been missing for two years."

"Two years!" Lieven exclaims. "Why not twenty?"

"Two years and one day," says the prefect. He gulps down the rest of his wine, pushes his plate aside, and wipes his hands on his pants. Then he takes out a clean sheet of paper and rummages around in the vase full of goose feathers until he finds a straight quill. As far as he's concerned, this conversation is over.

"She'll be back, my dear Lieven," Father tries.

Lieven says nothing.

"Listen," Father continues. "I understand that you are displeased, but I'm sure . . ."

"Displeased," says Lieven coldly. "I'm displeased?"

Father doesn't finish his sentence. Another silence falls over the Austrian Salon. All we hear is the creaking of the prefect's chair and the sound of the quill dipping into the ink. The prefect acts as if we've already left.

"I transferred forty thousand francs to your French bank," Lieven says. "I've paid your debts. You owe me forty thousand francs, Cloghead, and you're going to work for me until you've paid it all back. Starting today, you're going to use those brains of yours to design that cannon in my name."

The prefect glances at Father and Lieven, looking disturbed.

"But we would still be partners," says Father, like a child receiving his punishment. "That's what we agreed. Our company would be called Hoste and Goeminne."

"Yes, on the condition that your daughter bore me sons," Lieven roars. "But if that is not the case, there is no Hoste and Goeminne. That was our agreement."

Father says nothing.

"Now that your daughter is gone, you are no longer my business partner; you are my servant. You will work for me until every last cent of your debt is paid. Until that day, you are my engineer, and your inventions are my inventions."

By now, Lieven is so angry, steam is almost coming out of his ears.

"But my cannon, my design, Hoste's Cannon . . ." Father sputters.

"It will be Goeminne's cannon!" Lieven declares.

All the color has drained from Father's face.

"No," he squeaks.

"Think of your family, you idiot. Think of your son who should be in school. He is a smart boy. I expect great things from him."

Lieven looks at me and nods encouragingly.

The prefect leans back. His chair creaks. "Gentlemen," he says, "it seems that the rest of this matter does not concern me. May I ask that you kindly continue this conversation elsewhere?"

Lieven walks up to the prefect's desk, his heels clicking on the parquet floor, and slams a cloth sack on the table. A couple of gold napoléons roll out.

"If you cannot dissolve this marriage," Lieven says, "then I want Constance Hoste tracked down. Immediately!"

"Of course," says Prefect Gijsens. "But my authority does not extend beyond the city gates, and if you ask me, your wife stepped through one of those gates five days ago. She could be anywhere by now. Thus, I cannot offer you anything in exchange for your gold coins. I suggest you keep them. I wish you a pleasant day, sir."

◎ ◎ ◎

Once we're outside, Lieven says, "I want you to write to your family and your wife's family. Constance must be somewhere, with an uncle or an aunt. There's nowhere else she could be."

Father shakes his head. We already know she's not staying with our relatives. I wrote the letters myself.

"Tomorrow you'll show me your preliminary designs," Lieven demands.

"You're not getting my designs," says Father.

"What did you say, Clog?" Lieven asks.

"You and I were supposed to be partners," Father says.

"And your daughter was supposed to be my wife. I want to see your designs."

"No!" Father roars.

Stunned, I look at my father and then at Lieven, whose whole face is burning with rage. For a moment, I think he's going to slap Father, but he manages to control his hands.

"Leopold, don't be stupid. Bring me your work."

"Never!"

Lieven sighs and looks at me. I think my father is treating him unfairly. Not only has the man been abandoned by my sister, he's now been abandoned by my father too. But Lieven's the only one who can save Father—he's the entrepreneur who has paid off Father's debts, the man who expects great things from me. Finally, Lieven walks away. I stand there next to my father on the steps of the Town Hall.

"Forty thousand francs," I say with disbelief. But my father doesn't hear the outrage in my voice. He looks down at his pocket watch and winds it up, as if it's all a matter of time.

◎ ◎ ◎

Father pulls his tie a little tighter. He asks if I'd like a glass of wine and doesn't wait for an answer. I follow him to a pub across from the Town Hall. We plop down at a table by the window without bothering to take off our coats. Father orders two glasses of wine and smiles at me. It's not a genuine smile but the awkward, forced smile of someone who has just sat down on a pile of broken glass and doesn't want to admit it.

"What are you going to do now?" I ask.

His hand is shaking. He drinks the wine in one gulp and then holds the empty glass up in the air. The innkeeper hurries over to refill it. Apparently Father is a good customer here.

"He's not an inventor," Father says. "I am the inventor. Lieven knows about as much about mathematics as a crow knows about the days of the week."

He tosses a few coins onto the table. It's too much for three glasses of wine.

"You owe our friend Lieven forty thousand francs, and you're leaving tips?" I ask.

"That man is no friend of mine," Father says. He bids the innkeeper adieu as if he were some kind of count and walks out. The little bell over the door dings.

I chase Father down the alley and tug on his sleeve.

"So what happens now?"

"I'm afraid I'll have to declare bankruptcy," he says without looking at me. "Then we'll have nothing. They might send me to the Rasphuis."

"But I want to go back to school!" I cry. "Grandfather

did everything in his power to make sure that you could study at the Latin school."

Father stops and looks at me. I want him to reassure me that no matter what I'm still going back to school. I want him to say that Father Charles surely misses me in his Latin classes and things like that.

"What does that Lieven think?" Father growls. "That I am going to design the 'Goeminne cannon' for him? Preposterous!"

No, it seems that he's not going to offer me any reassurance.

"Preposterous!" he repeats.

So I gather my courage.

"But, Father, you signed a contract. Without Lieven, the bank would've already declared you bankrupt. Lieven saved you with his own money. Money that he earned honestly. He's a good man."

"Our company was supposed to be called Hoste and Goeminne."

"Design that cannon for him, Father," I say. "See to it that he earns back his forty thousand francs. What difference does it make?"

"You're just a stupid boy. You don't understand a thing."

He marches off in front of me.

"Surely the two of you can talk it out," I shout.

"Whose side are you on?" he barks. "Whose son do you think you are?"

I stare at him in bewilderment.

"He called me Clog," he says.

"What?"

"He used to call me Clog back in school too. He made sure that everyone knew that I wasn't like the other boys with their fancy surnames and stupid pedigrees, that they never forgot that my father was just a humble shoemaker."

One week later, the court declares Father bankrupt. The bailiff comes to our house with two gendarmes to take him to jail. They'll keep him locked up until all his debts are paid. Father puts on his best shirt and his most beautiful coat. He packs a bag with some clothes, pencils, compasses, rulers, a bundle of paper, and a sketchbook. He looks at Mother and tells her he'll be home soon. He hugs Rozeken and Eddy and nods at me. I'm too big for hugs.

The whole neighborhood has gathered in front of our house to watch my father be carted off like a criminal. But he walks out with his head held high. He takes a pinch of tobacco from his snuffbox, pushes it up his nose, and sneezes hard.

"Let's go," he says.

Eddy doesn't understand what's happening. He looks at us and then at Father. He asks over and over again what's going on, and when Rozeken explains it to him he starts crying and screaming because he doesn't understand. Mother is as cold as stone. It's as if she always knew this would happen.

The local tramps and peasants shout at him. "Swindler!" "Con!"

And one of them starts chanting that old schoolyard rhyme: "Shoemaker, shoemaker, dirty little lice raker."

II

PIER

Mother lights a candle in the front room every evening. The flame burns for the absent. After five days, Eddy asks how many times he has to go to bed before Father comes home. Rozeken tells him to be quiet and eat his bread. Eddy shouts that she's "a stupid child," because that's what Mother shouted when she came home with the laundry basket and a shirt was missing. The more Rozeken screams at him to stop, the louder he yells, "Stupid child, stupid child."

After the fifth scream he starts coughing. It's a deep, guttural cough that spews spit on the freshly ironed tablecloth. The spatters on the white linen are dark red. The silence that falls over the living room is so heavy it's almost palpable.

In the minutes after the coughing attack, Mother makes the sign of the cross at least a hundred times. Then she rushes off to fetch Doctor Buyck, mumbling Hail Marys all the way out the door. I even see her stop and kneel in front of a statue of Mary on our street.

"The white plague," the doctor diagnoses later that evening. Mother lets out a cry so raw that I think she's broken her voice forever.

"A fate that befalls God's weakest lambs," says Doctor Buyck. He says that Eddy shouldn't sleep with me anymore but in a separate room. We shouldn't get too close to him or talk to him for too long because the white plague spreads like a spirit that attaches itself to words. It can enter through the ear and infect the entire body. It's important that Eddy not overexert himself. He should drink half a liter of black beer every three days to create fresh blood and a glass of warm milk with sage every day. The doctor prescribes him some medicine and reminds Mother that miracles can happen. If she prays hard enough, God will hear. After the doctor is gone, Mother balls her fists and waves her arms around in the air. Then she falls silent and gazes up at the crucifix above the doorway. I hear her mumbling, "It's my fault, it's all my fault."

The next day Mother is up before the bells. She's wearing her best clothes and ironing a Sunday dress for Rozeken. I ask her what she is doing.

"I won't let them make a fool of me," she says in a steely voice.

She and Rozeken head off to the wealthy part of town in search of odd jobs—mending clothes, washing shirts, cleaning carpets. Mother divides the chores between her and Rozeken, who is twelve and old enough to work. Grandma wants to help with the sewing, but her eyes are too bad. Before long, our dining room is transformed into a sewing workshop.

"You can go work at the wool factory," Mother says to me.

"Factory work is for women," I say.

"It's boys your age out there laying cobblestones," she says.

"You expect me out there on my hands and knees hammering from morning to night?"

"I'm sure they could use the help."

"I wouldn't dream of it!" I shout.

"Well, aren't you a haughty one," Mother retorts. "If you don't want to work, then you'll stay home and take care of Eddy."

"I'm not a governess!" I exclaim.

But she's not listening anymore. She prays her first rosary of the day: fifty Hail Marys and five Our Fathers.

Mother sends me and Eddy down to Steyaert's pharmacy on Veldstraat, but she doesn't have any money to pay for the medicine. We stand outside shuffling from side to side, the crisp autumn air tickling our noses, and watch the customers walk in and out of the shop. We close our eyes and inhale the scent of healing herbs drifting out of the store. Every now and then one of them will hold their freshly bought herbs under our noses and tell us their names. We smell ginger, vinegar, and raw opium as well as anise, lemon seed, and thyme from the south. We make up stories.

"My brother is sick," Eddy says, and I nod.

"Poor boy," the people say.

"He can't speak," Eddy continues.

I shake my head.

"How terrible," they say.

"He only has a few days left to live," Eddy explains. "As soon as there's a place for him in heaven our good Lord will take him."

"The poor creature," they say.

On one of the last days of autumn, I take Eddy down to the Rasphuis to visit Father. The prison is located on the outskirts of the city, on the left bank of the Coupure. There, the prisoners work from dusk to dawn in exchange for bread, soup, and a couple of measly copper coins. They scrape the bark off of tree branches, which is used in factories to make paint.

Mother sent us with bread and wine. I'm surprised to see Father with a white beard. His clothes are dirty. He smells terrible. Apparently he's run out of eau de Cologne. He takes the bread, breaks it into pieces, and gives one to each of his fellow prisoners, who scarf it down in no time. Then he takes a sip of the wine and passes around the bottle. The men drink it as if it were nectar from the gods. Their clothes and faces are as rough as Father's. Misery looks the same on everyone. Father rubs his hand through Eddy's hair and murmurs, "My son, my son." Eddy beams. He's on strict orders not to speak so as not to infect Father, but it's hard for him to keep his mouth shut. There's so much he wants to say. He steps six feet back and asks, "When are you coming home, Papa?"

Whenever he manages to pay Lieven forty thousand francs plus interest, I think to myself, but I don't dare to say it out loud.

"I have a writing desk here," Father explains. "I have my instruments. I can make technical drawings, sketch designs."

He points to a rickety table with a missing leg in a corner of the cell. On it are a couple of scraps of paper, a compass, and a triangular ruler.

"I'm working on my cannon," he says. "Here I can work undisturbed."

"Why don't you just work for Lieven?" I ask.

"Lieven doesn't understand what's in my head," Father says. "I scrape bark during the day to earn my keep, and in the evenings I work on my invention."

I let out a heavy sigh.

"Don't sigh, Pier," Eddy says.

"Quiet!" I shout at him. "And you're standing too close."

Eddy sulks off into the corner of the cell and won't look at us anymore.

"Winter's coming," I say. "Mother and Rozeken work all day, but there's not much money coming in. It's barely enough for wood and coal. Think of them, at least. Think of Eddy."

"I think about Eddy constantly," Father growls.

And think of me, I want to say, *your eldest son who has had enough of all this misery.*

Father wriggles his hands as if his conscience is gnawing at his fingers. Then he points to his three-legged table.

"That is my life's work," he says.

"We believe in you, Professor!" shouts one of his toothless cellmates.

"They believe in me," Father says gravely.

He has lost his mind. I can't believe what I'm hearing. Two months ago, I was getting ready to go back to school, and now my entire existence has been shattered.

"This is all Stance's fault," I say. "That witch!"

"Stance is not a witch," shouts Eddy from the corner. "She's my best friend."

"Be quiet," I bark.

"Where could she have possibly gone?" Father muses. "I've searched all of Ghent. We wrote letters to uncles, aunts, and cousins. Nobody has seen her."

After all that Stance has done, all of her antics, all the hair that's been pulled out of her head, all the financial ruin she's caused, Father still misses her. And what about me? Me, the son who never does anything wrong. The son who is always obedient. Stance has brought us nothing but misery. If anyone deserves a beating, it's her! But who's Father thinking about here in prison—her! At first, I don't say anything, but eventually it comes out: "Father, you still have Eddy. And Rozeken. And me."

He refuses to look me in the eyes. Someone passes the bottle of wine back to him. There's still a little left in the bottom. Father tips back the bottle and gulps it down.

"Bertie can't take notes for me forever," I say.

He looks at me as if he has no idea who Bertie is anymore.

"What? Are you going to cry now?" Father sneers.

I feel my eyes welling up with tears. Why can't he understand that I just want to go to school?

"Don't be stupid," he snarls. "What are my friends supposed to think?"

A couple of prisoners turn their heads toward me. They look at me as if I'm some kind of imbecile who's too stupid to see that his father has been locked away along with the rest of them. An idiot who is of no use to his father.

Eddy and I walk back across the bridge over the Coupure and down a narrow, winding street until we come out on Hoogstraat. I'm so absorbed in my thoughts about how to escape this vicious circle of misfortune that I don't even notice that Eddy is no longer behind me. I turn around and shout his name, but there is no answer. My thoughts turn into panic.

I run back, searching left and right, shouting like a madman. People stare. I ask them if they have seen a little boy with red hair walking down the road. But no one can help me. Are they all blind? A boy with bright-red hair—how could you possibly miss him? When I reach the bridge, a terrifying thought occurs to me. What if Eddy climbed over the railing and fell into the water? It's all my fault. I wasn't paying attention. I look down at the water and spot something floating in it. A bundle of clothes? An old bag? Or is it . . .

"Pier!" a small voice calls out behind me. Tears fill my eyes at the sight of my little brother carrying a giant loaf of bread in his tiny arms. He drops it on the street before he's even reached me. I hug and kiss him, even though I'm not supposed to do that kind of thing anymore.

"I thought I lost you," I say. "Where were you?"

"Somebody gave me this loaf of bread," he says. "I shouted after you, but you didn't hear me, Pier. You just kept walking."

His lower lip is quivering.

"I shouted and shouted, but you didn't even look back," he wails. "The bread was so heavy. I couldn't carry it all by myself. And you didn't even look back!"

"Who gave you that bread?"

"I don't know. I couldn't see his face. An old man."

I look around, searching for the man who gave Eddy the giant loaf of bread. But there's no one there. Eddy wipes away the snot on his face.

"I'm sorry, little brother," I say and take the bread under my arm. He's right, it is heavy. I grab hold of Eddy's hand, and we walk home.

"Mother will be happy when she sees the bread," Eddy says proudly. "And I got it."

Mother puts a pan of vegetable soup with a few chunks of fish floating in it on the table. She seasons the soup with exactly two crushed peppercorns. Then she counts how many peppercorns we have left and calculates exactly how many meals she can get out of them. Then she starts slicing Eddy's bread. Two slices in, a silver napoléon rolls out. Mother stares at the coin in amazement, and, all of a sudden, another coin rolls out. She starts hacking into the bread like a madwoman.

One napoléon after another tumbles out onto the table. Once the bread has been hacked into a pile of crumbs, we examine the lot: ten shiny pieces of silver. Each one worth five francs. Pressed into the front of the coin are the words *God Protect France,* and on the back is the profile of a head with wild, curly hair and the words *Emperor Napoléon.* Mother makes ten signs of the cross. One for each coin.

"It's a miracle," she murmurs.

"God gave it to me," says Eddy, his little face beaming with pride.

I stare at the money. And all of a sudden, I know exactly where Stance has gone.

12

STANCE

That first day we follow the road from Ghent to Lille. The sleepless night catches up to me. I can still feel the rough journey from Lovendegem to Ghent in my bones. I struggle to keep up with the group. We finally stop for a break around noon, and we all drop to the ground where we're standing. My legs are numb. They pass out crackers as hard as floor tiles and some kind of watery soup that looks like it came straight from the ditch. Everyone dips the crackers into their soup, and I tear off a chunk of my bread. I'll feel better once I've got something in my stomach. I'm surrounded by at least thirty men. Most of them haven't said a word all morning, but now that we're taking a break, one of them introduces himself and another starts talking about the hamlet he's from. Only Geoffroy de Soudan remains aloof. At first, I assume it's because he thinks his shit smells better than everybody else's, but then I remember the gossip that was going around about him. Geoffroy was having an affair with Lucie Boone, his family's maid. I've seen her at the market. The Lord has certainly been generous to that girl. She has big, green eyes that sparkle like gems; a head of shiny, raven-black hair that sticks out from under her bonnet; a mouth full of white teeth; and a beautiful figure. God must have been so busy with her looks that he forgot about her brain because the stupid hen went off and got herself pregnant with the squire Soudan's child.

"Don't worry, darling," Geoffroy had allegedly reassured her when she came to him in tears and told him the news. He would tell his parents that he was going to marry her, that they were perfect for each other. Word has it, he joined his parents in the parlor that evening, where they were having their usual glass of sweet wine before dinner, and said that he had something important to tell them. His parents looked up from their glasses, slightly concerned, and listened to what their son had to say. When Geoffroy declared his intention to marry Miss Boone, his father dropped his wineglass and fainted on the Italian rug. The thud was heard all the way down in the cellars, where the cook was sautéing green beans and roasting a lamb. The beautiful Lucie Boone was sitting there at the workbench twiddling the cut-off ends of the beans in her trembling fingers.

Marquess Soudan finally came to after someone held a glass of gin under his nose. He crawled to his feet, gulped down the liquor, and declared that, as long as he breathed, there would be no more contact between his son and Miss Boone.

"Precisely," Geoffroy's mother agreed. The poor girl couldn't even read or write! The marquess's wife could tell by the way the girl washed and ironed their sheets that she had little to no character. Geoffroy's mother concluded that, like Adam, her son had been seduced by a devious Eve and led astray by her evil feminine tricks.

"A beginner's mistake," Marquess Soudan added, with a second glass of gin in hand, as if he knew all about the deviousness of women.

"You know," Geoffroy's mother continued, "every maid dreams of marrying the master of the house."

Geoffroy resisted. He declared that Lucie's love for him was as pure as well water.

"Typhus water!" his father bellowed.

That same evening—as soon as the green beans and the lamb were cleared from the table—Lucie Boone's two brothers were summoned to the drawing room. Marquess Soudan laid a sack of gold napoléons on the table, and the matter was settled. Lucie was sent away to a distant cousin in the country where she could give birth later that fall. She left no message for Geoffroy. A few weeks later, when he was drafted into the army and his father had just four days to find some poor boy who would take his son's place in exchange for a few thousand francs, the inconsolable Geoffroy said he didn't want a replacement. He'd rather take his broken heart into the army.

"His mother is just devastated," Mie De Peeze said on the docks.

It seems that I'm not the only one in our group who recognizes Geoffroy de Soudan. A couple of guys point at him and call him "Geoffie."

"It's Geoffroy," Soudan corrects them in a bossy voice. They laugh. He has no power over them here. In Napoléon's army, we're all equal.

That afternoon, our company walks through the open fields where you can see the horizon in all directions. We pass through a damp, musty forest that smells of pine needles, earth, and mushrooms. The wind rustles through the trees. Dead leaves swirl around us. I listen to the farm boys banter and try not to think about how exhausted I am. One of them tells a story about how, where he's from, people always kiss their pigs before the slaughter; it's tradition. Another one talks about how his mother makes her blood sausage (with lard, bacon, and gingerbread), and we all agree that that's one thing we will all miss in the army—blood sausage. With sautéed onions on the side. Then they start talking about sugar beets, which are apparently quite profitable now that there's no more sugar coming in from America. That evening, a rope maker from Mariakerke whines that he can't walk any farther because all the blisters on his feet have opened. A gendarme examines the soles of his feet and says he better start growing some calluses. Then the gendarme jabs him in the stomach with the butt of his musket, and before long the rope maker is walking with the group again. The gendarme told him the stomachache would make him forget all about his blisters.

That first night we sleep at an inn near Kortrijk. The innkeeper sells us soup and black bread. There are chickens scurrying around the taproom, and they hop up on the table to eat our crumbs. The only one not sitting at the table with the group is Soudan. He eats off on his own. His mother has sent him with a month's provisions: sausages, dried fish, oat bread, pots of honey, and quince marmalade. As he enjoys his feast, three skinny cats stare him down, hoping for a bite to fall from the table. But he shares nothing with the cats, let alone with us.

The boy who told us that he kisses the pigs before slitting their throats has a deck of cards with him, and he asks if anyone wants to play bouillotte. I raise my hand, though I have never seen playing cards up close before. The guy buys a candle from the innkeeper and sticks it into a raw potato with a hole in the middle. We sit close to the warm ashes smoldering in the fireplace. There are six of us. I'm immediately hooked and forget all about my fatigue. We stay up late playing cards. None of us wants to turn in for the night and go lie with all the other guys on the straw mattresses full of fleas. By the hundredth round, I can't keep my eyes open anymore. My head hits the table with a smack. I vaguely hear the others laughing, but I'm so tired I don't even feel the beans I won squishing into my cheek. When I wake up, the sun is rising. Geoff Soudan is still tossing and turning in his sleep. It's not every day that the fleas get to feast on the son of a Marquess for breakfast. Later that day, we stop at the big market square in Arras. Soudan hurries over to a butcher's stand to replenish his provisions with a slice of meat pie and a bottle of wine. Some of the guys stop to pee against a wall. I need to go too, but I hold it.

Peeing is a problem for me. During the morning and afternoon breaks, when the gendarmes go off to smoke their pipes, the guys all line up on the side of the road to pee. I walk on a bit until I find a bush to squat behind. Nobody has said anything about it yet, but I'm afraid I'll be discovered. In Arras, I find an old fireplace bellows on a trash pile. It's torn, but the wooden nozzle where the air is pumped through is still intact. That evening I manage, with the help of the nozzle, to pee standing up against a tree. I grin like the Devil in a convent. I can't shake the smile from my face. That night, I dip my bread in my nettle-and-chestnut soup and chuckle with glee. One of the guys asks me why I'm so happy. Since I can't really explain that I'm happy because I just peed against a tree with my new wooden member, I say that I'm looking forward to seeing Paris. After all, don't they say it's the center of the world? Home to the grandest bridges, the most beautiful shops, and houses as high as cathedrals? My companions shrug. They couldn't care less about seeing Paris. They miss their pigs, their blood sausage, and their sautéed onions.

"I've already been to Paris," Soudan the Silent says suddenly.

"And what did you think?" I ask.

He shrugs. He'd rather have his Veldstraat.

"They got pretty girls there?" the rope maker with the blisters on his feet asks.

"I guess so," Soudan says without a hint of enthusiasm in his voice. "They wear their hair short, they're all skinny, and they walk the streets with their necks and shoulders bare and sprinkle their skin with flour to make it look white. They color their lips and cheeks red."

"Why?" the rope maker asks.

"Well, the Emperor has all these paintings and statues from Italy in his museum. And the Parisian girls want to look like the women of ancient Rome. That's why they paint their lips and cheeks red. They even wear long dresses with ribbons tied high above their waists and sandals on their feet."

Soudan cuts off another piece of his sausage and shoves it in his mouth. We try to imagine the women in Paris.

"What are sandals?" the rope maker asks.

In the afternoon on the sixth day, we arrive at a fort about ten miles from Paris. It's a rectangular building with four floors, but it's still not big enough to house all the recruits, so they've added several rows of small, makeshift barracks with straw roofs in front of the entrance and along both sides of the road.

We report for duty in the courtyard. Two men inspect our papers and direct us into a hall to pick up our uniforms. The walls are covered in banners that, judging by all the rips and bullet holes, have clearly survived a battle or two.

A gray-haired soldier sizes me up from boots to hat. He's

lost his right arm, probably left it on the battlefield. The man barks to his comrades that he's got another half pint on his hands. All the old soldiers handing out uniforms at the long table look up at me and laugh.

"Now there's a colt," says a man with an eye patch.

I don't laugh along with them. I haven't walked two hundred miles to be the butt of their jokes.

"Just be careful not to break those delicate wrists of yours when you fire your first musket," says the man, and he slaps a bundle of clothes on the table. Two pants, a jacket, a pair of shirts, belts, and gaiters.

"Of course, sir," I say.

"It's Corporal!" he barks. "And remember that your jacket is not to be washed. Under no circumstances should the color fade. You can dust off your uniform with a dry brush. Any stains can be removed with tobacco. Only your pants, shirt, and leather may be soaked in a bit of chalk."

He adds a shako to the pile, along with two pairs of shoes. I hardly dare to touch the shako. The tall hat made of felt and leather looks like a stovepipe with a visor on the front. It's stiff and adorned with a plaque with the number fourteen on it. On the top is a vertical red plume.

"I have three shoe sizes, and this here's the smallest," he says.

I nod. I want to say that my father could make a lot more shoe sizes than that, but I figure I'd better keep my big mouth shut.

Corporal Left Arm wraps his thumb and forefinger around my skinny wrist and sizes me up. He shakes his head.

"If you're twenty, the Emperor is my uncle," he says.

"If the Emperor is your uncle," I say, "you must not be his favorite nephew."

His comrades burst into laughter. Corporal Left Arm is not amused.

"What are you still doing here?" he shouts. "Go get dressed."

I turn around but am not prepared for the spectacle unfolding before my eyes. All of my travel companions are taking off their clothes. I am surrounded by naked men. The gray-haired corporal repeats the command "Get dressed!" and points at his buttons as if I don't understand French.

"Yes, sir," I say. All of a sudden, Geoffroy de Soudan is standing right in front of me. He pulls off the white pants that he's just put on.

"These pants are way too tight," he complains and walks half naked back to the table with his aristocratic manhood bouncing in all directions. I lower my eyes and feel my cheeks burning. I walk out of the room and frantically search for a place to get dressed. A place where no man will see me. But the fort is teeming with soldiers like ants in a sugar bowl. Everywhere I turn is the clinking sound of sabers on belts and spurs on boots. I spot a stone staircase leading down to the cellar and seize my chance. It's pitch black down there, and the only sound is the dripping of water. I peel off my clothes and put on my infantry pants first, but they don't fit very well.

Damn, I'll probably have to exchange them later.

But then it occurs to me that I've got the pants on

backward. I laugh. I turn them around and stuff a sock into the front of my underwear to create a manly bulge. I inspect the cloth bandage wrapped around my breasts and tell them to stay put. I put on the jacket and notice that the buttons are on the right side of the buttonhole instead of on the left. I button it up.

I head back up the stairs in uniform. Once I'm back in the light, I look down at my dark-blue jacket with the white lapel. The buttonholes are lined with yellow. My pants are white, and the gaiters reaching over my knee are black. And just look at those fancy epaulettes on my shoulders—bright red with tassels. Someone get this handsome young man a mirror, shouts a voice in my head. But, of course, there are no mirrors anywhere. There's no way for me to admire myself. I put the shako on my head and tighten the strap under my chin. Look at me, the voice in my head cries, I'm in the Emperor's army.

Geoffroy de Soudan is fiddling with his belt.

"So, how do I look?" I ask him. I have to remind myself not to spin around for him like a girl.

"Yes," he says without looking at me. He asks if I can help him with his gun belt. He can't figure out how to get it crossed across his chest. I help him. There's a cartridge box hanging on the belt and a loop for a saber.

He grunts, which I guess means "thank you."

"Where were you just now?" he asks. "They came to tell us where to go. We're in the same company."

He picks up his linen bag of delicacies and walks out of

the room. If you ask me, that Lucie Boone was as stupid as coal. How could she ever fall in love with such a lout?

Soudan walks down the path between the barracks. It's getting dark. The red evening sky has faded. He stops in front of a group of soldiers smoking a pipe around a fire. He asks them in that haughty Veldstraat voice of his if this is "the Fourteenth." The men stop talking. They look at him, annoyed, as if he has just accused them of wearing women's clothes.

A boy in uniform—barely twelve years old—jumps up and grabs a drum. He announces us with a thirty-second drum roll, and after his last stroke he shouts: "Fresh recruits!"

"And who wants to know if this is the Fourteenth?" asks one of the men in broken French.

"Pardon?" asks Soudan, who doesn't seem to understand him very well.

"Pardon? Is that your name or something?"

"No, I beg your pardon, my name is Geoffroy de Soudan."

"No, your name is Pardon," says the other one. The soldiers who have gathered around nod in agreement.

"He's Breton," says an older man. "That's why he speaks such bad French."

"You're one to talk, Rabbit," says the Breton. "You people from the Auvergne can't even pronounce the *s* right."

"I can pronounce the *s* just fine, *shergeant*," says Rabbit. The man has a stern face with deep grooves carved in it. His hair is white, and his arms are covered in thick veins.

The Breton stands up. He's a lion of a man. Tall, dark, muscular, with scars on his hands and face. He sizes Geoff up from head to toe.

"Pardon, you're quite the pale little fart, aren't you? Have you been dipping into your mother's powder box or something?"

The other soldiers roar with laughter.

"Enough with the nonsense, sir," says Geoffroy harshly. "Just tell me whether this is the Fourteenth."

"Nonsense?" shouts the Breton. "We're the hungry Fourteenth, and you're not joining us until you've given us something to grease the pot with."

"Grease the pot?" Geoffroy repeats, as if he's trying to figure out whether he's understood the Breton's bad French correctly.

"Either he's an idiot," one of the soldiers laughs, "or he's as deaf as a cannoneer." The guy has no chin and a pointed nose. Later, I'll find out that they call him "Mole," not because of his nose but because he used to be a miner.

"If you don't have anything to grease the pot with, *Monsieur* Pardon," Rabbit continues, "then we'll have to hang *you* on the spit. We're starving."

The way he says it, it sounds like "shpit" and "shtarving." Geoffroy turns as white as a wafer.

"My name is not Pardon. My name is . . ."

But that's as far as he gets. Four men push him to the ground, tear his uniform off his body, and tie him to a lance by his ankles and wrists, using his brand-new black gaiters as straps.

"Are you out of your minds?" Geoffroy shouts. "Where are the officers? I demand to see an officer!"

"I'll take one of those ribs, Sergeant, and make sure it's well done," says Mole.

"Give me a breast," says the Rabbit. "And give the thighs to the Dutchman."

The Dutchman is a tall fellow with hands as big as coal shovels. He just shrugs. He couldn't care less.

"The Dutchman doesn't talk much," says the sergeant. "He speaks about as much French as a tobacco leaf, and his parents were too poor to buy a donkey."

"Donkey expensive," the Dutchman mumbles.

All the while, Geoff is shouting his head off. Two guys carry him over to the campfire. His loose shirt flaps in the wind.

Geoff looks at me and says my name for the first time: "Binus."

The men of the hungry Fourteenth whip around to face me. They all just stand there, staring at me for a moment—I'm a recruit as fresh as they come.

"And who are you, beanstalk?" the Breton asks.

He marches in front of me. He's enormous. At least three times my size.

"B Binus Serlippens," I stutter.

"These recruits are getting younger by the day," the sergeant complains. "Did they knock you out at the school gate and smuggle you into the army?"

I shake my head.

"Look at the kid's uniform," he says to the others. "The

smallest size, and he's swimming in it. My coat rack has wider shoulders than you do, kid. And what a dainty little chin. Boy, you'd make a peach jealous."

He rubs his finger under my chin. The others laugh. Then he points at Geoff.

"Our giant hare on a spit, here—is he a friend of yours?" he asks.

"No," I say. "I don't know him. I didn't even know his name was Pardon."

I try to smile, but the Breton's not impressed.

"I'm burning!" Geoff screams, but he's exaggerating. He's hanging more than three feet above the fire. What a whiner!

"Don't try to pull a fast one on us now," says the Breton. "I'll bet you're more tender than Pardon here. You've probably got less hair on your legs too."

"That'd be pretty stupid," I say. "I'm skinny as a heron. And if you hang me on a spit, you'll miss all the delicious treats I've brought you."

Geoff, dripping with sweat and bright red over that fire, looks at me in amazement.

"Unless, of course, you don't like meat pie and red wine."

I open Soudan's linen bag, pull out the bottle of wine and toss it to the Breton, who catches it. Then I pull out the meat pie—it weighs at least a pound. It's wrapped in newspaper and black from the ink. I toss it to Rabbit, who's risen to his feet. The sergeant and Rabbit both have their hands full, so they can't grab me by the collar. Rabbit sticks his thumb into the pie and licks it.

"Now that's what I call a first-class pie, Sergeant."

"There's more where that came from," I say cheerfully.

The sausages, the dried fruits, the marmalade, and the honey are accepted with an equal amount of enthusiasm. Only the dried fish—which smell like cheap soap—are left untouched.

"You see this grasshopper here," the Breton shouts at Soudan hanging over the fire. "This little guy has manners. He knows how to grease the pot."

The two pikemen drop Soudan into a puddle of soft mud. The edges of his shirt are charred.

"You got any money on you? Every soldier has to pay his dues to the company," says the Breton. I give him the few copper coins I have left. I've spent all the money I took from my husband over the past few days.

"With a bit of luck, you'll receive your salary of fifty-seven centimes a day at the end of the month," the sergeant says. "Half goes into the company's pot. We use the money to buy tobacco, wine, and food. We also pay the laundress to wash our shirts. You can send the rest of it home if you want."

I nod.

"And I know you've got some money for the company on you too," he shouts to Soudan.

The young nobleman climbs to his feet. He pulls his pants back on and says, "Yes."

The sergeant gives him a kick in his burnt behind.

"You mean, 'Yes, Sergeant,'" he shouts.

The Breton grins and slings his arm around me. My knees almost buckle under the weight.

"I like this little tyke," he says to the others, scratching his stubble. "My name is Perrec, and that"—he points at Rabbit—"is Corporal Gérard. He's from the Auvergne. That's a region with mountains, wolves, goats, and rabbits. Gérard was a poacher in his past life. Then he got caught by a gendarme with five rabbits and two pheasants under his coat, and they gave him a choice: forced labor or the army."

"Pleased to meet you, Corporal Gérard," I say.

"Call me Rabbit, kid," he says. "Everybody else does."

Perrec tells me that Rabbit has two guns. The Emperor's gun and the one he was using when he got caught poaching.

"Rabbit can pop a sparrow out of a tree at a hundred paces," Perrec says. "It pays to have a poacher in the company. Even if he is a grandpa."

The two guys who hung Geoff on the spit sit down with a chessboard between them.

"That there's the Basque," says Rabbit. "The man's as proud as a peacock of his old Basque country, where they've got more mountains and sheep than people. The guy he's playing chess with is Bouchon. He's from Gascony. He grew up among the vines."

The Basque and Bouchon, both young men with short black hair and dark eyes, give me a nod as they chomp on a piece of sausage and set up their chess pieces.

"That guy who's a head taller than the rest of us is the Dutchman."

The Dutchman gives me a wink.

Someone tosses Geoff a piece of bread and sausage. We search each other's gaze. He nods at me. Is that a thank you? I nod back. In the army, he's not the son of a marquess anymore. He's my equal—a soldier in a blue uniform, carrying a cartridge box.

"You play any bouillotte, Binus?" Mole asks as he pulls a deck of cards out of his inside pocket.

"You bet," I say. He hands me the cards, and I shuffle them as if I've been doing it all my life.

13

PIER

Mother spends the ten silver *napoléons* on medicines for Eddy. She is skeptical of Steyaert, the Veldstraat pharmacist, with all his powders, pills, and syrups. They're as expensive as mustard. She prefers the cures offered by traveling miracle doctors. They have an encyclopedic knowledge of plants, and their healing herbs come straight from the womb of Mother Earth. Their brews are prepared according to recipes that have been handed down for generations. Of course, there are all kinds of con artists out there too, and Mother knows that, but some of them are actual miracle workers, true healers. They come from faraway places, wear strange hats, and carry crazy amulets around their necks. They all have some kind of potion or powder or porridge that will cure the white plague that's ravaging my little brother's body. Mother buys them all, and Eddy swallows every one of them. Sometimes he'll do better for a few days, and we all feel hopeful. But then, at night, he'll have another coughing fit, and Mother will see the blood spatters on his white pillow in the candlelight.

Advent turns into Christmas, and before we know it, it's the new year. The silver napoléons are all gone. The guards at the city gates fire gunpowder into the air after the bells strike midnight on the last day of the year one thousand eight hundred and eight—a year that has brought our family nothing but misery. On Epiphany, the frost chases the sparrows from the trees, and we wrap ourselves in blankets to save coal for when it really gets cold. I have a feeling I'll never see my school again. We can't go on like this. On the first mild day in January, I decide to pay a visit to the only man who can help me.

I walk for two hours along the canal to Lieven Goeminne's estate in Lovendegem. I ring the bell at the gate. A maid with a heavy limp hobbles up to me and tells me to get lost. I introduce myself as Pieter, Lieven's brother-in-law. The maid eyes me suspiciously. Then she walks back into the house. A moment later the old coachman comes out, opens the padlock on the gate with a giant key, pulls off the chain, and slides back the bolt. The fence grinds open. He points his head toward the house. As I make my way up to the house I hear the chain rattling along the fence and the key turning back in the lock.

I'm led into the drawing room, which smells of dust, coal, and tobacco. The curtains don't let in any daylight. The only light in the room is coming from a candelabra with seven arms, only two of which are holding stubs of melted candles. The entire candelabra is covered in dried, dripping wax, as if it's burnt out on life. Lieven is sitting in an elegant, dark-red upholstered chair with curved legs and gilded lion's heads in the armrests. He's aged dramatically over the past few months and grown fatter. He looks like a shot animal bleeding to death in the expensive chair. He doesn't even look up when I walk in. He pours himself a glass of wine. It fizzes and runs over the edge of the glass.

"How are you, sir?" I try.

"Where is your sister?" he asks.

His voice does not sound friendly.

"I don't know. We have not heard from her. She hasn't written."

He slurps his wine.

"And your father, how's that invention of his coming along?"

"I don't think he is getting much work done in prison."

One of the two candles sputters and dies out. Now the whole room is illuminated by a single flame.

"I have always respected your sister," Lieven concludes. "I gave her coffee every day. She didn't have to sweep or scrub. She didn't even have to bathe herself. Everything was done for her. The Empress herself doesn't have it as good as she did."

I nod. It is embarrassing. There are no words to describe Stance's stupidity.

He rubs the lion's heads on the armrests of his chair, as if they are the only thing that can give him comfort.

"You're a good boy," he says. "In truth, you are the greatest victim of this whole situation."

I nod. He knows exactly how I feel.

"Sir," I start quietly. "I've been thinking about Stance. About where she might have gone."

He looks up.

"At the end of October, we came into possession of ten napoléons in a very unusual way. My mother declared it a miracle and has been lighting candles in gratitude at the cathedral ever since. But I know better. That money was from Stance. She feels guilty for abandoning us. And she tried to buy off that debt with fifty francs."

Lieven sits up straight.

"Well, perhaps she sold my walking stick and Sunday suit," he says. "I can tell you those things were worth more than that."

"Fifty francs is exactly the amount that new recruits receive when they join the army."

"So?"

"Maybe she asked one of those recruits to send that money to us. And in exchange, she followed him into the army. To take care of him. Wash his shirts and things like that."

"Who would she have followed?"

"Alfons De Keghel," I say.

"Who?"

"Well, actually they call him Fons, or Mr. Adonis."

Lieven gives me a dark look. I feel myself blushing.

"But that nickname is a gross exaggeration," I say in a

hurry. "His parents are grocers from Sint-Jacobs. He and Stance, they . . ."

I get so caught up in what I'm saying that my brain starts to hurt. Lieven just stares at me.

"Alfons De Keghel used to stand at our window, and I heard Stance . . . uh . . . talking to him. Later she called him a calf. But I think she still went to him. That's the only thing I can think of."

The information seems to bring Lieven back to life. Even the curved legs under his chair seem to stand a bit straighter. He walks over to the cupboard and pulls out a glass. He wipes off a layer of soot with his finger, reaches into a bowl with his hand, pulls out a dripping ice cube, and drops it into the glass. He holds the bottle high above the glass and pours. The wine foams like soap. He slides it toward me.

"I buy this wine from the widow Clicquot in Champagne," he says. "It's much cheaper than regular wine but actually quite delicious. When the Emperor heads out on a campaign he always takes a cart full of this stuff with him. He likes to celebrate his victories with foaming wine."

The fizz tingles against my nose. The wine is delicious. The bubbles dance in my mouth.

Lieven pulls the old wax stumps out of the candelabra and replaces them with new candles. He does this with quick, nervous movements. He strikes a match and lights the candles one by one. Slowly, the light chases the darkness into the corners of the room. Only now do I see how fine the wallpaper is, the magnificent desk in the corner, and the beautiful prints of the Emperor in Egypt.

I take another sip of the frothy wine, and soon the glass is empty. Before I know it, Lieven's dropped another ice cube into my glass and is pouring me another drink.

"That sounds like a solid theory," Lieven says. "Constance followed her sweetheart soldier to the war. There are other women who do that."

I nod.

"I had hoped that Stance would come back when she heard that her father was in prison," says Lieven. "Believe me, I'm worried about my friend Leopold."

I feel the bubbles celebrating in my empty stomach. A warm feeling rushes over me.

"And I take it things are not so easy for your family at home?"

"I can't stand it at home," I blurt out. "My mother and sister are constantly saying that I don't do anything and that I'm only in the way. They say I'm too lazy to go work in the factory. They won't light the stove, and apparently all I'm good for is to play nanny to my sick little brother. All the while, my father is sitting in jail crying over Stance!"

The tears start rolling down my cheeks.

I haven't cried in front of my parents in a long time, but somehow, with Lieven I can't hold back the tears. My whole body is trembling. I want to kick myself.

"I'm sorry," I say, wiping away the tears.

Lieven stands up and presses my head against his chest. He pulls me into his arms. I let it happen. He gently pats me on the shoulder. His jacket stinks of tobacco, but I don't mind.

"You don't have to apologize, my boy," he whispers. "I'd be proud to have a son like you."

"I want to go back to school," I say. "To my room with Bertie and Toine. I miss Latin. I miss the Romans. I even miss math."

"A young man as smart as yourself should be in school," he says, stroking my head. "When I think back on my days in Pecq, the battles in the orchard. Three to a room. The smell of paper, chalk, and ink in the classroom."

In my mind, I can smell it too. The feeling of homesickness rips through my stomach. Lieven lets go of me.

"Will you help me?" he asks.

I nod. Of course I'll help him.

"Will you go find your sister for me?" he asks.

I choke on the wine.

"Where? In the army? But, I-I wouldn't know where to start. I guess I could write a letter to the army. To the regiment that Alfons De Keghel is in and . . ."

"And your sister will make a run for it as soon as she hears that I'm on her trail. No, I don't think that's a good idea. But you can go look for her. According to the newspapers, the Emperor's army is still in Paris. I don't think they'll go on another campaign before the spring. Find Alfons De Keghel. I'm sure your sister is with him."

"But I have to go back to school," I mumble. "I've been gone for more than six months. That's half a year!"

"When my wife is back with me," says Lieven, "I will

personally cover your school fees for the next four years. I promise. You won't have to miss another day of school."

"That's very charitable of you," I say. "But I'm only fourteen years old, I can't just go to Paris."

"I know just the man to help you," he says. "He's a business associate of mine. He used to be in the military. Artillery. He's a decent, civilized man. With him, you'll be more than safe. He'll help you find Fons, and you'll be back in three or four weeks or so. With your sister."

"But what if Stance won't come?"

"I think my friend will be able to persuade her. And when she's back I'll chain an iron ball to her ankles."

I stare at him.

"I'm joking," he says with a chuckle. And I laugh with him. He pours the rest of the bottle into my glass.

The next day I go visit Father. It's snowing heavily. My shoes and pants are soaked by the time I get to the Rasphuis, and I warm up by one of the burning coal baskets. It's as cold inside as it is outside. Father looks thin. His clothes are covered with soot. He's wearing a wool cap full of holes. His beard is long and white. He's starting to look a bit like Archimedes. He can't move the fingers on his right hand anymore. They're crooked and stiffened from grating tree bark in the freezing courtyard. His nose is running, and he wipes the snot with his sleeve. He earns just enough to pay for his daily soup with bread and lard. He sketches on scraps of old paper and cast-off newspapers. In a small box, he's got a couple of goose-feather quills and a dozen pencil stumps that are so small I can't even imagine how he still holds them between his fingers. He accepts the tobacco I've brought for him and tells me to thank Mother. He flashes his rotten teeth at me, but it's not really a smile. He looks to the side and passes the tobacco to his cellmates. One of them takes it and pulls a few pipes off a rack. One of them is busy pinching fleas between his nails, and the other is writing a letter to his creditors. Their cloaks are threadbare.

"I'm going to Paris to get Stance," I say. "I think I know where she is. If I bring her back, Lieven will pay my school fees."

My father looks at me, stunned. But I feel strong and in control. I'm the man of the house now. And I've come here to tell him what's what.

"If I find her and bring her back to Lieven," I continue, "he's willing to let you out of here. This is all Stance's fault. By deceiving Lieven, she has also deceived you. Once she's back, Lieven will be more accommodating."

"You're going to Paris?"

My father sounds impressed, and that makes my shoulders swell with pride. In a few words, I tell him about my theory about Fons De Keghel.

"Are you going alone?" he asks.

"A friend of Lieven's is going to accompany me."

The room falls quiet for a moment. My father massages his fingers. The cellmate writing letters looks up.

"It's ready," the man whispers.

"What's ready?" I ask.

"The invention," he says, pointing at Father with his quill. "Hoste's Cannon."

Father pushes himself up and walks over to the three-legged table with his stiff knees. With his crooked hands, he pulls out a dirty leather portfolio full of papers. He hands it to me. I open it. On the first sheet of paper, it says in French: *The Cannon of L. Hoste, by Leopold Hoste, Professor of Mathematics.*

"You're not really a professor, are you?"

"I could have been one," Father says.

For a moment, I'm sure that my father has lost his mind, that what little sense he had left in his head has leaked out of one of those holes in his hat. The portfolio contains twenty-three pages of text written in such extravagant French that I barely understand it. This is followed by another forty pages of drawings—the cross-section of the cannon, an impression of it in the hold of a ship and sketches of various cannonballs: round cannonballs with a flat side, cannonballs connected by a chain, and a cannonball covered in short pins that can drill into the wooden hull of an enemy ship.

"A cannon for the navy," says Father, tapping on the pages with his crooked finger. "The future."

"How do you know if the cannon works?"

"It works. My calculations are correct. It's pure mathematics."

"Like your sawing machine?"

"Everything starts with theory," he says excitedly. "Even

the wheel started with theory. With a drawing in the sand. Without theory, there is no invention."

The cellmates nod as if they were the ones who invented the wheel.

"Wait a second, Father," I say as quietly as possible. "This changes everything. Everything. Invite Lieven to come visit you. Show him your work. If he sees money in it, he'll invest in it. Then you can negotiate a deal."

"Never!" Father shouts.

"I understand you're still angry with him."

"Angry!" he roars as if I've grossly underestimated the entire situation. "You understand nothing!"

"Give me those papers. I'll take them to Lieven. I'll talk to him. He's very reasonable. I'll make sure he gets you out of here, that he pays you—"

Father slaps me so hard on the head that his cellmates all look up. I gaze at him, frightened. Usually, Stance is the one who gets the blows. Not me.

"Traitor," he hisses. "Judas! These papers aren't for Lieven. And don't you dare take any money from him."

The cell falls quiet for a moment. Then I gather my courage.

"Lieven agrees that I should be at school. He thinks I'm clever."

With that, Father slaps me again. The leather portfolio falls from my lap, and he scrambles to pick it up. He could just say that Lieven is right. That I should be in the old Porpoise's Latin class. Just say it, Father. Say it, and I'll kiss your hands. Say I'm clever, and I'll do whatever you want.

But he doesn't say it.

"That Lieven is quite the talker," Father growls as he puts the papers back in the portfolio. "But that's all it is. Talk, talk, talk."

One of his cellmates passes him the burning pipe. Father takes it between his crippled fingers and inhales. He savors the tobacco smoke filling his lungs. Father's cellmates are lighting their pipes as well. They exhale through their noses. Soon the room is enveloped in a cloud of smoke.

"You're going to help me," Father says suddenly.

I look at him hopefully. Tell me what I have to do to make you proud, Father. Tell me what to do, and I'll do it.

"I'm trusting you with my invention," he says without looking at me. "Go to Paris with that friend of Lieven's. But do not let him see these papers. Once you're in Paris, run away and find the Emperor."

My jaw drops.

"Find who?" I can't believe my ears.

"Napoléon Bonaparte," says Father impatiently. "Tell him you've come on behalf of Leopold Hoste. That you're there to sell him my invention. Tell him that you want one hundred thousand francs for the design. And then another hundred thousand for me to build the cannon and test it."

I'm speechless. My father has completely lost his mind.

"You don't have a factory anymore!"

"Four walls and a roof are all I need. There are plenty of empty monasteries around Ghent. I can rent one for a pittance."

"We'll help you, Leopold," his cellmates agree. "You can count on us."

"What if the Emperor asks why Leopold Hoste didn't come to present his famous cannon himself?"

"Then you tell him that I am currently being deprived of my freedom."

"You want one hundred thousand francs from the Emperor in exchange for fifty sheets of paper," I say.

"For a revolutionary invention," he says. "That seems very reasonable to me."

"A bargain!" one of his cellmates adds.

"You're not right in the head!" I shout.

I jump up and take a step backward so he can't hit me. Then, he finally looks me in the eyes. All I see is disappointment.

"A son doesn't say such things to his father," he murmurs.

"Just talk to Lieven."

"Never. It's my cannon. Don't you dare say a word about it to Lieven. You will obey your father."

His cellmates look at me as if I were Judas who just kissed Christ. But what my father is demanding is insane.

"You are asking me to go find the Emperor, knock on his door, and tell him about your cannon? We're talking about Napoléon the First, for heaven's sake!"

"Why not?"

"I am fourteen years old," I say.

"Well, you were talking like a big man just now," he says, raising his voice.

His cellmates chuckle. They shake their heads. They're

laughing at me. I stare at Father. I want him to look me in the eyes. I want him to see that I'm not a traitor.

"Go to the Emperor and sell him my plans. Don't say a word about it to your mother. She doesn't understand these things. And don't you dare say anything to Lieven. Understand?"

"Yes."

"Show me that you've got some marrow in those bones," Father says. "Show me you're worthy of being my son."

He arranges the papers neatly in the old leather portfolio. He ties the three strings around the cover and pushes it into my hands.

Then he stands up and stumbles over to his cellmates, who are sitting in a fog of tobacco smoke. They slap him on the shoulder encouragingly as if to congratulate him on the way he has just negotiated the sale of his invention.

That evening I study my father's plans. I can't follow the theoretical explanation, and I can just barely decipher the drawings. I'm angry at myself because I don't understand things. Angry because I'm only fourteen. For my brother-in-law, I'm supposed to go to Paris to find Stance. For my father, I'm supposed to go to Paris to find the Emperor and ask him for a hundred thousand francs in exchange for a bundle of papers. And another hundred thousand francs to manufacture the thing.

Mother is at home sewing a shirt by candlelight. I tell her my theory—that I think Stance has run off with Fons. She thinks I'm right. Where else would she have gone? I tell her that I'm going to go look for her with a friend of Lieven's. We'll find Stance and bring her home. Mother just stares at me.

"Who is this friend of Lieven's?" she asks.

"A decent man who knows Paris and the army like the back of his hand."

"I don't know," she says. "You've never even been out of Ghent."

"Lieven is a fine man," I say. "He knows the man he's sending me with. Even Father trusts him."

"How is your father doing?" she asks.

I shrug. I don't feel like talking about Father.

"He still doesn't want to work for Lieven?"

"No," I say. "He is working on his new invention."

Mother closes her eyes. She can't stand to hear the word *invention* anymore. I don't breathe a word about what Father has asked me to do for him.

Mother puts down her sewing and stands up.

"My eyes are tired," she says.

Everything about my mother is tired.

"Tomorrow I will prepare a bundle of clothes for you," she says finally.

Lieven's business partner arrives a week later. His name is Auguste Dupin, and he is a giant of a man. His face looks like a battlefield. A long, purple scar curls around his mouth, and there's a black mark on his cheek. But other than that, he's immaculate. His hair is pulled back into a ponytail, his face is clean-shaven, and there's not a spot of mud on his dark green suit. He is kind to my mother and promises to bring me home safely.

"We'll find your daughter, madam," he says with a wily smile that makes the curly scars around his mouth slide up and down on his face.

"And you won't hurt her?" Mother asks.

"Madam, I left the artillery five years ago, and since then, I haven't hurt a fly," Dupin says gravely. "I've seen enough suffering."

Mr. Dupin looks strong, determined, and honest. I look forward to becoming his friend. But Mother is not convinced. I don't understand why she has to be so difficult.

"I'm not about to let my son go out in the world with the first adventurer who shows up at our door," she says. Oh, Mother can be such a nag! Can't she see that this man is an artillery hero? I'll be fine.

"I want to see your papers," she says.

Dupin smiles amiably and grabs his coat.

"Be polite, Mother," I whisper.

"Bite your tongue," she snaps.

Mother reads the papers, which confirm that our man is who he claims to be and also that he is a customs officer of the Emperor. Mother hands them back to him. She shakes her head.

"I'm sorry. The answer is no," she says.

"So you're just going to run Mr. Dupin off?" I exclaim. "Come on, Mother, let me go."

"I'll care for him as if he were my own son," Dupin says.

"Are you a Catholic?" Mother barks. "Or a heretic like the Emperor?"

Dupin reaches under his shirt and pulls out a rosary.

"The Lord is my shepherd," he declares, flashing a row of slimy, yellow teeth.

"Swear that you'll protect him," she says. She glares at him with fire in her eyes.

"Mother," I say, "there's no need to insult the man."

"I swear," Mr. Dupin says, and he kisses the little cross dangling around his neck. Mother locks him in her gaze. Finally, she lets him go with a sigh. She turns to me.

"Make sure to dress warmly enough," she says. "Put on your overcoat when it rains. Wash your feet at least once a week."

"I will," I say impatiently.

"And be careful."

"I promise, Mother," I say and smile at Mr. Dupin. Maybe he had an overprotective mother once too.

"And make sure you come back alive and well," Mother says.

"Mama," I sigh.

Suddenly, she slaps me across the face. Rozeken and Eddy jump with fright. My cheek burns. I've been getting knocked around quite a bit lately. I feel the tears coming on.

Mother shakes her finger at me and says, "That's to make sure you don't forget that you have to come back alive and well."

I look at Mr. Dupin. But he looks away discreetly. He

doesn't laugh. He refuses to look at my shame. We're going to be friends.

Mother gives me my best shoes. They have thick soles, and the tips are reinforced with iron. They're virtually indestructible.

"You can't travel in bad shoes," she says. "You're the son and grandson of a cobbler, after all."

The sole of the shoe feels firm and the iron tip taps against the cobblestones when I walk. Mother has packed an extra pair of pants in a burlap sack, along with three shirts, a blanket, and, of course, a Bible. I keep the leather portfolio with my father's plans under my shirt.

Rozeken hugs me and says she loves me. Grandma Blommaert kisses me with that toothless mouth of hers and leaves two smacks of wet saliva on my cheeks. She tells me to watch out for the Austrians. I almost don't dare to look Eddy in the eyes. I squat down next to him. His red hair is so bright against his pale skin that it looks as if someone painted it.

"My little red monster," I say. "Don't you worry. I'm going to get Stance."

He looks at me and coughs. A splash of blood shines on his lower lip. My little brother looks so small and fragile and alone. If there was ever a picture of misery, it's Eddy standing there in front of our house on Kraanlei. *Stay alive!* I want to shout. *Don't die until I get back.*

"Who's going to read to me?" Eddy asks.

"I don't know."

"Who's going to take me to the pharmacy?"

I don't answer.

"How about I bring something back from Paris for you?" I ask finally.

"Stance," he says. "I want Stance."

And so, I leave home, my Ghent, on a late January day. I climb onto Achilles's back and follow Mr. Dupin. Rozeken and Eddy watch me go and wave every time I look back. Mother doesn't wait until I'm out of sight. She's already walking back into the house. She's got better things to do. The sewing is waiting. Tonight she'll light the candle in the front room again. This time, for three souls instead of two.

14

STANCE

We sleep three to a bed. We take off our socks and lay them on the chair with our jackets. Pants and shirt stay on. We lie head to toe on a straw mattress. This means that I, as the skinniest of the three, get the middle with my head at the bottom of the bed. That way they get to enjoy the smell of my feet, and I get to enjoy theirs.

One of my bedmates, Mole, won't stop chatting. He's talking to my feet, but I can still hear what he is saying. He tells me that he used to work in the mines and that they were haunted. When I say I don't believe him, his story gets even bigger. Once, he saw it with his own eyes, he says. A dozen miners lying dead on the ground, surrounded by greasy lumps of coal. Their mouths gaping open, their eyes white orbs. Some of them were holding their own throats as if they'd strangled themselves. And down in the tunnels of the mine he heard laughing.

"Laughing?" I ask his feet incredulously.

"Yes," says Mole. "I'm pretty sure it was laughter. I had to get out of there quick and warn my mates. Some drew their knives and others grabbed their pickaxes, ready to kill the ghost. But that ghost that killed twelve of our mates? Nobody ever saw him. A week later, I joined the army."

"I didn't have a choice," I lie. "I drew a low number. What about you, Cornelis?"

"No Cornelis. Me name Cor," says my other bedmate, the Dutchman, in his broken French. He speaks slowly and carefully, as if letting the words ripen in his mouth for a moment before pronouncing them. He is nineteen years old and took the place of a notary's son for a few thousand francs, all of which he gave to his parents.

"So they can buy donkey," he says. He tells us he doesn't mind being in the army. It beats pulling peat out of the ground. But he does miss Holland, where you can pull lobsters right out of the tide pools.

"A man either spends his whole life pulling something out of the ground—coal, peat, beets—" Mole says philosophically, "or he has to face the fire."

Then I hear him sniffing loudly above my toes.

"Hey, Binus," Mole says, "your feet smell pretty good. Did you wash them with soap or something?"

"Yes," I say. "And it would be nice if you could too. It doesn't exactly smell like honeysuckle down here."

Cor and Mole laugh. Easy for them, they're at the head of the bed.

"I've never washed my feet with soap," says Mole.

"You dirty bastard," Cor says.

They both burst out laughing.

After a while, my bedmates are asleep, and I suppose that if I breathe in the cheesy smell of their unwashed feet long enough, I'll be drowsy enough to sleep too. But for now, I can't sleep in the crowded barracks, so I lie on my back and listen to the sound of hundreds of soldiers snoring.

Less than four months ago, I was wearing a wedding dress and a silver hairpin.

You used to have one snoring man to deal with, says Stance the Bride in my head. *Now you've got hundreds. I don't know if that's progress.*

This is where the heroes of Austerlitz slept, I say. *Of Tivoli, Marengo, and the pyramids.*

And where are they now? All dead, says Stance the Bride.

Shut up, you old nag, I say.

She shuts up.

Every new recruit is trained by a veteran soldier. Sergeant Perrec is in charge of training me and about fifty others. On the first day, he has us stand at attention for a full hour: one hand behind our backs and our pinkies placed exactly on the middle seams of our pants, heads motionless, chins up, and gazes fifteen paces ahead.

We learn to march in step at a standard tempo of sixty-seven steps per minute and at higher speeds of ninety and one hundred and twenty steps per minute. The little drummer keeps the beat, and the sergeant checks it against the second hand on his pocket watch.

We each get a musket.

The thing is a foot and a half long and weighs nine pounds. We learn how to take them apart and put them back together and how to grease them with cloths. Shooting a musket amounts to a series of twelve commands, twelve steps that we have to be able to perform in under a minute. Over and over and over again. We rip open paper cartridges with our teeth, sprinkle gunpowder into the priming pans, close the frizzens, and let the torn powder cartridges fall to the bottoms of the barrels with a crack. Then we draw the ramrods and load the cartridges. We pull back the cocks, shoulder the things, aim, and pull the triggers. The cocks hit the flints down, creating sparks; the powder in the barrels ignite, and the flames hit the torn cartridges; and the bullets whiz out of the barrels. The first few days they give us practice cartridges with no bullets in them and we fire clouds of sulfur. After that we get real bullets.

"The musket is reasonably accurate at seventy yards," the sergeant explains to us. "A good marksman can hit his target at a hundred yards. At one hundred and fifty yards, you'll need more luck than in the lottery, and at two hundred and fifty yards you have a better chance of hitting the moon than your enemy."

The sergeant teaches me how to improve my aim by holding up my left thumb next to the barrel.

"Your right eye is your good eye," the sergeant says over

my shoulder, "which means you should close your left to shoot."

It turns out I'm good with the musket. I rarely miss the target at a hundred yards. I call the weapon "Monsieur Charlesville," after the town where the guns are made. Monsieur Charlesville and I are going to get along just fine. Since I'm able to quickly load and aim, they assign me to the voltigeurs, the acrobats. Perrec teaches us to reload as we run and tumble. In a battle, we are on the front line, the first marksmen to engage the enemy.

The women in the camp are always busy. They wear army jackets on top of their dresses and a cloth in the French Tricolore around their heads. While one woman cuts turnips for the day's soup, another hangs washed shirts. There's one who walks around with a wine barrel, filling soldiers' cups in exchange for a few coins. She has thick arms and coarse facial features. They say she's the lieutenant's sweetheart. She notices me looking at her with the wide eyes of a new recruit.

She winks and says I'm a handsome fellow. I get my first cup of wine for free. I smile and blush. She pinches me on the cheek. I walk back along the barracks, past thousands of infantry soldiers—grenadiers, fusiliers, scouts—never have I seen so many men in one place. I breathe in the fresh air of freedom. I can't stop grinning.

Weeks go by. Our training continues. We disassemble our muskets, wash, and dry them. We wipe them clean, grease them, and count our flints. We also practice with the one-and-a-half-foot-long bayonets, which we call the fourchettes.

When we attach them to the ends of our muskets, they become spear-like weapons, almost six feet long. We practice stabbing our fourchettes into straw dummies, then using our feet to push the dummies off the blades, resuming position, and stabbing again. Stab, kick, reposition, and stab again. The key is not to lose your balance. Anyone who falls is an easy target. We also learn to fence with the briquet, an infantry sword that is lighter and shorter than the ones the cavalrymen carry. We sharpen the blades so that they cut through flesh and bone like butter.

Sergeant Perrec is quite the talker. He goes on and on about his beloved Brittany, a land of giant boulders and ancient oaks, where every road runs to the sea. When his French fails him, he speaks Breton. Sometimes I don't understand a word he's saying. He likes having me around because I don't mind listening to his gruff voice that creaks like a barn door. One afternoon he lets me practice shooting pistols. I have no trouble making my arm, the gun, and the bullet follow the direction of my right eye. I almost never miss the target. Perrec is delighted with my marksmanship. One afternoon, he takes me to see Cathérine, the sutler, who sells stationery, ink, shoelaces, buttons, alcohol, and candy from her covered wagon.

"So, Binus," the sergeant asks, stroking the stubble on his face. "I know you can read, but can you write too?"

"Yes," I say. "My mother taught me."

"I mean *really* write, like difficult words and stuff. *Armistice*, for example. Can you write that?"

"Yes, I think so," I say.

"Could you write a letter for me? A letter whose contents must remain between us?"

"Military secrets, Sergeant?" I ask mischievously.

He looks at me, annoyed.

"Of course not, you idiot," he says. "Who tells military secrets to a sergeant? I want you to write a letter to a woman. An actress. You've probably heard of her. She's almost as famous as the Emperor himself—Mademoiselle Mars."

I've never heard of her, but I'm not about to admit it.

"Ah," I say with raised eyebrows. "Mademoiselle Mars."

"Stunning, isn't she, la Mars? And what talent!"

"Oh yes," I reply like an idiot.

"I met her once at the theater, after a play. I had kicked out a bunch of proles who were whistling during her performance. She was very grateful. We struck up a conversation."

"What should the letter say, Sergeant?"

"That I have to see her again."

"That sounds a bit short and demanding," I say and think for a moment. "Perhaps you should write that soon you'll be off to war and you need to see her again up close so that you can recall every line, every curve, every birthmark, every movement of her face as you charge into battle. After all, you are but a humble sergeant of the line, who doesn't earn enough money to commission a portrait of his beloved and have it placed in an amulet. You're just a poor, wandering knight, committing the noblest of deeds for the woman he cannot have. And that woman is Mademoiselle Mars, your unattainable beloved."

The sergeant looks at me in amazement and then slaps

me on the shoulder. I lose my balance and fall against the side of the wagon.

"You're one sharp kid, Binus," Perrec says. "You're going to write that letter for me. With real ink."

"What else would you use?"

"Water mixed with gunpowder," he says. "Works just as well and costs nothing. But it doesn't look as nice."

"Ink seems better to me," I agree, and that afternoon I write a letter to Mademoiselle Mars, a letter full of hunger and thirst, so simple and sincere in its vocabulary, so smoldering with desire, so feverish with love that for a moment I'm afraid the paper might catch fire on the spot.

"What exactly does it say?" asks Perrec.

"Oh," I say as I close the envelope, "just the usual nonsense that women like to hear."

The sergeant trusts me, but if he could read, he wouldn't have dared to send that letter.

A week later, Perrec receives a reply from Mademoiselle Mars. My sergeant, hero of the white saber, trembles like a child as I open the envelope from his muse.

"Careful," he says.

Mademoiselle Mars's letter smells of violet perfume, and her handwriting is exquisite: her letters curl, her words twist, and her sentences slant downward. The letter is addressed to "My brave sergeant and wandering knight, defender of the higher arts."

Mademoiselle Mars writes that as she read his letter, she felt her blood run hot and cold. The feelings that her sergeant has so elegantly expressed, as if he were the natural-born son of Molière and Racine, made her lose all sense of time and place and caused her mind to wander off into that misty no-man's-land between dream and consciousness. It is only thanks to her maids—armed with fans, perfume, and glasses of frothy wine—that she managed to stay on her feet. And yes, she wants to see her sergeant again, the lover of fine literature who saved her from the whistling barbarians. And yes, she wants him to recall her face when, somewhere, far from her stage, he clashes steel with the enemies of France. Next Sunday she will be enjoying an ice cream at the Grand Tivoli. Between four and four thirty. If it's not raining.

The sergeant looks dizzy. I ask him how anyone can be the illegitimate son of Molière and Racine. Weren't they two men? But he doesn't hear me.

"What's the Grand Tivoli?" I ask.

"A park, gardens, near Saint-Lazare," he answers flatly. "I'll take you there."

He has one more request. He asks if I can read him the letter again. And then again. Until the smoking break is over and we have to go back to our bayonet training. There's only one thing on my mind: next Sunday, I will see Paris.

As the big day gets closer, Sergeant Perrec can't help but boast about his appointment. He has his weekly bath and shave one day earlier than usual, puts on a fresh shirt, and has his uniform ironed. When the day arrives, my sergeant looks like he just stepped out of a painting.

⊚ ⊚ ⊚

It is a beautiful Sunday. We follow the Seine for two hours until we reach the Cathédrale Notre-Dame. The sergeant explains that the cathedral's bells were melted down into cannons and that the Emperor almost ordered the entire building to be demolished. We walk along a wide boulevard. All around me, the city is buzzing. Carts creak. Hooves clatter. All of Paris must be out on the streets. Here and there, we see an acrobat or a fiddler performing for a handful of onlookers, hoping to collect a few copper coins. A little farther on, in the streets behind the Church of Saint-Séverin, is an Italian who claims that you can see fleas wrestling under his microscope. And along the quays of the Seine are stands selling books. I spot three women on a bench, each reading her own book as if it were the most ordinary thing in the world.

We cross the Pont Neuf over the Seine and walk through the market halls. I have never seen so much food in one place. There's a woman selling oranges and shouting "Portugal!"—as if the country of origin is supposed to tell us something about the fruit. Another is selling crushed apples and pears that have been baked in an oven and covered in icing and sugar. I want to taste everything. At one of the covered stands, I see fish lying on a bed of ice, a deer hanging upside down from a wooden awning, and poached rabbits being chopped in half by butchers and wrapped in newspaper. A vendor who seems to know my sergeant greets him warmly and hands him a bundle of vegetables to grease the pot. Leeks, turnips, and a couple of dried peppers. I've never seen such a pointy, wrinkled, red vegetable before.

"Can you eat those peppers?" I ask.

"No way, it would set your mouth on fire," says the sergeant. "But one is enough to flavor a whole pot of soup."

A little while later, we arrive at the Grand Tivoli. At the park gate, the sergeant pays the entrance fee of twenty sous for both of us. The park mostly consists of grassy fields with dirt paths in between. There are some bare trees, a few replicas of antique columns, and a little waterfall. The entire beau monde of Paris, all of the city's high society, seems to be gathered in the park; the murmur of voices drowns out the violinists playing in a corner. I hear French as I have never heard it before—beautiful, flowing, and full of dancing vowel sounds. In my company, we all speak French with a bumbling accent. The language creaks in our mouths. But here in Paris, in the cradle of the French language, I hear words and expressions that I've never heard before.

Mademoiselle Mars is sitting on a bench. She is wearing a simple dress with lots of jewelry. Around her are at least a dozen elegantly dressed ladies and gentlemen in opulent hats—all admirers. They shower her with compliments and remind her of her fabulous performances in plays they have all seen. They talk and talk and talk. The actress nods politely and caresses the furry little dog in her lap. She has beautiful black hair that's partially hidden under her delicate hat. Her bare neck and shoulders are draped with fur, and her arms are covered by long gloves with jewels stitched along the sides. In her right hand, she's holding a silver ice-cream coupe.

"We shouldn't have come," the sergeant says. "Look at all those chickadees fluttering around her. Listen to that gibberish. I don't understand half the words they're saying. We should go.'"

"Are you scared?" I ask.

At that moment, Her Divinity sees the sergeant standing there. A faint smile appears on her lips. I take Perrec by the arm and pull him forward.

"What are you doing, soldier," he says. "Stop that."

I make a deep bow to the actress and smile broadly.

"Mademoiselle, may I introduce Sergeant Perrec," I say. "He is an admirer of yours and the bravest man I have ever met."

The sergeant looks at me furiously, as if he's going to skewer me with his saber tonight and roast me over the campfire like a hare on a spit. He takes off his hat and greets Mademoiselle Mars with an exaggerated triple wave. The goddess's admirers chuckle at his clumsiness. But la Mars doesn't care.

"Please, come and sit beside me, Sergeant Perrec," she says, and the sergeant, the man who has charged straight into Russian and Prussian fire, trembles like a reed in the wind as he sits down on the bench. The actress's lapdog jumps up and barks. The sergeant tries to reassure the pup with a pat on the head, but the furry little yapper nips at his fingers as if he were a predator.

"Calm down, my little Tartuffe," Mademoiselle Mars says

to the little monster. Then she smiles at the sergeant. Her teeth are as white as pearls. Not a single tooth is missing. The sergeant beams.

If only my mother knew that I was here, surrounded by members of the beau monde in a park full of Roman columns in the middle of the City of Light. I beam like a child at a table full of sweets.

"What amuses you so, soldier?" a voice asks.

I look behind me and into the eyes of a woman with plump cheeks and thousands of freckles. A cheerful accent dances through her French. I instantly assume the most manly position I know, with my right arm on my back and my little finger against the seam of my pants. Under my left arm, I'm still holding the bundle of vegetables.

"Are you the cook's helper? Are you going to make soup?" she asks, pointing to the leeks.

I shake my head.

"Did you lose your tongue in battle?"

"No, no," I say. "I hope to never lose my tongue, miss. It's my favorite weapon."

She chuckles. She has short hair and nothing on her head. Nothing! And all she has on her bare shoulders is a scarf—in the dead of winter! She'll catch pneumonia. Like Mademoiselle Mars, the freckled woman with the round cheeks is wearing a simple dress and a lot of jewelry: red teardrop earrings, a glass ring with a mysterious Egyptian symbol in it, and a necklace with a Roman ring on it.

"Would you like some more lemonade, Fortuna?" asks a

man in expensive clothes and a top hat. He makes a swift motion with his head as if to say she'd better come over and stand beside him.

"I'm just having a word with this funny greengrocer, my Charles," she says in a tone that could cut through glass.

Her Charles looks slightly hurt. He turns to the vendor and orders two lemonades.

"You look as young as a spring chicken," says the freckled Fortuna. "You don't even have fluff under your nose yet. How did they ever let you into the army?"

"I've been known to lie about my age," I reply.

"Well, you're not the only one." She smiles.

"I'm sure you'll stay young forever," I say.

I feel myself blushing as I say it. Sometimes stupid things come flying out of that big mouth of mine.

"What a charmer you are," she sighs, sounding bored. "You men are so predictable. Now would you like a compliment back?"

"Please," I joke. "About my broad shoulders, perhaps?"

She smiles with her eyes. The she squeezes me right under my epaulette, where the butt of my rifle has left a giant bruise.

"Ouch!" I cry.

Now she's smiling with her mouth too. Her grin is big enough to swallow the sun in one bite. Her Charles looks up from his lemonade in annoyance.

"Take care of that tongue of yours in the next battle," she says.

"Oh, I find it easier to talk to a lady than a soldier," I say, cursing myself again. You're talking too much, Stance.

You're going to give yourself away in no time. I feel my cheeks burning.

"So you're one of those soldiers who gets nervous in the company of men?" she asks.

For a moment I don't know what to say.

"Don't worry. The army is full of men who prefer a gentleman's love." She winks. "So is the theater, for that matter."

"I don't know much about theater," I say. "I've only seen clowns at fairs. You're the first actress I've ever met."

"Actually, I'm a ballet dancer," she says. "There's always dancing in the shows. But my suitor, that good man Charles over there with the two lemonades, talking to his banker and his tailor, he thinks I should give up the stage."

"Why?" I ask in surprise.

"He says he'll only marry me if I leave the theater. He is not very keen on the idea of my going to Salzburg and Vienna with Mademoiselle Mars to perform. He says he can't guarantee that he'll still be here waiting for me when I return. My mother thinks I should marry him while I still can. While I still have all my teeth."

She's talking so fast I can hardly follow what she's saying.

"What do you think? Should I quit the theater?"

"Personally, I would be delighted to be engaged to a dancer," I say. "If I told my bedmates that I was marrying a ballerina, they'd be thoroughly impressed."

"Your bedmates?"

"Mole and the Dutchman. Fine fellows. Except for their feet."

She laughs. Her freckles dance around on her cheeks. Her Charles looks up in surprise, along with his banker and tailor. I remain firmly standing at attention with my arm behind my back and my little finger against the seam of my pants.

"Fortuna, are you coming?" Charles calls.

"Is that your real name?" I ask her.

"My real name is boring." She smiles mysteriously.

"Too bad you prefer gentlemen," she whispers shamelessly.

Then she gives me a kiss on the cheek.

"When you wipe my red lipstick off your face later," she says, "you'll know it wasn't a dream."

I feel the heat rising all the way up to my hair. I'm turning as red as a tomato.

"Or maybe gentlemanly love isn't for you after all," she teases.

At that, she walks over to her Charles. The men welcome her warmly. I can't take my eyes off her. She says something to Charles that makes him smile. What a rotten face he has. She takes a sip of lemonade and wipes a drop from her lower lip with her index finger. Then the banker launches into some long explanation, with an incredibly serious look on his face, as if the entire French Empire depends on his bank. Fortuna pretends to listen and turns her head toward me. Her eyes twinkle at me for a moment, and I feel my heart leap. Then she turns to the banker again and gives him a reassuring nod—no, the French Empire surely won't go under as long as he is at the bank. She runs her hand through her hair, and Charles catches it. He caresses her fingers, then lifts her hand and kisses it with that repugnant mouth of his. He's just another fool with a walking stick. Just like Lieven.

Lieven had your best interests at heart, says Stance the Bride in my head. *And what are you standing there looking at? You're not jealous, are you?*

No, I say in my head. *That Charles doesn't interest me. He can choke on his lemonade for all I care.*

I wasn't talking about Charles, says Stance the Bride.

What a nag she is, that Stance the Bride.

Leave me alone. I'm just standing here in this fancy park among the highest echelons of Parisian society. Now isn't that something?

Yes, that's something, says Stance the Bride in my head. *Pretty impressive for a shoemaker's daughter pretending to be a soldier—and for your friend over there too, the illiterate sergeant pretending to be a brilliant man of letters.*

Suddenly, I'm jerked back to reality by the sound of excited voices. The bench where my sergeant was sitting with his actress is empty. I spot them a little ways away, speaking to a hussar with a bearskin hat under his arm and a saber on his belt. The people around them take a step back. A violinist stops playing.

"That's Captain James Lemoine, the heroic hussar of Austerlitz," I hear the lemonade seller say.

The captain makes it clear to my sergeant that it is unbecoming of a low-ranking military man like him to be sharing a bench with the goddess of the Parisian theater. Him parading around with her at his side is about as inappropriate as a guillotine in the Palace of Versailles. The sergeant gives Mademoiselle Mars a brief nod and beckons me with his head. Then he marches toward the exit. The hussar follows him. I follow the men to the edge of the park, and that's where the sparks really start to fly.

"You would have been wise not to trumpet your amorous plans around the campfire, Breton," the hussar says, the braids in his hair dancing on his epaulettes.

Perrec doesn't respond.

"And who is this fellow who wrote that letter for you?" snarls the hussar. "You can't even spell *cat,* for God's sake, which is why you'll never be more than a stupid sergeant of the line. You're cannon fodder, Breton, and you always will be."

The way he says *Breton,* it sounds like a curse.

Meanwhile, Mademoiselle Mars and her admirers have gathered around and overheard everything.

"Well, tell me, Breton, who wrote that letter?"

Sergeant Perrec says nothing.

"Go!" he says. "Back to the barracks. And don't let me see your face again."

The captain turns and beckons the street boy who, in exchange for a couple of copper coins, agreed to hold his horse. The boy moves toward me, followed by the hussar's massive stallion, which pushes past me and almost steps on my feet. The stupid beast. The horse is so tall that my shako barely reaches the top of his withers. His enormous backside sways back and forth as if to show off just how muscular each thigh is. He swats away the flies with his tail. Then the horse's rear end comes to a halt right in front of me. Before I fully realize what I'm doing (*Why don't you think before you do something stupid, Stance?* I can hear my father cry), I extract one of the small red peppers from the bundle of vegetables under my arm and push it into the horse's ass. The giant beast feels nothing, but the street urchin looks back. I hold my index finger, which is now smeared with horse dung, in front of my lips. Don't say a word. But the boy looks suspicious.

The hussar apologizes to Mademoiselle Mars for the interruption, but he feels it is his moral duty to warn her that she has an infantry-level imposter on her hands. The goddess looks annoyed and tells the captain that she can take care of herself. He's gotten her little dog all wound up. The fur ball is barking itself hoarse from all the commotion. She kisses it and walks back into the park, followed by her admirers, who look back in disgust at the officer with his little braids who barged in and caused such a fuss.

"Watch yourself, Breton," the captain growls. "If I were you, I wouldn't want to cross my horse in the next battle." The words spew out of his mouth. He puts his foot in the stirrup and hoists himself up onto the horse's back. He kicks the animal's flanks with his boots. The stallion slowly plods forward. I watch his gigantic thighs sway back and forth. The beast doesn't even feel the pepper.

"I shouldn't have come," the sergeant says.

"Of course you should've," I say.

"Enough, soldier," he says. "We don't belong here."

I look back at the captain again. His horse has stopped and is kicking at the cobblestones with his hind legs as if there were a pebble in his shoe. He whinnies. The muscles in his hindquarters start twitching spastically. The captain yanks on the reins and, in a booming voice, tells the animal to calm down. But the horse makes a funny little jump with all four legs.

The captain scratches his head.

Then the animal bolts.

I had no idea that such a tiny red pepper could have such an effect. That the horse might buck a little, sure. That it might plop down in a puddle of mud to cool off—why not? But that it would tear off as if it had smelled a pack of wolves—that I could not have predicted. The red pepper must be burning his insides and driving him mad. The horse's hooves spark on the cobblestones. He's foaming at the mouth, galloping at breakneck speed. The hussar's bearskin hat with the golden tassels goes flying off his head, and slowly but surely he starts to slide off the saddle.

My heart is pounding with fear. What if the animal slips on the smooth pavement and breaks his legs? What if Captain Lemoine breaks his neck?

The people on the street run out of the way. A woman with children shrieks that it is forbidden to gallop in the city. The horse barrels past the Église Saint-Lazare with its stone saints looking down from their pedestals. There, with the courage that comes with desperation, the captain gives a hard tug on the reins, so that the horse abruptly stops and falls to its knees. Lemoine jumps out of the saddle and twists the reins around his fist. The animal is still kicking at the ground with its hind legs, but then it finally stops, snorting and steaming with sweat.

"Maybe we should get going," I say.

"Right. Double time, soldier," Perrec says with a nod.

I look back at the captain one last time and see him kneeling before the church as if all its saints on pedestals have just saved his life. He makes at least a dozen signs of the cross.

We meet up with the rest of our company at Café Corrazza on Rue de Montpensier near the Seine, where patrons can dance until dawn. The walls of the small café are covered with mirrors, which makes it look twice as big. The candlesticks are made of copper, and the wine is served in crystal glasses. Men sit at tables playing chess or dominoes. There's not a woman in sight.

"You don't walk in here with a woman on your arm," the sergeant explains. "It's a man's place."

We greet the men of the Fourteenth and order a round of frothy wine. The sergeant tells everyone how the hussar's horse went berserk. Cor and Mole are practically rolling on the floor with laughter. The Basque and Bouchon, who, until then, were deeply absorbed in their chess game, ask to hear the story again. Even Rabbit, with his tight, wrinkled face, can't help but chuckle. But I've got an uneasy feeling in my stomach. I'm afraid that silly street boy saw me pushing the pepper into the horse's ass and that the captain will come storming into the café and demand the scalp of the scrawny foot soldier who molested his horse.

Strangely enough, it is Geoff Soudan who cheers me up.

He has spent the afternoon at the Musée Napoléon, which is housed in the Louvre, the former palace of the French kings. There's a room full of marble statues and Roman busts that the French army stole in Italy and an Egyptian room with a sphinx and a statue of a pharaoh chiseled out of desert rock and all kinds of columns with strange characters carved into them—hieroglyphs they're called—that no one has ever been able to decipher. Soudan can't stop talking about it. He seems to have forgotten all about Lucie and the Veldstraat.

The Dutchman Cornelis went to the Jardin des Plantes, where he saw lions from Tunisia and an elephant named Parkie. There is still so much to discover in Paris, I think to myself, and I should enjoy the evening while I still can. In a few weeks, the army might be marching into battle, where death lies on the horizon like a red sunset. I look at my friends in the company. Some can't wait to go to war; we're invincible. The Emperor is outsmarting everyone. We raise our glasses and shout, "Long live the Emperor, long live the Fourteenth." We wish each other luck. We slap each other on the shoulders.

It's there, while I'm drinking and laughing and enjoying my freedom in Paris, that I hear, for the first time in three months, someone say my name.

"Stance," the voice says. "Help."

15

PIER

Fog hangs over the fields. When I look behind me, I can no longer see the towers of Ghent.

"I don't know if that horse of yours is going to make it to Paris," Mr. Dupin says. "He looks pretty worn out to me."

"He's just stiff," I say. "He's been in the barn for a few years."

My horse stops, lowers his head, and chomps on some thistles between the cobblestones. I pull on the reins, press my knees into his shoulders, and yell, "Forward!"

The animal couldn't care less. He keeps right on chewing. Dupin is already way ahead. He stops and looks back.

"Do you even know how to ride a horse?" he asks.

"Of course," I say.

I pull the reins and push with my knees. Forward! It has

no effect whatsoever. The horse just keeps chomping on the thistles.

"It was actually my sister who took care of Achilles," I explain. "He just doesn't know me very well."

"You call that walking bag of bones Achilles?"

"Yes, that was his name when my father bought him fifteen years ago."

"Methuselah would be more fitting."

I laugh because I sense that my new friend is making a joke.

"Sometimes I think the horse hates me."

Mr. Dupin shakes his head like Father did. I feel desperate and start tugging on the reins like an idiot. Then my new friend clicks his tongue. Achilles immediately lifts his head and trots up beside Dupin's horse. Achilles is a lot smaller than his steed. Dupin taps his horse's withers with his riding crop and the animal steps forward. Achilles follows meekly behind. I'm dumbfounded. The Emperor's customs officer is apparently a master of horses too. We ride out of the city, our horses walking side by side. Off we go, two adventurers heading south.

I ask Mr. Dupin how he and Lieven met. He says he doesn't remember. I ask him about his adventures as an artilleryman and if he's ever caught any smugglers red-handed. He says he can't remember that either. He is not much of a talker, my friend Mr. Dupin.

That evening we stop at a roadside inn. We're served stew with bread. I'm starving and scarf down every last bite. After the meal, my travel companion stuffs a bit of tobacco into his pipe. He looks rather glum. I know what will cheer him up. I take a sheet of paper and a pencil from my burlap sack.

"Want to play hangman?" I ask.

Mr. Dupin growls something unintelligible and waves his hand as if swatting away a fly. Maybe not hangman, then.

"Noughts and crosses is fun too." I draw a grid on the sheet of paper and draw an O in the middle box. I slide the paper toward him. He looks at it dully.

"Now you draw an X or an O," I say. "It's a fun game." He only looks up when the innkeeper arrives with a bottle of liquor. The innkeeper pours him a glass, which he drinks in one gulp. He closes his eyes and savors the taste.

"Cognac," he says.

The innkeeper fills the glass again. And again.

I know a few more games, but I decide to keep them to myself. Mr. Dupin sets his gun on the table.

"Here, clean this," he says.

One afternoon, near Amiens, we stop at an inn to give the horses a rest and have a bite to eat. Mr. Dupin always gets thirsty at the sight of a roadside inn. He says it's because he's got a dry liver.

"A day without cognac," he says, "is a lost day."

I wait outside. He's just barely out of sight when four men come strolling up to me. They're wearing wide-sleeved shirts and old clogs. I smile because I recognize them immediately—they're monks of the order of Saint Francis, who were driven from their monasteries years ago and now roam the country praying for humanity. One of them asks if I can spare some bread for him and his friends. I make the sign of the cross, kneel before him, and say, "Of course, Reverend Brother, as Yahweh gave manna to Moses and his followers, so I share my bread with you and yours."

The monk looks at me, confused. I take the bread out of my bag and break off a piece. I present it to him as solemnly as a priest presents the wafer.

"Here is the bread that gives life," I say, proud of my Biblical knowledge. He takes the bread and looks nervously in the direction of the inn.

I tell the good friar that I have been to the Franciscan monastery of Ghent—to his temple—and that the beautiful building has been spared the demolition hammer for the time being. Even the masterful ceiling fresco of Saint Francis and the wolves is still intact.

I say it slowly and in the universal language of our faith, Latin. The monk, who has a rather unpleasant odor, looks at me in total confusion, which makes me wonder if I used the wrong Latin inflection. Then I see that his three brothers are standing by our horses and that one of them is taking the reins of Mr. Dupin's steed.

"Wait a minute, Reverend Brothers," I call out to the monks. "That is the horse of my friend the customs officer."

"We are so poor," says the friar in faltering French. He looks down at my shoes with their iron tips. "May I have your shoes? God will repay you."

Mr. Dupin's horse snorts and whinnies.

"What's going on here?" Dupin bellows. He storms out of the inn, waving his arms.

I turn to say that I have shared our food with the followers of Saint Francis. But the monk drops his piece of bread, grabs me by the collar, pulls me against his body, and puts a rusty knife to my throat.

Reverend Brother, what are you doing? I want to ask him, but the words won't come out. The monk twists my collar into a knot and squeezes my throat.

Mr. Dupin moves swiftly. He lurches forward and takes hold of the monk's wrist, then he yanks his arm away from me. The rusty knife tilts in front of my face. He twists the monk's arm onto his back and kicks the legs out from under him. The monk hits the ground and whimpers in pain. The three others charge at Mr. Dupin, one with a club, another with a piece of a spear, and the third with a tiny blade that looks like a dessert knife. My friend laughs. It's the first time I've seen him cheerful in three days.

"Are you going to attack me with that?" he shouts. I can smell the alcohol on his breath. The monks hesitate. Then Mr. Dupin draws his saber and shouts, "Give me your worst!" The brothers pull their mate to his feet and run off into the thicket. Dupin calms our anxious horses and grins at me.

"Brigands," he says.

I nod, speechless.

"You're not hurt or anything, are you?" he asks.

I shake my head. He slaps his palm on my head, so hard that my mouth is slammed shut. But I don't complain. My friend is giving me affection.

"Good thing you stayed calm and called out, kid," he says.

I nod. He hands me a cup of wine.

"Drink up. You'll make a good customs officer yet."

I drink the wine and hand the cup back with a smile. He smiles back, exposing his gold teeth.

As we approach Paris, we steer our horses to the muddy side of the road. The middle of the road is overrun by the dark, covered postal wagons that come thundering past every few minutes. The wagons are pulled by two horses galloping at breakneck speed, urged on by shouting coachmen. Everyone moves aside for the postal wagons. We ride to a fort about ten miles from Paris where new recruits are trained. Mr. Dupin has documents stamped and signed by Prefect Gijsens and can easily persuade the officers to check whether there is an Alfons De Keghel stationed at their fort and insist that we need to speak to him about "an urgent family matter." At the second fort, we get lucky: De Keghel is on the list of the gunners. Fons walks out in his dark-blue artillery uniform and black-and-white shoes. He looks worried and doesn't seem to recognize me.

"Is there something wrong with my parents?" he shouts from a distance as he marches toward us.

"I'm here with the brother of your sweetheart," Mr. Dupin says.

He looks at me.

"You're the brother of Lewieze La Belle?"

I shake my head.

"Of Marie Scheldewaert, then?"

"I am Pieter Hoste."

"The snotnose brother of Stance?"

I try not to look annoyed. I explain to him in a few words that Stance has disappeared without a trace and that I thought she might be with him. Fons looks at me with such genuine surprise that it's immediately clear we're on the wrong track.

"No, little brother," he says. "I haven't seen Stance. But she might be with another regiment. It's possible. There are tons of regiments and hundreds of thousands of soldiers. Maybe she's looking for me."

Then a grin spreads across his face, as if he's used to old sweethearts knocking on the fortress gates every week or so and throwing themselves into his arms.

"If you find her, tell her I'm here and that I wouldn't mind having someone to warm my bed and wash my shirts."

"She's married," I say. The smile disappears from his face. He casts a worried glance at Mr. Dupin.

"Excuse me, sir," he says. Suddenly, he looks a lot less tough. The fool.

"Not to him," I say. "To one of my father's old schoolmates. She ran away three months ago, and we haven't heard from her since."

Fons brightens up.

"Stancie from the Kraanlei quay," he muses. "That girl's got gunpowder in her veins, I can tell you that."

"And sawdust in her head," Dupin retorts.

"That too," Fons says, more cautiously. "But what are you going to do when you find her? I'll bet you anything that she'll scream her head off, rally the troops, and refuse to go back to Ghent."

"We have her marriage contract with us," says Dupin, "and unless Miss Gunpowder has a letter from her husband authorizing her to work for the army as a laundress, cook, hairdresser, or a God damned dentist's assistant, she will have to come with us, even if we have to drag her by the hair behind our horses."

Fons is very quiet now.

"Well, in any case, I haven't seen her," he says finally. "Now, if you'll excuse me, I'm going back to my cannon. If you see Stance, give her my regards."

We've only just left the fort when Mr. Dupin pulls his horse to a stop and whistles to mine. Achilles walks right up to him like a little lamb. As soon as our horses are side by side, my friend whips my ears so hard with his riding crop that I almost fall out of my saddle. The pain stings. I look at him, flabbergasted.

"Did your sister have any other suitors she danced the fricassee with?" my friend demands, though he might not be my friend anymore. I suspect that "dancing the fricassee" has something to do with passionate kissing, but I decide not to ask. "Any other suitors who might be in the army?"

"I don't know," I say. "She used to dabble with the Sint Jacobs gang. Those guys were too lazy to dance for the Devil and liked to get up into mischief. Alfons was one of them. The others I don't know."

He sighs.

"I'm sorry, Mr. Dupin," I say. "I hope we didn't come all this way for nothing."

He shrugs.

"I needed to come to Paris anyway."

He clicks his tongue, and his horse starts walking. Achilles plods along behind him. Maybe I won't make such a good customs officer after all.

When we get to Paris, we turn down a dead-end alley with horse stables at the end. We're greeted by a woman who's barely five feet tall. She watches us suspiciously from under her hood, smoking a pipe.

"Where's the old stable master?" asks Mr. Dupin.

"I am the stable master," the woman says, "Josée is the name."

He nods.

"Two horses," he says. "We're staying over at Widow Delasalle's."

He hands her some money. I stand there, staring at the tiny woman. She notices.

"Men die in the war, young man," Josée says to me. "Which is why I'm the stable master now."

"Of course," I mutter.

We leave the horses with her and walk on until we come to a tall, narrow house on Rue des Rosiers. A chair maker works on the ground floor. He displays his creations on the sidewalk every morning to attract buyers. His workshop and the entire stairwell smell of wood, glue, reeds, and rushes. The second floor—the most beautiful floor in the house—is home to a notary, his wife, and their three daughters.

The war widow, Madame Delasalle, lives on the third floor. She is a large woman with black hair piled high on her head. Her face is sharp and angular, but her eyes sparkle with light. A rosary hangs around her neck. When she sees the customs officer, she throws herself into his arms and holds his embrace for at least a minute. Two children peek out from behind her long black skirt. The girl's name is Dédée and her older brother is Germain. That night, I learn that the widow was married to a captain who was hit on the head by a Russian cannonball at the Battle of Austerlitz. She then married a lieutenant who succumbed to diarrhea on the Prussian campaign before he ever saw an enemy uniform. From her captain and her lieutenant, the widow received two children and two military pensions. Now it appears she has her eye on the customs officer from the north, who's sitting comfortably at her side.

The apartment is small. I have to sleep on the floor in the stairwell, against the front door of the apartment. I roll up in a blanket and use Mother's Bible as a headrest. Out there on the landing, I get to know the rest of the tenants. They walk by in the morning and evening, greeting me with a polite "Bonjour" or "Bonsoir." The fourth floor is also home to three lace makers, and the fifth is occupied by a yarn spinner and his family. The attic room, where the rain seeps in through the roof and it must be freezing this time of year, houses two law students. They trip over me in the pitch-black stairwell on their way home from the pub.

Every day, Mr. Dupin and I go out looking for Stance. He checks every fort and army station around Paris. He requests and receives lists of all the laundry maids, sutlers, cooks, barbers, and seamstresses who have joined the army. You never know. But nowhere on any list does he find the name Constance Hoste. He suspects that she registered under a false name. She must have forged her papers. From a distance, we watch the morning roll call and listen to the soldiers and army women shout "Present!" when their name is called. But nowhere do we hear or see Stance. Every evening, before heading back to the widow's for dinner, Mr. Dupin stops for a drink at Café Corrazza behind the Comédie-Française theater. He stays there reading the newspaper for a while, and I continue back to the apartment to give the children lessons.

I teach Dédée and Germain a bit of arithmetic and Latin. Germain is eleven and bores quickly. He runs out of the room after half an hour and tries to sneak out of the apartment to play in the street. The widow usually catches him, gives him a few flicks on the ear, and brings him back. Germain might be as slow as the seasons, but his sister is exceedingly bright. Dédée is nine and laps up the new words like rice pudding. She's always asking for more. More words. More arithmetic. As if she's afraid that after we're gone there will be no one left to teach her. Her eyes are a pale shade of blue and look so light and innocent that they seem to hold the entire sky.

Every morning, I wake up to the sound of the law students clambering down the stairs to go to class. A half hour later, I hear Dédée's steps in the apartment. I climb to my feet and greet her with a little bow.

"Maître Pierre," little Dédée says, "I wish you a pleasant day."

"Why, thank you, Mademoiselle Dédée," I say. "I wish you a pleasant day as well." It always makes her smile. The sky in her eyes smiles along with her. Then she directs me to my first task: emptying the full chamber pots lined up in the hallway. At least I don't have to go into the widow and Dupin's bedroom to collect theirs. And that's how my days in Paris begin: I stack the three pots of piss on top of each other and walk carefully down the two flights of stairs, hoping I don't cross any neighbors on the narrow staircase. Out on the street, I tip them one by one into the gutter and carry them back upstairs.

Dédée insists on combing my hair every morning. She bundles the matted lump of hair on the back of my neck into a silk pouch and ties it up with a big bow. The pouch is supposed to hang just above the collar.

"So you'll look like a gentleman," she says, "and not like some crude potato farmer like Dupin."

"The customs officer is a respectable man," I correct her.

"Look at that fat ponytail of his. He looks like a peasant," she says. Even Dédée has short hair.

"Short hair is fashionable for girls nowadays," she says. "Especially the coiffure à la Titus."

"Titus?" I repeat.

"A dead Roman emperor in the museum."

The happy reunion of the customs officer and his raven-haired widow doesn't last very long. A week after our arrival, I hear them arguing from my bed in the stairwell. She wants to know when he's going to take her to the altar, and he tells her that he has to stay in Zeeland because that's where his customs duties are. She shouts that his job is no excuse—there's no reason he can't marry her and keep working in Zeeland. He tries to soothe her with a "Calme-toi, chérie." And she dares him to say that one more time. She asks whether he thinks she'll bring him bad luck, whether he's afraid of ending up like her other unfortunate husbands. He replies that he's not afraid of anything, that superstition is for soldiers, sailors, and miners—not for him. He promises to take her to the altar. He just needs some more time. She says his time is running out. If he won't marry her now, she'll find someone else. It falls quiet for a while; then I hear the widow cry, "Oh mon Dieu, oh mon Dieu," as she gasps for air. I don't think I've ever heard anyone pray quite so passionately before. I make the sign of the cross.

I've been wearing Father's portfolio under my shirt for weeks now, and the leather sticks to my stomach. There are blisters on my belly, and my navel itches like ants. I think it's time I sneak away from Mr. Dupin, find the Emperor, hand him the papers, and ask for a hundred thousand francs. And another hundred thousand to build the cannon. Maybe it won't be so hard after all. One morning, I strike up a conversation with the chair maker on the ground floor. As he sits there braiding a seat, he tells me that the Emperor lives at the Château de Saint-Cloud, a few miles southwest of Paris. That's where he usually stays when he's not out on a campaign.

Later, I tell Dupin that I'm going to stroll around Paris for a bit and look at the wild animals in the Jardin des Plantes. He doesn't respond. He just gazes at the widow, who is in a particularly bad mood. It's been several evenings since I heard her pray.

"Shouldn't you go with him?" she says. "You're more use to those wild animals than you are here."

He motions at me with head, as if to say, *Get out of here.*

I find the road to the Château de Saint-Cloud without much trouble. There's a lot of traffic. Carriages and horsemen gallop past me at full speed. After a few hours of walking, I see the castle looming in the distance, through the branches of the bare trees. When I reach the entrance, I'm stopped by the sentries at the high iron gate. They're not just any soldiers, they're members of the Imperial Guard—giant men covered in medals and wearing earrings the size of rings. Their mustaches look like paintbrushes and their headgear makes them seem even bigger than they already are. I've heard of these veterans. Everyone has. They're the elite of the elite. They're depicted on triumphal arches in the city, and it is said that the Emperor loves them as if they were his own sons. He calls them his "Immortals."

I look up at the three guards and, in the deepest voice I can manage, announce myself as Pieter Hoste from Ghent. I pull out the leather portfolio from under my shirt and wave it at them as if it were some kind of passport. I tell them that my father is the Archimedes of Ghent and that he's invented a new kind of cannon. A cannon more powerful than any cannon on Earth. A revolutionary cannon with which the Emperor can win the war. The soldiers look at me as if I've just told them that I'm from the moon.

"That sounds like a lot of cannons," says the one with the biggest mustache, incredulously.

"Your father's name is Archimedes?" asks the one with the most medals, even more incredulously.

"And you know how to win the war?" asks the one with the largest earring, sounding the most incredulous of all.

"My father is a mechanical engineer," I say. "An inventor, and his name is not really Arch—"

"Then why doesn't he come here himself?"

"He's indisposed," I say. "He's in jail."

At that, the three men burst into laughter.

"Is the Emperor here?" I finally ask. "Surely, he will understand what I am talking about."

"Go away, kid," says the big mustache. "The Emperor can win the war all by himself. He doesn't need Archimedes's cannon."

"You don't understand," I say impatiently. "A good cannon is the result of high mathematics."

"High mathematics, go on," says the one with the medals.

They can't stop laughing.

"Get out of here," says the huge earring, "or we'll set the dogs on you."

The Immortals hiccup with laughter. Big Mustache lights a pipe. I guess I have to be strict with them.

"Gentlemen, listen carefully," I say. "When I speak to the Emperor I shall be obliged to inform him that the three of you have prevented me from handing him the plans for a new cannon."

They stop laughing. Earring asks Medal to hold his musket for him. He draws his saber and walks right up to me. The thing is huge. I turn and run back toward Paris. After a few hundred yards, I look back. The Emperor's elite are laughing so hard that one of them drops his hat. When they notice me watching them, Medal takes his musket and points it straight at me. I take off running and don't look back.

Later that afternoon, I stop at one of the fountains in the main square. I tuck the leather portfolio back under my shirt. Then I walk into the Café Corrazza where my travel companion is probably enjoying a glass of cognac and reading the newspaper. Inside, everyone is talking and drinking. Standing at the bar is a group of soldiers in black boots, white pants, and blue-and-white jackets. There's something familiar in the jumble of their voices, but I can't put my finger on it.

"Pieter," I hear Mr. Dupin call out from a small table behind me.

He smiles. I smile back, glad to hear him calling my name.

My friend points to the empty stool at his table. I sit down. He slices a few pieces of dried sausage with a knife and offers one to me. I'm famished from the long walk and take it gladly. It tastes delicious. I hear the soldiers at the counter shouting and look back at them again. Something about them grabs my attention, but I'm not sure what.

"And how is the Emperor?" Dupin asks.

I look at him, stunned.

"The Emperor," I repeat.

"The chair maker told me you asked him the way to Saint-Cloud," he says. "So my guess is little Pieter wants to speak to the Emperor."

"Oh, I just wanted to see where the Emperor lives," I say. "Out of curiosity. Since I'm in Paris and all, I thought, why don't I go and see where the Emperor lives."

I take another piece of sausage as if there's nothing more to tell. I hear laughter again and look up. I've heard that laugh before. My friend jerks my chair toward him. I almost fall backward.

"Do I look like some kind of stupid cake baker to you?"

I can smell the mix of cognac and sausage on his breath. His golden teeth glisten with saliva.

"No, Mr. Dupin," I say. "You definitely don't look like a cake baker to me."

"Then enough with the stories," he says. "What are you hiding?"

"Nothing, absolutely nothing," I say quickly. "What would I have to hide?"

Dupin sighs.

"Just go home. The children need their lessons," he says and waves his hand at my chest. I feel it smack against the leather portfolio under my shirt.

He looks at me. He felt it too.

"What's under your shirt?"

"Nothing," I say, and I feel my stomach sink through my bowels.

"Nothing?" he asks.

"My shirt is dirty," I say as casually as I can. "It's all crusty and stiff. From all the sweat, I think. It was a long walk."

I should have come up with something better than that. My travel companion smacks me on the ears, first left, then right. It happens so fast I don't even see his hand coming. I feel dizzy on the stool. The whole café is spinning.

"Show me what you've got under your shirt," he says menacingly.

I'm trapped. If I give Mr. Dupin the papers, he'll immediately send them by post to Lieven Goeminne in Ghent. Then Lieven can just take Father's design and sell it, and our family will never see a centime. Then I'll have really betrayed my father. Then I'll be the Judas.

"What's under your shirt?"

I search desperately for a way out. I could run away, but it's so crowded in here. I'll never get out. My heart is pounding so hard it feels like it's going to bounce out of my throat.

"I'm sorry, Mr. Dupin," I say, "but that's not for you." He hears the fear in my voice. He gives me another slap. Harder this time. My face stings.

"Show me what you've got."

There's nothing I can do. On the table is the knife Mr. Dupin used to cut the sausage. A knife I might be able to use to defend myself. I could hold him off with it, walk backward toward the exit, and then make a run for it. Run back to the palace, perhaps. Why not? I could climb over the fence and enter via a back door, find a maid, and ask her if I can go with her when she takes the Emperor his breakfast. Then he can read over the plans while he spoons out a soft-boiled egg. Yes, of course! Why didn't I think of that before? That's got to work. It will work. But first I need to get out of here. Just grab the knife, and the rest will come. It all comes down to making a move.

Forward, Hoste! I hear Bertie whispering in my head. *When we pointed our guns at the Russians, we didn't hesitate.*

"Well?" Dupin roars.

I grab the knife, spring to my feet, and brandish it in front of me as menacingly as possible.

"Don't move," I say. Before I know it, the customs officer grabs ahold of my wrist and is bending it onto my back. My God, he's fast. He slams my head against the table. The knife falls to the floor, and he rips the portfolio out from under my shirt. The hard leather cuts into my throat. I hear shouting around me. A waiter asks Mr. Dupin what's happening, but he doesn't answer. He rips off the strings, opens the cover, and flips through the papers. He does all this with one hand while holding me by the hair with the other.

"You dirty, sneaky brat," he says.

He flips through the papers.

"Give that back to me," I shout. "Thief!"

He smothers me into the table again. My ears are ringing. I feel blood dripping from my nose. I hear him telling the waiter that I stole documents from him and that I threatened him with a knife when he realized what I'd done.

A very small knife, I want to add, but I can't speak. He's pressing me down so hard that it's as if he wants to crack my skull like a walnut. Why won't he release me? Isn't he supposed to be a model of decency and civilization? Let go of me, Mr. Dupin, I will be good, I promise. I will never threaten you with a knife again. I'll make a good customs officer. We'll be friends again.

I try to push up from the floor and wriggle myself free, but my legs are as heavy as lead. There's no strength left. Out of the corner of my eye I see the soldiers at the bar. They don't even look at me. You'd think it's perfectly normal for a boy who knows his Latin conjugations to have his skull cracked like a walnut on a café table. And that's when I see him. A soldier who is slightly smaller than the rest, a soldier who nods, waves his hand, and lets out one of those awful cackles that I know so well.

"Help," I shout with my cheek against the table. "Help me, Stance."

The soldier turns his head toward me.

He sees me.

She sees me.

Mr. Dupin jerks me up.

"What did you just say?" he demands. "Did you just see your sister?"

I don't answer. He shakes me.

"Where is your sister?"

"The soldiers," I groan. He looks at the soldiers, who are now looking at us. They seem to be wondering whether they should intervene. Dupin's eyes narrow to slits. And then he grins.

"Well I'll be damned," he says.

He too recognizes the young soldier with the narrow shoulders. The soldier with the blushing cheeks and the chin as smooth as porcelain.

Mr. Dupin lets me go. He points his finger and makes that curly *you come here right now* gesture that the Porpoise makes when someone interrupts the lesson, and whether the student deserves it or not, he has to go to the front of the class and receive a rap on his fingers. The soldier approaches us with his head bowed and a glass of frothy wine in his left hand. He's as skinny as a reed next to the giant Mr. Dupin. The soldier raises his head.

"Having trouble keeping that child under control, sir?" he asks.

For a moment, Mr. Dupin is surprised by the sharp tone in the soldier's voice, but then he grins. The gold in his mouth twinkles in the light of the oil lamp.

"Playtime is over," he hisses. "You come with me, or I'll

rip that ridiculous costume off that skinny body of yours so all your drinking buddies over there can see what God gave you."

"Ridiculous costume?" the soldier shouts so the whole café can hear. "This is not a carnival costume, sir. This is a uniform. The uniform of the line."

For a moment, my travel companion is lost for words. The whole group of soldiers, alarmed by the shouting and the insult to their uniforms, push their way toward us. Men at other tables have jumped to their feet as well. Mr. Dupin tries to grab Stance's military jacket and rip it off her body. But she takes a step back, causing Dupin, who has had just a little too much cognac, to lose his balance. He just barely manages to stay on his feet by leaning on the head of a man playing chess. Kings, rooks, and knights clatter off the board. The chess player jumps up and calls Dupin a drunken lout. Mr. Dupin gives him a shove, causing him to fall back onto his chair. When he turns back to Stance, the tip of her saber is already at his throat. She drew it with lightning speed. I can't believe what I'm seeing. By now, the entire café is in an uproar.

"Settle down!" someone shouts.

The waiter comes running out in a panic. "Arrêtez, messieurs. Gentlemen, please stop!"

A sergeant grabs Stance by the sword arm.

"Don't," he says. "That's murder."

Mr. Dupin is grinning like a coffin maker during a bloody battle. He's not afraid of the tip of a sword pressed into the V of his throat.

"This man insulted our uniform," Stance shouts so the whole café can hear. A grim silence falls over the room.

"Enough, gentlemen!" the waiter cries, stomping his foot. "Stop this nonsense at once, or I'll call the gendarmes."

"You do that, sir," Dupin says.

Stance lowers her sword.

"You see," he continues, already tasting victory, "I am indeed a gentleman, but this soldier here is a—"

At that, Stance throws a glass of wine in his face with her left hand. The glass shatters to pieces in Dupin's face.

"Come on, I dare you, asshole. I dare you," Stance shouts with a fury that makes the whole café gasp. "You ridiculous excuse for a man. You coward. You had your front teeth pulled to get out of the army. I will not stand here and be insulted by a deserter. Long live the Emperor!"

"Long live the Emperor!" the soldiers roar.

"Long live the Emperor!" repeats every chess and card player in the café.

"Long live the Emperor!" repeats the waiter.

There are lines of blood running down Mr. Dupin's face. The shards of glass have cut his nose and forehead.

"Well," Stance calls. "Do you accept my challenge, or do I have to shove a piece of garlic up your ass to see if your organs are connected properly?"

At first he looks at Stance in confusion. But then his gaze hardens.

"Name your weapon," he says.

"The pistol," Stance replies.

"Where?"

Stance looks to the infantrymen around her.

"The Bois de Boulogne," says the sergeant to Mr. Dupin. "Tomorrow at dawn. You'll need to bring two witnesses with you."

"Agreed."

"I'll provide a doctor," says the sergeant.

"There will be no need for one," says the customs officer.

"Get lost, fool," says a soldier with a Dutch accent, "or you'll have two duels tomorrow morning." He smacks Stance on the shoulder.

Mr. Dupin turns around, leaves a few coins on the table for the cognac, and picks up the portfolio with my father's sketches inside.

"That broken glass will cost you an extra five francs, sir," says the waiter.

My travel companion nods and throws a silver napoléon on the table. He doesn't hurry. I've been standing there the whole time watching, like a wax doll. I try to catch Stance's gaze, but she looks past me. Her eyes are fierce and wild. Her whole face is trembling. Maybe she hates me just like Dupin hates me. But, Stance, sister, I had no choice but to betray you. He was cracking me like a walnut. And none of this is my fault, by the way, it's yours. I didn't take marriage vows at the altar before God. I didn't disappear like a thief in the night. I didn't do anything. I just want to go back to school. To Bertie and the Porpoise! How dare you put on an army uniform? It's preposterous! All right, maybe it's not wild enough for a carnival, but it's still absolutely mad. I want to scream at her, but the words fall apart in my throat.

◎ ◎ ◎

Mr. Dupin grabs me by the collar, twists it a half turn, and almost strangles me to death as he drags me out of the café. I can hear the customers booing at him. "Coward!" and "Deserter!" they shout, and "Long live the Emperor!" But I can tell by the look in his eyes that he doesn't care.

Tomorrow he'll have his revenge.

Tomorrow at dawn.

16

STANCE

I doze off for an hour or two at a time. As soon as I fall asleep I'm plunged into a nightmare. I see Dupin standing in front of me. A Goliath with a golden grin. His pistol is pointed straight at me. He fires, and the bullet rips my heart out of my chest. Blood gushes out of my body like wine from a bottle. I'm jolted awake and feel around for the hole in my chest. But there's nothing there. The two men beside me growl that I'm keeping them awake with all my tossing and turning. But I can't sleep anymore. I wonder about the dilemma Dupin has gotten himself into. He must have promised my husband that he would bring me back unscathed. But for the Zeeland smuggler, it's a lot easier to put a bullet through my head. My husband will be furious, of course, but Dupin can tell him that he had no choice. If he kills me in a fair duel with witnesses, he won't be charged with murder.

And if it ever comes out that this so-called soldier is really just a stupid woman who, in a fit of lunacy, put on her husband's clothes and ran off and joined the army, then Dupin won't even get a fine. The case will be kept quiet, and Binus Serlippens, the draft evader, will be tracked down. His parents will be fined. Binus will be chained and beaten and sentenced to a few years of hard labor. And with the proof that I'm dead, my husband will be able to remarry immediately.

Pier. Spiering. The Godforsaken oracle of the Latin school. How on earth did that milksop find me in Paris? In the largest city in the world. A city with hundreds of thousands of inhabitants. And that knucklehead finds me. *Moi.* The Emperor's soldier. The needle in the haystack.

A little after five, I hear the night watch coming to wake me up. I'm already out of bed when he walks in. Shivering with cold, I pull on my coat and shoes, run a belt through the loops on my pants, put my stovepipe hat on my head, and walk out to the entrance of the fort. Sergeant Perrec, Corporal Rabbit, and a field doctor named Percy are standing there waiting for me. The doctor is a potbellied man of about fifty with almost no teeth left. His salt-and-pepper hair hangs down in greasy locks. The sergeant tells me he's the Emperor's finest doctor.

"You mean this colt is going to fight a duel?" Percy says.

"Yes he is, and we're proud of him," the sergeant says.

"Good morning to you too, sir," I say.

"This boy's as skinny as a grasshopper," the doctor exclaims. "There's no fat on him to catch a bullet."

"You'll be taking the bullet out of my opponent's body," I say as confidently as I can. "And he's got plenty of fat on his bones. Trust me."

The doctor sighs.

"Since the duel is so early in the morning, I presume it's to settle a serious matter," the doctor says, "and not to attract a large audience and impress women."

"We have been insulted, and this soldier is going to avenge that insult," Sergeant Perrec says.

"Will the duel be stopped at first blood?" the doctor asks.

None of us says a word.

"Until there's a man down, then," observes the doctor dejectedly.

The sergeant nods.

"You know you only have one life, son," the doctor says.

"No need to frighten our soldier," says Rabbit. "It is what it is."

The sergeant has rented a yellow coucou, a carriage with room for six. The coachman has already harnessed up two horses. The doctor climbs into the coucou with his pillow and installs himself in the corner of the carriage, hoping to get just a little more sleep. The corporal and the sergeant climb in as well. There's a lantern burning inside the coach box. In the halo of light, I can see the coachman's snarling face.

"You coming, Binus?" the sergeant asks.

Without a word, I climb aboard. Inside, it smells like a chamber pot. I hear the reins slap against the horses' backs and the sound of horseshoes clicking against the cobblestones. The ironclad wheels grind down the road to Paris. My stomach is churning, and there's a sharp pain in my bowels. We're only a few minutes into the journey when I say I need to stop and relieve myself. Perrec knocks on the ceiling of the carriage. The coachman stops. I climb out and walk a little ways down the road. Paris rises like a dark wall in front of me. There are people walking down the street with a lantern on a stick, but no one looks as I squat over the gutter in the middle of the street to empty my bowels. My legs are shaking. An endless stream of diarrhea comes out of me, as if I'm letting go of everything inside. Finally, I wipe myself with a bit of straw and climb back into the carriage. Perrec holds the little door open for me. For a split second, it feels like I'm going to burst. That I'm going to scream. That I'm going to start whimpering and begging the three men in the carriage to save me. That I'm going to tell them I don't want to die. That I'm only eighteen. That I want to live a long, full life. That I only challenged that idiot Dupin because I had to. Otherwise he would have revealed my secret and ripped off my shirt. Then, my life here would be all over. My real life. My life with the soldiers. My life around the campfire. My life wearing pants. I'd have to give up the bed I share with two men who think I'm one of them. The bed I used to share with my husband might as well be on the other side of the world. In the damned Himalayas for all I care. I feel the tears welling up my eyes and bite my lip. Don't cry, Stance, don't cry for God's sake. You stupid girl. I pull myself back into the carriage and sit down. My legs are still trembling.

"Every soldier has had the fouran," says Perrec.

I gaze up at him with a dazed look on my face.

"*Fouran* is Breton for the shits," Rabbit specifies. "I remember a cavalry general who jumped off his horse right before an attack, pulled down his pants, and dropped a load in the grass before charging at the enemy with his saber drawn. The battle was a smashing success, and afterward the Emperor asked if he could visit the spot where the general relieved himself. And you know what the Emperor said?"

I shake my head. The sergeant chuckles. He's already heard this one.

"'Now that's what I call a good pile of shit,'" Rabbit says with a snort. "'My compliments, General.'"

Perrec and the corporal double over with laughter, and pretty soon I'm laughing too. The only one not laughing is the doctor. He's sound asleep. Then a silence falls over the carriage. We start passing the dark façades of Paris, and I think of the dancer with the thousand freckles who I'll probably never see again. After a few minutes, there are no more houses. We're riding under trees. This must be the Bois de Boulogne.

The wheels plow through the thick mud. The coucou slows down and finally comes to a halt. I push open the door and climb out. We've stopped in a soggy clearing that's completely sheltered by vaulted trees. The place seems abandoned by God. A ghostly mist hangs in the bare branches, and above it I can see the last remaining stars. The morning chill sends a shiver down my spine. I skip back and forth a bit to warm up. "Stop trembling," I say aloud to myself. Stop it.

Perrec unfolds a small table and places a red velvet-lined

box on top. Inside are two pistols. He walks to the middle of the path and sticks a saber in the mud to mark the spot where I'll stand. Then he walks forty paces and sticks a second saber in the ground for Dupin. The doctor climbs out of the carriage. He yawns and stretches his arms as if he were still in his bedroom. Then he lays out a pair of pliers, a saw, and a few bandages. The purple sky turns gray, and it starts to drizzle. What a miserable day to die, I think. Then I see a carriage approaching.

That professional lout of a man has rented a boguet—one of those open, two-wheeled carriages that rich Parisians use to go to the market. It has two seats. In one of them, Dupin, the Philistine, is clutching the reins, and in the other is a woman dressed in black. It's as if Dupin has brought Death along for the ride. And sandwiched between the two of them, narrow and almost completely tucked away in the wool blanket over their legs, is a third passenger—my traitor of a brother, Pier.

Dupin jumps out of the carriage and takes off his coat, which he passes to the woman in black. The giant horse is skittish and wants to keep moving. Dupin pulls the animal's hair. The horse whinnies and stays put. That Dupin is one strong man. Then, with his shirt sleeves exposed, he steps up to the sergeant. Pier follows him like a puppy. Dupin lays his gun on the folding table.

"You don't have a spare?" Sergeant Perrec asks.

"There's only going to be one shot," Dupin says.

His voice and attitude are so confident that my insides burn with fear.

Perrec checks Dupin's loaded pistol.

"This duel really isn't necessary," Perrec says. "If you apologize to soldier Binus Serlippens here, I'm sure he will accept it, and we can all go home."

Dupin grins, and his gold teeth sparkle as if he's polished them for the occasion. The vanity of this man!

"Bi-nus Ser-lip-pens," Dupin says in a voice dripping with condescension. "No, I will not apologize to Bi-nus Ser-lip-pens."

Perrec asks if Dupin would like to inspect his opponent's gun, but he shrugs.

"Let's not waste time," he says. "I'm hungry. We bought croissants on the way here. They're still warm. I really prefer to eat them warm."

Sergeant Perrec remains impassive.

"Very well," Perrec says, and he accompanies Dupin over to the saber stuck in the ground. Then he takes me to the other saber, forty paces from Dupin.

"He's a head taller and three times as wide as you are," Perrec whispers to me. "So you're more likely to hit him than he is to hit you."

I nod.

"If I die," I say, "I don't want that bastard to touch me. Don't undress me. Just wrap me in a sheet, put me in the ground, and forget about me."

He looks at me dully.

"Promise me," I ask.

"Of course," he says. "But the important thing right now

is that you stay calm so you don't accidentally fire your weapon."

I nod.

"Keep your left eye closed, and aim with your right," he says. "Don't tremble. Breathe in, breathe out. Aim low. The guy's body is so wide you can't miss. On the count of 'two,' hold your breath. And when you hear 'three,' pull the trigger. That's all you've got to do. You think you can do that?"

I nod.

"Then you shouldn't have any trouble at all," he says with a smile, as if he's just explained how to weigh a pound of beans.

I don't smile. I take off my coat and hand it to my sergeant. A duel is something you do in shirt sleeves.

Perrec's pistol feels good in my hand. It's a beautiful, well-maintained weapon with a brand-new flintlock. The barrel is not too wide, so the bullet—that little ball of lead that can rip through skin, muscle, and bone—won't deviate from its trajectory.

It's starting to get light. The winter birds greet the dawn. Those vile, obnoxious creatures actually sound cheerful, as if they've already caught their first worm. They're not the least bit interested in the game of life and death that's about to take place below. I'm trembling like a little dog in the arms of a Parisian demoiselle. I can see the golden teeth in Dupin's mouth from where I'm standing. He, on the other hand, is perfectly calm. He's thinking about his croissants.

If this is where it ends, so be it. If I have to go out with a bullet in my head from that walking piece of shit Dupin, then so be it. If I'm going to die here under these bare branches, to the excruciating sound of birds chirping, with my bowels churning, then so be it. Better to die here than to return to Lieven, kneel before him like a sinner, and bear his offspring like a slave. I have chosen my path, and I refuse to regret it. Regret is for the weak. Mademoiselle Courage didn't give up in the boxing match. And she, too, was up against a Goliath. Dupin is my Mad Nel. I picture Courage up on her stool, her lips mouthing the word "Never." I've got a hard head too. And I'm not about to give up now. I ran away from home. I bashed in the skull of a rabid dog. I learned to shoot in the army. This duel is nothing.

"On the count of 'three,'" Perrec says. "Arms at the ready."

I raise my gun and point it straight at Dupin's silhouette. Suddenly, the edges blur.

No, no tears now, damn it.

"One."

I quickly wipe away the tears with my sleeve, sniff away my snot, and extend my arm again. My heart is racing. There's no stopping it.

"Two."

Stop that God damned trembling, Stance. That bullet is going to go exactly where you tell it to. You know where it needs to go—into that haughty lump of flesh standing forty paces in front of you. You can't miss. My heart is pounding in my chest. Suddenly, I realize I'm not holding my breath.

"Three."

I pull the trigger toward me. I see the spark hit the pan, and then I feel it—the blast against my head.

This is it, I think, before everything goes black. There's a bullet in my head.

17

PIER

I sit in the boguet beside Dupin's widow.

Already at the count of "one," I can't watch. I don't dare to look at Stance. I have to look at something else. At the widow beside me, at her hands in her lap. One hand is clasping the fingers of the other. I hear her say "two" along with the count. She's wearing lace-up bottines with old-fashioned heels like the ones Mother took to Father to repair, back when they first met. I don't even hear the count of "three." The two bangs knock all thoughts out of my head and startle the horse in front of our carriage. The animal takes two steps forward, but the widow gives a tug on the reins and pulls it back again. I hear the flapping of birds taking flight. And then the widow whispers in relief, "Dieu soit loué." Praise be to God.

◎ ◎ ◎

Stance is lying in the mud. The customs officer is still standing tall on his feet like one of the Bois de Boulogne's massive oaks. The sergeant and doctor run over to Stance. Her face is covered in blood. Only her right foot is moving. The doctor kneels beside her head and rinses her face with water to see where the bullet went in. I want to rush to my big sister, but the widow pulls me back by my jacket.

"You stay here," she says.

The murderer Dupin strolls over to us as if he has just taken a morning walk. He doesn't even glance sideways at Stance and her two witnesses. He takes the bottle of cognac the widow hands him and passes me his gun. The burnt powder smells like rotten eggs. The barrel is still warm.

"Clean it," he says.

The customs officer pulls the widow toward him and kisses her on the mouth. He pulls the cork out of the bottle and takes a giant swig. He groans as the fiery alcohol burns his throat and immediately takes a second sip.

I pour water down the barrel of the gun to wash away the remnants of the burnt powder. I use a strip of cloth to dry the inside of the barrel. My hands are shaking.

The doctor pushes a wad of linen against Stance's wound and wraps a bandage around her head. It looks like a strip of her skin or maybe even a piece of her skull has been blown away. She's going to die. Stance, my tormentor and playmate. My nagging big sister who made me help her with the laundry, who saved me when I almost drowned in the Lieve as a little boy. She will never call me "Spiering" again.

"Is she dead?" Dupin asks as he pulls the widow close and she rests her head on his shoulder. Stance's foot is still twitching. Damn it, sis, how am I going to explain this back home? They'll ask me why I didn't do anything. It'll be all my fault. I let you get shot. I'll be the coward. The king of the Judases. But there was no stopping Dupin. And I couldn't stop you. I couldn't do anything. Why didn't you just come with us?

"Is she dead?" Dupin asks again.

"She's dying," I mutter.

My travel companion takes another sip of cognac.

"You know, mon amie," he says to the widow, "if you want to get married, we shall. Today. Then you can finally take off those hideous black clothes."

The widow lifts her head from his shoulder, looks at him with watery eyes, and kisses him on his golden teeth.

"Mon ami," she repeats.

Mr. Dupin smiles like Hercules after completing the twelve labors. He presses the widow against him and kisses her head, as if to promise that nothing bad will ever happen to her again. I stare at my sister, lying fifty yards away in the dirt. Her foot is no longer moving. Dupin taps me on the shoulder to get my attention. His breath reeks of alcohol.

"In a moment, you're going to walk over there and tell those soldiers that she's an imposter. That she tricked them. That she's your sister," he says. "We'll follow them to the morgue to procure written confirmation of her death. Then we'll go back to Ghent and tell Lieven what happened. I had no choice, you understand!"

I say nothing. My eyes are flooded with hatred.

"Repeat it. I had no choice."

I don't move.

He slaps me across the head. I say nothing. I don't even feel the blow. The hate is dripping from my chin. He hits me again.

"You had no choice," I murmur.

Dupin takes another sip of cognac. This time he doesn't groan. The burn of the syrupy grape liquor is gone. The widow combs her future husband's hair with her fingers as if preparing him for a hero's portrait that will hang in her parlor forever. Her eyes are full of love for the disgusting brute. She's not going to be a widow anymore. The third husband is the charm. Never again will she have to wear that black veil. She kisses the scar above his mouth and the black powder stain on his cheek.

"Lieven will be furious," the customs officer tells me. "But I'll calm him down. His anger will subside once I give him the plans for your father's cannon."

I couldn't care less. What are those plans to me? My big sister is dying. I feel empty.

"I wasn't in the navy myself," he says, "and I don't know much about math, but those technical drawings look very precise. And your father's description sounds pretty logical to me."

Then he looks at the widow and smiles. "But first we need to find a priest, a chapel, and two rings."

"Mon ami," the widow exclaims.

And at that moment—I can't believe my eyes—I see Stance sit up.

Her voice sounds like a little bell over the chattering birds. "Did I get him?"

The murderer whips around. The widow gasps and throws a hand over her mouth so the cry surging up in her body can't escape her lips. Stance leans on the doctor and pulls herself to her feet. She staggers a bit, and the doctor tries to get her to lie back down, but she pushes him away and tells him to go take a nap. Then she kicks around in the mud a bit, as if searching for solid ground. A few seconds later, she's steady on her feet. She looks at us. Thick, wet mud is dripping from her pants. Her shirt is drenched with blood—a lot of blood. There's a dark stain soaking through the bandage around her head and left eye. She looks terrifying. She glares at my travel companion with her remaining eye, like the Cyclops staring down Odysseus.

"You call that aim?" she shouts hoarsely. "You deserter, you coffee smuggler, you customs officer, my ass! I'm not scared of you."

The widow clutches the cross around her neck and starts rattling off Hail Marys. She says that she brings bad luck. That she always has.

Dupin snatches the gun out of my hands and looks down the barrel to make sure the thing is clean. He tucks it under his armpit and cracks open a cartridge with his fingers. It doesn't work. The paper is too stiff. You're supposed to use your teeth, but he's afraid he'll pull out a gold tooth. He picks at it with those thick fingers of his. Gunpowder falls to the ground. He curses.

"Don't do it, Auguste," the widow says.

"Why don't you stick to your prayers," he growls.

He taps a bit of gunpowder into the pan, closes the frizzen, pushes the cartridge into the barrel, and rams it down with the ramrod. He seems nervous.

"Think you can manage?" Stance calls out as she takes her position with her second pistol in hand.

All of a sudden, she seems different. She's no longer the skinny soldier who was standing there like a reed in the wind a few minutes ago. It's as if she's risen from the dead. She's turned the tables on the Devil and his wife. She stands there waiting, a goddess of dirt and blood.

Dupin walks back to the saber that marks his spot. He steps in a deep puddle and staggers. He curses. Clearly, the cognac—four big gulps on an empty stomach—has gone straight to his head. He stands beside the saber and turns to Stance.

"You can still apologize," the sergeant says, more as a formality than anything else. Dupin looks so fierce and grimy that I can't imagine him apologizing to anyone ever again.

"This time, I'll blow that wench's head off," he shouts.

The sergeant doesn't flinch at the word *wench.* Even he was probably called a wench a few times as a new recruit.

"On 'three.' Arms at the ready," the sergeant calls. A pair of magpies perch on the bare branches overhead, as if looking for a front-row seat.

◎ ◎ ◎

Stance's left arm hangs down at her side. She makes herself narrow. Her right eye burns like a lantern. Dupin takes position too. But his body seems heavier; his movements are slower and less precise. He shakes his head like a wet dog, as if trying to slosh the alcohol out of his body.

"One."

Stance straightens her arm and extends it out in front of her. Dupin stretches his arm too.

"Two."

The pistols are aimed at each other in a straight line. Their silhouettes are perfectly motionless, as if they are made of stone. I hold my breath. No, this time I will not close my eyes.

"Three."

The bangs are almost simultaneous, but Stance's shot is a fraction of a second faster. The birds flutter out of the trees. Two black clouds of gunpowder hang in the air above their pistols. Neither one falls down. Did they both miss their shot? Then I hear the widow whisper, "Oh mon Dieu."

Dupin curses. It is an exasperated curse, as if he has stepped into a puddle again. But he has not stepped into a puddle. There is a hole in his chest. And around that hole, his white shirt is turning dark red. The customs officer looks down as if he can't believe it. *This can't be right,* I see him thinking. *No, this is impossible.* Then I hear the widow scream. She jumps out of the boguet and runs toward her fiancé. Only then does he collapse. His golden teeth are smeared with blood. The widow screams that it's all her fault.

"Don't worry," he mutters. "We'll find a priest, a chapel, and . . ."

But he's speaking Flemish, and the widow doesn't understand. The doctor bends over him, along with the sergeant and the corporal.

Stance marches up to me. There's fury in that one wild eye of hers. I just sit there in that open carriage like a birdbrain. I can't escape. I'm afraid she's about to give me the beating of my life.

"You Judas," she says.

I say nothing.

"How dare you betray me, you stupid swine."

"You're the stupid swine," I say, as if we're back home, sitting on the hardwood floor in the dancing shadows of the honeysuckle bush while Mother reads us a story.

"What the hell are you doing here?"

"Father is in prison because of what you did," I say. "He's forced to grate bark in the freezing cold. You should see his crooked fingers."

"How did he end up there?"

"Lieven made him file for bankruptcy," I say. "Now Father owes him forty thousand francs."

"Lieven's money has blood on it," Stance says. "He makes his fortune from smuggling in Zeeland. And anyone who dares to report him will be found dead with a rotten fish down their throat."

I stare at her. Is Lieven a criminal? What about Mr. Dupin? I don't know what to say. But regardless, Stance must come home. So that everything can go back to the way it was. So that I can go back to school and all this misery will go away.

"Father wants you to come back," I say.

She doesn't answer.

"Mother and Rozeken have to mend clothes to survive."

"You betrayed me," she says. "I never want to see your face again."

I've saved my best argument—and yes, I'm ashamed of it—for last.

"Eddy is dying," I say. "He's got the white plague."

She turns even paler than she already is. Her whole face is shaking. She takes a step back. For a moment, it looks as if she might fall. She steadies herself against the carriage.

"I promised Eddy I'd bring you home," I say.

She's still leaning against the carriage. Her one eye looks deeply aggrieved.

"Eddy, my little Coppertop," she murmurs.

The widow wails. The doctor is pressing a cloth against Dupin's wound. The sergeant and corporal help the doctor tie a bandage around his chest and shoulder. They have to stop the bleeding. This is his only chance.

"I'm not going back to that disgusting man," Stance declares. "You can tell me whatever you want about Eddy, about Father, about Mother. And even if it is true, I'm not going back with you. I'm never putting on a dress again."

"What good does it do?" I say, more belligerently.

"Dressing like a man. How long are you going to be able to keep it up? What will your comrades say when they find out you've been lying to them this whole time?"

"They aren't going to find out," Stance says.

"All I have to do is walk over there and tell your sergeant who you really are," I threaten. "That is, if Dupin hasn't done so already."

Stance glances over at my travel companion, who is being pushed up into a seated position by the sergeant and corporal. He is unconscious. His head is limp against his chest.

"I don't think he's got much talk left," Stance says.

She looks at me with that one haughty eye of hers, and I imagine that her other eye, under that bloody bandage, looks equally haughty.

"What do you want me to do?" I ask. "What am I supposed to tell Lieven? How's Father going to get out of prison? How, Stance? Because I really don't know. I'm only fourteen years old."

I blink back the tears.

"Go home, Spiering," she says, more softly now. "Tell them I'm dead."

The sergeant walks up to us.

"Well? What are you two talking about?" he asks.

"Nothing," Stance says. She lets go of the side of the boguet and leans on the sergeant's arm. "I have a terrible headache."

"Must be all that wine from yesterday," he says with a grin.

"Very funny," she groans.

"Your bullet is between that man's ribs. The bleeding has stopped, but the doctor wasn't able to extract it. It's a delicate wound."

Then he looks at me with sympathy in his eyes.

"I'm sorry about your father, kid," he says.

I could say that Mr. Dupin is not my father and that the widow is not my mother. And that Stance is my sister. But I don't know what to say anymore. I feel nothing but miserable in this gloomy forest in the middle of this awful city. It's true, I betrayed Stance. But yesterday in that café, she could have just said, "Well, you found me. Thank you. It's been fun fraternizing with soldiers. But I'm ready to go home now with my little brother, to my hot bath, to my daily coffee, and to my husband, for whom I'm going to bear a strapping baby boy. Nothing to worry about." But no, Stance had to call a duel. She had to put a bullet into the ribs of her husband's business partner and best friend.

"Did you hear what I said, kid?" the sergeant asks.

Stance glares at me with that Cyclops eye of hers. She's afraid of what I'm going to say next. Afraid I'll betray her.

"I'll take care of Father," I say.

I walk back to the boguet. The widow is clinging to her fiancé with all her might. I squeeze between the two of them and take the reins. She looks at me with confusion.

"Hold him tight," I say, trying to sound as manly as possible.

She nods. I slap the reins against the horse's back, but the stubborn beast won't budge.

Then I click my tongue the way Dupin does. And what do you know, the horse moves forward.

The boguet lurches into motion.

"Gee-up, gee-up," I call, and the animal actually breaks into a trot.

18

STANCE

In the carriage on the way back to the barracks, the throbbing pain in my head becomes unbearable. The doctor and my two companions light a pipe as we ramble down the bumpy road, and the carriage quickly fills up with smoke.

"The look on that guy's face when you got up," the sergeant says. "That was golden."

"That boy he brought with him almost wet his pants," the corporal adds.

"What kind of man brings his wife and child to a duel?" says the doctor.

"It wasn't his wife," the sergeant says. "She was a widow. Perhaps the boy was her son. Isn't that right, Binus?"

Their voices sound far away, and the interior of the creaking coucou is a brown blur. I can feel that I'm about to faint, just like that idiot father of Geoff Soudan, who hit the carpet when he heard that his son wanted to run off with the kitchen maid. I'm terrified that I'll pass out and be carried off to the infirmary by my two witnesses, where the doctor will unbutton my uniform and immediately see the cloth wrapped tightly around my chest. Upon further examination, he will discover the sock stuffed into the front of my pants and the bellows nozzle hidden in my stovepipe hat. I have to stay awake at all costs. I push down the window in the door and hang my head out of the small, square opening, letting the cold morning wind and icy drizzle hit me in the face. The door shakes and rattles. Carriage doors are held shut by tiny brass handles, and all it takes is one pit in the road for them to spring open. The sergeant grabs me by the belt to keep me from falling out of the carriage.

We stop before we get to the fort. With the last strength I have left, I follow the doctor into a church that serves as a makeshift hospital. I'm given a mattress which, the doctor promises me, I won't have to share with anyone else. What a luxury! With tremendous difficulty, I manage to kick off my shoes, take off my coat, and lie down under a blanket. The doctor says that I need to take it easy.

"Don't worry," I say. At last, I can close my eyes. Finally. I let myself fall into the blackness. I'm back home in the old shoe shop on the Kraanlei quay. The dining table is covered in dust. The sideboard is empty. The hands on the clock are gone. No one is home. Even the mice have left. Out in the courtyard, the lid over the pit is missing. The pit that Grandpa used to soak his hides in, that the neighborhood bums and children used to pee in. I'm drawn to it like a magnet. There's nothing I can do. I try to grab hold of the edge, but my arms are too heavy. I'm sucked in and falling into the abyss. My stomach tingles from the speed of the fall. That speck of daylight high above me is getting smaller and smaller. The closer I get to the monster at the bottom, the monster that swallowed Father's brothers and mother, the sharper the smell of piss. I can hear him gnashing his teeth.

When I wake up, it's dark. I need to pee. Moonlight pours into the church windows. My head is throbbing. It's as if there's an entire regiment of drummers drumming as hard as they can underneath my skull. Tears leak out of my eyes. Then comes the fear. I must have slept a whole day. My clothes. Did they take off my clothes? I push the furry blanket off me, but I still have my clothes on. I breathe a sigh of relief. I try to sit up, but the drummers in my head do not agree. The whole room is spinning. And it's so incredibly cold. Freezing! I rest my hand on the floor and look around the room at the motionless bodies stretched out on the other cots. I grab the chamber pot next to my mattress, pull down my pants and pee sitting down. Then I pull my pants back up.

"They're worried about you, you know," says a voice in the darkness.

I look around and see a man sitting up in his bed near the pulpit. The moonlight illuminates half his face.

"The doctor came to check on you every few hours to see if you were still moving," he says. "That's not a habit of his."

"No?" I ask.

"I've been here for three weeks," the man says. "And only once has he asked me how I'm doing."

He shows me the stump where his left arm used to be.

"Blown off by a Spanish priest," he says cheerfully. "And after that two peasants came at me with pitchforks."

At that, he pulls up his shirt. There are welts in his chest where the points of the forks were jabbed into his body.

"I still managed to draw my saber," he says, "and the parish priest didn't have time to take the peasants' confessions before I showed them the way to hell. When I got back to my regiment I was more dead than alive. The doctor thought I wouldn't make it. Fortunately, it is winter. The flesh around a wound doesn't rot as quickly in the cold. When a wound like that turns black, it's all over."

Somewhere in the church someone shouts.

"That's Jules the Fool," the one-armed soldier says. "Don't pay any attention to that. He fought in Spain too. The doctor says he's not right in his head. God knows if he'll ever heal. Terrible country, Spain."

I lie down and slip back into the blackness. I'm back in the pit. The monster has me in his jaws.

I wake to the smell of burning tobacco. The doctor is crouched beside me, sucking his pipe. Through the open church door I can see that it's the middle of the day. Red-and-blue spots dance around on the floor. The sunlight streams in through the stained-glass windows, lighting up the church in hundreds of colors.

I try to sit up, but the drummers in my head are awake too. They're drumming the attack march, the pas de charge. I lean on the ground with one hand to keep from falling over.

The doctor places a cup of soup and two pieces of dry bread next to my mattress.

"With a crack in your skull like that, I was afraid you'd never wake up," he says. "But your wound seems to be healing nicely."

I can see his breath when he talks.

"It's freezing outside," he says. "Eat your bread before it gets dark, or the mice will run off with it."

I nod. I feel as limp as wet laundry. The doctor walks out of the church. Up near the pulpit, the man with the stump waves.

I drink the soup and nibble on the stale bread. But I immediately vomit it all up again. I leave the rest for the mice. Somewhere in the room, Jules the Fool starts shouting again. I lie back down. Into the blackness. The pit. The monster.

Then there is light. An explosion of light. Someone has me by the wrist and is pulling me out of the darkness. The blinding light comes from the burning wick of an oil lamp. The light sparkles on the brass buttons of the uniform of the man bent over me. I don't recognize him. Around him, everything is as dark as an inkwell. His hair hangs in braids.

"Do you remember who I am, soldier?" the man asks in beautiful, unaccented French. I can see his breath too.

Then it hits me. It is Captain Lemoine. He's wearing a

long, dark, hooded cloak over his uniform as if he doesn't want to be recognized. His breath smells of wine.

"The boy who was holding my horse told me you were up to something," he hisses. "That poor animal almost broke his legs. What did you do?"

His voice sounds calm and toneless, as if he were ordering a baguette and some Sainte-Mathilde cookies at a bakery. I don't think it's a good idea to tell him the truth. My eyes dart from left to right around the infirmary, but I can't see anything. The light from the lantern burns my eyes. He grabs me by the throat. His fingers are so long they almost reach around my neck.

"I didn't do anything," I say.

I can feel the calluses on his fingers. He squeezes. I reach for his wrist and try to pull him away. But there's more strength in his fingers than in both my arms combined.

"Don't," I squeak. The drummers in my head are beating with all their might.

"Everyone is talking about your duel," he whispers. "That you, a soldier in training, challenged an experienced customs officer. That you took a bullet to the head and stood back up. That you rose from the dead like a Godforsaken Lazarus. You know what they're calling you in your company? Ironhead! But I don't believe a word of it. I think you just got lucky."

For a man who came here to strangle me to death, Captain Lemoine sure has a lot to say. I want to apologize for hurting his horse. I even want to beg for his forgiveness. But he won't let me say a word. He keeps his mighty fingers clamped around my throat. My legs start twitching. My vision blurs.

"Angel," I croak.

"What?" he asks.

"Angel. I saw an angel."

He loosens his grip.

"I was dead. And then an angel kissed me."

He stares at me. Then he curses. He must think that I—the shrimp who got his head cracked open—am trying to make a fool of him. But I was there when he finally regained control of his runaway horse in front of that church. I saw how he climbed out of the saddle, knelt before the church, kissed the rosary around his neck, and made the sign of the cross—as if it were those stone saints staring down at him from the portal, with miters on their heads and staffs in their hands, who had tamed the wild beast. Captain Lemoine is more pious than the apostles.

"The angel's breath was sweet," I continue. "He blew into my lungs. I felt my cheeks grow warm and death leave my body."

I tell the story slowly. Each word falters in my throat. Every syllable hurts. Lemoine looks around, as if to make sure no one has woken up. His gaze lingers on Christ hanging on the cross in the center of the church. The altar has been removed. He looks at me again; the anger has melted from his face. Maybe he didn't even want to strangle me to death. Maybe he just needed to lash out a bit. Then he smiles like a little boy who has just received his First Communion. To him, I am living proof that it's all true: the baby in the manger, the wise men from the East, the water turning into wine, and the afterlife where rice pudding simmers over the fire all day without burning. He lets go of my throat. My lungs fill with air.

"What did the angel look like?" the captain asks.

"Beautiful," I say.

And Captain Jacques Lemoine, hussar of the Emperor, captain of the cavalry at Austerlitz, admirer of Mademoiselle Mars, and master of horses with a pepper up their ass, nods.

He nods.

"An angel," he repeats.

Then he stands up and takes his coat.

I watch him leave. The lantern swishes back and forth and slowly fades. I can still feel the imprint of his fingers around my neck. I close my eyes, but this time I don't slip into darkness. I'm wide awake and can hear every drumbeat ringing in my head. "Make the drummers stop," I mumble. "Make them stop."

It takes two weeks for the headache to subside and the dizziness to disappear. I am happy to leave the church. I say goodbye to the one-armed soldier and hear Jules the Fool shouting as I step outside. I walk the mile and a half back to the barracks alone. There's still a bandage wrapped around my head, which means I can't put on my heavy shako. I carry it like a broken stovepipe. I tuck the nozzle away under my jacket. The road to the barracks is a stream of mud now that the thaw has set in, but the air is still cold. The soldiers along the road nod at me as I walk past. The story of my incredible duel must have spread through the fort like wildfire. When I walk into my regiment's barracks, the sergeant stands up. His whole body is beaming.

"Well, if it isn't our duelist," he shouts.

The men of the Fourteenth spring to their feet. They shake my hand, slap me on the shoulder, and tap my uniform. Everyone wants to touch me; it's as if I've experienced a miracle and by touching me, a piece of that miracle will be passed on to them. They hand me a tin of onion soup with two chunks of chicken in it and a piece of bread. Bouchon, the chess player from Gascony, comes up and scoops a piece of chicken from his tin into mine.

"You need to put some meat on those bones," he says.

His chessmate, the Basque, gives me an extra piece of chicken from his tin too.

Cor the Dutchman seems happy to see me. He had vowed to challenge Dupin to another duel if I didn't pull through.

"We missed your ugly mug," says Geoff Soudan, the nobleman from the Godforsaken Veldstraat.

"Oui, the bouillotte games were much less intéresshante," says Rabbit, the white-haired poacher from the Auvergne.

"Well, you got out of some training, you lucky bastard," says Mole, the miner from northern France.

The sight of all these boneheads brings tears to my eyes. I quickly wipe them away. No one laughs. They're all just staring at me.

"Well," I say, "I'm glad to see your ugly faces too."

They chuckle.

"You're just in time," the sergeant says. "Rumor has it

things are shaking up in Austria. We might be headed out on a campaign as soon as the weather improves."

"That's good news," I say. "We were getting bored here anyway."

They laugh.

Mole hands me the deck of cards. I shuffle them, and my six comrades gather around so I can deal them in.

19

PIER

The doctor is having breakfast with his family when I storm into his house on Rue de Rivoli. With sweeping arm gestures, I tell him everything: about the customs officer, the duel, and the ride back to the widow's apartment. Less than a minute later, he's walking behind me with his napkin still tucked into his collar and his medical kit in his hand. His instruments rattle in the bag. The chair maker from the ground floor, the notary from the second, the yarn spinner from the third, and one of the students from the attic all help carry Mr. Dupin up the stairs by his arms and legs. The unconscious man is so heavy and cumbersome that the four men groan and curse as they lug him up the winding, narrow staircase. The stairs creak under their weight. His head bangs against one of the steps.

"Careful!" says the widow, leading the way.

The doctor and I follow the entourage up to the third-floor apartment. The children's jaws drop as the neighbors carry Mr. Dupin into the house like a dead bull. They hoist him up onto the bed by his clothes. His shirt is black with dried blood. The neighbors, exhausted and panting, wish the widow strength and head back to the stairwell. The widow asks me to take the children for a walk. Then she steps into the bedroom to help the doctor and hold her betrothed's hand. Dédée looks startled, but I try to reassure her with a smile and help her into her coat. The children head out the door. I look over my shoulder at the China cabinet. That's where the widow stashed my father's portfolio yesterday.

I walk out into the street with the children. Germain runs off to play tag with his friends. Dédée stays with me. She gives me her hand.

"Is Monsieur Dupin dying, Maître Pierre?" she asks.

"Weeds don't die," I say.

"Shall we go and see the elephant in the Jardin des Plantes?" she asks.

"Good idea," I say, but at this very moment, the parlor is empty, and my father's plans are just lying there in the China cabinet. If I ever want to get them back, it's now or never.

"You two wait here," I say. "I forgot something upstairs."

I walk back up the stairs and into the parlor. I glance down the small corridor that leads to the bedroom, where the doctor, armed with clamps and scissors, is searching for the bullet in Dupin's body.

"Why wasn't he wearing a shirt made of silk?" I hear the

doctor complain. "Silk just tears, but cotton rips off and goes into the body. Now I have to scrounge around like an idiot looking not only for a bullet but also for a piece of cloth."

The China cabinet is an imposing piece of furniture. The entire room seems intent on pleasing the cabinet. On the left, the pendulum on the wall clock ticks away the time, and on the right, two small portraits of the widow's late husbands, their heads painted in profile, forever encompassed in their oval frames, stare at the piece of furniture out of the corners of their eyes. On one of the cabinet doors is a medieval helmet with the year 1707 painted under it. The widow opens the cabinet every day to take out the cutlery. I have seen the valuables on the shelves: twelve crystal glasses, one of which is cracked; the silverware in a felt box; and the stacks of porcelain plates, teacups, egg cups, and butter dishes. In the bottom of the cabinet are rolls of yellowed paper gnawed away by mice, and somewhere between them is my father's leather portfolio. And in that portfolio are the plans for Hoste's Cannon, the weapon of the future, the invention that will change the course of the war. Those plans are my only hope of ever having a normal life again. The widow keeps the doors locked with a giant key, which she keeps deep in the pocket of her skirt. But as Bertie would say—that lock is nothing!

The lock plate is made of copper. It's at least a hundred years old. That old lock that Bertie picked with the tip of his compass was just like this one. I frantically scan the room, and—yes!—there's a letter opener on the table.

I stand in front of the cabinet and slide the letter opener

into the lock. All I can do is hope that the widow is still in the bedroom holding Dupin's hand and that the children are patiently waiting down on the street. I push the tip of the letter opener deeper into the lock and wriggle it around, but the rusty latch won't budge. Dupin roars in pain. The pendulum on the clock seems to tick louder and louder. Then, all of a sudden, the lock starts to give.

"I'm coming back, Bertie," I whisper. "Get my bed ready."

I hear a click. One more second and that cabinet will be open. Just one more little push and—

The letter opener snaps. I crash into the cabinet. The China inside rattles. My heart skips a beat. The tip of the letter opener is stuck in the lock. I try to pull it out, but it's too small and slippery to wrangle out of the mechanism with my fingers.

You with your two left hands! Bertie groans in my head.

"Shut up, Bertie," I say almost audibly. "Think, Pier, think!" I take a step back and peek into the hallway. Through the open door of the bedroom I can see the bleeding coward lying there with the doctor and the widow beside him. They haven't extracted the bullet yet. There's still time. Then I notice that the cabinet is propped up on four legs. What if I just push up on the bottom shelf a little bit and pull the portfolio out from underneath? Now there's an idea, Bertie!

I crawl under the cabinet. I have to tilt my head to get under it, but I manage. I push the bottom shelf up with both hands. You see that, Bertie—you cheater, you pain in Father Charles's ass, you champion lock picker—it worked! It's not even nailed down, for God's sake. What luck! Two left hands, my foot! I balance the plank between my hands. It's not heavy. I extend my right arm and hear the rolls of paper shifting from right to left. I push the shelf even higher to create a small opening, and the rolls of paper fall out onto the floor, one after the other, each one landing with a light thud. Then I hear something heavier shift inside the cabinet. That's it! My father's portfolio! Hoste's Cannon! It hits the left side of the cabinet, but it's too wide to fit through the opening.

"My Emperor, stay where you are," I hear myself whispering. "I'm going to bring you my father's cannon. The weapon that will rule the seas."

I push again on the shelf, which is now tilted at an almost forty-five-degree angle. One corner of the portfolio is still stuck on the ledge. I lift the shelf a little more—and yes! The portfolio drops to the floor under the cabinet with a plop. It's the most wonderful plop I've ever heard.

And then I am buried in porcelain.

For a moment, I think the pretentious cabinet did it to me on purpose, but then I realize that with all my pushing, I accidentally lifted the heavy bottom shelf out of its brackets. The shelf with all the porcelain. All the cups, saucers, butter dishes, and plates have come crashing down on my head. The broken shards cut into my scalp. Just my luck—defeated by dinnerware! You better get out of here, Pieter, you've got what you came for. I tilt my head to pry myself out from under the cabinet. I scrape my ear on the bottom edge of the China cabinet and scramble to my feet. An egg cup that survived the avalanche falls out of my hair and shatters on the floor. The room is spinning. I have to run. In five steps, I'll be at the door of the apartment. Then I'll take the stairs five at a time. But I can't move an inch. There's a saber poking into my chest, Mr. Dupin's saber. The widow has caught me red-handed. Her rosary is dangling around her wrist, and her two children are standing right behind her.

Germain grins with excitement.

Dédée looks at me in horror.

"That was the China from my first marriage," she hisses. Her eyes are red and fierce.

"This portfolio is mine," I mumble.

The tip of the saber pricks into my chest.

"Mr. Dupin stole it from me," I try again.

She knocks the portfolio out of my hands with the sword and aims the pointy tip at my neck. The heavy, curved weapon doesn't so much as tremble in her steady hand. The widow is as strong as a bear.

"Get out," she shouts.

Behind the widow, the doctor appears. He's holding up a pair of pliers with a bullet in between them.

"Would you like to keep it as a souvenir?" he asks.

The widow doesn't even look at him.

"Out!" she shrieks.

I don't know where to go. I pace around the neighborhood for an hour or so. The back of my head stings. My hair is wet with blood. I stick my head under a city pump. My scalp must be pretty scratched up. When I turn back down Rue des Rosiers, I'm met by Germain and his friends. They throw stones and horse droppings at my head and call me a thief. I run away. I'll hide out in the stables with the only creature in the world who doesn't want to bash my head in. I greet Madame Josée, and she seems to sense that I'm on the verge of tears.

Then I hear whinnying in the stables.

"Your horse hears your voice," she says. "I think he misses you."

I walk over to Achilles. He snorts and stomps. The fur around his mouth and along his spine looks a little grayer. His mane hangs limply down his side. I wrap my arms around his neck. Achilles calms down, as if he understands that I need to hug someone, even if it's just a stupid old horse.

That evening the widow comes down to the stables. I don't dare to look her in the eye. I stammer that I'm sorry about all that broken China.

"Mr. Dupin has regained consciousness," she says.

"Thank goodness," I say and make the sign of the cross.

"He says he still needs you."

"Why?"

The widow shrugs. "I have to take you back into my home."

"Thank you," I say.

"You broke at least thirty francs worth of China."

I nod.

"In return, you will give three months of lessons to my children."

"Three months?"

"And if you ever go near my cabinet again," she says, "I'll throw you out the window."

I swear on the Bible and on everything I believe in that I will never go near her China cabinet again.

20

STANCE

By early March, the time has come. We begin the march to Austria. We sing a marching song about onions as we march. About how much we love onions. About how onions taste so delicious when they're fried in oil. All it takes is one fried onion to turn us, the men of the line, into lions ready to storm the enemy. One onion for us, and no onions for the enemy. Not even a shallot—nothing for those bloody Austrians! The onions are for us! And so we march away the miles singing about onions while we wear out our shoes.

We march from sunrise to sunset. The hussars and light infantry on horseback lead the way. They scout the area and make sure the coast is clear. We march behind them, and the rest of the convoy follows. Behind us are the cuirassiers with their helmets, armor, and giant horses. Then come the heavy cannons pulled by even bigger horses, then the wagons carrying equipment and the carts full of provisions. The cavalrymen look fantastic in their uniforms. But we—the foot soldiers, the scum—we take our uniforms a little less seriously. Some soldiers are wearing their spare pants, which are more comfortable than the ones that go with our uniforms; others have taken off their headgear. It's easier to walk without a giant stovepipe on your head. No one seems to mind as long as we're wearing our uniform pants and shakos when we're eye to eye with Hans and Jürgen in Austria. We need to be able to recognize one another in the smoke and fire of the battlefield, and the only way to do that is by the color of the uniform.

We take one smoke break in the morning and one in the afternoon. At dusk we stop for the night. The cavalrymen tend to their horses. We, the infantry, drop down wherever we're standing. The straps on my cartridge box, rucksack, and musket cut into my shoulders. After just one day of marching, I'm already exhausted. My shoulders are screaming in pain. As soon as I sit down, I fall asleep. The sergeant has to wake me up. The kettles are bubbling over the fires. I need to eat. Restore my strength.

"Why do we have to go all the way to Austria?" I ask.

"Four years ago we defeated them," Sergeant Perrec tells me. "We took their muskets and melted their cannons down to stove pokers. But the Emperor's spies have heard that the archdukes are inciting a revolt. On Sundays, there are cries for deliverance from the pulpit. Dear God, deliver us from the stomach flu, the boils, and the wicked French! That's what those Austrian priests are praying, and all the church mice in the congregation repeat the prayer after them. Young men are joining the army in droves. But officially there is no war yet."

"Maybe it will all blow over," I say.

"It might," Perrec says casually. "And if that's the case, we'll spend the summer picking strawberries, plucking cherries, and lounging in the sun."

"That sounds good," I say.

"Yes," he says. "That does sound good, doesn't it?"

Soon, I come to love the evenings out on campaign. I love the kettles bubbling over the fires, the beets and potatoes that, until just a few months ago, I always thought were animal fodder. Now they float in the soup along with bits of wild rabbit, pheasant, or squirrel, and salt and pepper. Lots of pepper. We set mousetraps for a little extra meat—a bit of cheese on a stick over a bucket of water usually works. The mice fall in and drown by the dozens. And they're actually pretty tasty in the soup. We pass around the tin cups and spoons. We eat standing up and slightly hunched so as not to get grease on our blue uniforms and white pants. We sleep sitting against trees or huddled under thin blankets. On the third day, the temperature fell below freezing, and I was searching for a spot by the fire when the sergeant said don't be silly—soldiers lie against each other when it's freezing to keep warm. And so I curl up with twenty other men by the slowly dying campfire. If only they knew! The officers take shelter in a comfortable farmhouse or with a local village priest, who undoubtedly has a barrel of Communion wine to spare. We sleep until the thirteen-year-old drummer wakes us with a drumroll. There's no bathing. I've never felt so dirty in my life. My clothes stick to my skin, but I don't mind. I was born for this campaign.

In the second week, my headache returns. The sergeant lets me sit in the sutler's cart. Cathérine, the sutler, promises to take good care of me, and she's certainly well-equipped to do so with all the provisions in her cart. She is about thirty years old and has two little girls with her in the cart. Her husband was killed, and she was left alone with their two young daughters. She makes me herbal tea during the smoke break. In the evening, she lays wet rags on my forehead, but the drummers keep drumming in my head. She has beautiful, gray eyes, and her loud voice turns soft when she talks to me. She sleeps beside me, and in the morning she changes her clothes before my eyes.

Cathérine's cart is the last one in our convoy. When we roll out in the morning, I see the crows, pigeons, and sparrows swoop down to pick up the crumbs we've left behind. There are dozens of women traveling with Cathérine's cart. Most of them are the wives and sweethearts of soldiers. Others are following the army because they have nowhere else to go. They wash the soldiers' shirts or sell themselves for money. Cathérine tells me that she was one of them before she became a sutler. The cart bumbles along behind the army. In the afternoon, three little drummers, tired from walking, come ride in the cart too. Our convoy stretches at least two miles down the narrow road. It looks as if all humanity is on the move. Cathérine urges her horse onward. Her two helpers pick up provisions in the villages and farms along the way: cheese, beets, bread, and hay for the horses. Cathérine sells it to the troops during the breaks and in the evenings. She smokes her pipe all day long, and in the evenings she doesn't shy away from the wine.

Finally, in the evening on the eleventh day, the drumming in my head stops. I tell Cathérine that tomorrow I'll go back to marching.

"Stay," she says.

"I can't."

She takes my hand.

"Stay," she repeats.

I feel short of breath. She's got me trapped in the cart.

"You're different," she says. "So refined. So respectful. So different from all the other men here."

She puts her hand on my knee, but I gently push it away.

"What's wrong? You think I'm too old?" she asks.

"No," I stammer.

"Is it the children?"

She nods at her two daughters, who are sleeping under a blanket.

I shake my head. No, that's not it. Her hand caresses my face.

"What soft skin you have," she whispers.

I can smell the tobacco and wine on her breath. She reaches to unbutton my shirt.

"I have a fiancée," I lie.

Her eyes don't believe me.

"She's a ballet dancer," I say as convincingly as I can. "She dances in Mademoiselle Mars's company. We met in Paris."

"A dancer?" she says mockingly.

"Fortuna is her name."

"That's not even a name!"

I don't dare to tell her that I don't even know Fortuna's real name. She lets go of my hand. She empties her pipe and fills it with fresh tobacco. Her love affair is over before it started. I thank her for all her care, but she won't even look at me.

"Go off with your mates," the sutler snarls. "Go sleep in the dirt."

We march. All around us, spring is awakening. On the fifteenth day, late in the afternoon, when our shadows are long, we hear cheering rising up behind us. The men are shouting, "Long live the Emperor! Vive l'Empereur!" The cries are repeated over and over again as the cheering comes closer. The marching slows. We bump into one another and step on one another's feet. A magnificent carriage is cutting through our ranks. Wagons and cannons are pulled to the side of the road. Occasionally, the carriage has to stop and wait until the road is cleared. Officers stand at attention. The twelve or so riders accompanying the carriage have beautiful helmets with plumes, and their hair is pulled back into braids. One of the escorts is wearing a turban, puffy red pants, and a crooked dagger in his wide belt. The carriage approaches. The horses' hooves stomp in the mud. I only catch a glimpse of the Emperor, but I recognize him instantly. I know his face from the coins. He smiles. He is happy to see his troops. He is loved by every living soldier—but, as Rabbit likes to say, the dying soldiers and widows all curse his name.

"Vive l'Empereur!" I shout. A moment later, the carriage is gone. We keep shouting. "Long live the Emperor!" We shout so loudly that they can probably hear us all the way in Austria. The only person not shouting is Geoff Soudan. He looks at me.

"The Emperor is on his way to Austria," he says in Flemish. "That can only mean one thing."

"What?"

"The war has started."

Encouraged by the sight of our leader, we march late into the night. It's as if we want to catch up with him, as if we're afraid of arriving late in Austria, as if we don't want to miss a single minute of the war. Eight days later, we join the rest of the army units. The masses of infantry and cavalry stretch across several hills. Everywhere, the French colors are flying high. Rumor has it the war is already almost won. With every attack, the Austrians are being pushed back. The campaign has only been going on for two weeks, and already the enemy is in retreat. A portion of the Austrian army is entrenched on the other side of the Traun in the town of Ebelsberg.

The Traun is a nasty little river whose waters are divided into three or four tributaries. This means that the wooden bridge leading to the gate of Ebelsberg has to cross over not one river but four small rivers. The bridge is one hundred and fifty meters long. On the other side is a town that backs up to a hill, and on top of that hill is a castle, a white stone fortress with four round turrets and square windows around the top.

We wait in a meadow amidst thousands upon thousands of infantrymen in blue-and-white uniforms. Then come the first musket shots. They sound like branches snapping in the distance. A drumroll follows. It's the pas de charge, the rapid trill to sound an attack. We hear the cannons roar and the endless fire of muskets. We are more than a mile from the city and can already smell the gunpowder fumes blowing in our direction. The Austrian army is resisting. Up in the windows of the castle, we see the white smoke of muskets being fired.

The day is over before we know it. The town is in flames. Finally, as the sun is going down, the musket fire stops. Word spreads that Ebelsberg is ours. The sergeant calls for us to prepare to march through the city. The cuirassiers with their plumed helmets and iron armor go first, followed by the Emperor's carriage, and then by the heavy carts and artillery. We, the men of the line, are the last to go. We march across the long, wooden bridge. Whole sections of the railing are missing. There are so many corpses floating in the water that they form a dam.

The city is completely destroyed. There's not a house left standing. Even the castle is on fire. We walk past the black skeletons of houses consumed by flames. Hundreds of soldiers and civilians have lost their lives.

"Keep moving," the sergeant says.

We wipe away the sparks that hit our uniforms. The burning town is trembling with heat. We're all drenched in sweat. The stench of molten flesh clings to our noses, creeps down our throats, and lodges itself in our lungs. We walk across Ebelsberg's main square, where the bodies of dead soldiers are being piled six feet high, as if it were some kind of macabre market where death is sold by the pound. All around us are the groans of the wounded.

"Keep moving, men," the sergeant says.

The façade on one of the houses has been blown completely off, and on the second floor I see a baby bassinet. Every alley we pass is full of dead horses and human remains. Finally, we arrive at a stone gate on the east side of the town. The cavalry, the Emperor, the cannoneers—they were all in such a hurry to cross the bridge and leave this hell behind that they rode right over the corpses. Flesh, bones, and skulls have been crushed by thousands of horseshoes and flattened by hundreds of cart wheels. The ground is covered with a red, slimy slush that's too gruesome for words. A small group of men with cloths around their mouths use shovels to clear a path for the infantry.

"Keep moving," the sergeant shouts. "I said keep moving, God damn it."

We march on. Two by two. Our shoes sink into the soup of mud, blood, and bone. I don't look down. I stare at the back of Cor the Dutchman in front of me. Geoff Soudan stumbles and falls forward. Mole and Rabbit pull him back to his feet. I hear someone vomit. We walk through the town gates, leaving the hell behind us. No one speaks—not Cor the quiet Dutchman, who is probably thinking about the sun setting over the long, flat fields back home in Holland; not our sergeant, who doesn't even curse in his native Breton but just clutches the pebble in his pocket, thinking of his childhood home by the sea where old men pick the nets clean every day; not the Basque, who receives love letters from home with lavender and dried espelette peppers in them; not Bouchon from Gascony, the land of the ancient vines; not Rabbit, whose wrinkles in his old leathery skin seem deeper than before; not Geoff Soudan, who is dreaming of his father's house on Veldstraat and Lucie's warm body; and not me. I am thinking of the back room of our house, where the sunlight streams in on clear days, where the shadows of the honeysuckle dance across the floor. Mother's soft voice is ringing in my ear. She sings old church hymns, and I sing the lines after her. She teaches me to write French, and when I do it right, she caresses my cheek and gives me a kiss on the head.

"Who loves onions?" the sergeant shouts suddenly.

No one answers his call. We march on in silence, our noses still raw from the stench of dead bodies, our lungs full of the putrid smoke, our shoes dripping with black blood, and our eyes seared with the image of human slush. If only we could shake the horror of the past hour out of our heads.

"Are you men deaf?" the sergeant asks. "You're not cannoneers, are you? You should still have your ears! Who loves onions?"

"We love onions!" Rabbit chants back.

"And how do we like our onions?" the sergeant calls.

"Fried in oil," we all chant now.

"And what are we?"

"Lions!" we roar.

"And do the Austrians get fried onions?"

"No! They get nothing!" we shout. "No onions! Not even a shallot!"

Finally, we come to a halt. Behind us, in the dusk, we can still see the black clouds and burning glow over Ebelsberg, the town that has been wiped off the map. No one is hungry. No one wants to play cards. We spent the whole day lying around in the grass, playing cards, and smoking pipes, but those last few miles through Ebelsberg were more exhausting than a month of marching. We buy extra wine from the sutler, and we drink and drink and drink. But no one becomes merrier. All I want is to sleep. Sleep and forget this horrifying day.

Around midnight, I'm shaken awake by the sergeant. Around me I see my comrades stretching awake and rolling up their bedrolls. The Basque is still drunk. He can't even stand up straight.

"What's going on?" I ask.

"I only want men who are not drunk!" shouts the sergeant.

"Pack as light as possible. Rifle and cartridge box, nothing else. Overcoats on."

"Overcoats, Sergeant?"

"We might have to go through enemy territory, and I

don't want their armed lookouts spotting us from a half a mile away in our blue uniforms," he says.

"Enemy territory?" asks the Dutchman in an accent thick enough to spread on toast.

"We're going after a bunch of deserters," says the sergeant. "A group of idiots from a German regiment who didn't take very well to our little stroll through town. They've run off. They're trying to reach the Austrian army. We've got to get them back."

"Can't the German regiment get them back themselves?" asks Bouchon, with a yawn so big that I can practically see down to his empty stomach.

"The marshal is afraid that more Germans will try to desert," says the sergeant. "It's not unthinkable that they'd rather join their German-speaking brothers in the Austrian army."

"But why us?" I ask.

"Because, Ironhead, Captain Lemoine has apparently told the marshal that, of all the Godforsaken sergeants in this army, I'm the best one for the job."

"Ready, Sergeant," says Rabbit. There are twelve of us.

"I don't want a single musket loaded," the sergeant says. "If one of those damned things goes off by accident, those idiots will know we're on their trail."

We walk out of the camp and meet Captain Lemoine. He is standing in front of a large campfire fueled by the beams of a destroyed barn. Lemoine grins when he sees me. His cheerfulness makes me suspect that the task he's given us is not going to be pleasant. He hands the sergeant the maps of the area.

"The group of deserters consists of roughly twenty men," Lemoine says.

"I've only got twelve, Captain," the sergeant says. "The rest are still too drunk."

The captain shakes his head as if that were the sergeant's fault.

"Well, at least you've got Ironhead here with you," Lemoine says. "If you need a miracle, just ask him."

The men all look at me. I stare at the ground. Captain Lemoine seems to be relishing the chance to ridicule me in front of the others. The sergeant doesn't respond.

"I'm counting on you, Breton," Lemoine says.

"You can count on us, my captain," Perrec says and takes the maps.

We march off into the night.

"That lunkhead Lemoine, he gives me a map," the sergeant snaps at me. "I can't read a map!"

But orders are orders. So we head out with our muskets, cartridge boxes, lanterns, and a map our sergeant can't read.

21

PIER

In the week following the China cabinet avalanche, the doctor comes to the widow's apartment every day to check on Dupin's wound. Through the doorway, I can see him lying in bed, gray as the dead. He's lost buckets of blood. The doctor reminds him how important it is to take it easy. If the wound were to reopen, he could really take a turn for the worse. Dupin falls in and out of a fitful sleep full of death sweats and feverish dreams.

It's up to me to do the daily shopping. At the end of the morning, I head out hand in hand with Dédée, and together we walk to Les Halles, the giant indoor market in the center of Paris, where hundreds of sellers all try to shout louder than the others. Germain uses the free time to run around the streets playing battlefield. In the afternoon, we continue our lessons. The busy schedule helps take my mind off of things. I can put all my energy into my teaching, the daily errands, and the chores I have to do. But every morning, as the students from the attic clamber down the stairs past me, I hear my father's voice in my head:

Have I ever asked anything of you, Judas? Father asks. *Go to the Emperor and sell him my plans. Prove that you're worthy to be my son.*

Well, it hasn't exactly been smooth sailing, Father.

Three weeks after the duel, Dupin is back on his feet. The man is indestructible. He walks a bit stiffly and his left arm hangs limply beside his body. But it'll come back to life, he blusters, and he orders me to get his horse from Madame Josée and rent us a boguet. I walk to the stables and ask for my master's horse.

"Your horse isn't doing very well," says Madame Josée as she leads Mr. Dupin's steed out of its stall. "He hardly eats anymore. He's wasting away in there."

Achilles refuses the carrot I offer him. He whinnies as I walk away.

I lead Mr. Dupin's horse down the street to the carriage rental company, where they harness him to a boguet. Then I drive back to the widow's and pick up my master. The carriage bounces over the cobblestones. Mr. Dupin clings to the side of the coach and winces with pain. He feels every jolt and turn in his torn flesh. Occasionally, he tells me to go left or right. We cross the Pont Neuf to the Île de la Cité.

"Stop here," he says. I pull on the reins a little too hard. The carriage lurches to a halt, throwing my recovering companion forward and back again in his seat. The customs officer curses like the Devil in a barrel of holy water. He tries to punch me with his good arm. But I jump down before his fist hits my ribcage.

"You did that on purpose," he shouts.

"I didn't, I swear," I say. He gingerly steps out of the carriage. A boy comes up to us, and Mr. Dupin snarls at him to guard the horse and carriage. He tosses the boy five centimes. We walk into a sand-colored building, where we're immediately engulfed in a cloud of incense. I've heard of this place. They call it the mortuary for the drowned. I feel the hairs on the back of my neck stand up. This is where they keep the bodies of unidentified souls who have been lost in the waters of the Seine. Women, mostly. They call the men who work here the corpse fishers.

Mr. Dupin taps on the wooden counter with his walking stick. The sound echoes through the dark, empty hall. It looks like the inside of a crypt. Incense swirls upward from a small cauldron.

"That's to mask the smell of the dead bodies," Dupin says.

I hold my handkerchief to my mouth.

"Why are we here?"

"You'll see."

Just then a door creaks open, and a bald, pale man in glasses approaches us. He doesn't look particularly healthy. He dips a quill into an inkwell and scratches our names and place of residence into a large book.

"Are you looking for a child or a woman?" the corpse fisher asks.

"The boy's sister. She's been missing for a few days," Dupin lies. "Almost a week. She was quite desperate."

I look up at Mr. Dupin, confused.

"My sister didn't throw herself into the Seine," I say. "Why would she do that?"

"My friend is still young," he says. "He doesn't know that desperate women often throw themselves from bridges. Young women without money or property who are at their wit's end and have nowhere to go. Women like his sister. It's their own fault, of course."

The corpse fisher nods as if he too understands the cruelty of life. He takes an oil lamp and leads us down a stone staircase. We enter a basement. The vaulted ceiling is high and rests on narrow columns. The heavy, putrid air reminds me of the smell of the Devil in our classroom. High in the basement wall is a tiny window that lets in a feeble streak of daylight. The wall facing the street is made of large stone blocks, like the ones used to build castles. It's as if they wanted the thickest possible wall to keep this chamber of death, this holding cell to the underworld, separate from the world of the living. The corners of the room are hidden in the shadows. Dupin's face is little more than two white eyeballs surrounded by hostile flesh. In the middle of the basement is another steaming pot of incense. Next to it are three stone tables. On one of them lies a corpse.

Dupin pushes me forward. The body is a girl in a maid's uniform with long, pleated skirts, a stained blouse, and a mobcap on her head. She is missing a shoe on her left foot. Her remaining shoe is sticking straight up, looking somewhat abandoned. There is a hole in the sock on the left foot, and I can see the white flesh of her sole. I make the sign of the cross.

"That's your sister," Dupin says somberly. "God rest her soul."

"My sister? But that's not Stance, is it?" I ask.

"It's her," Dupin says to the corpse fisher.

He lays his bear claw of a hand on my shoulder and squeezes it. It feels like he wants to crush all the bones in my shoulder.

"Take a good look," he says. "It's most certainly her."

I look at the dull hair under the cap, the colorless lips, the marks on her gray skin, the closed eyes. Her belly is bulging and hard.

"She's been lying here for four days," says the corpse fisher.

"Poor soul," says Mr. Dupin. "Do you recognize her now?"

The pain in my shoulder is too much to bear. I nod. I taste the salty drops running down my cheeks.

"He's emotional," Dupin says to the man as he lets go of me. I massage my crushed shoulder. I think he might have broken a bone.

Dupin shoots me a menacing look. His eyes say: *Dare to contradict me, boy, and I'll leave you here to rot in this house of death.*

I turn to the pale corpse fisher and say, "Yes, that's Constance Hoste, born in Ghent in the year 1790 and married to Lieven Goeminne."

"Lieven is good man; he'll be incredibly distraught," says Mr. Dupin to the corpse fisher, as if he might know Lieven from somewhere. He sounds as sincere as the Devil's tailor.

"I will prepare the documents," says the man, and then he turns to me. "You may say your goodbyes."

I look at the young woman who has been lying here for four days. Her body smells rancid. The heavy incense and the stench of decay make me feel nauseated.

"Kiss her," says Mr. Dupin.

"Kiss her?" Absolutely not. The girl will fall apart! Or death will seep into my mouth. He grabs me by the neck with his one good arm and presses my face against hers. I taste her lips. They are cold and weak. He pulls me back again. I rub my sleeve over my mouth.

"Now say an Our Father," Dupin, the heretic, demands. I fold my hands and say the prayer, my eyes locked on her lifeless body. A fly crawls out of one of her nostrils. I can't look anymore. I turn around and walk past the corpse fisher, up the stairs, and back to the world of the living. Behind me, I hear the heretic say, "Amen."

The next day the young woman is tossed into a mass grave outside the city. A man shovels lime on top. The weather is wet and gray, as it should be at a funeral. I watch from the boguet with Dupin at my side. Goodbye, girl with no name. Goodbye, girl with one shoe. You were the first girl I ever kissed.

Dupin sends the documents confirming Stance's drowning and burial to Lieven. I suppose word will reach my parents too. Mother will get the news at home and Father in the debtor's prison. They'll wear black. They'll burn candles in the cathedral and hold a Mass. Maybe Mother will sing during the service so that her daughter can slip in through the back door of heaven.

Dupin is in good spirits, as if the visit to the mass grave really cheered him up. He only has one arm to eat with, which does nothing to help his table manners. I hear him say that he intends to deliver my Father's plans to Lieven in person.

"How long is Maître Pierre staying with us?" Dédée asks.

"Pieter owes you two more months of lessons," Dupin says. "Enough to pay your mother back for all her broken China. Isn't that right, Pieter?"

I nod. Dupin looks at me as if nothing's happened. As if we never stood in front of the corpse of that unknown woman lying on the table. As if he never shot my big sister. As if he never stole my father's papers from me. As if he were a model of decency and civilization.

"So your sister is dead?" Dédée asks.

I look at her and don't answer.

"Sadly, she drowned," the widow says. "We will pray for her."

"My sister did not drown," I tell her. "And those plans are mine."

Dupin rises from his chair. He swings his good arm across the table, grabs me by my ear, and gives it a quarter turn. The movement is so swift, it's a wonder he was on the brink of death four weeks ago.

"Repeat after me," he roars. "My sister is dead, and those papers belong to you, Mr. Dupin, to you and no one else."

The pain burns through my head, but I say nothing. Hatred boils up in my eyes. He turns my ear upside down. Any farther and it will rip off my head.

"Careful with your wound, mon ami," the widow cries.

"Say it," he shouts, wheezing with exertion.

"My sister is dead, and those plans belong to you, Mr. Dupin," I cry. "To you and no one else."

Only then does he let go of my ear. His nail has cut so deep into my flesh that blood is dripping from my jaw. Germain hiccups with laughter and immediately gets a slap from his mother. There's no laughing at the table.

Dédée looks at me and then at Dupin. Her sky-blue eyes are wide with horror.

The next morning, it's not the students heading down the stairs with their books who wake me up but little Dédée. I don't understand. Did I sleep late? Is it already time to wake up, wish her a pleasant day, and empty the chamber pots in the street? She looks at me with her big, blue eyes. The sky inside them looks sad.

"Promise not to forget me, Maître Pierre?" she asks.

"What is it?" I ask back.

She hands me a wallet and an orange. Then she passes me my father's portfolio. I look down at it in shock. She unties the three strings and opens the cover. Inside are my father's notes. Every sheet. I don't dare to touch them.

"There are twelve francs and fifty-five centimes in that wallet," she says.

I look at her.

"The orange is for breakfast," she murmurs.

I don't know what to say. I'm sure the coward Dupin will appear behind her at any moment and throw me down the stairs.

"My mother will be up soon."

I sit up on my knees, fold the portfolio shut, and retie the strings. I clamber to my feet, roll up my blanket, and collect my bag. I need to get out of here.

"You're an angel, Mademoiselle Dédée."

She shrugs.

"No one has ever called me Maître Pierre," I say.

"No one has ever called me Mademoiselle Dédée." She smiles.

I gaze at her, and she gazes at me. I want to say that I'll never forget her. That I'll come back to Paris and see her, but that's nonsense.

I hear footsteps above us on the stairs.

"I wish you a pleasant day, Mademoiselle Dédée," I say finally.

"I wish you a pleasant day as well, Maître Pierre," she says.

I tiptoe down the stairs in my socks. I hear Dédée go back into the apartment and lock the door. Once I'm out on the street, I put on my shoes. Here and there, the light of candles and oil lamps can already be seen glowing behind apartment windows. Paris is waking up.

◎ ◎ ◎

I race down the dead-end alley to the stables and pound on the gate like a halfwit. After several minutes, Josée finally opens the gate, still blinking the sleep from her eyes.

"What's the matter?" she barks. "Is Paris burning or something?"

"I'm here to get my horse," I say.

"At five thirty in the morning?" the woman asks.

"Please," I beg.

She curses and hands me a bucket.

"Go fill it for me at the pump first. The horses are thirsty."

"But—" I protest.

"Just do it," she says. "I'll saddle up your horse."

I take the bucket and run the seven blocks to the nearest pump. What a waste of time. I lug the full bucket back to the stables. The water splashes over the edge and onto my pants. I walk into the stables, and for a moment I am afraid that Dupin's hand will grab me by the neck and strangle me to death once and for all.

Achilles gulps up the water in the bucket. Josée buckles the saddle. The animal snorts restlessly and stamps his feet. The gray beast looks even uglier than usual.

"Give Mr. Dupin my regards," says Madame Josée.

"Will do," I say, feeling slightly guilty about the lie.

She walks back inside and closes the gate behind her. She's off to sleep a little longer.

◎ ◎ ◎

I'm free and have my father's plans. But where should I go? Instead of digging my heels into the old animal's flanks, I just sit there. I have to go to the Emperor, to his castle. I need a moment to get my bearings. Then I remember—I need to cross the Seine, then keep going straight until I reach the city gate. Now I wonder which of these little streets leads to the Pont Neuf. And that's when I see him coming around the corner. Dupin the Savage.

He's headed straight for me, and I just sit there like the stupidest calf in creation, frozen like a pillar of salt on my horse while the customs officer charges at me. Finally, the alarm bells go off in my head, and I kick Achilles in the flanks. But Dupin grabs the reins. Achilles rears and whinnies. I almost fall off his back.

"Where do you think you are going, you little brat?" Dupin shouts. The sound of his booming voice rattles all the courage out of my body. I'm speechless.

"Get off that animal," he shouts.

But Achilles won't go without a fight. He takes a step back. His hooves clack on the cobblestones. He's trying to help me. I have to do something. Bertie would do something. Bertie would be ready with a response.

"He's my horse," I say.

"Get off or I'll break your neck," he growls. His left arm is hanging limply at his side and his right hand is clutching the reins. If he had the use of both of his arms, he would've thrown me to the ground already. But a one-armed savage is still a savage.

"Give me those papers!" Dupin shouts as he pulls down

on Achilles's head. The animal snorts and jerks, but Dupin is stronger.

I have no choice but to obey. If I don't, he'll throw me down onto the cobblestones, break every bone in my body, and leave me to bleed to death in the gutter, the same gutter that thousands of chamber pots are emptied into every morning. He will tell the widow and her children that I deserved it. I take out the portfolio from under my shirt. A look of relief spreads across his face.

"Did that little serpent help you?" he says without expecting an answer. "I'll whip some manners into that girl."

I feel my blood turn cold. You can shatter my bones in this alley, but you're not going to lift a finger against that little girl with the sky in her eyes, you scoundrel! I've only got one chance. I slide my right foot out of the stirrup.

"I'm sorry, Mr. Dupin," I say as submissively as I can. "I'm sorry."

I reach out to hand him my father's masterpiece. He looks annoyed. If he wants to grab hold of the leather portfolio, he has to let go of the reins.

"Drop it," he growls.

"Drop it?" I repeat, as if I don't understand. I keep my arm extended. All he has to do is reach out and grab it.

The opportunity is too good. He does exactly what I hoped he'd do: he lets go of the reins and grabs the portfolio.

He doesn't even see my kick coming. It's not easy to kick someone while you're on a horse. But I know exactly where to aim my foot—right where my crazy sister pierced him with a bullet. I kick as hard as I can, and the iron tip of my shoe drives into the wound under his shirt. The first kick jerks him to a halt. The second one brings him to his knees. He lets go of the portfolio and flops sideways on the cobblestones. I jump—well, fall—off Achilles's back. One foot gets caught in the stirrup, and I bang my shoulder against the ground. The horse steps forward and drags me on the cobblestones. "Stop, Achilles." Fortunately, he obeys.

I crawl back to my feet and pick up the portfolio. Dupin growls as he tries to get back up. A ring of blood appears on his shirt. I pull Achilles away by the reins. Away from the alley. Dupin tries to grab at my ankle, but I'm too quick. Once I'm a few feet away, I pull myself into the saddle.

"Gee-up, Achilles," I call. "Gee-up."

And the animal actually listens. Achilles, the poor horse with the old joints, who has been languishing in the barn for weeks, takes off down the street. I bounce in the saddle as we gallop out onto the boulevard. It's still early. There's hardly anyone on the street. Someone on the sidewalk yells at me to slow down. I tug on the reins and slow Achilles to a trot. I don't want to be stopped by a gendarme, but I have to get out of the city before that idiot Dupin comes after me. We arrive at the banks of the Seine, where a bookseller is just setting out his prints. We cross the Pont Neuf, and I make a sign of the cross as we pass Notre-Dame.

Fifteen minutes later, we reach the city gates. It is not even six o'clock yet, so the gates are still closed. There are about four carriages and a couple of riders in long coats waiting to leave the city. Vendors walk around peddling bread, wine, and newspapers. A newsboy, who looks about twelve, shouts that the Emperor has arrived in Austria and was met with cheers from his troops.

"Austria," I groan, "The Emperor is in Austria?"

"Read all about it in the paper!" shouts the newsboy.

I look behind me. I still can't believe I kicked that cowardly cognac-guzzler to the ground. He will find me—the words keep pounding in my head. He will find me, and he will crush me. I scan the seven streets leading up to the city gate. On one street, a few soldiers are walking; on another, a couple of workers are smoking pipes. Two women step out of a door carrying baskets. But there's no sign of the savage with a hole in his chest. Finally, the gates creak open. The carriages roll out of town. The whips crack, the coachmen shout. I let myself be carried out by the stream of horses and people leaving Paris.

And all of a sudden, I'm on the other side of the gate. I ride past meadows, fields, and forests. I pass merchants coming to the capital with their carts. I urge Achilles forward. We trot—no, we gallop—down the open road. Every few minutes, I look over my shoulder, but no one is following me.

After a half hour, I finally let Achilles slow down. The animal is sweating, and there's foam around his mouth. We trot on for a little longer, and then I stop so he can rest. I'm still reeling from the excitement of it all. Only now do I feel the pain of the fall in my shoulder. But I can't stand still. I pace back and forth while Achilles grazes. I rip the peel off Dédée's orange and toss the pieces into my mouth. I barely taste the sweetness.

All I have is an old horse, a Bible, and a wallet with twelve francs and fifty-five centimes. Before me is a long stone road that runs through an unknown world of forests, mountains, and farmlands. I only have one option: go to Austria and find the Emperor. But how? I'm only fourteen years old.

When we pointed our guns at the Russians, we didn't hesitate, I hear Bertie saying in my head. *You only have to ride one mile on the back of that horse. Repeat a thousand times, and then you'll be there.*

No, it can't be that easy.

And while you're at it, start working on your proposal for the Emperor, Bertie says.

Up ahead, an old man shouts at three pigs being herded into the city. The magpies are chattering. The wind rustles in the fresh spring leaves. Achilles plucks a thistle out of the ground and savors it. I scratch his neck and hoist myself back into the saddle.

22

STANCE

We run behind the sergeant through the night. After half an hour, Perrec stops. He unfolds the map on one of the soldier's backs. Geoff Soudan holds up the lantern. The sergeant takes out his compass and presses it against the map. He looks around, but everything is dark. The moon, which is little more than a feeble arc, has slipped behind clouds. Sergeant Perrec curses in Breton and squints his eyes. He can barely make out the dots and lines on the map. He looks up and glances from left to right. It's still just as dark as before.

"We're here, Sergeant," says Soudan, pointing to a line on the map that runs parallel to the river.

"You can read maps?" Perrec asks, somewhat redundantly.

"My uncle was a monk. He spent his time mapping the

monastery's properties. We used to visit him once a year, and—"

"You think now's the time to tell us your life story?" the sergeant snaps. "Just read the map!"

The sergeant takes over the lantern. The hero of the Veldstraat bends his nose over the map.

"The deserters took off to the south," says the sergeant. "They're probably looking for a way to cross the river. But there are no bridges there, I believe."

"These dots could mean there's a ferry," Soudan says, pointing to the map. "The deserters will most likely follow the path along the river. But as you can see, sergeant, there's a quicker way."

"What makes you think that, soldier?" the sergeant says, without looking at the map.

Soudan points to a greenish-brown patch on the map.

"That must be a forest or a hill with some kind of donkey trail through it," he says. "If we can find the trail and follow it, we might get there before them. We should go that way."

Soudan points to the black rock face to our left.

"That's not a hill," the sergeant barks. "That's a mountain."

"I'm just trying to help," the soldier says, already handing back the map.

"Give me your musket and your cartridge box," Perrec says. "You lead the way."

Soudan can't believe his ears.

"Come on, let's go find your donkey trail, Mr. Map Reader. And hurry up. We haven't got all night."

Proud as a hussar who's just received his first medal, Soudan turns off the road and into a forest. We all run after him. Our shoes sink deep into the soggy mud. We step over fallen trees. Branches swish against our heads. One man falls. Another slips. We cross a fast-flowing stream, and our shoes get soaked. Then the ground hardens, and we start climbing over boulders. Everyone curses. Mole shouts to Soudan that he'd better find that donkey trail soon. The sergeant snarls at Mole to shut up.

"Found it," Soudan says suddenly. And there, in the glow of our lantern, we spot the donkey droppings. The path is less than half a meter wide.

"Some damned skinny donkeys they've got here," says Rabbit.

But a path is a path. Soudan runs ahead, and we run after him. Higher and higher we climb. After twenty minutes of running, we've reached the top of the hill. We're all out of breath, panting from exertion. We come out in a clearing surrounded by spruce trees. There is no view, but somewhere on the other side of the hill must be the river.

"Put out that light," the sergeant says. "We don't want the deserters to see us."

Geoff Soudan trots down the hill as if he were born in these woods. We walk so fast through the dark that I'm afraid I'll veer off the path and crash into a tree. My back and knees are aching. We kick up more dust than a team of runaway donkeys. In no time, we reach the bottom of the hill.

Back on the road, we run into a farmer who almost

wets himself at the sight of us. Bouchon asks the man, with the help of hand gestures, if he has seen a group of soldiers come through here. The farmer says something back to him.

"Our uniforms, five minutes ago," Bouchon translates. "Moving south."

"You were right," the sergeant says. "They're headed for the ferry."

We run on and finally see, five hundred yards upstream, a group of men on a raft. A rope has been stretched across the river. They pull on the rope, and with every jerk the ferry moves closer to the opposite bank. It's slow going.

"Blast! We're too late," the sergeant curses.

"They'll see us coming," Rabbit says. "Maybe we can take down one or two of them before they reach the other side. But we'll never catch them all."

No one says a word. Soudan shows the sergeant something on the map and leans in to whisper into his ear.

"Don't go blowing in my ear, man," the sergeant growls. "Just say it."

He uses his fingers to draw the course of the river on the map. The sergeant nods and turns to us, "Who here can swim?"

I immediately raise my hand. Then Cor follows. And finally, after a little hesitation, so does Rabbit, who, judging by his body odor, is really just looking for a bath.

The sergeant tells me, Rabbit, Bouchon, and Soudan to follow him. The five of us run a little ways downstream, toward the bend in the river. The others stay behind with

Mole and keep an eye on the ferry. Behind the riverbend, the raft is out of our sight.

"Hand me your rifles, belts, and cartridge boxes," the sergeant says as he begins gathering large branches and snapping them in half. All of a sudden, my heart starts pounding.

"Listen to Soudan," the sergeant says.

"You swim to the other side," Soudan explains. "Then you run straight ahead, three hundred yards through those fields over there, until you come to the road. The deserters will follow that same road from the ferry, but you can take a shortcut through those fields."

"Understood," I say as the sergeant starts lacing the branches together with two belts. Bouchon bundles up our rifles and cartridge boxes in two overcoats and places them on the stack of branches.

"This is your raft," the sergeant whispers. "Don't lose it."

"Raft" is a big word for the pile of branches with our bundle of weapons on top.

"Now undress," the sergeant orders. "Quickly!"

Cor and Rabbit immediately kick off their shoes, take off their jackets, and pull their shirts over their heads. I gape at the sergeant like an illiterate staring at the Bible. Undress? Why do we have to undress? Why didn't you keep your big mouth shut, Stance?

"I can't swim," I say.

"Then why did you raise your hand, you idiot?" Perrec roars.

Apparently, Soudan can't keep his stupid mouth shut

either. "But you told me you saved your brother from drowning when you were kids," he says.

Perrec looks confused. Cor and Rabbit are already pulling off their knee socks.

"All right, then," I say as I take off my shoes and knee socks. "But I swim with clothes on."

"You'll take them off," says Perrec sternly. "You have to swim more than a hundred yards, and that water is freezing. Your uniform will take on water after a couple of feet and weigh a ton. You won't make it across. I didn't train you to end up as fish food."

Cor and Rabbit toss their pants to Bouchon, who ties them onto the raft with their shirts. They walk down to the riverbank with their butts bare and their cocks swinging back and forth.

"Take off your uniform, soldier."

It's dark but not dark enough. This is it. All is lost. How could you be so stupid, Stance! I stand there frozen with fear in my shirt and pants. I feel sick with shame.

"What the hell are you waiting for?"

The sergeant shouts the order again. I push down my pants, and the sock falls out. My sergeant looks at the sock, then at me. I throw my shirt, jacket, and pants to Bouchon, who is still busy tying the others' pants and shirts onto the raft and doesn't notice anything. I unwrap the bandage around my breasts and let it drop. Then I walk down to the water, naked as a jaybird. I hear the sergeant cursing in Breton. Cor and Rabbit are already up to their necks in the river. Soudan and Bouchon are knee-deep in the water, gently pushing the bundle toward Cor. I pass them. The cold water sears into my flesh. My entire body is covered with goosebumps.

"Good luck," Soudan starts to say, but he doesn't get further than "good." The "luck" falters in his mouth as he watches me sink down into the river naked. Now they know the truth. But there's no time to think. I have to swim. The moon is no longer hiding behind the clouds. I can see the crowns of the trees on the other side of the river outlined against the night sky.

Cor is an excellent swimmer. He pushes the raft in front of him and kicks his legs vigorously. He reaches the other side first and pulls the dripping bundle of branches carrying our weapons and clothes up onto the bank. Then he helps Rabbit out of the water. For me, it's more of a struggle. The current is relentless, and the water weighs against me like lead. Cor walks back into the water, meets me and pulls me to shore. Rabbit is already almost dressed. His mouth falls open. I feel him watching my every move. I turn around and pull on my pants. I push my arms into my shirt and button up my coat. I shiver—and not just from the cold. I hardly dare to look at Cor and Rabbit.

"Come on," Cor says, and he gives Rabbit a shove. They run ahead of me, and I hurry after them, my socks soaking into my shoes.

The three of us dash across the field. Our clothes stick to our wet bodies. We can hear the voices of the deserters. They talk loudly in German. One of them is laughing. They feel safe now that they've made it across the river. Just another hour or two of walking and they'll reach the Austrian troops. They'll remove their hats and hold them up on the tips of their swords so that it's clear to everyone that they are defectors. The Austrians will receive them with open arms. They will be given fresh bread, salted meat, and mince pie. They will be given new uniforms. All white. Austrian uniforms.

We dig around in the cartridge box until we each pull out a cartridge. But the paper is wet and rips. The powder crumbles between my fingers.

Rabbit pulls a leather tobacco pouch out of his bag. In it are four extra cartridges.

"Bone dry," he says. It pays to have a poacher in the infantry. We hear the voices getting closer, and we load our weapons. I rip the stiff paper off the cartridge with my teeth, shake some powder into the barrel, close the frizzen, drop the cartridge into the barrel, and pound it down with the ramrod. I pull back the cock. I'm ready. I see Rabbit looking at me.

"You *shtupid, shtupid* wench," he says.

I stiffen. I'm red with shame. It occurs to me that I accidentally put the cartridge in backward—with the paper side down and the torn side up, which means the bullet is on the wrong end of the cartridge and the spark can't hit the powder. The musket won't fire. How many times have I loaded that God damned gun during training? I've pulled that trigger a thousand times. And now, in the moment of truth, when a bullet is the difference between life and death, right after they've found out that I'm a girl, I mess it up. I turn my musket upside down and shake it. The cartridge is stuck in the barrel. Why am I doing everything wrong? I'm worse than Pier the Blunderbuss. I could cry. Scream. You stupid hen, Stance! You're the stupidest hen that ever hatched.

Meanwhile, the poacher has loaded both of his muskets. I can hear the deserters laughing. They're getting closer.

"Give me one of your guns, Rabbit," I say.

"Why don't you go knit a sweater," he snarls.

Cor peeks over the edge into the clearing. He can see the deserters approaching.

"There are at least twenty of them and only three of us," he says.

"You mean two," Rabbit growls.

"What do we do now, Rabbit?" Cor asks.

Rabbit curses and looks at me as if his life's tragedies were all my fault: the war, this hopeless mission, and maybe even that fateful morning when he was stopped by an old gendarme in the Auvergne with five rabbits and two pheasants under his coat.

"What the hell is a *shilly* broad like you doing in the army?" Rabbit asks, without expecting an answer.

Cor remains calm. That boy never panics.

"What do we do?" he asks again.

"There's nothing we can do," Rabbit says. "We tell the *shergeant* it's all Miss Ironhead's fault."

We hear the deserters' shoes thumping in the mud. In a moment, they'll have passed us. It is my fault. I failed the mission. They'll throw me out of the army. They won't even let me stay on as a sutler. They'll laugh at me and send me away with a hunk of bread and a couple of copper coins in my pocket. *You'll have to travel home all by yourself,* cackles Stance the Stupid Bride in my head, *one thousand miles along muddy roads, prey to robbers and rapists, only to scratch at your husband's door like a dog and beg to sleep in his bed again. You should've stayed where you were.*

Never! I hear Mademoiselle Courage shouting in my ear. Never. I see her standing up again with the scratches on her face.

"Look at you, Rabbit," I say. "You're already shitting your pants. I can smell your crap all the way up to here."

Then I click the bayonet onto the end of my musket and stand up.

The deserters can't see me through the thick brush along the side of the road. They're five yards from me at most. Then four. Then three. My Charlesville is even more dangerous with its companion, the fourchette. Every move I'm about to make has been repeated countless times in training. Six feet to go. I take two steps forward and stand in the middle of the road. I glare at the deserter in front and jab the butt of my musket into his face before he knows what's happening. He bounces back as if he's just crashed into a wall. I don't even see him collapse. I thrust the butt of my gun into the next guy's stomach, tilt the musket, and in one fluid motion—butt back, bayonet forward—stab. Then I turn to the third in line and slice his cheek to shreds. Finally, I shoulder my musket and point it at the fourth in line.

"Arms down," I shout, "or I'll blow your brains out."

The group of men stare at me in utter amazement.

They're young. New recruits. I'm lucky. All Germans who have been forced to fight for the Emperor. Boys not yet twenty who've never seen the battlefield and long for a cup of warm milk on their mother's lap. None of them look particularly bright. Their mouths hang open in shock. All I hear are the groans of the men on the ground.

"Belts off," a voice shouts from the left. "Drop everything."

Rabbit and Cor are standing there, muskets at the ready.

"I said belts off!" Cor repeats.

"Belts off," I shout.

All of a sudden, one of the deserters makes a run for it. Rabbit shoots, and the guy goes down without a sound. The poacher drops his musket and immediately shoulders the second.

"Belts off," he roars.

The boys loosen their belts and drop their weapons.

The deserters cry as we march them to the ferry. One of them mumbles, "Mutti, Mutti." He can cry for his mother if he wants, but she isn't going to save him. We take as many of their weapons as we can carry. The boy who was shot by the poacher is carried by two men. He howls in agony. His shoulder is destroyed.

"There are only three of them," I hear one of them mutter in German, but his men have already been caught, humiliated, and defeated. They no longer have the courage to fight back.

We arrive at the ferry. On the other side is the sergeant, waiting with the others. Their muskets are pointed at the deserters. The men step onto the ferry that they so cheerfully stepped off of less than fifteen minutes ago.

"We'll stay here," Rabbit says to Cor and me. "They could easily overpower us on that raft."

We sit down on the bank as the deserters pull themselves back across the river. They have no choice.

The night slowly gives way to day. The stars disappear from the sky. Rabbit and Cor are sitting across from me. For the past hour or so, all I've been able to see is the whites of their eyes. But now our features become visible. Our lips are black with gunpowder from tearing the cartridges with our teeth. Cor can't stop smiling. A grin spreads across Rabbit's old face as well. All three of us are grinning. Then we laugh. We can't stop laughing. We laugh ourselves silly.

A little while later, the sergeant and Geoff Soudan come back to get us with the ferry. They've brought tobacco and pipes.

"Glad to see you all back in one piece, mes enfants," he says. "The captain wasn't expecting us to actually return with the deserters."

"Permission to speak, *Shergeant* Perrec," Rabbit says seriously.

"I'm listening, Corporal," the sergeant replies.

"Ironhead here stepped out on his own with just a bayonet and shouted with the loudest bark you've ever heard from a soldier, 'Arms down, or I'll blow your brains out.'"

Cor can't stop laughing.

"I don't know if that's worth a promotion," Rabbit says, "but I'd be happy to recommend him."

"Thank you for the recommendation, Corporal," Perrec says.

We smoke the pipes. Then, we take turns pulling the raft back across the river. The water sloshes under the wood. The sergeant hands me my cloth bandage and sock. I turn around, remove my jacket and shirt, wrap the bandage around my breasts and push the sock back down into my pants. How good it feels—that sock in my pants.

"Better," says Rabbit as I turn back around.

"Better," says the sergeant.

Cor doesn't say anything. He just nods.

"There are things we can't keep secret though," the sergeant says. "Bouchon saw our friend jump into the water, and he's about as discreet as the Emperor's washerwoman."

We're almost across. I stand next to the sergeant and see all the men in the company gawking at us in the early morning light.

"What are you all staring at?" the sergeant yells. "Soldier Ironhead has just received a recommendation from Corporal Gérard for exceptional bravery. It's the first time Rabbit has ever recommended anyone, so that says something. I'll report it to the captain, and I wouldn't be surprised if Ironhead is soon promoted to corporal."

That shuts them up. I step onto the bank. They all pat me on the back and offer their congratulations.

"Let's save the celebration for later," the sergeant says.

"Line up, men. Time to take these deserters back where they belong."

And so we march back to camp with the group of deserters between us as the first rays of sun break through the clouds.

23

STANCE

From a distance, Vienna looks peaceful. The sun glistens on the city's thirty church spires. Flags and pennants fly; swallows skim through the sky. It's as if no one in Vienna realizes who is at their gates—me, Ironhead, with my musket and thirty-five cartridges. With my bayonet and razor-sharp briquet. If I were Viennese, I would surrender to this mighty corporal; to his Fourteenth company; and to the Emperor's one hundred thousand soldiers waiting in the hills with horses, cannons, and muskets.

"You need new shoes," Rabbit says to me. I look down. My soles are cracked, and the leather is dried out. There's a hole in my right shoe.

"This is already my second pair," I say.

"I always get hungry when I see a city like this," Rabbit says. "Think of the huge stocks of butter and meat and sugar they've got stored in their cellars. No more mouse soup."

We hear shouting. A French officer comes riding out of the city. His horse is galloping, stirring up dust on the dry road.

"That's the negotiator," Rabbit says. The officer stops his horse a few feet from us. He has lost his hat. He is furious. We hear him shouting. That a rabble of angry citizens nearly tore him to shreds. That they pelted him with dung and rotten food. Him, a negotiator for Napoléon the First. He marches into the camp and heads straight for the Emperor's tent.

"No, they're not surrendering yet," says a voice I recognize. "This is going to be fun."

I look his way. "Fons?" I ask.

He turns and glares at me in exasperation. "That's Corporal Alfons De Keghel to you." He puffs up his chest as if he's a direct descendent of Charles V himself. It's the first time I've ever heard him speak French.

"Corporal De Keghel," I correct myself.

I turn my eyes back toward Vienna. I just hope that Fons, Mr. Adonis, won't recognize my face. My entire body feels hot. He's going to recognize me. There's no way around it.

"So you're from Ghent too, Corporal?" he asks me in Flemish. "Have we met?"

At my window, you useless windbag, I want to say. *Your tongue was in my mouth, you squeezed my breasts, and I felt something hard in your pants, remember?*

But I don't say that.

In a voice as deep as I can muster, I tell him we met at the Black Magpie on the day the numbers were drawn.

"You had quite a few beers in you," I say. "You got up on a table and shouted that the Emperor and the French army could all go to hell. Then you fell off the table. They had to carry you home from the pub."

Or that's what they were saying on the wash rafts the week afterward.

"You were there?" he asks incredulously.

"You had quite a few drinks in you."

His eyes narrow to slits. Where do I know this guy from, he wonders. I can see him racking his brains, opening all the closets and drawers. Where have I seen that face? I can almost hear the thoughts whizzing in his head.

"So you're in the artillery, Corporal?" I ask, interrupting his train of thought.

He nods proudly.

"I look after the Emperor's daughters," he says.

That's what they call the cannons—the Emperor's daughters. Sounds like a good job for Fons.

"Too bad they want us to blow this place to smithereens," I say. We gaze at the beautiful city before us. The sunlight sparkles on the towers as if they were made of gold. From here, Vienna looks like a giant crown nestled in the hills.

"Nah, it doesn't look so sturdy," Fons says. "Those towers look pretty flimsy to me. And see that little wall over there?"

The city is encircled by an old, crumbling wall topped

with merlons and embrasures from the days when damsels were slayed by dragons and the knights just sat around picking their noses. Back when the Devil was just a naughty little boy.

"We'll piss it down," Fons says.

Still as charming as ever.

"What's your name, Corporal?" he asks.

Then it occurs to me that he knows Binus Serlippens. They stood side by side on the Botermarkt during the lottery last spring, both begging for a lock of my hair.

"Ironhead," I say.

He frowns, surprised that I don't say my real name.

"I'm off to find some new shoes," I say. "My soles are cracked, and the leather is worn out. Adieu, Corporal. Take good care of the Emperor's daughters."

"They're in good hands." He grins. I walk toward the camp. He goes back to his weapons. He holds his shoulders straight and his chest high as if he personally dragged the cannons to Vienna.

I walk up the road to the hills. There are hundreds of carts and wagons with food, ammunition, and all sorts of things that might come in handy in battle. I walk past carts of rope weavers, butchers, and sellers of frothy wine, until finally, I come to a shoemaker. There are a dozen soldiers waiting in line, all chattering excitedly.

"A couple of stagecoaches arrived this morning," one of them says. "Full of actors and musicians."

"All the way from Paris?" I ask.

"Yes, even Mademoiselle Mars is here," says the soldier. "With lots of ballet dancers."

A couple of men whistle. I think of Fortuna. Fortuna with the thousand freckles, whose face dances when she smiles. *Too bad you prefer gentlemen,* she said. Suddenly, I feel awkward. My heart is racing.

"But here in Vienna," the soldier sighs, "only the officers get to see them perform."

"Aw, don't pout, boys," I say. Then it's finally my turn at the cobbler's cart. The shoemaker sizes me up.

"The smallest size, I take it?" he says.

"Yes, and a jar of your best shoe polish. I want to march into Vienna in shiny shoes."

As the sun sets and night falls, the Emperor's daughters are awakened for duty. The cannons are lined up, and that night, the night of May 11, two thousand red-hot balls of lead are fired at Vienna. The cannons are aimed at two specific districts, which are lit up in flames within an hour. Black smoke billows up from the city. No one sleeps that night. Around midnight, we hear the first building collapse.

The next morning, the Austrian soldiers leave the city, blowing up the bridges across the Danube behind them, one by one. But Vienna is ours. An officer warns us not to rob the poor peasants and not to be haughty. It is thanks to God and the artillery that Vienna has fallen back under the control of the Emperor. But we, the hungry Fourteenth, don't get to enjoy ourselves yet. By order of Captain Lemoine, we have to spend the next three nights guarding the camp outside the city, stuck with the carts and cannons.

Three sergeants from the company march up to Sergeant Perrec, address him disrespectfully as "Breton," and say that it's all his fault that we're not allowed to enter Vienna. Because the captain's got it out for him. Perrec brushes his sleeve to show what he thinks of their whining. But they keep hurling their accusations at him. He shouts a few words in Breton, which are probably not very polite. Then the pushing and shoving starts. One of the sergeants, a small bully of a man with a stubbly beard, points at me.

"Is that the wench you've got under your command? Does she keep you warm at night?"

In less than a second, Perrec's saber is drawn. The bully who called me a wench barely has time to draw his briquet. The group disperses. The short infantry swords clash a few times; sparks fly from the blades like burning fleas. Then Perrec smashes the hilt of his weapon into his opponent's face. The man hits the dust like a sack of coal. His mouth is full of blood. Then the shouting really begins. The two other sergeants fly at Perrec. We jump to his aid. Other soldiers come to help their sergeants. A uniform is ripped apart. A cup is smashed over someone's head. There is cursing. Shouting. Then a shot is fired.

Before us is a lieutenant holding a smoking gun.

"Enough!" he shouts. "Or you'll get three more days of guard duty. Save that fighting spirit for the Austrians."

That calms everyone down.

"It's his fault we can't go into Vienna," says Sergeant Bully as he spits blood and chunks of tooth from his mouth. "I want to celebrate too, you know, because next week could be my last."

Perrec stows his sword and extends his hand to Sergeant Bully. They shake hands, but not cordially. In any case, he won't make any more comments about me, the wench of the Fourteenth. Apparently I'm an open secret in the company. When I walk through the camp, I see how the soldiers look at me and gossip. Even Cathérine, the sutler, treats me differently when I buy bread and tobacco at her cart.

"Need anything extra?" she whispers. "Something against bleeding, perhaps?"

I tell her my needs are the same as any other soldier's.

"Don't be silly," she says with an accusing look, and she slips me a bundle of cotton cloths when no one is looking.

"I knew there was something different about you," she whispers.

After a night of keeping watch, we sleep in the next day. We might not be able to enter Vienna, but at least we can sample all the pies, sausages, and breads that the sutler's helpers have bought or stolen in town and that Cathérine sells at some profit.

After four days, they finally let us enter the city. At last. Tonight Vienna is ours. We'll take whatever we want, drink whatever we find, and eat whatever we can steal. Anyone who dares to object will get a slap in the face. We haven't marched a thousand miles for nothing, we haven't plodded through the blood-drenched streets of Ebelsberg and spent three nights on watch not to enjoy our reward. We haven't received our soldier's pay in weeks and are unlikely to see a centime until we've faced the Austrians. The French State prefers to pay after the battle. No point in paying the dead.

The members of the Fourteenth spread out across the city. Vienna is teeming with French soldiers—there are plenty of low-level infantry like us, but we also see majors and colonels who've seized people's homes and taken over the better restaurants. Almost everyone on the street is in uniform. There is not much left to be plundered. The city is like a chicken that has been thoroughly plucked. The Viennese citizens do their best to stay out of sight. If they do have to go out on the streets, they keep their heads bowed and their eyes fixed on the cobblestones. The last thing they want is to get into a skirmish with some drunken French soldier demanding the coins hidden in their belt or the silverware in their sock. The pubs are packed, and the stores are empty. On a sidewalk, I spot two soldiers carting off a large gilt mirror. They claim they found it on the street, and after searching in vain for its rightful owner, they plan to sell it for a pittance. On the next street, there's a corporal peddling paintings. He has cut the canvases out of their frames and laid them out on the sidewalk with a stone on each corner. Most of them are portraits of wealthy landowners with fancy collars, but there is one of the Virgin and Child that seems much older. Another soldier has gotten his hands on a set of musical scores. He's trying to sell a violin concerto by some man named Mozart for one franc, but there are no takers. He rolls up the score and tosses it into a basket of glowing coals. Then he uses the flame to light his pipe.

Rabbit walks into a shop with a sign outside that says *Delicatessen.* But inside, all the shelves are empty. The sausages and hams have all been looted. The owner has locked himself upstairs with his family, and whenever someone enters his shop he shouts down the stairs that everything he owns was in that store. But Corporal Gérard is a wily old poacher for a reason. He finds a hatch under a few bags of coal. He pulls it open, walks down into the cellar, and comes up with a barrel and a few bottles of wine. He rolls the barrel out into the street, and the sergeant pries off the lid with his saber.

"Pickled salmon," Rabbit grins.

I've never even seen salmon, let alone tasted it. Rabbit rolls up a slice of salmon, grips it in his fist, and takes a bite. We follow his lead. It's delicious but extremely salty. Like swallowing a mouthful of sea water. But we can't get enough. We gorge ourselves on the salty, pink fish.

An officer on horseback rides up and tells us we are a bunch of barbarians. He says the salmon still needs to be smoked and demands we hand over the barrel for Marshal Masséna. He says he's Masséna's personal assistant, his aide-de-camp. But we're not about to listen to some prissy old aide-de-camp. We stand around the barrel and tell him to look go look somewhere else.

"We soldiers live on scraps," Rabbit shouts. "In Paris, all those bureaucrats are paid fat salaries to stroll along the Seine and scratch their balls. Why don't they do their job and send their foot soldiers food and pay. We don't have cooks like the marshals and the Emperor."

"Your name, soldier," the aide-de-camp shouts. "I'll make sure you see the whip."

"Come a little closer, and I'll carve it into your forehead with my fourchette," Rabbit retorts.

Applalled, the officer looks at Rabbit's rough, furrowed face, but then he decides to try his luck elsewhere after all.

After stuffing ourselves with pickled salmon, our mouths are as dry as sand. We pass around the bottle of wine. The shop owner and his family are watching us from the second floor. A girl who looks about ten presses her face against the window. She reminds me of Rozeken. She sticks out her tongue at us, and rightfully so. Rozeken would have done the same thing in her position.

With every sip of wine, I feel farther and farther away from Ebelsberg, with its burning houses, piles of corpses, and blood-soaked streets. Then Mole staggers out of a house carrying a large stringed instrument.

"Violin for sale!" he shouts.

"That's a cello," Geoff Soudan yells. That aristocrat really knows everything.

"Who here can play a tune?" shouts Mole, spilling wine all over the wooden instrument.

A young woman marches out on the street. She looks about eighteen years old, the same age as I am. She has dark eyes and thick eyebrows like upturned exclamation points. Her upper body is short, but there are long legs hidden under her wide skirts. She is undeniably beautiful. The men whistle.

"That is my cello," she declares.

The Basque says he has a flute and that the two of them are going to make music together. A couple of guys laugh, but I don't. He pulls the girl onto his lap. She tries to push away from him. All of a sudden his hands are all over her. Under her skirts. On her breasts.

"Leave her alone, Basque," I say. He looks at me defiantly and holds her tightly to his chest.

"What are you going to do about it, Ironhead?" he demands.

He's as drunk as a seagull.

"I'll knock your lights out," I say.

"Oh yeah?" he says, already removing his saber and cartridge box.

"Leave him alone," says Cor, stepping up beside me. Cor is always there when I need him.

"Why don't you go find a woman who's as ugly as you are, Basque?" says Rabbit.

"If you want to fight, you'll have to fight me first," says the sergeant.

The Basque is already letting the girl go.

"It was just a joke," he mutters gruffly, as if it wasn't him but the wine.

The girl doesn't run away. She straightens her clothes and points to the cello in Mole's hands.

"Why don't you play something for us?" asks Mole, who

clearly has no intention of giving up the cello. "Something Viennese."

"Herr Beethoven and Herr Haydn are worth more than all of you combined," the girl says bravely.

Soudan walks up and hands her two silver napoléons, almost three weeks' pay. He's out of his mind.

"Play something, please," he says, and he turns to Mole. "Give this girl her instrument."

Mole does as he's told.

"But that cello is still mine," he says.

The girl looks Soudan in the eye and sits down. She clamps the instrument between her legs and holds it slightly above the ground. Then she takes the bow.

"Only for you," she says to Soudan.

What a charmer that Geoff is. No wonder that maid Lucie melted for him like butter on the stove. The cellist watches him with her dark eyes—the noble squire in his blue uniform with that stovepipe hat on his head.

"I'll play a suite by Herr Bach," she says.

"By Herr Bach," Mole repeats, as if we haven't heard her.

When I sit down on the street, I feel dizzy. I've had too much wine. The girl closes her eyes and starts to play. Her fingers dance across the strings. The sound she conjures up from the belly of the instrument is the most beautiful thing I've ever heard. The melody is warm and soothing. It reminds me of Grandma Blom's voice before she lost her teeth and her mind, back when she would take me onto her lap and tell me stories about the miserly Blommaerts. We gather around the woman like sheep to listen to her play her cello. As evening falls on the Austrian capital—with its thirty spires, its crowded pubs, its hundreds of pianos, its famous composers—the girl plays the cello for a full fifteen minutes. Finally, she concludes with a long, slow stroke of the bow across the strings.

"You can take the instrument now," she says in German. "I've said my goodbyes."

Her eyes are sharp as knives. She looks at Mole. His face is dripping with tears. He doesn't want the cello anymore. He is too overwhelmed with sorrow to speak. He points to his cartridge box as if to say that the cello wouldn't fit in there anyway. It only holds thirty-five cartridges, after all. The girl glances at the rest of us. We're all speechless. She nods to Soudan to thank him and walks back into the house with her instrument. She locks the door behind her. I hear the latch click. We all just stand there like a bunch of idiots, overwhelmed with homesickness. As if we're all longing for one last sniff of our mother's perfume, for the softness of our childhood pillows, for the smell of soup simmering on the stove back home, the sound of a summer's day, our fathers' callused fingers . . .

"Why the long faces," the sergeant shouts. "We're going to eat and drink, and then we're going to eat and drink again. Until we fall. And we will fall. That's an order, men."

"I want to find me a woman," the Basque cries.

"Me too," says Mole.

"I'd rather drink alone," says Soudan, the romantic.

"Me too," says Rabbit. "I don't want to catch any diseases."

We buy wine and ham from a stand in the square in front of the cathedral. I feel nauseated from all the alcohol and dip my head in the basin under the public water pump. I'm so thirsty! That pickled salmon has left me parched. The men push their way into a rowdy tavern. The place is bursting at the seams. It's as if the entire infantry has crammed into a single pub. The women working inside wear plunging necklines and bright-red lips. They beckon to any man willing to pay for five minutes of love. I stay outside with the sergeant. He doesn't know what to do with himself.

"You're not going in?" he asks.

"In a bit," I say. "I'll wait until things calm down a bit."

He stands there for a moment and looks at me. I smile. He smiles back.

"I don't stand a chance with Mademoiselle Mars," he says suddenly. "She was going on and on in that park. I couldn't get a word in, and I only understood half of what she said."

I nod.

"I'm sure she's already forgotten me," he says.

"Her loss, then," I say.

He smiles at the compliment. He even blushes a little.

"You know something, Binus," he says, but he doesn't finish his sentence.

"What should I know, Sergeant?" I ask.

"You're really something," he says.

"Thank you."

"What's your real name? Your girl's name?"

"I'd rather not say."

He nods.

"I'm not that old yet, you know. I'm only thirty. I've been in the army since I was twenty."

I wonder where in God's name he's going with this.

"Never married," he says. "I didn't have the time for it. Always out on campaign. Always marching into the fire. But you know, someday this war will end, and someday you and I will be just plain old citizens again, and . . ."

He searches for his words. I feel my stomach sink. I'm afraid to hear what's he's going to say next.

"Well, I was wondering if you would, you know, later, ever consider sharing your days with a poor, old sergeant."

He utters the question in one long breath so I can't interrupt him.

"With me, I mean," he adds to be precise, something they teach you in the army.

"Sergeant," I say.

"You can call me Yves. At least, for tonight, now, just this once. Until, well, you know what I mean."

The last thing I expected in the Emperor's army is a marriage proposal. I want to die with shame. The sergeant is my best mate. I'd do anything to make him proud. But mates don't ask for each other's hand in marriage, do they?

"Sergeant," I say without looking at him, "I'm sorry, but I . . . I don't know . . . You're my sergeant . . ."

I don't get any further than that.

"No problem, no problem," Perrec says immediately, as if he's relieved that I rejected him.

"Think nothing of it," he adds quickly. "Forget I ever asked. Just forget it."

I look at him, but now it is he who avoids my gaze. He straightens his uniform and looks toward the rowdy pub full of giggling women and drunken laughter.

"Well," he says finally. "I guess I'll go in, then."

"Give the ladies my regards," I say. "Let me know which one's the prettiest."

He steps up to the entrance, pushes aside a drunken soldier, and pulls open the door. Inside, he's greeted with cheers from the company. Then he disappears into a sea of blue uniforms and colorful dresses.

I stroll through the city. While the Viennese are sleeping, the French are out celebrating. And then, as fate would have it, I spot Mademoiselle Mars, walking arm in arm with a colonel whose mustache is so long he could use it to clean his ears. His magnificent uniform is covered with ribbons and the epaulettes on his shoulders are the size of bricks.

"Mademoiselle Mars," I call after her. The colonel looks extremely annoyed, but Mademoiselle Mars smiles. She recognizes me.

"You are the young man who was with Sergeant Perrec," she says. "How is he?"

"He's in good company, thank you."

I bow politely to the goddess of the Parisian theater. The

colonel looks at me as if he's going to have me executed at dawn.

"I was wondering," I say. "Is your dancer, Mademoiselle Fortuna, in Vienna?"

"Have you forgotten your rank, Corporal? Look at those rags you're wearing!" the colonel says.

"Oh Colonel," Mademoiselle Mars says, "don't forget what Molière wrote in *The Learned Ladies*: 'It's a rag, perhaps, but one of which I am fond.'"

She says it with a broad gesture, and the officers around them nod in unison as if they know Molière's entire oeuvre by heart.

"You'll find Fortuna in the traiteurie in the alley by the Heaven's Gate," she says. "It's just over there. But she's in high company tonight. I'm afraid you don't stand much of a chance. Good luck, Corporal."

I bid her farewell with a bow before one of the officers can ask me which company I belong to and have me put on latrine-digging duty for a month.

I walk down the alley and find the entrance to the restaurant. There are posters advertising concerts hanging on the wall outside. Inside, patrons are eating at tables covered in white tablecloths and drinking wine from elegant glasses. The place is packed with officers in neatly pressed uniforms. But Fortuna must be in there somewhere—Fortuna with the thousand freckles.

24

STANCE

I'm just a lowly infantry corporal, little more than a cannon target. I'm not welcome among these officers and elegantly dressed women. Inside the restaurant, people are talking and shouting. Men in black coats bring dishes to the tables and have to squeeze their way through the crowd of officers standing around chatting and smoking. They flaunt the ribbons and medals on their chests so that everyone can see what great war heroes they are. The place is so full, there's almost no way in.

Forget it, Stance. Why don't you just go join your company at the pub, even if it's just for fun? You can chat with some other young soldier who's not going to get lucky tonight. You can wink and flirt with the girls while your mates from the Fourteenth enjoy themselves. But then I spot Fortuna sitting at a little table in an alcove. I instantly recognize her round cheeks and curly hair. She's sandwiched between a lieutenant and a captain. She's smiling and nodding and talking so giddily that she barely touches her bread and meat. Her hair hangs loose, and her freckles dance on her cheeks. The neckline on her dress reveals the curve of her breasts. Mother would make the sign of the cross at the sight of her. The lieutenant has one arm around her shoulder and the captain has a hand on her arm. She says something that makes the two of them laugh. They release her and gulp down their wine like water. The captain has clearly had too much to drink, and the lieutenant is probably hoping that his superior will collapse soon so that he can have the beautiful dancer all to himself. Mademoiselle Mars was right—Fortuna is as far out of reach as the moon. Suddenly, I feel a hand on my shoulder. I turn around and find myself face-to-face with Captain Lemoine. Judging by the smell of alcohol on his breath, he's already consumed half the wine cellar. He shouts to his fellow hussars that I'm a friend of his.

"This boy was dead with a bullet in his head," he shouts, pointing to the wound under my stovepipe hat. "And then he was kissed back to life by an angel."

The captain is completely intoxicated. His tongue hangs in his mouth like a wet rag, and the hussars have barely understood a word he's said. But the scar on my head says it all.

"This kid single-handedly stopped a gang of deserters and drove them back to camp," he exaggerates. "We shot five of them to set an example."

"Shot?" I repeat in a startled voice, but Lemoine doesn't hear me.

"God loves this kid," he shouts. "He brings his company good luck. And you know what they say in the army—better an ounce of luck than a pound of gold."

An officer hands me a glass of wine. Another one pats me on the shoulder.

I glance to the side, but Fortuna is gone. The seat between the lieutenant and the captain is empty, and they're both just sitting there staring at the wine in their glasses. The crowded restaurant and the smell of alcohol, smoke, and sweat are giving me a headache. Those Godforsaken drummers are at it again. I push through the sea of uniforms and stagger out of the café. I lean against the wall and wipe the tears from my right eye.

It's late, but the streets are far from deserted. Shouts can be heard in all directions. There's not a soldier in the French army who wants to sleep tonight. But I need to put these drummers to bed. I have to get back to the camp and lie down.

"Well, if it isn't my soldier."

All of a sudden, Fortuna is standing in front of me. She pushes back the brim of my hat and touches my scar.

"Looks like you've got a scratch there," she says.

Her fingers are in white gloves. I nod, completely tongue-tied.

"A duel over a woman?" she smiles mischievously. "Or was it to protect your honor?"

"I won the duel," I snap. I don't like the mockery in her voice. She seems haughtier to me this time, with all her jewels and those ribbons in her dark curls.

"My, my, aren't you touchy, soldier," she says.

She looks at me, wondering whether I'm going to say anything else. Whether I'm still that sweet, charming boy from the Grand Tivoli that she almost gave up a glass of lemonade for. Whether I'm going to play another card in this game of seduction, in this bouillotte of love. *Say something,* I hear the drummers roaring in my head, *say something.*

Fortuna glances back at the door to the restaurant. She's starting to get impatient. She wants to go back inside.

"Are you going to perform in Vienna?" I ask.

My throat and lips are as dry as the desert. The words crack in my mouth. The drummers cheer me on.

"In a few days," she says. "After you boys have hammered those Austrians to the ground."

"I hope so."

"The Emperor is here," she says flatly. "The Emperor always wins."

"How have you been?" I ask. "How's your Parisian suitor?"

"Ah, my Charles," she says. "He begged me to stay in Paris. He wanted to drag me down the aisle. But I left with Mademoiselle Mars. The theater comes first. He sends me letters every day, wet with tears. Sometimes the ink is so smudged that I can barely read them. He's even written to my parents to tell them he wants to marry me and that a dowry is not necessary."

"That sounds familiar," I say.

"And then there are all the officers who write to me," she says. "Too many letters to read. My mother in Cologne thinks

I'm mad. She says I'm going to end up a depraved woman, a you-know-what."

"Why did you refuse to marry Charles?" I ask.

She shrugs.

There are shouts from the pub. She looks back at the curved windowpanes and the sea of colors swirling behind them.

"The captain said you were kissed by an angel," she asks.

I nod, slightly embarrassed.

"So how does an angel kiss?" she asks. "I'd really like to know."

Time to retreat. I take a step backward and feel the wall against my back. She comes closer, presses herself against me.

"Well, how does an angel kiss?" she asks.

And then she leans in to kiss me. I turn my face away. The kiss lands on my ear. Everything tingles. I feel her lips all the way down to my toes. She's surprised. I don't dare to look at her.

"Are you afraid of me?" she asks.

"I'm not afraid of anything," I say, trying to sound as tough as I can. "I've fought a duel. I've beaten back wild dogs. I've stopped a gang of deserters in their tracks."

"What a little tough guy you are," she says.

I look at her. Isn't it obvious why she can't kiss me? This beautiful creature with the thousand freckles and the wide mouth? She touches the patch of raw flesh under my hat with her gloved fingers.

"You were lucky," she says.

I nod.

"I'm going back inside, poor soldier," she says.

She tries to turn around, but I grab hold of her hand. She doesn't get it. I bring her hand to my chest. I push it inside my open jacket and under my shirt. To the bandage that has been flattening my breasts for months. I slide her hand under the linen band. I see the shock in her eyes. She pulls back her hand and stares at me, as if God just boxed her ears. She says nothing more. I button my jacket.

"Your lieutenant and captain will be wondering where you are."

"They're too drunk to spell their own names," she says.

I nod. Look around, Stance. It's time to leave. A thousand paces and you'll be back around the campfire where you can lay your head and forget this night ever happened. Just a ten-minute walk. But I can't move.

"Why are you looking away?" she asks. "Don't you dare to look me in the eyes?"

I look her in the eyes. Her light, green eyes. At her freckles dancing on that big nose of hers, at all those teeth in her mouth. She pushes me against the wall. Her breath smells like wine and cloves. She kisses me again. Softly. Not like Fons, who wiggled his tongue around in my mouth as if he were wringing out a wet towel. Her lips are as soft as melting butter.

"I have to go," I say softly.

Her second kiss is fiercer. Our teeth collide. I push her away.

"Wait," I say. "I have to . . . this isn't supposed to . . ."

"Don't be such a girl," she whispers. She pushes her hand through my hair. My stovepipe falls off my head. Her breath is warm, and her tongue explores every nook and cranny in my mouth. Here, in this city with its thirty spires, time stands still. Here, in battered Vienna, robbed of its furniture, paintings, pickled salmon, and musical scores, in this mutilated city, I am being kissed by a woman. I am so parched that there's hardly a drop of saliva left in my mouth. But she quenches my thirst. I drink her in.

Fortuna doesn't go back to the restaurant, and I don't go back to camp. We walk through Vienna like a soldier and his sweetheart, down wide boulevards with tall houses, through squares full of soldiers. We talk incessantly. I love the German sounds in her French. Fortuna's real name is Elise; she is about four years older than I am, and I am not the first woman she's kissed.

"But I must be your first woman soldier," I joke.

And then we stop and kiss again.

We walk right up to the Theater an der Wien, where she'll be performing next week. It's a strict-looking building, angular, with capitals over the windows. We enter through a back door. Then we walk down the dark corridors until we reach the dressing rooms, where we lie together on a divan. The furniture is so narrow that we have to cling to each other's bodies. My limbs are heavy, but I'm not tired. We run our fingers over each other's goosebumps. We laugh, kiss, caress, talk, kiss again, and finally slip into a faint sleep until the early hours of the morning.

◎ ◎ ◎

We wake up to the sound of footsteps in the building. We get up and put our clothes on. It's easier for me than it is for her—just pants, socks, and shoes. My beautiful dancer searches around for her earrings and ring in the cushions of the divan. I hear the church bells strike the hour.

"I have to go back."

She looks at me. I twist the bandage around my breasts and try to wrestle it into a knot.

"No," she says.

"What?" I ask.

"You don't have to go back to the camp at all," she says. "Stay with me."

I can't believe my ears.

"But that's not possible," I say.

"Sure it is," she says. "You're not Binus. You're Stance."

"But my company," I say. "The sergeant, my mates. They need me."

"Don't you get it?" she says. "The Austrian Archduke is right across the Danube with God knows how many horsemen and soldiers and cannons. I'm not going to let you get shot."

"Please, Elise, I have no choice."

"You'd rather give your life for Napoléon? For that tyrant? That monster? The widow-maker of Europe?"

"You don't understand," I say.

"No, you don't understand," she says. "I won't let you go."

"Don't be stupid," I say.

She looks at me, her eyes burning.

"We're going to win," I say sharply. "And then I'll come back."

"I'm German," she says. "They destroyed my country. I don't want you to win at all. I want Napoléon and his army crushed."

"That's treason!" I exclaim.

"What are you going to do about it, Corporal?" she says. "Send me to the firing squad?"

For some reason I can't get the bandage tied around my breasts. I'm even clumsier than Pier the Blunderbuss this morning.

"I can't let my mates down," I say.

"Your mates," she scoffs, her voice dripping with disdain.

"My mates," I repeat proudly.

She stands up furiously, kicks over a table, and buttons up her blouse. Then she sits down in front of a mirror. She sets the red teardrop earrings in front of her.

"Fine. Go," she says.

My dancer pushes her hair to the side and puts an earring through her right earlobe. It's as if I'm already gone.

"Elise, I don't want the best night of my life to end in a fight," I say.

I see her watching me in the mirror.

"Then don't go."

"Don't be such a man," I say. "You have your theater; I have my war."

Her eyes soften.

"I'll come back tonight," I promise.

She doesn't respond. She stands up, takes the bandage out of my hands, and wraps it around my breasts. She helps me put on my shirt and jacket. Then she buttons up the jacket and places the stovepipe on my head. She looks at me.

"You're the most beautiful soldier I've ever seen," she says.

"And you, you . . ."

I want to tell her how beautiful I think she is. I want to say that I'll miss her every second of the day. I want her to know that I'm already longing for the touch of her skin. That I love her. All that sentimental nonsense. But she puts her finger to my lips. She doesn't want to hear promises I can't keep. She kisses me one last time.

"Don't die, beautiful soldier."

I walk the one thousand paces back to camp just as the sun is starting to rise. There are feathers in my shoes and ants in my belly. The only thing that feels heavy is my head. This time I really have been kissed by an angel. The sun peeks up over the tents. That's it, Sun, you better rise and set as quickly as possible because tonight I'm going back into the city. I reach my company and fall asleep in the sand beside the doused campfire. By the time I wake up, it's already afternoon. The sergeant hands me a tin of soup and a piece of fresh baguette to dip into it.

"Long night?" he asks.

I smile and savor the pepper, garlic, and thin strips of meat. I don't ask if it's rat or squirrel.

"Enjoy it," the sergeant says. "Tomorrow we're headed into the fire."

25

STANCE

We pack up our camp in the late afternoon on the twentieth of May in the year one thousand eight hundred and nine. Time to leave Vienna behind. Fortuna, I'm afraid we won't be seeing each other again tonight after all. But maybe tomorrow night or the night after that or even later, after we lay down our weapons and the Archduke of Austria bows to the Emperor. Then I'll come back to the theater, and we'll lie on our divan. Skin to skin.

It's a clear night with a bright moon and thousands of stars. We cross the Danube on the long, floating bridge that the Emperor's engineers have built over the past few days. It's a ramshackle construction, made up of hundreds of boats and rafts in all shapes and sizes tied together with ropes and beams. The water below is as black as ink. The river is high and wild. The rushing rapids thrash and pull at the makeshift bridge beneath our feet; it's as if we're walking along the spine of a monster who wants to shake us off his back. The infantry has to cross first, then the cavalry, followed by the cannons, each one pulled by four horses, and finally the supply wagons loaded with cannonballs, ammunition, and gunpowder. We march across the bridge, and I can't help but feel relieved when we finally step off of it and onto an island in the middle of the Danube.

The island is an untouched wilderness, full of rustling trees as high as towers. They remind me of knotty old sleepless giants, all whispering to each other about the thousands of soldiers passing by. The sounds of waterfowl and frogs fill the night. A pheasant flutters up from the bushes. After half an hour of walking, we arrive at the other side of the island, where a second bridge rigged from boats has been built across the rest of the Danube. This one is shorter. In the moonlight, I can see the silhouettes of two church towers up on the hill, one in each village. We cross the second bridge. On the opposite side are areas where the river has burst from its banks and flooded a field. We march through streams and up the hill until we reach the village of Aspern.

The main street is lined with trees. The houses are low and wide. Roses bloom in the front yards. In the backyards, the tomatoes and cucumbers are probably just starting to grow. There are still bedsheets hanging on the clotheslines—the citizens must have left their homes in a hurry. The two streets in the village lead to a small square, where there's a church with a walled cemetery beside it. We march through the village and down the hill. Before us is a landscape of rolling hills and valleys. The morning is still a ways off. The thin ribbons of smoke floating above the forest are a sign that there's an army of men sitting around campfires in those trees. We stop to rest. I shiver with cold and my eyes sting with fatigue. I fall asleep with my arms wrapped around my shoulders.

By the time someone pokes me awake it's almost light. In front of us is a wide cornfield. The stalks are still green and bushy—it's early in the year. We hear the bells ringing for the first Sunday Mass in Vienna, about five miles away. Then all is quiet again. A silence as heavy as lead. We don't dare to disturb it. The entire army moves up the road that connects Aspern to the neighboring village of Essling. The villages are at least a mile apart, but the road is completely packed. The thousands of cavalrymen are dressed as if they're going to a ball and carrying heavy sabers and lances. Their helmets and weapons sparkle in the morning sunlight. We grip our muskets as if we're afraid we might drop them. We've put new flints in our flintlocks. We've counted our cartridges and spare flints at least ten times. Our bayonets—our fourchettes—hang on our belts, sharpened with stones.

There are no drumrolls or trumpets. All we can hear is the chirping of the birds. There's no enemy in sight. All we can do is wait. The Basque and Bouchon have set up their chessboard in the grass and are playing a game. The morning hours slowly creep by.

"Battle is so boring," Mole says as he entertains us with

stories about the mines, claiming that his snot used to be as black as coal.

Geoff Soudan pulls a sausage out of his rucksack.

"Nom de Dieu!" Rabbit exclaims. "Look who brought breakfast."

"Of course," says Geoff. "We can't fight on an empty stomach, now can we?"

We each take a piece of Geoff's sausage.

Cor the Dutchman lies down on the side of the road. "Wake me up when the Austrians get here," he says in his broken French.

The whole scene reminds me of one Sunday in Ghent. The day that the six of us—me, Father, Mother, Pier, Rozeken, and Eddy—headed out of the city gates and walked along the creeks under the pollard willows, where the birds were building their nests. A spring day a thousand years ago, it seems.

The drummer is bored to death. He jumps up every few minutes and cranes his neck to see if the enemy is here yet.

"Stop fidgeting," says Sergeant Perrec.

As the morning drags on, we run out of things to talk about. Up in the white church tower with the black slate roof, the marshal is scanning the area with a telescope. Mole kisses an amulet with a drawing of his sweetheart inside. Rabbit twiddles the silver coin his mother gave him for his First Communion between his fingers. Bouchon rubs a pendant of Our Lady. His rough fingers have buffed away the image on the plate over the years. The sergeant is sucking on the pebble from his old harbor in Brittany, as if he hopes to draw some kind of taste out of it. Geoff Soudan uses an old pencil to write yet another letter to his child, whom he's never met and maybe never will. He has already asked me if I could deliver the letters to his son or daughter if he dies. My sweetheart's name is Lucie, he says, and he tells me where she lives. But of course, I already know all about Lucie from the gossip on the washing rafts. Then I tell him we actually know each other from Ghent, that he visited my father's saw factory once. He looks at me for a moment and then smiles.

"You're the inventor's daughter," he says. "You were there with your brother. You're Constance."

"Don't tell anyone," I say.

Off in the distance, I hear the bells of Vienna striking noon. I put my hand in my pocket. Inside is the bullet that cracked my skull, the one that almost killed me. I roll the lead musket ball around in my fingers as if it is my amulet. I kiss the portrait of Saint Rita around my neck. Two good luck charms are better than one. I look back and see that the marshal is no longer standing in the tower with his telescope. He rushes out of the church waving his arms, shouting orders I can't hear. The sergeant has seen it too.

"They're coming," he says.

Bouchon looks up from his chess game.

"Can't they wait a minute?" he says. "I've almost won."

"That's what you think," the Basque says.

"Five moves and you're in checkmate," Bouchon says.

"On your feet, men!" the sergeant shouts. "On your feet. Stand tall."

Bouchon sighs and puts the pieces in the wooden box.

Cor the Dutchman stands up. He's the tallest one of all of us. He's worried they'll aim for his head first. One time he told me that whenever a pub fight breaks out, he's always the first one hit simply because he's so big.

The last one on his feet is Bouchon. He puts his chess set in his rucksack. All is quiet again. My throat is in a knot.

They're coming.

We see them approaching over the hill. Their black headgear bobs above the green lines in the landscape. Their bayonets glint in the sun. They come without drums. Without shouts. A line of silent, white uniforms. The first line is soon followed by a second. And then a third, a fourth. No problem, I think; we've got four lines of infantry behind us in the village. But then comes a fifth line. A sixth. They keep appearing over the top of the hill, line after line. I count ten of them. Now I understand why the marshal was waving his arms. There are a lot more of them than there are of us. The lines disappear behind a gentle slope only to suddenly reappear. In the undulating landscape, it's hard for us to estimate how close they are. Is it two miles? Or a mile and a half? Or is it less than a mile? No one says a word. I recall the image of myself standing in front of the mirror. Stance the Bride with her white teeth, dark-blue dress, and her mother's silver hairpin. But when I think back to Lieven groaning on top of me like an old boar, I know where I'd rather be—here, in this green cornfield in the sun, with death marching toward me. I am not that bride anymore. I'm the soldier who got shot in the head and lived to tell the tale.

I'm Ironhead.

"Mes enfants," the sergeant roars. "Today's the day we fight against tyranny. Against the kings, dukes, and counts who don't care if we starve, who would have us believe that we are no more than beasts. We fight against the Church that wants control of our souls and to tell us what is sin and what is not. We are fighting for a new age. There is no middle way. Freedom, equality, or death. We are freedom. We are the Revolution. We are the best infantry in the world. Long live the Emperor!"

"Vive l'Empereur!" we shout.

Mole shoulders his rifle.

"Hold your fire, Mole," the sergeant shouts. "Don't waste the Emperor's gunpowder."

Mole points the barrel of his rifle back toward the ground.

I catch the sergeant's eye. He gives me a confident wink.

After all, we are the voltigeurs. The acrobats. The tumblers. We charge. We spread out, running down one hill and up the next, and then we see them coming. They march calmly. None of them seem to be in a hurry to finish us off. They trust their bayonets, which are so shiny you'd think they've never been used. Their uniforms are as white as chalk. They're less than a hundred yards from us now. The sergeant raises his saber. We shoulder our muskets. Then he swings it down: "Fire!"

We fire a hundred men at a time. The butt of my gun slams back into my shoulder. For a moment, I think I might've broken a bone. A cloud of black smoke hangs in front of us.

The air stinks of burning sulfur, coal, and saltpeter. I have no idea if I've hit anything. I run forward, tear a cartridge with my teeth, throw gunpowder into the barrel, flip down the frizzen, and ram the cartridge into the barrel—with the right side down this time. I'll never make that mistake again. I fire like a machine. After fifty seconds, my Charlesville is loaded again. But there is no wind to clear the smoke, and we can't see the white uniforms we're supposed to be aiming at. But I point my gun in the direction of the Austrians and fire. And then I load again. And shoot again. The Austrians charge and fire back, but we throw ourselves to the ground. And after their salvo is finished, we jump to our feet and fire again. Finally, I hear the Emperor's daughters roar. One by one, they spew fire and lead at the lines in front of us.

Fons. His face shoots through my mind.

We fire again and again, until our drums start to rumble. The pas de charge, played by a band of twelve-year-old drummers, echoes over the hills. It's the attack march that pushed the Emperor's soldiers forward from Portugal to Poland, from Egypt to Lisbon. The drumroll that makes the enemies of the Revolution tremble in their boots. The French infantry is coming. Ten companies, at least. We, the voltigeurs, run down the ridge and join them. A moment later we're marching in their ranks, side by side or single file—rows and rows and rows. We form lines that stretch across the cornfield. There are more than a thousand of us. We are a wall.

We want blood, the drums roll. *We are ruthless. We will stop at nothing.*

"Marchons!" shout the sergeants. "Forward march!"

The drums give us courage. We stand shoulder to shoulder. Straight as candles. We screw our bayonets to the ends of our muskets and carry them upright in front of our bodies. We march forward. Not too fast. Not too slow. At just the right pace. Into the fire and steel. "Vive l'Empereur!" we shout over and over again, as if the cry will make us invincible. The ground is soft and uneven. The corn is thick.

"One line!" the sergeants shout at anyone who falls out of step. We march through the black clouds of gun smoke until we see the white uniforms again. But they are not in formation anymore. They're running in all directions.

The Austrian troops are panicking. Their officers are shouting. They're supposed to hold their ranks, but they can't. The cannonballs have ripped through the front line, bounced across the ground, and continued their slaughter in the lines behind them. From the second to the tenth, leaving blood and bodies behind them. This is the first battle the Austrian infantry has seen. As it is for me and many men in my company. But our sergeants and corporals have seen every corner of Europe. They know what they're doing. We march on to the next hill. Sergeant Perrec shouts orders. We stop, kneel, and shoulder our Charlesvilles, each one loaded with a deadly, lead musket ball.

"Aim low!" Perrec shouts.

We fire. Then comes the black smoke. The smell of rotten eggs. We reload. Marchons! Marchons! But then we hear the trumpets blast. Beyond the cornfield, at the edge of the forest, I see them coming out of the trees by the dozens, no, by the hundreds—horsemen. The Austrian cavalry. They appear out of nowhere, like spirits of the forest brought to life by the sound of the horns. They are the hussars, light cavalry without helmets or breastplates. They look shiny and new in their dark-green jackets covered with ribbons. Their tall hats each have a plume in the middle that sticks straight up like an exclamation point. The cavalry dresses for war as if it were Easter Sunday.

The horses form one long line at the edge of the forest. The trumpet blares and the riders pound their spurs into their horses' flanks. They kick the animals into a gallop. Together they roar and extend their right arms. Their saber arms. The long, curved blades of their heavy sabers sparkle in the sun. The sabers they'll use to break heads and split shoulders. Cavalry sabers are like chopping axes. The ground beneath our feet trembles as the hooves trample through the corn. They charge at us like a tidal wave of flesh and steel. There is nowhere to hide. No wall to protect us. No moat. Not even a cluster of trees.

We're trapped.

26

PIER

The road from Paris to Vienna is crowded with traffic. Carts carrying ammunition and wine, carriages of all shapes and sizes, postal wagons, groups of hussars and cuirassiers—they're being pulled to Vienna like nails to a magnet. I let myself be carried by the current. Achilles almost seems young again. The old horse is reinvigorated by the new horizons, the clean mountain air, the mossy smell of the forest, and the fresh spring thistles along the side of the road, which seem to grow more tender and delicious as we travel. Achilles can easily cover sixty miles a day. I, on the other hand, am getting tired of the road. My behind is covered with blisters, and my spine is as stiff as the Latin school benches. The leather portfolio is safely buckled in the saddlebag that never leaves my side. I buy soup and bread at the inns, use the saddlebag as a pillow, and sleep in the stables next to

Achilles so no one can steal my swift-footed steed. Somewhere in Bavaria, we stay in a barn that doesn't have any hay or oats. I remember how Stance used to feed him newspaper sometimes, so I tear a page out of the Bible that Mother gave me, and Achilles eagerly grinds it down with his teeth. He's just barely swallowed it, and he's nudging me with his head for more. That night, Achilles consumes the entire book of Genesis. Only then is he satisfied. The next day we continue along the valleys and mountain trails, and every night Achilles begs for more Holy Scripture. By the time we get to Regensburg, he has finished the entire Old Testament. By Linz, Paul's Letters have been devoured too. By the time I see the towers of Vienna on the morning of the twenty-first of May, all that's left is the Book of Revelation.

The day is warm. It almost feels like summer. There are no clouds. Not a breath of wind. At the city gate, an unshaven French corporal checks my papers. I ask the good man if he knows where I might find the Emperor. He gives me a serious look and says that the Emperor has not yet communicated his plans for the day to him. Another soldier, who is checking a grocer's papers, finds his remark incredibly funny. The corporal tells me to come back in a few hours. Perhaps he'll have received some news from His Imperial Highness by then. At that, his friend bursts into laughter. The corporal, too, chokes back a coughing fit. I'm annoyed. You just wait, you nitwit. I'll get those hundred thousand francs from the Emperor. We'll see who's laughing then, jackass! But I remain polite and pull Achilles by the reins.

◎ ◎ ◎

"Your first love was the cannon, Your Highness," my proposal begins. "You grew up with the cannon at your side. It is thanks to your artillery and, of course, your genius and perseverance that you have become the Master of Europe. You already rule the Continent from Lisbon to Warsaw. Now is the time to conquer the Seven Seas. Here, in this portfolio, I have the plans for a new cannon, a revolutionary weapon that will make you the Emperor of the Waves."

The fingers of Napoléon the First will tremble as he takes the papers into his hands. He will look at the sketches of Hoste's Cannon with awe. He will read theoretical explanations and—being as versed in mathematics and geometry as he is—he will nod. He will understand that the future of artillery is before him, that this revolutionary invention will reduce the English navy to fish food. He will close the portfolio, take off his hat, and look at me with glistening eyes. Then he'll stand up and take me in his arms, squeeze my ears, and whisper, "I am proud of you, Pieter Hoste." Tears come to my eyes just thinking about it.

All I have to do is find him.

I walk through Vienna with Achilles at my heels. The city seems deserted. The stench of excrement and spoiled food drifts from the alleyways. In the distance, I hear the roar of thunder. There are hardly any soldiers in sight. All the stores are closed. There's no army here. Two women hastily shut their front door behind them. I want to ask them if they know where the French troops are, but they quickly walk off in the other direction. One is still wearing her apron; the other has her sleeves rolled up. Their clogs click against the paving stones. In the square, a group of children dash through the streets behind the women. They're carrying sticks, drums, and shields, ready to play battle. No one has time for questions. Everyone is rushing in the same direction. The thunderstorm in the distance is now a steady rumble. I walk toward the south side of the city. There's a burnt smell in the streets that makes Achilles restless. I have to jerk on the reins like an idiot to get him to follow me. We walk past collapsed houses and through streets filled with rubble.

Then I see where all the people are going in such a hurry. They're crowded up on the crumbling city walls with weeds growing out of the cracks. They seem to be watching something going on outside the city walls. I tie Achilles's reins to a tree limb and walk up the wooden stairs to the ramparts. At the top, there's an optician renting telescopes.

"One franc a minute," he shouts.

"I'll take one," says one of the spectators.

I push through the crowd and look over the battlements. The Danube glides through the valley like an animal, heavy and wild. There are white rapids in the water. And to the left of the river, about three or four miles south of town, a battle is underway. The rumbling I heard wasn't an approaching thunderstorm; it was cannon fire. Over the light-green hills, clouds of gun smoke hang like black mist. Flames shoot out of cannons. A village is on fire. A few women with binoculars are watching the battlefield.

There's so much pushing and shoving that I almost get knocked off the wall. A man takes my place. I pass one franc to the optician at the top of the stairs, and he hands me a telescope. I hold the heavy brass contraption up to my right eye. At first everything is blurry, but then I see the French cavalry lined up on the road beyond the burning village. Their brightly colored uniforms and plumes are easy to spot. The sun sparkles on the cuirassiers' armor. The green fields are teeming with white uniforms and, across from them, blue uniforms. To the right of the battlefield, where the Danube bends, is a large, wooded island in the middle of the river. Thousands upon thousands of French cavalry and infantry are stuck on the right bank while the battle rages across the river. They seem to be waiting to cross a bridge. On the bridge, soldiers are trying desperately to keep the sloops that are being pulled downstream by the current from hitting the bridge. One of the sloops crashes into the bridge in a spinning motion, causing the structure to break in half. Several men fall into the water. A cheer rises from the crowd on the wall. A portion of the bridge is swept away by the current.

"He's trapped," one of the Viennese citizens hollers. "The Emperor is trapped!"

The optician takes the telescope from my hands and passes it to someone else. Everyone around me is shouting their commentary. Based on what they're saying, I understand that the Austrians lured the Emperor across the Danube. Then they sent sloops full of stones down the river to sabotage the bridge. In other words, they managed to split the French army in half. And if the Emperor doesn't get his reinforcements, his men are done for. But the Viennese won't be cheering for long. The Emperor has never lost a battle on the mainland. His engineers will repair the bridge, and the army will cross the Danube and rip the Austrians to shreds. And then I'll take my father's plans to the Emperor and remind him that the cannon was his first love and that, one day, he'll rule the seas as well. I wriggle out of the crowd of spectators and run down the stairs to where Achilles is gorging himself on Viennese thistles.

"Come, my swift-footed steed," I say as I climb onto his back. "We are going to find the Emperor."

27

STANCE

The avalanche of horses thunders toward us. Their hooves don't even seem to touch the ground. We don't have time to gather and form a group. We're scattered in a sprawling line hundreds of yards long. The Austrian cavalry hold their sabers out in front of them. I'll never see Fortuna's thousand freckles again. The sergeant doesn't order us to fire, or maybe he does and I can't hear it over the roar of the horses. Rabbit is one of the first to shoot. A rider tumbles from his horse. I crash into Cor.

Another rider comes charging at us. His horse is monstrous. Only the biggest stallions are used in the cavalry. Cor and I both fire at the same time. One of us hits him in the arm. The other misses. The hussar drops his sword, but the horse storms forward. It charges at us and knocks us off our feet. A hoof hits Cor in the thigh. A second rider is coming for us. We dig the butts of our muskets into the ground, pull in our heads and shoulders, and point our bayonets up like spears, six feet in the air. There is no time for a Hail Mary. The rider turns his horse away in the nick of time and lowers his heavy saber. At that moment, Cor raises his musket just a little bit, and the saber chops the weapon in half. Then the rider swings his saber again and cuts a gash into Cor's long body. The Dutchman is so surprised he doesn't even scream. I stick my bayonet into the rider's thigh and pull it back out. The man howls. I see his saber barreling toward my arm. But he misses—the blade only tears the sleeve off my jacket. I duck, dive into a somersault, and land under the giant horse. Cor tries to get up—God, what a wound!—and the Austrian jerks his horse forward. He raises his saber to beat Cor's brain to fricassee. I pull back my bayonet and thrust the foot-and-a-half-long blade into the horse's belly. The animal whinnies and rears up. I roll out from under the beast. Its legs flail around me and just miss my head. The horse falls and rolls onto its back. I hear the rider's bones crack. The animal continues to kick and cry.

Another hussar struggles to get his horse under control. The animal is wild from the smell of blood. As soon as the hussar catches sight of me, he slams his spurs into the horse's sides. He raises his bloody saber, but he doesn't see my mate, Cor. The great Dutchman, the biggest man in our company, wields his musket by the barrel and slams the butt into the rider's face. He hits him straight in the eye. The hussar's hat falls down into the grass. He pulls his horse away. Away from us. Away from this doom. Away from this trampled, blood-splattered cornfield. He rides off into the forest. The hussars are regrouping for another attack. Cor slumps to the ground.

"Come on, Cor, don't lie down now," I call out.

He looks at me, his eyes dark with fear. The gash runs all the way down his chest. I can see the white of his ribs.

"Get up!" I call. If he doesn't get up now, he'll be food for the crows.

"Gather up, men!" the sergeant shouts.

My Charlesville is crushed under the horse kicking in agony. I pick up the rifle of a fallen soldier and rush over to the sergeant. Everywhere I look are the bodies of dead linemen. The wounded groan in pain. They cry out for help. They cry out for their mothers. They curse the Emperor. The wounded will have to fend for themselves, for helping someone means sacrificing yourself. The air reeks of blood and shit and rotten eggs. We gather around our sergeant.

"Line up!" shouts Rabbit. "Three lines."

"Load your weapons!" the sergeant shouts.

My heart nearly stops as I carry out the twelve movements. My fingers tremble. I rip open the cartridge with my teeth, taste the salty gunpowder, and ram the cartridge down into the barrel. I watch the horsemen at the edge of the forest. How they bring their horses under control, how they line up again, how their officer shouts orders. I cock my new gun. It's loaded. There are about forty of us.

"Gather up!" the sergeant shouts.

Infantrymen run toward us. The sergeant pushes them into position.

"Load! Load!" he keeps saying.

Cor, leaning on his rifle, inches toward us, step by step. He moves as if he's walking through water, slow and laborious.

"Come on, Holland!" I call out. "Don't be so pathetic. It's just a scratch, man. Not even big enough to write home about."

"I can't write," he moans.

Other infantrymen, two hundred yards away, are scrambling to regroup too. The trumpets signal the second charge. The braying of horses can be heard from a couple hundred yards away. The Austrian hussars shout. The hooves thunder. The ground trembles. The avalanche of horses comes roaring at us again.

My sergeant, the Breton, didn't spend ten years in the army to die in this wretched cornfield. We're all depending on him. He knows how to lead his men.

"First line, kneel!" he shouts. "Second line, stand! Shoulder your weapons! If you fire before I give the order I'll shoot you myself! Only the first and second lines shoot!"

He grips his saber and holds it high.

A few more infantrymen join our ranks. He points them to their positions.

"Third line!" the sergeant orders. "Load!"

Cor finally reaches our group and is pulled to the center. He falls to the ground.

The horses are galloping. Side by side. They cling to one another, as if they're offering one another support. As if they're sharing one another's hopes and fears. The riders cheer one another on. They keep their knees clamped against the horses' flanks. Their arms are outstretched with their heavy sabers, ready to split skulls and slice bodies once again.

"Hold your fire!" the sergeant shouts.

The horses come closer and closer. I can smell them. I can see the whites of their bulging eyes, the snot dripping from their giant nostrils.

"Hold your fire!" he calls again. I can see the hussars' faces. They grit their teeth, as if clenching away their doubts.

"Fire!" the sergeant orders with a giant swing of his sword so that everyone in our group—including the deaf and the village idiots—understands the signal.

We pummel them with lead. There's no missing the target. Our musket balls rip through dust, flesh, muscle, and bone. The first row of cavalry collapses. The horses behind them stumble over the fallen men. We hunch down and slam the butts of our muskets into the ground, raising our bayonets like a hedge of steel for any rider who dares to try to leap over the dead and break our ranks with his saber. But that doesn't happen. The hussars who try get a bullet from the third line shooting over our heads. I stand back up and look to the right and see that the company beside us wasn't so lucky. They too set up three rows deep, but they were crushed by the hussars. The sabers are crashing down, splitting their skulls and shoulders. There's nothing we can do.

"Reload!" the sergeant shouts. "And round up every cartridge box you can find."

◎ ◎ ◎

We march in formation back to Aspern. The Basque and Bouchon help Cor, who's still bleeding heavily.

"March!" they yell at him. "March, or you'll die." Cor dribbles his feet the best he can between Bouchon and the Basque. I pick up two cartridge boxes and hang them around my shoulders. I pick up a cavalry saber but quickly let it drop. My God, that thing is heavy! I hear the trumpets again. Another charge. But this time we're ready. We turn around and line up again. Four lines deep this time. The first line kneels. The second remains standing. We shoulder our weapons and pull back the locks. We hold up our left thumbs beside the barrels and take aim. We are a wall. This time the horses slow their charge. The hussars steer them away when they see us in formation, ready to treat them to another round of iron and lead. The horsemen make a wide turn, but some of them are already within shooting range.

"First line, fire!" shouts the sergeant. Three horsemen and two horses go down.

"Reload!" the sergeant commands. "Turn around and march!"

We reload as we march. We move up the hill toward the village. Another charge is coming. We turn back and see the horsemen charging across the flattened cornfield. We move back into our lines, and at a hundred and fifty yards they're already pulling out.

"Turn around and march!"

◎ ◎ ◎

Fifteen minutes later we reach the cemetery wall in Aspern. We're exhausted. Our faces are black with gunpowder. The eyelashes on my right eyelid have been singed off. My face burns where the flaming powder licked my skin. All the houses are on fire. A tower of black smoke rises from the village. I think of the cucumbers, the tiny green tomatoes, the laundry hanging on the lines in the backyards. The flames are eating through the attics. Only the thick stone walls are left standing. The heat from the glowing embers makes the sweat drip down my face. The streets are covered in a layer of ash. Cannonballs are lodged in the walls of houses. Only the church is still intact. My legs feel like they weigh a thousand pounds. I look around and search for my friends. They're all there. We grin at the sight of one another's black, exhausted faces: Geoff Soudan; Mole; the Basque; Rabbit; Bouchon from Gascony; and even Cor the Dutchman, who is being helped onto a cart. All of a sudden, a cannonball explodes over the cemetery—a shell full of nails. Blood sprays as five men fall to the ground. They scream. We run between the toppled graves to the church. Behind the church wall we catch our breath. The cannons continue to bombard the churchyard. I see an entire headstone fly into the air.

"Clean your muskets!" the sergeant shouts.

Some of the guys open their pants and pee down the barrels of their muskets. I think of my nozzle, but there's no time. Bouchon grabs my musket and pees into the barrel. Then I push a rag down the barrel with my ramrod and pull it out again. It's completely black.

In the direction of the other village, I hear trumpets and

see the French cuirassiers charging with their armor, helmets, and plumes. The cuirassiers are the army's battering rams. They're the best horsemen in the cavalry. They thunder up the hill, straight into the cannon fire. Come on, win, I think, make those Austrians drop their weapons and run. Somewhere in the village a house collapses. We hear drumrolls, trumpet blasts, and creaking—the endless creaking of thousands of muskets. The sergeant joins us and tells us that the bridge is broken. We have to hold out until it's repaired. I look around the corner of the church at the flattened green cornfield in front of the village. The Austrian foot soldiers are forming lines again. They march over the hills, which are already strewn with bodies. They're coming back.

There are shouts. Wine barrels are rolled out onto the main street and set upright. An officer smashes them open one by one with an ax. The salty gunpowder, the heat of the burning houses, and the clouds of black smoke make our throats drier than those of Moses's followers after forty years of wandering the desert. Some men take their cups out of their rucksacks and fill them up with wine, drink them empty, and fill them again. I don't have a cup anymore, so I make one with my hands and drink like a madman. I am the goddess of parched men. I slurp up cup after cup after cup. I even splash the wine into my face. When I finally take a step back, the whole world is spinning. Behind us, muskets crack to life. The Austrian infantry, the white uniforms, are climbing over the cemetery wall and entering the square.

"Come on, mes enfants!" an infantry lieutenant shouts.

"We'll drive them back. Give 'em a kick in the ass. Vive l'Empereur!"

"Vive l'Empereur!" we roar. Suddenly, our fatigue is gone. We laugh in the face of the enemy. And we, the men of the line, fresh with courage from the wine, form a blue wall and charge at the enemy. And every time I see one of my comrades collapse, my fury grows, and I shout louder. I don't even realize that I'm running out in front. I don't shoot at the line of white uniforms. I charge at them with my bayonet. I feel the bullets whizzing past me. One of them rips my jacket and shaves off a bit of skin. It only makes me angrier.

The clash is gruesome, but I know what to do. I don't think. I stab, I kick, I yank my bayonet out of one body and into another. I whack away a saber with the butt of my gun. I stay on my feet. I stab again and duck. I'm standing at the edge of life and eternity, and my mates are standing there with me. They, too, are machines. We keep each other standing. Anyone who falls we pull up again. Warm blood gushes. Sabers clank and chop. Men scream. Soldiers fall. A corporal vomits blood. A lieutenant cries for his mother. One soldier tries to crawl away. Another one plays dead. The sergeant hacks at the Austrians with his sword like a savage. They start to give in, and ultimately they retreat. We run after them. They jump over the wall. The graveyard is ours again.

"Reload!" Rabbit shouts. We run back into the graveyard, or what's left of it. Just about every cross and headstone has fallen, and right in the middle, where a grenade exploded, there's a coffin sticking out of the ground. It's been blasted open, and there's nothing—not even a skull—left inside. As if the skeletons have fled too. The Austrians don't know where to go; they're gathered at the foot of the hill. They try to line up again, but we aim and fire. We drive them even farther back. Then they flee. We shout after them and cheer.

"This time we'll keep the graveyard!" shouts Rabbit.

We are surrounded by the dead, both above and below the ground.

Why is Rabbit shouting orders? Where's the sergeant?

I look around to make sure they're all still there. My mates. I see Mole, Soudan, Bouchon, and the Basque. But I don't see the sergeant. I look back, and that's when I spot him bent over a broken tombstone. I rush over to him. Blood is gushing from a hole in his throat—so much blood. His eyes are full of anger and despair. He grins when he sees me. He can no longer speak. He pulls me close and kisses me. I taste his lips—they're salty with gunpowder and sweet with blood. Then he collapses. His body slides off the headstone. My sergeant is dead. I sink down on the grave. The headstone says Weber, but this is the grave of Yves Perrec, sergeant of the Fourteenth.

A shell explodes in full flight, sending shards and nails flying in all directions. The Austrians have their cannons pointed at the cemetery. The soldiers who were entrenched in the village rush in to fill our ranks.

"Stand your ground, men, stand your ground!" a captain shouts.

"I'm out of cartridges!" Soudan exclaims.

"Me too!" shouts Mole.

"Where are the reinforcements? Where's the ammunition?" shouts the Basque.

"Stay calm," says Rabbit. "We just have to hold on until nightfall."

"With what?" shouts Soudan. "Are we supposed to throw rocks or something?"

The cemetery wall is all but destroyed. But we have to hold out. Show them that the French army does not give up. We raise our muskets and bayonets. We make ourselves look big. A cannon blasts, and a second later another cannonball bounces across the cemetery. It rips a man in two and then smashes into the church. There it remains—a lead ball, dripping with blood. I pee in my pants. How many cannons are pointed at us, right now? Two? Four? Surely no more than five. It takes half an hour to reload a cannon. We have to hold on. Stand our ground. Behind us, the village is burning. We're in hell. The sun is going down. Come on, let it get dark. Hundreds of yards away in the field, we see another flame blast from a cannon. A moment later we hear the bang.

"That one's for us," cries Mole, who's standing at the front.

"I'm right behind you!" shouts the Basque. "I'm not going anywhere."

"And I'm behind you!" I shout. "Let the Devil come."

The shell explodes in the graveyard. Two men go down. Blood spurts. A third soldier hits the ground, trying to hold in his intestines. I stick my hand in my pocket and touch my lucky charm. My lead musket ball. I start to pray. Please, God, let it get dark. Let it be night soon. A few minutes later there's another boom. Mole shouts that this one is for us too. "So be it," the Basque yells back. "Let the Devil come," I roar.

And this time, Mole is right.

The cannonball knocks off his head, slams the Basque square in the chest and tears my arm to pieces. I see the blood pour around me. I fall into the blackness, into the bottomless pit where the monster is waiting for me.

28

PIER

By the time the cannons fall silent, it is evening. I reach the Emperor's army at the foot of the pontoon bridge over the Danube. Hundreds of carts full of supplies and ammunition are standing idle. Tens of thousands of soldiers and horsemen are lying around in the grass, waiting for the bridge to be repaired. I can just barely make out the names on the sloops in the semi-darkness: *Sonntagsruhe* and *Die schöne Donau*. It's as if these Viennese summer boats now being used as a bridge are mocking the French army. Tonight, with its dark waters and foaming rapids, the blue Danube is anything but calm and beautiful. The river is eating away at its own banks, and the broken pontoon bridge dances atop the raging waters. I let Achilles stop for a drink. I crouch down and wash my hands in the water. Even here on the bank, I can feel the strength of the current.

◎ ◎ ◎

Soaking-wet soldiers frantically try to weave the barges together with ropes. They anchor the boats in the raging river with cannonballs. Officers use telescopes to track the Austrians, who continue to send boats loaded with stones and massive tree trunks down the river. They pick up speed in the swirling current and come spinning toward the bridge. Upstream, the engineers have stretched chains to stop the treacherous projectiles from hitting their makeshift construction, and soldiers pull them to shore with boat hooks. Every sloop that's captured is welcomed with cheers and used to repair the battered bridge. Soon it will be fixed, and tomorrow the rest of the French army will be able to cross the river. All of a sudden, for a split second, I see him. There, on a white horse on the island in the middle of the Danube—Emperor Napoléon. The tens of thousands of men on the bank shout, "Vive l'Empereur!" I stand up and wave at him like an idiot. Then he's gone, disappeared into the island's wilderness.

The hills around Vienna are lit by a crescent moon and thousands of stars. Here and there, fires burn. People are eating, drinking, and smoking. A lancer comes up to me. His helmet is dirty, and his lance is two meters long. He tells me his horse got sick and died. He needs another one for tomorrow's attack. He offers me five francs, a ridiculous sum. Even for an old bag of bones like Achilles.

"My horse is not for sale," I say. "And Achilles isn't

much of a charger. He'll run off at the first sound of the cannon."

But the man doesn't listen. He thrusts a silver Napoléon into my hand and takes hold of Achilles's reins.

"He's not for sale!" I shout and snatch the reins out of his hands. The lancer pulls off his helmet and hits me in the head with it. I feel the blow all the way down to my knees. I fall down in the grass. For a moment, I can't breathe. The lancer pulls Achilles with him. The horse's tail swings back and forth, and I watch his stupid hindquarters plod off into the night.

"Achilles, stop!" I shout.

And praise the Lord, Saint Peter, and Saint Mark—Achilles actually stops! The lancer pulls on the reins, but my Scripture-munching steed, my Greek hero, the terror of Troy, won't budge. I rip out the last chapter of my Bible, the Book of Revelation, and wave it in the air.

Achilles tries to walk toward me. The lancer curses and pulls at the reins. A couple of artillerymen playing cards look up, annoyed.

"Let go of that animal!" I shout. "It's mine."

"Shut your trap!" the lancer shouts. "This horse is mine. I paid you for it."

"Five francs for a horse," I screech. "You're out of your mind, you dirty thief!"

Then Achilles stomps his hoof on the lancer's foot. The man screams in pain and drops his weapon. What a brilliant old clodhopper that Achilles is.

The foot soldiers and cavalrymen lying in the grass laugh at the lancer, which doesn't improve his mood. I run to Achilles and take hold of his reins. The lancer, limping and cursing, picks up his lance and points it at me. The tip dances in front of my chest. There are red-and-green ribbons hanging below the blade.

"Let go of those reins!" he shouts.

But I haven't traveled a thousand miles to be robbed by some plumed soldier with a spear.

"Enough!" shouts a man wearing a uniform covered in ribbons and medals. He has stars on his epaulettes.

"This here farmer's son won't sell me his horse, Major," shouts the lancer.

The major looks at me as if I were a bug that's just crawled out from under a rock. But I give it everything I've got.

"I have traveled a thousand miles to see the Emperor," I say. "My father is a mechanical engineer who has designed a new cannon. I have the plans with me. I have explicit instructions to present them to Napoléon the First."

"He's mad," the lancer shouts. "Absolutely insane."

The major walks up to me. His buttons sparkle in the moonlight. He has a giant mustache and an earring in his ear. He's from the Emperor's Guard; he's one of the Immortals.

"Plans?" he repeats.

I take off my coat and pull out the portfolio from under my shirt. I untie the three strings and hand the papers to the major. It's risky, I know that. The major could simply say thank you and promise to deliver them to the Emperor and send me home. And my father would never see a cent of his one hundred thousand francs. The major opens the cover and calls over a lieutenant with a lantern. He flips through the sixty-three sheets of paper. Finally, he closes the portfolio and hands it back to me.

"I'll make sure you see the Emperor," he says.

Then he turns to the lancer and tells him to leave me alone. The man sulks off in search of another horse to buy for five francs. Good luck, numbskull!

The men around the campfire look at me. They're all grinning. One of them says, "Good job, kid."

I am awakened by the shouting of men. In the moonlight, I see a cart full of equipment being pulled across the bridge. The bridge creaks. The weight of the cart almost pushes the sloops underwater. In the middle of the bridge, the horses stop. The drivers shout and jerk the reins until the horses move forward again. The crossing is slow. An entire army is waiting. Most of the cavalry are still lying in the grass. All of a sudden, we hear a cannon fire across the river. One of the two armies has launched an offensive in the dark of night.

Morning comes, and the stars disappear. The army is still crossing the river. The major seeks me out in the crowd.

"Come with me," he says, and I pull Achilles behind me. At the bridge, there is a line of men with horses. We wait.

"That water looks pretty wild," I say, but the major doesn't reply. Then it's our turn to cross. I pull on Achilles's reins. We step onto the bridge. I walk with my horse beside the major's.

The water below our feet foams and sputters. Downstream, it spirals into whirlpools. The wood groans. The chains clatter. We are exactly halfway across the bridge when they sound the alarm.

"Arrêtez, arrêtez!" I hear someone behind me shout. The horsemen behind me try to turn around on the narrow bridge. The major and the men ahead of me rush forward with their horses. I look upstream and can't believe my eyes. The Austrians have dragged an entire barn or mill onto a set of barges and lit the whole thing on fire. A tower of burning wood is barreling down the river toward the pontoon bridge. In front of me, there's a clear path across. Behind me, men with sticks are running up the bridge to try to stop the behemoth.

"Get out of here," they call, and I yank on Achilles's reins. But he won't budge. My swift-footed steed refuses to take another step on those wobbly planks. The boats under our feet bob up and down in the raging water. The animal stares at the burning tower growing larger and larger as it approaches. The fire roars and crackles. Hissing chunks of wood crash down into the water. But the tower remains gigantic.

"Courage, men," shouts an engineer wielding a stick. I throw myself onto Achilles's back and dig my heels into his flanks.

"Come on, you stupid beast," I shout, and at last Achilles slowly starts to move. He doesn't trot; rather he gingerly places one foot after another on the smooth, wet wood. As if he's got all the time in the world.

"Come on, Achilles," I call, but the animal has no intention of breaking his legs on this funny little bridge. The burning tower breaks through the chains. Two men in a small boat try to push it toward the bank with sticks, but their boat collapses and disappears into the black water. Finally, Achilles breaks into a trot. We're almost there. I can see the tall trees on the island. I can almost smell the forest. Thirty yards to go. Twenty. And then the giant flaming raft crashes into the pontoon bridge with a bang that shatters the night. The impact sends us flying. Achilles and I fall into the black river. The icy water pounds the air out of my lungs. Achilles flails around trying to get a foothold. The soldiers with the sticks who were standing on the middle of the bridge are hurled into the river too. We're done for. I cling to the saddle as the current drags us downstream. The bank is only a few feet away, but there is nothing I can do. The water has us in its icy grip. A man on shore throws me a rope with a plank attached to the end. It crashes into the water right in front of me.

"Leave the horse!" he shouts. "Leave the horse."

But I clamp my legs around Achilles as I grab the rope. I won't let go. You stay with me, you stupid beast. Somehow Achilles manages to swim toward the bank and his feet find the bottom. I hold on to the rope, and the man pulls me onto the bank. I climb out of the water. Achilles scrambles up the bank behind me in a tangle of low-hanging branches and thorny bushes. In the middle of the wide river, where the water is cold and wild, I see the bobbing heads of soldiers. One by one they disappear under the water. A loose barge spins around in the foaming rapids. The burning tower has broken the bridge in half and hooked itself into the network of ropes and chains. The fire rages. Achilles snorts and shakes himself dry. Water drips from the saddlebag. The plans!

I undo the straps on the saddlebag and pull out the portfolio. I untie the strings and open it. The paper is soaked, and the pages are stuck together. I walk to a clearing in the trees where, trembling with cold, I lay out the plans, sheet by sheet. I weigh down the corners of the pages with rocks. I make sure to arrange them side by side and in the correct order. If only they'll dry, I think, if only they'll dry. Only then do I notice that my teeth are chattering. My clothes cling to my shivering body. I walk with Achilles to a campfire to warm up. My clothes begin to steam.

The two halves of the bridge float in the water like broken scaffolding. The burning raft is still crackling and hissing in the middle of the river. The poor Emperor. Just when he got his bridge fixed, the whole thing was destroyed. There are still so many carts of ammunition and supplies stuck on the wrong side of the river. So many cannons. So many thousands of cavalry and infantry soldiers. A general shouts orders to repair the bridge. Get to work! But when I see the pitiful remains bobbing in the river, I'm afraid we'll be stuck on this island forever. The two men who rescued me look crestfallen. I walk back to the clearing. As soon as the sheets of paper are dry, I'll take them to the Emperor. I'm almost there, Father.

29

PIER

Thanks to the early morning sunlight, the papers are as good as dry an hour later. They're wrinkled from the water, but otherwise everything is still legible. I collect them in the right order and carefully place them back in the leather portfolio and tuck it under my arm. I climb onto Achilles's back, and we cross the island in search of the Emperor. The island is a wilderness of ancient trees. The brush has been trampled down by horses and people.

At the other end of the island, I come to a small pontoon bridge that crosses the narrower arm of the Danube. Here the current is less strong. On the other side, I see medics, men, and women assisting the wounded. There's a man carrying an old rake with helmets hanging from it; one woman is collecting plumes and another medals. They notice me watching them.

"You looking to buy something, boy?" the woman asks. "A helmet, a feather, or a medal?"

I shake my head in surprise. I can smell the fire, gunpowder, and rotting flesh drifting across the river.

"This way, Achilles," I say. "The Emperor has got to be over there somewhere."

I steer him across the bridge, and we trot up the hill. Soldiers stare at me—a boy in his Sunday suit and white knee socks stained by the mire of the Danube. After a mile or so, I come to a village. The church tower is on fire. Most of the houses have collapsed or are completely charred. I hear the cannons roar and the muskets crackle. And that's when I see him—the Emperor on horseback. He is standing in the stirrups and looking through a telescope. Beside him, the major is waiting.

"You're her brother!" I hear someone exclaim behind me.

I look back and see a soldier looking up at me. At first, I don't recognize him. He has a bandage around his head. His face is black with gunpowder. There's a dark blood stain where his ear is supposed to be.

Then I recognize him.

"Squire Soudan," I say.

"The corporal is wounded," he says.

"Who?"

"Ironhead."

I stare at him. What is he talking about?

"Constance."

"Constance," I repeat stupidly.

There's something I'm supposed to understand here, but I don't.

"She's badly injured," he says.

"Still?" I ask confused.

How can Stance still be badly injured three months after the duel? Stance isn't a corporal. And besides, she's back in Paris.

"She's here," Soudan says impatiently.

No, she can't be. Stance wouldn't charge at France's enemies with a musket and a bayonet. She's crazy, but she's not that crazy.

Soudan looks at me as if I'm some kind of dimwit. A good-for-nothing weakling who ought to be at home looking after the geese. He grabs my hand and squeezes it, trying to bring me back to reality.

"Go find her," he says. "Right now. Go."

I want to tell him that I'm not here for my sister. That I don't want to see her, and she doesn't want to see me either. We hate each other. We always have. She's a monster.

"We got hit with cannon fire," Soudan says.

I feel my stomach turn.

"I saw her fall," he says. "In the cemetery. We helped her onto a cart. She was more dead than alive. The medics, they took her."

Now is not the best time, Squire Soudan. I've got better things to do than to try to find my more-dead-than-alive sister. Like speak to the Emperor, for instance. I need to give him this portfolio that's under my left arm. I have to remind him that his first love was the cannon and all that. I've got my whole sales pitch ready, Soudan, you've got to understand. I didn't memorize the whole thing for nothing. Soudan frowns. Only then do I notice Achilles take a step back. The smell of gunpowder and blood makes him nervous. He wants to get out of here. I look at the path over the ridge, at the Emperor and the major. They're less than two hundred yards from me. The major catches sight of me and says something to the Emperor. He turns around. The Emperor looks at me. He sees me! The major beckons me over. I have to go to them. I'm coming, my Emperor, I'm coming!

Soudan takes hold of my horse's reins. I flinch.

"Listen," he barks. "She's on the island. Go to her. Go to Stance."

Constance. Stance. It was the first name I ever said. Mother used to tell me that. "Ance," I'd say as a toddler. Stance. How she used to smile under her bonnet. How she swam after me when I was drowning in the Lieve. How she shamelessly looked the boys at the market straight in the eye. She called me Spiering. Killjoy. Milksop. The oracle of the Latin school. She made me help her carry the laundry basket. She made me hike up to that wretched old convent with her to watch a women's boxing match. She said it would give me something to brag about at school. Just five minutes, she said. We'd be home before lunch, she promised.

"If she's still alive," Soudan said, "she's on the island."

The major beckons me again.

"Petit," he shouts, "Come here, boy."

He looks annoyed to see me dawdling. His giant mustache

blusters up and down. But, Major, sir, your Immortal Highness, my sister is on the island. The medics took her. She's more dead than alive. I'm so sorry.

"I'll be right back, Major," I call, but he doesn't hear me through the thunder of the cannons. I kick Achilles in the flanks, and we trot back down the hill. No, we don't trot, we gallop as if the Devil were biting at our calves. In less than a minute, we're back at the river.

I have to wait to cross the small bridge to the island. Soldiers are walking back and forth, helping the wounded. I dismount and shout that I have to get across now. I pull Achilles behind me and clamp the portfolio under my arm. I push and shove my way across the bridge. I hear men cursing at me. Someone hits me. Someone pulls on my coat. Someone kicks at me. But I make it across. I pull myself back up onto my horse, kick him in the sides, and we head off in the wrong direction. I make at least five wrong turns, and it takes me an hour to find the field where they're keeping the wounded. There are more than a thousand of them. There's hardly an empty spot in the grass. At the edge of the field is a cart carrying a wooden statue of Saint Luke with a few candles lit in front of it. I'm so nervous that I try to dismount before Achilles has come to a complete stop. I jump, stumble, and roll into the grass, crashing headfirst into the cart. Typical clumsy me. But I scramble to my feet. I have to find Stance. She is one of these thousand victims. I leave Achilles by the cart and start scanning the rows of wounded soldiers. Most have already seen the medics and been bandaged up. Some are lying on beds of straw. Others are just sprawled out in the grass or mud. There are coats, cloaks, and bags hanging in the trees. People have strung up canvases here and there to provide shade for the wounded. Everywhere is the sound of moaning, cursing, and wailing.

After fifteen minutes of searching, I finally see Stance lying on the ground in a torn uniform. The right sleeve of her jacket is gone, and there's a bandage twisted around her arm. It's covered in flies. She is awake, but she doesn't recognize me. Her eyes turn away. Around her neck hangs the amulet of Saint Rita. A lot of help she's been.

"Stance, I'm here," I say. "Stance!"

She mutters something unintelligible. She's delirious. Her wound smells like a dead cat. At first, I don't dare to touch it. I take hold of the linen bandage and loosen it so that I can bind it tighter. The wound has been sewn shut, but the threads are coming loose again. I see a shiny piece of bone. Her flesh is teeming with maggots. The wound looks as black as the Devil. She's going to die. I feel the vomit rising up in my mouth. I take hold of her hand. She's hot. She's boiling with fever. What can I do? Beside her, I see a man using a branch to swat the flies off the stump where his leg used to be. On the other side lies a soldier with a waxen face. He's already gone. In the middle of the field, two surgeons are trying to save as many as they can. Each one works at a wooden table. Their two assistants, both civilians in blood-stained aprons, remove one wounded soldier from the table and place the next one on it.

"Stance is dying," I say, but no one hears.

◎ ◎ ◎

I try to reach under her armpits and lift her up, but she's too heavy. I pull her up into a seated position by her left arm. Then I get down on my knees and hoist her up on my shoulder. Now it's just a question of standing up without toppling over. I push up on my right leg, wobble a bit, and manage to catch myself on my left just in time. Stance's entire body is hanging over my shoulder. I won't be able to carry her like this for long. The one-legged soldier stares at me as if we might collapse on top of him any second now.

"Get out of here," he says, waving his branch.

I make a quarter turn. How far to the tables? A hundred paces? Two hundred? I drag Stance on my shoulder through the rows and rows of wounded soldiers, some dying and others already dead. She's as heavy as lead. How on earth am I going to make it all the way over there with her on my shoulder? But it's like the thousand miles to Vienna. Just put one foot in front of the other. I have to save my sister. My sister with the big mouth. My sister with the cackling laugh. One Holy Rita isn't enough for her because of all the hopeless cases, Stance is the most hopeless of them all. I manage to take the two hundred steps to the middle the field.

Around the tables, wounded soldiers are waiting their turn. One of the doctors is an older gentleman with long, bushy sideburns and glasses. The other one is young. The doctor with the sideburns has just barely finished sewing up a wound when his unconscious patient is pulled off the table by the two assistants. The table is dripping with blood. The surgeon wipes it away with a black, soaked rag as if it were spilled wine. He wrings out the rag and rolls his shoulders.

He's stiff from hours of operating in an open field. His clothes cling to his body from the sweat. The young surgeon is sawing off a lieutenant's leg, but all of a sudden something goes wrong. Blood sprays from the wound, and the lieutenant starts convulsing violently. His eyes roll into the back of his head. His mouth gasps for air like a fish on dry land. Then it's all over.

"You cut into an artery!" the older doctor shouts. "You graduated from medical school, didn't you?"

"Yes," the young man says, looking sheepish. "Three months at the École de Médecine. Graduated cum laude, sir. But there we had the right materials. Here I have to amputate with a carpenter's saw."

"Our instruments are in a cart on the other side of the Danube," the older surgeon barks. "Your excuses are of no use to this poor lieutenant. This young man's just lost his life."

The younger surgeon takes a sip from a bottle of wine while the assistants pull the poor lieutenant off the table and toss him onto a cart full of corpses. There, next to that cart, is—I have to blink a few times before my eyes will believe it—a pile of sawed-off arms and legs. At least a hundred of them. Or more, even. The pyramid of limbs is nearly a meter high, and when the young doctor throws the lieutenant's leg on top, a cloud of flies buzzes up and immediately returns to its feast of blood, flesh, and bone.

The older surgeon wipes the sweat from his brow with his sleeve and swats away a fly. He looks up angrily at the sky, as if he blames the sun for making this horrible day so hot. Then he looks over the rim of his glasses at the wounded. Dozens of soldiers are raising their arms at once.

"Me!" one shouts.

"It's my turn," shouts another.

"I'm next," shouts another. "You promised."

Only now do I see that some of the wounded have numbers written on their foreheads in chalk, while others are marked with a straight line. I can't help but notice that the ones with the line are in pretty bad shape. Probably too bad to be treated, I think, but they give them a chalk mark anyway, so they think their turn is coming. I step forward with Stance on my shoulder. I can't carry her anymore. With every step, I think I'm going to collapse among the rows and rows of wounded.

"Hey! Don't cut the line," one shouts at me.

"Wait your turn, peasant," another moans.

"Get lost, jackass," yells another.

"Step back," the old surgeon barks at me. "We've already done that one."

"Please," I say. "This is my sister. She's going to die."

The surgeon looks dumbfounded, and the soldiers stare at her in amazement too. "A woman?" he shouts.

"Yes, a woman," I repeat. "Her name is Constance."

The surgeon looks at me for a moment. Is it because I'm only fourteen? Or is it because I'm carrying a young woman in uniform? I don't know. In any case, the surgeon points to me, and the two assistants take Stance and lay her on the table. The old surgeon nods to his young colleague.

"She's for you," he says. "Make sure she survives."

The young surgeon takes another swig of wine. He must be drunk—how could he not be? The older surgeon points to a badly injured sergeant, bleeding from one eye. They carry him to the second table, which is buzzing with flies.

A wounded soldier to my right gives me a shove. He has blood on his lips and is pressing a cloth into his neck. His hand is trembling. Part of his neck has been torn away and the flies are swarming around his raw flesh.

"It was my turn," he gurgles.

"I'm sorry, sir," I say. "You'll be up in a moment. Stay strong."

I know it sounds stupid to say something like that to someone who can barely gurgle, but what am I supposed to say? The man pulls at my sleeve as if clinging to life itself. His lips seem to be saying all sorts of things, but his gurgling is barely intelligible.

"What number is on my forehead?" he asks.

I look at his forehead. He's been marked with a line. Meanwhile, the young surgeon pulls off Stance's coat and shirt. Yes, now he can see for himself that she is indeed a woman. The man next to me keeps gurgling and tugging at my sleeve.

"You've got a one on your forehead," I say. "That means you'll probably get your turn very soon."

"Good," he gurgles. "Thank goodness."

He wants to say something more, but he's out of strength. I hold his hand. That calms him down a little.

"I have to bring my sister home," I explain, just to say something. "Eddy wants to see her."

But he's not looking at me anymore. He shakes his head as if to stave off Death and makes a gesture that says, "No, not me, I have a number."

The young surgeon ties off Stance's upper arm with a belt. Then he takes the furniture saw and places the crooked teeth on her arm.

"Wait," the older surgeon exclaims as he plucks iron from his patient's eye. "You forgot the stick."

The young surgeon mutters something that looks like "Let me do this." He picks up a bloody stick and places it between Stance's teeth so she won't bite her tongue off. The assistants hold her down by her shoulders and ankles. The surgeon begins his work. Stance jolts awake in pain. She screams so loud that her voice cracks. Her body jerks up and down.

The amputation takes less than half a minute. Blood gushes from the end of her arm. The young surgeon rips open a cartridge with his teeth and sprinkles gunpowder on the wound. He takes a twig from a firepit and presses it on the gunpowder. Her skin ignites. The stench of burning flesh fills the air. Stance is no longer screaming. She's lost all consciousness.

"Done," the young surgeon shouts.

The old surgeon looks over. He twists a bandage around the sergeant's eye.

"I didn't hit an artery this time," the young man boasts. "Next!"

◎ ◎ ◎

I look down at the numberless man beside me. He's no longer shaking his head. I slowly pull my hand from his.

"I'm sorry," I say. "But I have to go to Stance."

He can't hear me anymore.

An assistant pulls Stance off the table and hands me a bandage. I have to wrap the wound myself. The injured men lying on the ground begging for care gaze at Stance, at her battered, naked upper body, as if she were an angel from heaven. I pull her up by her armpits. I drag her back to where she was lying and put her shirt back on. The flies swarm above her, ready to feast on her smoldering arm. I swat them away. They can go find another stump. I wrap a nice, tight bandage around what's left of her right arm.

"Don't die," I say. "Please, don't die."

I keep repeating it. Like a prayer. A hundred times. A thousand times. And there I sit, Pieter Hoste, surrounded by the dead and wounded, in a field full of maimed soldiers, with all the flies in the world, sweating in the merciless sunlight.

I fall asleep and don't wake up until early evening. I turn over to Stance and lay my head on her chest. Her heart is still beating. I look around at the field full of wounded soldiers. It's starting to drizzle. The canvases protecting them against the sun are now flapping in the wind. The cannons have gone quiet. The battle must be over.

The Emperor! Suddenly I remember. The plans. Where

are the plans? I had them under my arm as I crossed the bridge and rode across the island looking for Stance, and then I fell off my horse. I tumbled into that cart. The portfolio must have fallen.

I spring to my feet. That cart with the statue of Saint Luke is still parked at the edge of the field, and Achilles is grazing around it.

"I have to go see the Emperor, Stance," I say, but she's still unconscious. I tell the man with the one leg that I'll be back. He looks back at me like an idiot. I rush over to the cart. I make the sign of the cross to Luke, the patron saint of surgeons and the author of the third book of the New Testament, which Achilles ingested shortly before we reached Linz. Achilles whinnies happily when he sees me. I immediately spot the leather portfolio lying under the cart. Phew. It's still there.

"Come, my hero, let's take these plans to the Emperor." I take a step toward him and hear something crunch beneath my feet. It's a sheet of paper. No, it's a scrap of paper. On the ground are eight more sheets just like it. Achilles is nibbling away at them. I don't understand. I don't want to understand.

I pick up the portfolio. The strings have been chewed away. There's nothing left inside. Achilles is munching on the paper as if it's the most ordinary thing in the world. I pick up the eight sheets. A bit of text here. A drawing there. The old bag of bones has eaten Father's plans.

"The Cannon of L. Hoste," by Leopold Hoste, Professor of Mathematics, has been fully devoured by Achilles.

30

PIER

The days come and go. The French army has retreated to the island. The soldiers look battered. They sleep, smoke, drink, and fight for a spot close to the campfire. There are so many wounded. The worst cases lie under tarpaulins, hoping that death will come for them. I don't leave Stance's side. She trembles with fever for two days. On the third day, she regains consciousness, but she doesn't recognize me. I make her sit up with her back against a tree. She is awake and can hold her head up, but that's all. She stares out into space. She doesn't respond to anything. I talk to her, but she doesn't answer. She just looks off in the distance at something very far away. She doesn't eat and pees in her pants. She stinks. I have to press a cup between her lips to make her drink. I figure that she must have a crack in her brain even bigger than Grandma Blom's.

◎ ◎ ◎

A white-haired corporal with deep furrows in his cheeks squats down next to Stance. I recognize him. He was at the duel with Dupin. He snaps his fingers in front of my sister's eyes and talks to her. Stance blinks, but that's it. The corporal shakes his head sadly. Then he looks at me. He says his name is Rabbit. He must be joking, I think.

In the evenings, I sit around the campfire with the men of the Fourteenth. They pass me a tin cup of soup with chunks of horse meat in it. It tastes terrible. Someone notices the foul look on my face as I hold it up to my lips and says that the spice wagon is still on the other side of the Danube. They've seasoned the soup with gunpowder, which gives it a salty-spicy flavor, they say.

At last, the bridge is fixed, but it will take another day and a half for the cavalry and cannons to cross. Rabbit and the men from the company give me a saber, a pistol, and a hat from the Fourteenth. For Stance. For if she ever gets better. They salute her and give her shoulder a little squeeze, but she doesn't notice. Then they leave with the rest of the army. On to the next battle.

I lift Stance onto a cart full of hay. Inside are twenty other wounded soldiers. The cart is part of a ten-cart convoy to transport the injured. Those who cannot be transported are left behind on the island to recover or rot away. The convoy heads west. Achilles, the horse who's ruined everything, is excited to be back on the road again. I click my tongue as he munches on thistles on the side of the road. He stops plucking at the grass and walks on. Stance still hasn't said a word. She just sits in the cart, nodding her head. In the afternoon, I feed her as best I can and carry her to the side of the road so she can do her business. The convoy moves slowly. Whenever a wounded soldier dies, I help them bury the poor soul under a couple feet of dirt.

All the men have lost an arm or a leg or worse. Their wounds and smell attract the flies. Some have bandages around their heads, and the lieutenant leading the convoy has lost an eye and a hand. The men are somber and don't say much. They're the scraps of the great French army, the refuse of the war machine. They don't notice the spring giving way to summer. They don't see the chickadees flittering about and the swallows swooping in the sky. The grass is high and a deep shade of green. Newborn creatures rustle and chirp in the forests. It's as if the world is mocking our somber convoy.

Somewhere near Metz, the group splits up. Most of the carts continue in the direction of Paris, and from there, the men will continue back to their villages. We say our goodbyes. The cart Stance is in continues in the direction of the North Sea. In Brussels, the group splits up one last time. I hoist Stance onto Achilles's back, loop the reins around her wrists, and we set off toward Ghent. At one point, she falls asleep and almost slips off the horse, but I push her back upright in the saddle. She's lost a lot of weight.

◎ ◎ ◎

I can't wait to see my Ghent. The journey from Brussels takes two days. By the second evening, I can see the city's three towers from the road. Even though I'm utterly exhausted, I race ahead, dragging Achilles behind me. Stance bounces like a rag doll in the saddle. I run along the marshy lakes at the edge of town. Bats skim over the water.

"We're here, Stance," I say. "We're home."

But Stance doesn't answer.

There are two gendarmes at the city gates. They ask to see our papers. It's not the first time I've been asked to show identification. I hand them Stance's papers.

"Binus Serlippens?" the gendarme asks Stance.

She doesn't respond.

"He was not only wounded in the arm," I tell them, "but also in the head." I point to the scar above her eye.

The two gendarmes shake their heads sympathetically and wish us luck. I lead us into the city, past the horse stables, then down Lange Violettestraat, past the Beguine convent, and then left onto Lammerstraat. I can see the sign outside the bakery, an old wooden paddle for pushing loaves into the oven. I knock on the door and untie the reins around Stance's wrists. She slides off the saddle and into my arms. The door opens, and there stands the baker in his nightcap. It takes him nearly a full minute to understand who is in front of him. Then he recognizes Stance. He lets us in and stands there gaping at her like a fool. He calls Binus. At least three times. Each time louder.

Before long, the whole Serlippens family is in the bakery. Binus, who hasn't left the house for months, no longer has pimples on his face. He has grown into a rather good-looking guy. His sister's name is Johanna. I hand him his discharge papers, which state that he has been released from military service due to serious injuries. There are no further details. The document is authenticated with a stamp of the French eagle and a signature of an infantry captain. Binus's mother keeps whispering, "Oh God, oh God," as she examines what's left of my sister—her sunken cheeks, her lifeless eyes, her wrists as thin as matchsticks.

"She hardly eats anything," I say.

They nod and don't say a word. I'm bringing home a living corpse.

"Stance has been gone for ten months," Binus says.

I nod. Johanna stares at Stance.

"Maybe you can lend my sister some clothes, Johanna," I say. "Comb her hair a bit. Then I'll take her home."

After Johanna and her mother have taken Stance into the back, Binus can't take it anymore. He hits himself on the head. Once. Twice. His father grabs him by the wrists and makes him stop. His face is twisted with shame.

"Binus," I say, "don't feel guilty. Stance didn't do it for you. She did it for herself. And for herself alone."

He nods but doesn't seem convinced.

The baker hands me two loaves of bread.

"Your family will never go hungry as long as we're here," he says.

Johanna brings Stance back in a long green dress that's way too big for her. She's practically drowning in it. They've covered her head in a bonnet embroidered with flowers. She smells like soap.

"At least she looks normal again," Mrs. Serlippens says.

But the clothes don't look right on her anymore.

"You'll visit us again, won't you, Pier?" Johanna asks. The torch illuminates her pretty face, and she doesn't wait for me to answer.

"Or I'll come visit you," she says.

"Johanna, mind your manners," her mother chides. I smile, and Johanna's eyes sparkle.

Night has fallen by the time Binus and his father hoist Stance back onto Achilles. We walk through the Brabantdam toward home. Even though it's late, there are still many people out on the streets enjoying the summer evening. Some are standing around the entrance to the pub. Others are sitting in chairs in front of their homes. They're not the least bit interested in the boy in tattered clothes pulling a horse carrying a young woman almost completely hidden under a dark cloak. We walk along the Botermarkt, where Stance and I watched the two hundred young men report for service. We walk past the café where Father and I stopped for a drink after his argument with Lieven. We turn down the Donkersteeg. The tears start streaming down my face. I can't hold them back anymore. I look over my shoulder at Stance in the saddle, but it's too dark to see her eyes. They're probably just as dull as they were this morning, as dead as they were when she opened them on that island in the Danube.

Then the crooked houses built against the ruins of the castle come into view. I can see the moored coal barges on the Leie River and the wooden cranes on the quay. Our quay.

"Look, Stance," I say. "There's our house."

But Stance doesn't look. Her mind is still in Aspern, in that cemetery by the burning church.

A candle burns in the front window. The tiny flame flickers. Mother's light for lost souls. Our neighbor, Gilbert, the stove maker, is outside smoking a pipe on the Empire chair he bought from us. He recognizes me. He jumps to his feet, and the chair topples over behind him. He starts banging on our front door like a madman.

It's Mother who opens it. She doesn't have her cap on. Her hair has turned gray. Suddenly, I can't go on anymore. I have no strength left. But Mother sees me. She runs toward me in her clogs, screaming. I don't understand what she's saying. I can't take another step. I wait for her to take me in her arms and press me against her and say something I will never forget. But she doesn't. She stops a few feet in front of us and falls to her knees. She looks up and makes the sign of the cross. And then another and another. She stares at Stance on the horse. She can't believe it. Stance was dead. Drowned in the Seine. Buried. Mother saw the official papers. The stamps. My signature. She burned candles for her dead daughter. Held a Mass. And now, here she is, Stance, in a baggy dress and cloak and with a bonnet on her head.

"Oh, Stance," she whispers. "Stance."

And then, finally, she takes me in her arms.

◎ ◎ ◎

In the kitchen, Mother lights an oil lamp. Rozeken walks in and throws her arms around me. She hugs me. She cries. She won't let go of me. "Pier, Pier," she keeps saying. Mother helps Stance sit down and takes her hand. She says her name and rubs her hands through her daughter's short, sticky hair. But Stance doesn't respond. I hear a creak on the stairs.

Father comes into the kitchen and sees me first. His hair is long. His white beard curls in all directions. I'm surprised to see him home.

"Shouldn't you be in prison, Father?"

"Did you sell my cannon?" he asks immediately.

I say nothing. But the answer is written all over my face. His expression darkens, but I don't look away. "What are you going to do about it, Father? Bite my head off? Call me a Judas?"

"What cannon?" Mother asks. "What are you talking about? That boy brought your daughter home. Pieter brought Stance back from the dead."

Only then does Father see his daughter. He looks at her and then at me. The anger vanishes from his face. He stares at me as if I were Orpheus who has descended to the underworld, crossed the River Styx, given Cerberus a few kicks in his beastly behind, and convinced Hades to give Stance back.

"Sit down, Leopold," Mother says. "Our children are back."

But Stance is not back. Her spirit is still trapped in the underworld.

Father looks as if he wants to touch Stance, to caress her face, but he doesn't dare. He doesn't even dare to ask. He looks at me. His lips quiver. This is all too much for him. He's at a loss for words.

"Achilles is home too," I say.

"Ah," says Father, relieved to have something to talk about. "That's good. I'm glad Achilles is back."

I nod.

"You wouldn't know by looking at him," Father says, "but Achilles is a strong horse. He's over twenty by now, you know. Twenty-two, I think."

I nod.

"I bought him when he was about six. I was working as a mechanic for a couple of factories back then."

I nod.

"He's smart too," Father says.

If only he knew.

Mother carries Grandma Blommaert downstairs. A moth flutters out of her dressing gown. She kisses my forehead, cheeks, and hair. She keeps kissing me with that toothless mouth of hers. Her drool drips off my cheeks. When she sees Stance, she moans. She caresses her face and her shoulder above the missing arm.

"Those Austrian bastards," she murmurs.

I hear another creak on the stairs. Eddy. Mother didn't wake him because he's so weak. But he heard the commotion downstairs and climbed out of bed. He looks like a ghost with his pale skin and white nightshirt. He doesn't see anyone but Stance. He walks up to her in his bare feet.

"At last, you're home," he says in that lisping child's voice of his. He climbs into her lap and rests his head against her chest. He looks in surprise at the stump where her right arm used to be. Then he takes her left hand and places it protectively around his shoulder. He clasps her hand in his tiny hand. He plays with her fingers. He counts all five of them.

"You're home," he repeats.

Eddy just sits there in her lap while Stance stares out into space with an empty look in her eyes.

Rozeken wants to hear what happened. The story of my journey, my odyssey, my descent into the underworld. But I'm too exhausted. I want a bed. I've slept in stables, on floors, on bridges, in the grass, and under carts. I've been eaten alive by fleas. Now all I want is my bed. My bed with its starched sheets and the faint smell of soap. I want my pillow. A blanket over my feet. Mother says there'll be plenty of time for stories later. I'm home now. And Stance is home. I must be hungry.

She heats up some stew. Father takes Achilles into the courtyard and gives him some hay. Mother whispers that Father was in such bad shape in the debtor's prison that they let him come home. He has to return to the prison after he's regained his strength. His cellmates miss him, Mother says. They're bored without him.

I chew Stance's bread and vegetables for her. I add some milk to her stew and spoon it into her mouth while the others watch. Eddy just sits in her lap and keeps saying, "At last, you're home." Stance swallows a little, but most of it drips down her chin. I wipe her mouth with the spoon and then with my sleeve. That's how I'm used to doing it. Mother just stares at me.

"Those clothes are going straight to the wash, young man," she says.

I haven't bathed in weeks. I must stink like that dead Devil in our classroom.

"I'll wash them in the Lieve tomorrow," Rozeken promises.

Father comes in and says Achilles is glad to be back in his stable. I nod. And then we fall silent. The clock ticks away the time. We're all together.

"You're home," Eddy says for the hundredth time.

And then, all of a sudden, Stance says, "Yes, Coppertop, I'm here."

31

STANCE

Rozeken watches over me and does her sewing while I sleep. She says I cry out. In my dreams, I still have both of my arms. In my dreams, I load my gun in twelve motions and ram the cartridge with my right arm. I shuffle the playing cards and split the deck with two hands. I caress Fortuna with all ten fingers. Even after I wake, I can still feel my fingers, my fingers that are no longer there.

When I look at Spicring, I can see how he has changed. He's no longer the blundering milksop who bumps into everything and is afraid of his own farts. A week after returning home, he went down to the Ghent Town Hall. Exactly what he said to the prefect, I don't know, but he started working there as a writer and a copyist that same day. Every evening Johanna

Serlippens comes over with a loaf of bread. She can't take her eyes off of Pier.

And he has plans, my Spiering does. He wants to study to be a doctor, he says, so he can do better than the genius who sawed off my arm on the island in the Danube. I don't remember anything about the island or the trip home. All I remember is the blast of the cannon. Mole shouting that this one's for us. The Basque shouting, "So be it!" And me, screaming, "Let the Devil come!" And then the agonizing pain, the cloud of blood, and the fall backward. After that, there was nothing but darkness. I never wanted to leave that darkness. It was warm there. Safe. Almost cozy. I slept in the arms of that monster as he slowly ate away at me, bit by bit.

But then I heard Eddy's voice. Faint at first. Then more clearly. I followed the voice and somewhere above me, out of that deep blackness, I saw a streak of light. All I had to do was walk toward it. Leave behind the darkness, where it was so warm and safe. I hesitated. I wanted to stay there, with that monster. But that little Coppertop kept repeating my name.

Eddy and I spend entire days together upstairs, where the sweet scent of the honeysuckle swirls in through the window. I tell him how big and beautiful Paris and Vienna are, and in his imagination they become even bigger and more beautiful. He asks me to go with him to the pharmacy and sniff healing scents, but Rozeken takes him. The fewer people who know I'm back, the better.

Within a week, Mother and I are bickering again.

Rozeken has mended my uniform and sewn a new right sleeve on my shirt, but Mother thinks my men's clothes are disgraceful. She doesn't want to look at them. She won't even touch them. The uniform is packed away in the bottom of an old trunk, buried under Father's Sunday suits that are all too small for him. The trunk smells of camphor. Mother demands that as long as I'm under her roof, I dress like the dignified young lady I'm supposed to be. She expects me to start living a virtuous life again. Because sooner or later I'll have to go back to Lieven.

"He got remarried," Mother says. "What do we do?"

She makes the sign of the cross.

"I've been declared dead anyway," I say.

"But if Lieven finds out you're still alive, then what?" Mother asks. "Officially, he's still your husband."

She could twist the hind leg off a donkey with her nagging.

I'm too tired to argue with her. Too exhausted to think. I spend most of the day sleeping.

On one of the last days of October, I hear voices downstairs. It is almost noon. Mother walks into my room. Her face is stiff with irritation.

"What are you doing lying in bed?" she barks.

I sit up and yawn.

"Button up your blouse," she says. "Put a bonnet on."

"Why?"

"You have visitors," she says, already reaching for my bonnet.

I get out of bed. My skirts are all wrinkled. Mother stuffs my blouse into my waistband, pushes me into a jacket, and buttons it up.

"I can dress myself," I snap.

"You behave yourself," she warns me and then pushes me out in front of her. I head down the stairs and almost miss the last step when I see who's come to visit. In the dining room are Rabbit, Geoff Soudan, and Cor the Dutchman. I just stand there, staring at them. I can't believe these men of the Fourteenth are standing in our kitchen. It doesn't make any sense. They're much too tall for our small dining room. Their stovepipe hats tap against the beams. They stare back at me. At my wrinkled skirts, my blouse, my jacket, and the bonnet with those hideous flowers on it. They're all speechless. They seem to be wondering if I'm really their old mate. I feel my cheeks burning with shame. How can they see me like this? What are they thinking? *Look at that! Corporal Ironhead is wearing women's clothes!* Rabbit points to my empty sleeve.

"I see your arm hasn't grown back yet," he jokes.

I hear Mother cluck disapprovingly behind me. I try to think of a comeback, but nothing comes to mind. My head is empty.

Soudan asks me how I've been. Fine, I say. I sound hoarse. All three of them nod, glad to hear my voice.

Pier invites the men to have a seat. Soudan, Rabbit, and Cor take off their cloaks; hang them over the backs of our chairs; and sit down. Their sabers scrape against the floor. Their belts jingle. Rozeken and Eddy come down the stairs, but Mother chases them back up. Mother asks if the soldiers would like a glass of warm milk. They nod. Mother takes the cups, saucers, and spoons out of the sideboard. The China clinks as she places it on the table. My mates don't know what to do with their hands. Their fingers seem too big for Mother's cups with their small, dainty handles. They hardly dare to look at me. And I'm too shy to look them in the eye.

"Soudan here knew exactly where you lived," Rabbit says.

Geoff smiles.

"We're on leave," says Cor.

"Leave?" I repeat, in an attempt to make conversation. Silence falls over the table. The clock ticks as the milk warms on the stove. Pier glares at me, amazed that I have nothing to say.

Mother pours the steaming milk into the cups. Rabbit says it smells very fresh and reassures Mother, "We won't be staying long, madam. We just came by to say hello."

Mother is happy to hear that. She takes some cookies from the cupboard. They're weeks old and hard as cobblestones.

"I'm glad you came to see my daughter," Mother says.

The three men nod.

"And as you can see, Constance is doing much better now," Mother continues. "My daughter is back to her old self. Well, almost."

The three men nod. They dip their cookies into the milk.

"It's nice not to be the only woman in the house anymore," Mother says.

"You must be happy about that," says Rabbit.

"Very happy," Mother says.

"You've got Rozeken too, you know," says Pier.

"Quiet," Mother snaps.

My mates shift and recline in their chairs as if they've got nettles in their pants. Rabbit scratches his head and glances at the door as if he wants to leave as quickly as possible. He points to the clock.

"My, is it three thirty already?" he asks, with a hint of surprise in his voice.

"Half past three," Mother confirms. "I synchronize our clocks with the one on the church tower every day."

"It's getting late," Cor says.

Soudan blows into his cup of milk, which refuses to cool. Pier glares at me again. *Stance, say something!*

I stand up. Cor, Rabbit, and Soudan spring to their feet at the same time, out of politeness, as if I were the wife of a marquess or something. Soudan spills his milk. Cor, the tallest of the bunch, bumps his head against a ceiling beam.

"I'm sorry," I say. What a stupid goat I am.

I don't wait for a response. I march back upstairs.

"Constance has always been an unusual girl," I hear Mother explain. "Capricious and stubborn and all that. But still, she's a good woman."

"Mother," I hear Pier say in Flemish so they can't understand. "They already know Stance is a woman."

"Enough!" Mother says. "You're too young to understand."

I walk into my room and rip off the bonnet. I struggle

with the buttons on my jacket, but I can't unfasten them. Rozeken looks up from her sewing. I pull the jacket over my head and toss it on the floor. God damn it! What must my mates of the Fourteenth have thought when they saw me? How ridiculous I looked! Why did they even come? They should have stayed away. Away from Constance Hoste. Any second now, they'll push back their chairs. Mother will be all too happy to show them the door. Maybe Pier will call upstairs and ask if I want to come downstairs to say good-bye. And then they'll be gone forever.

"Where's that old trunk?" I ask Rozeken.

When I stroll back into the dining room, my three mates have finished their milk. Cor is already at the door with his cloak on, ready to leave. But when he sees me, his face lights up. I fasten one last button on my uniform and brush a bit of lint off my two stripes.

"What are you doing standing there by that door, soldier?" I say. "Who told you you could leave?"

Cor tosses his cloak back over the chair. He sits down next to his mates. All eyes are on me. I look at the men one by one. They're dressed in their Easter best. Clean-shaven. Shoes polished. Their uniforms are immaculate.

"I've never been so happy to see your ugly faces," I exclaim.

The guys laugh so loudly the windows shake. Mother's jaw drops. Her face turns as pale as an altar cloth. She doesn't dare say a word. Pier grins.

"Do you have any more of that milk for us?" Rabbit asks Mother.

"You don't happen to have a little something for the flavor?" I ask.

Geoff Soudan pulls out a bottle of cognac and pours a splash into each of the cups. When he holds the bottle over Mother's cup, she almost screams and holds her hand over the top. Even Pier gets a drop. We clink cups. Milk sloshes over the edges. The clank is so loud I think one of the cups might have cracked. We drink the milk in one gulp.

"This milk is delicious," the Dutchman says to Mother.

"Very delicious," Rabbit agrees, smacking his lips.

"That's some cow," Geoff Soudan adds.

They bang their hands on the table with laughter. A candle falls over. The porcelain rattles. Mother pulls back her cup and saucer to protect them.

"You know what the worst thing is about having only one arm?" I say. "I can't deal cards anymore."

Rabbit slaps a deck on the table. They're in a rough state—brown, creased, frayed at the edges—and they reek of old tobacco. But all the cards are there.

"I'll deal," says Rabbit. "Is your brother playing?"

Pier looks hesitant but curious at the same time.

"Deal him in," I say.

"And your mother?"

"I have some sewing to do," she says.

Mother stands up, and the three men jump to their feet. Mother is startled.

"There's still some milk in the pan," she squeaks, and disappears.

We pour ourselves another milk with cognac and toast

to one another's health. We laugh. We shout. The dining room is much too small for my mates of the hungry Fourteenth with their big cloaks, wide gestures, and thundering laughter.

"God, I missed you guys," I say.

"We missed your *shtupid* head too," says Rabbit.

The next morning, when Pier goes to work, he finds us sleeping with our heads on the table in a cloud of tobacco, surrounded by empty bottles. My friends stick around for another day—our game of bouillotte isn't over yet. They give Rozeken money to buy meat and cheese, and the next evening, we feast. I laugh and drink and joke like a man. Mother makes the occasional sign of the cross. Father takes his dinner in his study. Grandma Blom thinks the Austrians have taken over the house.

They don't leave until late morning after the second night.

"Will there be another war?" I ask.

"No," says Rabbit. "Next summer we'll be picking strawberries, plucking cherries, and lounging in the sun."

"Thank goodness," I say.

And all four of us laugh.

32

STANCE

The day after my mates leave I still have my uniform on. It's still a little big, but I'm getting stronger every day. I toss a long cloak over my shoulders, the kind of cloak that hides everything. I take Achilles out of the stable and feel around in my pocket. My fingers land on my lucky musket ball.

It's an hour-and-a-half ride to Lieven's house, the same house I fled a year ago. The route is shorter than I remember and the house smaller. It's even started to sag a bit. The gate is still locked with a chain. I ring the bell. The little door to the back kitchen opens. The housemaid limps toward me. The maid who used to give me a bath every day. The stupid goat who giggled at the sound of the bed creaking.

"Can I help you, sir?" she asks suspiciously, as if I've come to sell poached rabbits.

"Good day, miss," I say. "I have come from Paris with a message for Monsieur Goeminne. I am a corporal of the Emperor."

I tap my left hand against my stovepipe. She doesn't recognize me, and it's true what they say, the clothes make the man. She smiles bashfully—what a gullible fishwife. She lets me in, and I fasten Achilles's reins to the fence. The maid leads me through the garden and shows me to the drawing room. "Would you wait here for a moment, sir?"

The candelabras; the horns of plenty on the walls; the armchairs with their elegant, curved legs and lion's heads in the armrests: nothing has changed. It smells like damp wood. There's a fire burning in the fireplace.

"Who are you?" I hear behind me.

I turn around and am surprised to see a girl in the doorway. She can't be more than seventeen years old. She's wearing a blue-gray dress with a white lace collar. My clothes. I bow slightly, and she does the same. She scans me up and down, from shoes to overcoat to stovepipe.

"Why, you're a soldier," she blurts out. "Don't you look fine."

"No, miss," I say, "you're mistaken. You're the beauty here."

The girl snorts in surprise. Her cheeks burn red, and she's so embarrassed she doesn't know where to look.

"It's madame, if you please," she says and then snorts again as if the thought of it still amazes her every day.

"How long have you been married?" I ask.

She thinks and counts on her fingers.

"Fourteen weeks," she says.

"Is there a little bun in the oven yet?" I ask.

"No, silly," she snorts. "Not yet."

The girl speaks with a thick Ghent accent. Her words sound rough and chirpy—like one of the daughters at the Black Magpie. She didn't grow up wearing silk. She's a natural beauty, with her black curls and full figure. Lieven must have found her attractive and given her parents a bag of money. Now all she has to do is give him a son. She is nothing but a walking womb with a beautiful body around it.

"What's your name?" she asks, as she takes a step closer, as if I am a miracle to her, as if I have just stepped out of a sweeping romance novel about war and love.

"My name is Corporal Ironhead," I say, and then I show her the scar on my temple.

"That must have hurt," she says, wide-eyed.

I decide to act tough and reply with a shrug.

"My name is Lewieze La Belle," she says. "At least, it used to be. Now it's Lewieze Goeminne."

I can't help but grin. So this is Lewieze La Belle, the daughter of the ironsmith on Onderstraat who was sweet on Fons De Keghel, protector of the Emperor's daughters.

In the hall outside, I hear my husband shuffling in our direction. My first impulse is to duck out of sight. Disappear. Run home. But I turn to face him. There he is—Lieven Goeminne. He doesn't look so well, the Master of the Blue. Like his proud manor, he has started to sag a bit. The lines in his face have deepened. The vestiges of youth and cheerfulness that were still evident a year ago are now gone. His nose has taken on a purplish color, which makes me suspect that he's been drinking more than ever.

"Corporal," he asks, "you've come from Paris?"

"Yes, indeed, Mr. Goeminne."

He doesn't recognize my voice.

"May I congratulate you on your new wife," I say.

He grins with his dark-brown teeth. His hands are covered with age spots.

"He asked if I was pregnant yet," Lewieze blurts out.

That immediately puts a damper on Lieven's mood.

"What business is that of yours, sir?"

"I knew your previous wife, and I know Mr. Dupin," I say.

Lieven's eyes narrow to slits. But he still has no idea who I am.

"You know Mr. Dupin," he repeats. "How is he?"

"Fine," I say. "Dupin is indestructible."

Lieven's eyes become even narrower than slits.

"He's dead," he barks. "Bled to death in front of a horse stable. Who are you?"

"Dead?" I repeat in surprise.

"He had a gunshot wound that reopened. He was shacking up with a widow," he says. "A woman who brought him bad luck."

"Is that so?"

"Who are you, sir?" Lieven repeats.

"My father did business with you," I say.

"Business," Lieven says, his voice filled with agitation and suspicion.

"You gave my father money," I say quietly. "And you got me."

He doesn't understand. He looks at me with a furrowed brow. But then his eyes widen. His face turns white as a sheet. Fear hits him in the heart like a musket ball. He has to lean on a chair to keep from falling over.

"What is it, little bear?" says the girl, and she actually takes his hand.

"Step outside for a moment, darling," he stammers. "I have business with this . . . with this . . ."

"With this gentleman?" she asks. "They call him Ironhead."

Lieven shows her out. Then he closes the tall drawing room doors.

"You're dead," he says. He almost doesn't dare to look at me.

"I've been dead," I say. "But I didn't like it very much."

He looks stunned.

"I've come to ask you to burn a contract," I say. "The contract you made with my father. If the contract no longer exists, my father no longer owes you a debt."

"You're joking?"

"No. Burn the contract, and I'll disappear from your life."

He straightens his spine and looks at me. All this talk about debts and contracts seems to restore his confidence.

"Do you know how much your father owes me?"

"Do you know what Prefect Gijsens will do if I tell him your good friend Dupin shot me in the Bois de Boulogne? What he'll say when he learns that you are the mastermind behind a major smuggling network? That they call you the Master of the Blue?"

"You don't know what you're saying," he cries. "Report me, and you're dead. They'll find you with a rotten fish in your—"

"The contract," I cut him off.

A silence falls over the room. He studies me. *She's just a woman,* I see him thinking. Just a woman.

"All right, then," he says. "The contract."

He turns and walks over to the secretaire in the corner of the room. He pulls a key from his pocket and unlocks the desk. He looks at the closed drawers and then slides one open. He stands there for a moment. And then I hear—as I expected—the click of a pistol being cocked. He's opened the drawer that holds his loaded gun.

"You shouldn't have come back, you bitch," he says and then turns around with the gun in his hand. But he's as slow as the seasons, the old lout. Far too slow for a veteran of the hungry Fourteenth. I already have my infantry briquet in my hand. The weapon isn't as heavy or as long as a cavalry saber. But it's long enough. And most of all, it's sharp enough. I swing the sword over my head and swipe the gun away, along with three fingers on my former husband's hand. The gun hits the floor and fires. The bullet blows a chunk of marble off the mantelpiece. The three fingers hit the floor without a sound.

I lay the saber down on the table as Lieven stares at the three fingers on the floor in disbelief. Blood flows from his mutilated hand. I open one of the drawers in the desk. Inside are a couple of contracts. I throw the entire contents into the fireplace.

"Stop," Lieven shouts. "Please, stop."

He looks dumbfounded when he sees that I have only one arm under my cloak. He doesn't know what to believe anymore. I dump the papers from a second drawer into the fire.

"Stop," he repeats.

Then Lewieze La Belle comes into the room. She sees Lieven on his knees with his bleeding hand pressed against his shirt. The maid rushes in behind her and screams. I shake the contents of a third drawer into the fire.

"I'm going to call the gendarmes," the maid shouts. She rushes toward the door.

"The gendarmes, yes, that's an excellent idea," I call after her. "Let them take a look in the cellars. Your master is a smuggler. He's an enemy of the Emperor, and you are an accomplice."

The maid stops dead in her tracks and makes the sign of the cross.

I throw every last one of the drawers, along with all of their contents, into the fire. The fire crackles and roars. Pieces of burning paper are blown into the room by the rush of hot air. They float down to the carpet. The maid frantically stamps them out. The entire secretary is empty.

I pick up the pistol from the floor, take my saber, and walk out of the room. The maid limps over to Lieven and places her apron on his bleeding hand. I walk through the hall and exit via the back kitchen. Achilles is waiting for me. I open the gate.

"Corporal," Lewieze La Belle says behind me.

I look back.

"Take me with you," she says.

She walks up to me and kisses me. Her mouth is red and full. She's a mischievous one, that Lewieze.

"I'll treat you real nice," she says. "I don't want to stay here with him."

"I can't take you," I say. "I'm sorry."

"You can," she sputters.

"No, I can't."

The disappointment wells up in her eyes.

"Good luck, Lewieze," I say and pull myself into the saddle.

33

PIER

Late one October evening, Stance brings Achilles back to the stable. She has been out all day in her uniform. She tells us that Lieven's contract with Father has been tossed into the fire. Father is free.

"How did you convince Lieven to do that?" I ask.

"He was glad to see me back," she grins.

"I must say I find that very hard to believe." But that's all she has to say about it. I can't have a normal conversation with my sister.

"Oh, and Auguste Dupin is as dead as a doornail," she says.

"What? He's dead?" I shout, fear rippling through my gut. "Surely it wasn't my fault? Not because I kicked him?"

"You kicked him?"

"Yes, in Paris, at the stables. He tried to stop me. He threatened to whip the little girl who helped me."

Stance looks at me, eyes wide. This makes me even more anxious.

"How did he die?" I ask, already making the sign of the cross.

"Don't worry," Stance says. "Some kind of flu."

I don't know whether to believe her or not.

"A vicious flu. He was already weakened by the gunshot wound."

Yes, of course. That sounds plausible. My worry starts to fade.

"The man drank like a fish," I say. "That didn't help either."

"He was already done for," she says.

I nod. Then Stance wraps that one arm of hers around my head and pulls me into her side with an iron grip.

"What are you doing?" I shout. "Let go of me!"

But she keeps my head pressed into her side with her strong arm. I try to wrestle myself free, but then I feel her nuzzle her face into my head. I feel her nose in my hair. I stop struggling. Her grip slackens. Her warm ear rests on mine. I feel her breath on my cheek.

"You're a real piece of work, Spiering," she says.

Eddy enters the room and is surprised to see us in such a strange position.

"What are you two doing?" he asks.

Stance lets go of me and wipes a tear from her face.

"Hey, Coppertop," she says.

Eddy smiles and throws himself at her.

The gout in Prefect Gijsens's fingers has gotten so bad that he can barely write anymore. He is satisfied with my work and pays me well. I've become the breadwinner of the family. I also help Father write letters to factories and entrepreneurs soliciting his services as a mechanic. He receives word from the entrepreneur in Rotterdam who bought his steam engine. The machine is still driving the pumps that they're using in Holland to empty their ponds and polders, but it needs maintenance. The man would like my father to come to Holland to service and recalibrate the machine.

"I'm an inventor, not a maintenance man!" Father sputters.

"Just do it," Mother says. "It will do you good to tinker with a machine."

"You can take a look at the man's pumps," I say. "Maybe you can design a better one for him."

"Those pumps probably date back to the wig era," says Stance.

"Invent a new one," Mother says. "There's definitely money in that."

"They'll call it Hoste's Pump," scoffs Stance.

Father looks aggrieved.

"Oh, Stance, you hush," says Mother. "What do you think, Leopold?"

A few days later, Father leaves for Holland on

Achilles's back. Mother has trimmed his hair and beard and washed his jacket, so he looks like a gentleman again. We wave him off.

One November morning Stance comes in and sits on my bed. She holds her finger up to her lips. I have to be quiet. Everyone is still asleep. She lights a candle and motions for me to follow her downstairs. I tiptoe down the stairs behind her. She's dressed in men's clothes. On the table are a rucksack, a blanket with spare clothes rolled up inside it, a saber, and a pistol. Her cloak is hanging over the chair. She tucks her arm into the sleeve and flips the cloak over her right shoulder.

"The stagecoach leaves in half an hour at the Korenmarkt," she says. "Will you come and see me off?"

"Where are you going?"

"Vienna," she replies, as if it were around the corner.

"But why?"

"I like Austria." She smiles mysteriously.

We head out the door and light a torch. Ghostly shadows flicker on the old, crumbling façades of Ghent. I carry her saber and her travel bag. The cold air stings our noses. All the world is still asleep. This is all so sudden. I can't say goodbye to her now. I still have so much to say to my sister. There are a thousand and one things I'd like to tell her, but as we walk, side by side, holding that torch, nothing comes to mind. We walk in silence. Our footsteps echo across the quiet city.

◎ ◎ ◎

Torches burn in iron rings outside the inn, where a squeaky, dilapidated stagecoach pulled by seven horses is waiting to take passengers out of town. I open the small door for my sister. Inside, the curtains have been eaten away by moths. There are people sitting on wooden benches, on cushions that are so worn down from all the behinds that have sat on them that they've lost all softness. But Stance doesn't climb in.

"I'm not about to spend my soldier's pension on a good seat," she says.

She hugs me with her one arm. I catch a whiff of tobacco in her short hair. Then she lets me go. She climbs up onto the roof where they keep the luggage, where every pothole hits twice as hard and there's no shelter from the wind and rain. It's the cheapest seat you can buy.

"It smells like a chamber pot in there," she calls down from above. "I'll take the fresh air any day."

A woman about to step on board overhears and looks up, disturbed at the impertinent young man on the roof. The coachman tosses Stance a blanket. She spreads it out across her legs and wraps herself in her thick cloak. My big sister. Crazy Stance. We gaze at each other as if it's the last time. As if we want to remember every detail of each other's faces. We paint a portrait of each other in our minds. A painting that we can put in an invisible amulet, lock in our memories, and open again later. One of the horses takes a few steps forward, and the coachman almost loses his balance. He tugs on the reins, curses the cross, and shouts at the impatient steed to hold steady. It's slowly getting light. The night breaks into a gray dawn.

The carriage jerks into motion. Stance raises her hand.

"You're going to miss me," she yells.

I swallow back a lump in my throat.

"Not for a second," I shout back.

GLOSSARY

ARRÊTEZ: stop

BEAU MONDE: the elite; the high social classes

BERLINE: a four-wheeled Berlin-style travel carriage for four people, with a hood that can be opened

BOGUET: a two-person chariot with two wheels

BONNE CHANCE: good luck

BOTTINE: a lady's small boot

BOUILLOTTE: a card game; predecessor of poker

BRETON: a native of Brittany; also the language spoken there

BRIQUET: a short, slightly curved sword with a brass handle that was carried by most infantry units in the Napoléonic Wars

CALME-TOI, CHÉRIE: calm down, my dear

CENTIME: one hundredth of a franc

CONSCRIT: a conscript; someone who has been drafted into the military

COUCOU: a Parisian coach on two wheels drawn by one or two horses, with room inside for six people on two benches

DIE SCHÖNE DONAU: the beautiful Danube, in German

ÉCOLE DE MÉDICINE: a famous medical university in Paris

EPAULETTES: shoulder pads worn by officers to show their rank

ESPELETTE: a pepper from Mexico used in the Basque region of Spain

FOURCHETTE: French for *fork*; also the soldiers' nickname for a bayonet

FUSILIER: a member of the line infantry

FRICASSEE: a dish of finely chopped meat in sauce; also a wild dance

GENDARME: a French police officer

GRANDE ARMÉE: the French Imperial Army of Napoléon

GRENADIER: an infantry soldier responsible for carrying and throwing grenades

GUILLOTINE: a device with a large falling blade designed for swift decapitation

HUSSAR: a member of the light calvary, known for their distinctive uniform

"LA MARSEILLAISE": the anthem of the French Revolution and still the national anthem of France today

MADEMOISELLE: title for a young, unmarried woman

MADAME: title for a married woman

MONSIEUR: title for a man

MAÎTRE: title for a teacher

MARCHONS: Let's march

MES ENFANTS: my children

MON AMI(E): my friend or my love

MON DIEU: my God

NAPOLÉON: a coin issued during the reign of Napoléon I; the silver napoléon was worth five francs, whereas the gold napoléon was worth either twenty or forty francs

NOM DE DIEU: Good Lord; literally, the name of God

POLDER: low-lying land that has been drained of water to be used for planting or grazing, typical in Holland.

SECRETAIRE: a secretary desk; a cabinet with a fold-down writing surface, compartments, and drawers

SHAKO: a tall, stiff military hat with a visor

SONNTAGSRUHE: lazy Sunday, in German

SUTLER: a provisioner, often a woman, who accompanies an army and sells useful things to soldiers

TRAITEURIE: a Viennese restaurant; this book depicts former court chef Franz Jahn's traiteurie, which was also a famous concert venue

VIVE: long live

VOLTIGEUR: literally, a tumbler or acrobat; also a light infantryman, known for being nimble, swift, and a good marksman

ACKNOWLEDGMENTS

I would like to thank the team at Querido and especially my editor, Belle Kuijken, for her enthusiasm and feedback. Special thanks to Professor of History Tom Verschaffel and Professor Emeritus of History Emiel Lamberts for their comments. City guides Roger Van Bockstaele and Xavier Perneel and the Patershol expert Guido De Wulf told me about the history of Ghent, and Mirjam Morad showed me around Vienna. Herr Böhm, who has a small tin-soldier shop near the Vienna cathedral, told me all about the Austrian and French army uniforms, and Margarete Pelikan and Johann Peschke welcomed me at the Museum Aspern-Essling 1809. I'd also like to thank readers Virginie Oltmans and Sanne Standaert.

SOME NOTES ON THIS BOOK'S PRODUCTION

The art for the jacket and case were illustrated and hand-lettered by Maria Elias, using Procreate for iPad, and refined in Photoshop. Stance's portrait on the jacket references both the military fame and the many unreliable portraits of Napoléon Bonaparte. The tricolor palette recalls the French flag, and is printed in three inks to simulate the quick printing and humanism of propaganda art. The lettering was inspired by the passionate, speedy, and explicit wartime love letters from Napoléon to his wife, Joséphine de Beauharnais. The body text was set by Westchester Publishing Services in Danbury, CT in Abrams Venetian, designed in 1989 by George Abrams, based on the Italian Renaissance letterforms of Nicolas Jenson. The display text was set in American Favorite Serif, an all-caps serif font designed by Mulkan Nazir for Great Studio in 2019. The book was printed on 98 gsm Yunshidai Ivory woodfree FSC™-certified paper and bound in China.

Production was supervised by Leslie Cohen and Freesia Blizard
Book jacket and case designed by Maria Elias
Book interiors designed by Christine Kettner
Edited by Meghan Maria McCullough